ABOUT *CON*

"*Connectedness* is a gripping ꜱ
struggle to be your one true self. An amazing read."
Linda Druijff, The Netherlands

ABOUT *IGNORING GRAVITY*

"Sandra Danby carves her believable characters with both their
fine points and their flaws."
Gwen Wilson, author of 'I Belong to No One'

"This contemporary tale of sisterhood and identity is immediately
engrossing. Sandra Danby writes with great empathy and wit."
Shelley Weiner, author of 'The Audacious Mendacity of Lily Green'

"All in all a really really great debut that definitely makes me
want to see what Ms Danby can come up with next. This will
appeal to fans of family drama with authentic real life issues
and I would highly recommend it."
Liz Wilkins, Liz Loves Books

"This book genuinely surprised me. Reading the first couple of
pages I almost put it down but I am really glad I didn't make
that mistake because as it drew me in I found it increasingly
difficult to stop reading. I love books about secrets and this
was no exception. Solving this puzzle was literally like peeling
layers off an onion. A chance discovery of an old diary turns
Rose's world upside down causing her to question her identity
and initiate her search for her other family."
Michelle de Haan, Shellyback Books

connectedness

sandra danby

For David, always

PROLOGUE
LONDON, SEPTEMBER 2009

The retired headmistress knew before she opened the front door that a posy of carnations would be lying on the doorstep beside the morning's milk bottle. It happened on this day, every year. September 12. And every year she did the same thing: she untied the narrow ribbon, eased the stems loose and arranged the frilled red flowers in her unglazed biscuit-ware jug. Then she placed the jug on the front windowsill where they would be visible from the street. Her bones ached more now as she bent to pick them up off the step than the first year the flowers arrived. She had an idea why the carnations appeared and now regretted never asking about them. Next year, someone else would find the flowers on the doorstep. In a week's time she would be living in a one-bedroom annexe at her son's house in a Hampshire village. She walked slowly back to her armchair beside the electric fire intending to tackle *The Times* crossword but hesitated, wondering if the person who sent the flowers would ever be at peace.

1
YORKSHIRE, MAY 2010

The clouds hurried from left to right, moved by a distant wind that did not touch her cheek. It felt unusually still for May. As if the weather was waiting for the day to begin, just as she was. She had given up trying to sleep at three o'clock, pulled on some clothes and let herself out of the front door. Despite the dark, she knew exactly the location of the footpath, the edge of the cliffs; could walk it with her eyes closed. Justine lay on the ground and looked up, feeling like a piece of grit in the immensity of the world. Time seemed both still and marching on. The dark grey of night was fading as the damp began to seep through her jeans to her skin. A pale line of light appeared on the eastern horizon, across the flat of the sea. She shivered and sat up. It was time to go. She felt close to both her parents here, but today belonged to her mother.

Three hours later, she stood at the graveside and watched as the coffin was lowered into the dark damp hole. Her parents together again in the plot they had bought. It was a big plot, there was space remaining.

Will I be buried here?

It was a reassuring thought, child reunited with parents.

The vicar's voice intoned in the background, his words whipped away by the wind. True to form, May was proving changeable. It was now a day requiring clothing intended for mid-winter, when windows were closed tight and the central heating turned on again. Or was it that funerals simply made you feel cold?

'Amen.'

She repeated the vicar's word, a whisper borne out of many childhood Sunday School classes squeezed into narrow hard pews. She was not paying attention to the service but, drawn by the deep baritone of the vicar who was now reciting the Lord's Prayer, was remembering her first day at art college. The first class. Another baritone. Her tutor, speaking words she had never forgotten. Great art was always true, he warned, and lies would always be found out.

In her handbag was a letter, collected from the hall table ten days ago as she left the house for Heathrow and Tokyo. She had expected to return home to London but, answering the call from her mother's doctor, had come straight to Yorkshire in the hope of seeing her mother one last time. The envelope, which was heavy vellum, and bore smidgens of gold and scarlet and the Royal Academy of Arts' crest, was still sealed. She knew what the letter said, having been forewarned in a telephone call from the artist who nominated her. It was the official invitation. If she accepted, she was to be Justine Tree, RA.

Later the same day, she stood again where she had lain at dawn, at the edge of land where East Yorkshire ended and the North Sea began. The teapots were emptied, cake eaten, mourners gone. She was glad to be alone, welcoming the wind in her face, the roar of the waves pounding hundreds of feet below, wondering how she could bear to be away from this bleak beautiful place. Finally she turned, the wind twisting the unfamiliar black skirt round her knees, hobbling her stride so she stumbled over a path she knew inch by inch, a path she had walked in wet and snow and sun, in mud and dust and wind for almost half a century. Rain arrived, lashing her face like spitting gravel as if it also wept for her mother. In her pocket her hand clasped a pebble. Stroking it was always a comfort, had been since childhood.

The path ran along the cliff to Seaview Cottage, her mother's house and now hers. On the sea side of the path, tufts of grass spread over the thin layer of earth covering the chalk beneath, growing outwards into nothing. At the other side was a field, in summer a golden flag of waving wheat, barley or oats, now the patchy bristle of new crops. Between the two, the path was well trodden. In summer there was a constant trail of hikers walking the coastal path. Most were headed from the nearby campsite loaded with cool bags and picnic rugs to the beach at North Landing. Others followed the cliffs towards the north, binoculars carried ready to see puffins, gannets, guillemots and razorbills. But today even the locals were indoors.

She stopped beside a rock known to her since she was five as the Sheep Rock because of its shape. It was kind of puffed-up and woolly, the shape of a ewe just before shearing.

This is the place.

Her unfamiliar black court shoes were edged with a muddy fringe of grass, the pattern of the storm clouds above reflected in the mirror of a puddle. At this particular curve in the path, her life had changed direction for the first time. It seemed like yesterday. Today, as the past re-opened to her, lots of things seemed like yesterday. It was here where the girl she had been, who loved drawing and making things, learnt a lesson. That real life, put into art, made it stronger. The hot days of holidays were spent here with Susie, each summer of primary and secondary school, stretched out on the grass, making magazines. They were inseparable, the writer and the artist. Susie wrote the stories and Justine designed the illustrations and front cover. The magazines were sold to long-suffering family, friends and neighbours for 1d each – then one new penny, after decimalisation – the profits spent on materials for the next issue and on Embassy records in Woolworths. Suzi Quatro. David Bowie. Queen. Tom Robinson. Wizzard. If time spent together equalled friendship, then Justine and Susie were best friends. This was their last summer before parting, Justine to the art foundation course at Scarborough Technical College and Susie to work in a local bank. They had arranged to meet at Sheep Rock at five o'clock to plan the summer edition of their magazine. Justine was confident she could fit in the design work with her holiday job at the RNLI ice cream kiosk at North Landing.

After school she went straight to a training session to be

shown how to use the till and the correct way to serve ice creams. Her head full of 99s, cones, wafers, Fabs, Mivvies and Zooms, she walked along an unfamiliar footpath towards home, climbing a five-bar gate and traversing the far end of the village past the bus stop. In the concrete shelter sat Susie, her arms wrapped around a boy. Justine knew it was Susie even though her face was hidden, because she could see Susie's favourite Suzi Quatro black trousers with metal chains sewn along the leg seams from hem to waistband. Justine couldn't see the face of the boy until a pause in the kissing. It was Kevin. Kevin, who she had walked out with last night until ten thirty, Kevin who kissed her goodnight in the shadow of the wall of Mellor & Sons garage, who asked her to go out with him again, and she said yes.

Knowing she might throw up, Justine ran until she had no breath left, sinking to the ground with a puff of summer dust. She cried for a long time, for lost love and lost friendship and then, recognising betrayal, she got angry. She opened her satchel and took out a sheet of drawing paper, orange furry pencil case and tube of paper glue. She weighed down the paper with lumps of chalk culled from beside the path and then, careless of the dust and grass seed flowing freely in the soft breeze, she created her first collage. A tangle of gull feathers, grass, dock leaves and smears of mud made of the dusty earth mixed with tears. She carried the half-finished jumble to her father's shed where she carefully dismantled it, sorted and re-assembled it, fixing it together permanently with some plaster-like stuff from his workbench. She rescued a Frosties cereal packet from the dustbin and then, imagining it was the boy's A-grade physics essay of which he'd been so proud, she tore it into strips. She sat holding a felt tip pen feeling empty of words until they spilled forth from a subconscious thesaurus: Traitor. Betrayal. Envy. Hurt. Jealousy. Theft. Unfair. Friend. Pain. Lies.

Her anger grumbled on and she picked at the hem of her school jumper, loosening a thread from its ribbing, pulling the crinkly wool until she had yards of the stuff. Next term she would wear bell-bottomed jeans, not an acrylic jumper, shiny skirt and American tan tights. She ran into the house to her mother's needlework drawer, selected what she needed. Back in the shed she used the dark green wool to crochet rhythmically, knotting, looping. Gradually she made a long chain, each dropped stitch representing a tear. The furious crocheting rubbed a raw patch on her palm but she crocheted on. Finally she chopped the chain into pieces, fraying the edges before gluing them to the cardboard in a broken line. Morse code for her sobs.

Two years later, 'Loss and Loss and Loss Again' opened the door for Justine into art college. 'The over-sentimentality of the title and the rough execution of the piece itself are unable to hide this student's ability. There is a raw truth to the complex emotions of a teenager,' said her acceptance report at RivesArt in London.

She wished she could see Susie again, to say thank you for everything.

It was my first collage, the first time I turned emotions into art, the first time I did more than just copy.

Justine stood at the cliff's edge and stroked the scar on her palm, the raised line of white flesh the only evidence of that frenzied night of crocheting. She wished she had never sold 'Loss and Loss and Loss Again' but she had been desperate for money. That had been her darkest time when she despaired of ever making art again.

No point dwelling on it, I can't change history.

When she returned home, a blue and red 'For Sale' sign had appeared in the garden. She struggled to light the portable gas fire in the kitchen. Finally the flame sputtered; the gas canister was nearly empty. Mains gas had never reached the few houses sprinkled along the cliffs and the electric storage heaters offered only background warmth. She filled the kettle and put it to boil. Her mother believed no decent cup of tea ever came from a teabag and now Justine followed the well-worn routine. From the shelf she took the brown-and-black patterned Hornsea Pottery teapot, spooning in leaf tea from the battered tin that had once held shortbread biscuits from Edinburgh. The tea was just as her mother had made it. Strong, the colour of rich earth, a splash of skimmed milk, no sugar.

She remembered the time when, alone and desperately in need, she had returned to Seaview Cottage and sat in this chair at this table, cradling a mug full of strong tea. With the benefit of hindsight, she realised her mother would have rushed to help without blame. But in her youth, Justine feared to disappoint, to let down and shame her parents who set such store by behaviour and appearances and 'not letting the side down'. So she had drunk the tea her mother made, hid her secret, saved herself from their disappointment. She had done so many things to protect her parents from the truth, but now they were gone, she wanted to tell them everything. She sipped tea from her mug and remembered clearly the day it began, the day she had stepped off the plane and into the September Spanish heat, not knowing what lay ahead of her.

If I'd gone to Paris instead, my life would have been so different.

2
SPAIN, SEPTEMBER 1982

The sausage-shaped yellow nylon bag was stuffed full of her gear, the zip almost pulling apart. Justine didn't like the colour but the price had been reduced and it did the job well enough. She was tired of hauling it round all day; many times she wished she hadn't forced in the last few books she couldn't bear to leave behind. The bus from the airport dropped her on a busy street, disorientating, exciting; a whirl of noise and light spun in her head as she tried to work out where she was. The walk through the town was the hardest, the strap of her bag cutting into her shoulder as she negotiated narrow shadowed alleyways, carefully following the map she had been sent by the college, her route marked with a red line. When she arrived at her lodging, the place which would be home for the next academic year, she was too weary to examine her surroundings. She was to share an apartment on the first floor. The stairs were narrow and dark and she was aching. She'd taken the first morning flight because it was the cheapest but that had meant getting to Gatwick airport in the middle of the night. The last two steps seemed bigger than the others and she arrived at a narrow landing, plain wooden floorboards, a door with a heavy black knob.

The room was dark and the ceiling light, when she located the switch, cast a dull yellow hue over the room. Justine King dropped her yellow bag on to the floor and carefully placed her rucksack, which contained her precious paintbox, beside it. Slowly turning 360 degrees, she examined her home for the next year. Dark brown heavy furniture that made her think of chapel, plain terracotta tiles on the floor, no rugs, and an open fireplace with a stack of logs waiting to be burnt. There was no sofa; instead the focus of the room was a large table swamped by a floor-length chenille tablecloth. Six dining chairs offered the only seating. The air was cool.

She crossed the room, threw open the blue-painted shutters and stepped out on to a balcony. The noise of the street rose up to meet her, loud voices, incomprehensible language, laughter and sun. Most of all the sun. The heat clung to her skin like a tightly fitting eiderdown so her insides simmered and her tiredness fell away. At one side of the balcony hung a thin slatted wooden blind, casting a light shade and flapping in the breeze. She stood still, eyes closed, allowing the sun's rays on her white face. She was dressed for September in London, not Málaga. She discarded her cardigan and boots, freeing her toes, regretting her selection of books over t-shirts. She leant eagerly over the peeling black railings, their curlicues interlinking in complicated *s*'s, and surveyed her surroundings. Dusty, slightly shabby; blue sky and noise from every direction. Sparrows jostled for the highest branches, a black cloud of starlings swooped at roof level, cars hooted and mopeds buzzed.

This is my new home.

Seaview Cottage would always be home-home. She was connected to it by a permanent cord, to her parents, to the cliffs. But this, this was exciting. This was different. The balcony walls were covered with pots from which tumbled red geraniums, dead leaves and red petals scattered round her feet. A waterfall of red. She wondered who did the watering; was it up to them now? She thought of the word 'them' with quote marks because she'd been allocated this shared apartment by the college accommodation office. She was to share three bedrooms, kitchen, bathroom and study area with A Masterson and M C Alba Roman. It seemed she was the first to arrive so she assumed the other two must still be travelling. Justine went indoors and examined the apartment with the benefit of sunlight. It was tidy to the point of empty. A faint smell of bleach hung in the air. The kitchen consisted of a fridge, hotplate and sink squeezed into an alcove at one side of the study room. No television, no record player, not even an ancient radiogram like the one in the common room at Parkville Hall of Residence at RivesArt. But there was a radio. She turned it on and stood back at the loud noise it emitted, the beat of fast guitar music which filled the empty room and brought it alive. She turned down the volume and continued to explore.

She chose the bedroom at the front. Its narrow balcony, really no more than a ledge, overlooked the square. It wasn't the biggest of the bedrooms but it had the best light. There was a rather nice table lamp with a delicate art deco glass shade which would cast a yellow-green light over the walls. A side table at exactly the right height for her to stand at and paint. The lamp she put beside her bed on a low cabinet, along with her wind-up alarm clock and a white pebble from the beach at Flamborough – it doubled as a reminder of home, and a paperweight. She put the table in front of the French windows knowing its position may change depending on the way the light fell in the room. It was different here, the light. Brighter, whiter, the tonal differences more pronounced. It would make painting light and shade more of a challenge and she couldn't wait to try it out. She was used to the wide horizons of home; shades of grey, not startling blue and yellow.

Her stomach rumbled. Wondering how and where one bought food and drink here, she opened the fridge and found a bottle of milk, a lemon, a loaf of crusty bread, half a dozen eggs, two onions and a crude orange-coloured pottery jug of still water with a slice of lemon in it.

A white notecard propped against the jug said simply: '*Bienvenidos del Departimiento de Alojamiento Estudiante*'. She found a tumbler in a cupboard alongside a tin of tomatoes, bottle of oil, bottle of vinegar and various small tin boxes.

Am I expected to cook?

She panicked. Before leaving home two years earlier for art college in London, her mother had taught her to make scrambled eggs on toast, baked potato, mashed potato, tomato soup and an omelette. It was too hot to contemplate eating hot food, so Justine carried a dining chair outside and sat on the balcony to eat a chunk of bread. She tore it into pieces and chewed. It had been hours since she had eaten but the bread was a challenge without margarine, the crust splintering and falling on the terracotta tiles at her feet as if she were feeding the ducks on the village pond at home. Realising she'd never be able to swallow even if she chewed for an hour, she spat the bread into her handkerchief and took a huge swig of water, savouring the taste of the lemon on her parched throat. She hadn't drunk since the paper cup of water handed out on the aeroplane and hadn't dared to ask for more, afraid she would be asked to pay. She had a wodge of peseta notes in her pocket. Thousands. It felt like a lot of money but she'd been given them yesterday at the bank in exchange for fifty pounds, her spending money, which had to last all year. She'd worked the last summer holidays not selling ice creams, but on the fryer in the fish-and-chip kiosk. Every pound symbolised the stink of wet fish and film of chip oil in her hair and on her clothes, a stink which no amount of detergent or showering removed. She had hated every minute of the job but it was the best paid work she could get while living at home for free. She emptied the tumbler and poured more.

I will forget what Mum said about the tap water not being safe to drink and will treat myself to lemons.

She liked it, it tasted like water in a hot climate should taste. For the first time since her alarm had gone off at two, she breathed deeply. She'd never done so many new things in one day. She was going to spend the next year living in the Plaza de la Merced.

This is it, the plaza where Picasso was born. The plaza where he sat with his father drawing doves. He started with doves and I started with pigeons.

Her fingers itched to paint, to sketch something no matter how ordinary. Because that's what Picasso did; he used ordinary objects and made them beautiful by decorating them. She had seen one of his pots in the Royal Academy's ceramics exhibition. He had painted a beautiful face on to the plainest household jug, not bone china, not Meissen or Ming, but exactly the sort of pottery jug that was in her fridge. And it had made her want to add painting to her collages, make them more substantial, but as yet she hadn't worked out how.

Were A Masterson and M C Alba Roman fine art students, or fashion students, sculptors or architects? She flicked through the much-thumbed brochure given to her at the careers office at RivesArt in London, the brochure she had relied on to plan her year abroad. On the cover was the title 'Escuela de Bellas Artes' and a montage of photos. Picasso, of course; an ornate cathedral which looked unfinished; a striped umbrella on a sandy beach; and a mountain. She had seen the hills from the bus window as it trundled into the city, rough bare outcrops of rock so different from the gentle slopes of the Yorkshire Wolds. She took a deep breath and felt the warmth travel deep inside into her lungs.

A motorbike roared by and she hung over the balcony and looked down at the square again. The sun cast deep shadows from the trees which enclosed the central paved area around a grand but crumbling obelisk. Perhaps she would sketch it later. The trees were unfamiliar; their trunks huge, as big as English oaks, though the upright trees themselves seemed young. Like lanky teenagers stretched by a growth spurt. The feathery leaves were familiar though, similar to the pinnate-shaped rowans in the park near Parkville, the rowans whose leaves and berries she had collected, dried and stored in a shoebox in case she could use them in the future. That shoebox was stored in the basement at RivesArt with her trunk and countless boxes of belongings. Two years of stuff accumulated at college but deemed unnecessary for her year in Spain. Also in the trunk was her tree book. She regretted that now.

Along one whole side of the square was a grand but derelict terrace of houses, some with stained glass windows, shutters closed against the sun, others with broken glass and rusted balcony railings. Shops filled another side of the *plaza*; at least Justine presumed they were shops because, while there were no signs outside people were coming and going with bulging bags. On the corner was a large café, the Café del Pintor. Opposite the grand houses was an empty space where the earth was bare and small black-and-white birds searched in the dust, their tails bobbing as their heads nodded.

In one of these buildings, Picasso was born.

The smell of roasting floated up to her and, leaning further over her balcony to survey the street below, she saw a cart loaded with a barbecue roasting chestnuts. Her stomach rumbled again. Roasting chestnuts meant Christmas shopping to her, but a queue was forming; businessmen with briefcases, women wearing headscarves and carrying baskets, schoolchildren wearing blue t-shirts and shorts, and two workmen in trousers splattered with white.

It was time to explore. She picked up her door key and went downstairs to buy a bag of chestnuts and find Picasso.

3
YORKSHIRE, MAY 2010

Sitting at her mother's square kitchen table, Justine considered the jobs to be done. Not knowing when she would next return north, the spare front door key had to be deposited with the estate agent. She made a start on clearing the house, sorting her mother's possessions, deciding what to keep. Boxes to fill and label for the man-with-a-van who would collect and distribute her mother's lifetime possessions round the neighbourhood. Boxes for the charity shop in Bridlington eight miles away. The good china and glass, furniture and electrical goods for the auctioneer's next 'general household goods' sale. A box of books – mostly Catherine Cookson, Mary Stewart and Maeve Binchy – sat by the door, waiting for the weekly visit of the library van. She planned to donate her grandfather's two watercolour seascapes to the RNLI kiosk. She would have been pleased to look at them, in the pauses between serving 99s and ice cream sandwiches. When she worked there, the wind-and-salt-bleached wooden walls were bare.

How quickly her mother's life would disappear, absorbed into the poor seaside community used to accommodating the possessions of its recently dead elderly residents. Everything had a use. The rural population struggled to live on earnings from agriculture, plus seasonal income from tourists with few spare coppers to spend on a holiday they scratched and saved all year to afford. She set aside one box to pack into the hire car; sentimental things, practical things, things she couldn't bear to leave behind. Her mother's sewing basket with its mixture of haberdashery items, silks, buttons, braid; her mother's knitting needles and crochet hooks, their silvery paint rubbed off over the years. Justine remembered the hours of crocheting, learning the basics, making chains using leftover wool. Painstaking hours. Fluffy blue leftover from something made for a baby. Scraps of cream wool oily with lanolin; remnants from three matching roll-neck Aran sweaters. Also into the box went the set of encyclopaedias bound in red leather bought by her father for an extortionate monthly payment to help her study for O levels. His bird books and binoculars. And her mother's three biscuit tins. The box fitted neatly into the boot alongside the ancient Singer sewing machine with its shaped wooden cover. Two photo albums full of faces Justine did not recognise, a connection to distant family: a man with her father's nose; a child, boy or girl she wasn't sure, with her own tiny earlobes. She wished she had met them.

The house felt empty. She had never slept there alone until now. Since she could remember, her mother not her father had locked the back door at night, checked the windows were shut, the front gate closed, so when Justine woke on the morning after the funeral, she realised she had gone to bed with the front door on the latch and the back door wide open.

She turned from the window and again walked a well-trodden route from room to room. The familiar house felt odd. It wasn't just the physical absence of her mother, the smell of her favourite wool jumper thinned by much wearing and washing, the sound of her fingertips tapping out a rhythm to a tune heard on Radio 2, the scratching of her pencil as she wrote the answers in *Puzzle* magazine. There was an emotional emptiness as if Seaview Cottage itself knew her mum had gone. Everything was still. Not waiting, but halted. The mahogany mantel clock in the front room was stilled at eleven thirty-five; it was that way when Justine arrived. It had been a wedding present from a great-aunt of her father and had to be wound every night with a small brass key. She wondered how many days, weeks, had passed since her mother had been downstairs and able to wind the clock at bedtime.

I should never have gone to Tokyo.

This was illogical. She had learned after her father's death fifteen years earlier that grief was unpredictable. She swallowed down the small bubble of resentment that her mother had not shared her illness, had not trusted her or was protecting her from the process of death. As if she would be a nuisance to her mother rather than a comfort.

She knew she was being unfair, but there was no getting away from the fact that a mother and daughter should be together at the end, no matter whose end it was.

Her phone buzzed with an incoming text message. Her agent, Maud Nettles, asking if she could do anything to help. That's all it took, that one buzz, to trigger the memory. Only a week ago, she had been in Japan.

She had never been anywhere so alien as Tokyo. If London was a million miles away then East Yorkshire was another planet. Waiting in the hotel lobby at the wide bank of lifts, standing next to the diminutive woman in the gold and blue kimono, Justine felt like a giant. Three days was insufficient time to shake off jetlag, but long enough to learn not to press the lift button and instead let Kimono Lady do it for her. Long enough to learn how to say *onegaishimasu* instead of please and *arigatōgozaimashita* for thank you. Long enough to learn it was rude not to arrive at least thirty minutes before the appointment time. Long enough to have collected a bundle of notes in her jacket pocket with her various destinations written in Japanese to give to the taxi drivers. On one side of the note were Japanese characters written beautifully with a paintbrush by another Kimono Lady at the Customer Relations desk. On the reverse side, in Justine's scrawl, were her key destinations. Her hotel, the New Otani. The Museum of Contemporary Art Tokyo. Last night's restaurant, Sekihotei. The previous night's restaurant, Ohara. The Ginza Six shopping complex. And her gallery, Project Sai.

Tonight was the official opening ceremony for 'Justine Tree: Retrospective' at the Museum of Contemporary Art Tokyo. Tonight she would be chauffeur-driven.

Tonight I will act.

22

Her face was projected on to the front of the museum, her name spelt out on a series of twenty-foot-high banners hanging across the street. In the foyer, everyone bowed to her, dipping from the waist. Breaking into the Japanese market was a big thing, Maud kept telling her. The Asia Pacific region was developing territory for art investors and Justine worried about the etiquette of her bowing. She stood on a raised platform, flanked by museum directors and sponsors, gazing out at an audience of businessmen, artists, art hangers-on; so many she could not count. For an hour there were speeches in Japanese, traditional dancing which was elegant, graceful and endless, and more speeches. She smiled throughout. The culmination of the ceremony was the robing in which she was dressed in a beautiful silk kimono, an acceptance into their culture; a great honour she knew from this most private of peoples who rarely invited strangers into their homes. She stood, her shoulders bowing under the weight of the silk, while effusive thanks were given for her attendance, her art, her grace. More delicate music, like raindrops falling on bells, and then dancers appeared to announce the serving of the food. Along each wall were long rows of tables covered in white floor-length table-cloths, weighted down with huge silver food servers, with a Kimono Lady standing beside each table. At two central tables stood chefs in tall white toques, waiting to cook to order. The underlying smell of green tea made Justine feel nauseous. The smell seemed everywhere, as if infused in the carpets. She smiled and did her neck bend thing; the beds and chairs here were so hard that every muscle in her body complained. Unsure how she would manoeuvre a plate of food and a full glass with the heavy golden sleeves that brushed her finger-tips, at first she politely declined each dish of food offered to her. But then aware she was offending her hosts, she attempted to push the sleeves up her forearms. During this struggle, her pocket began to vibrate. She'd meant to turn her mobile off. The vibrating stopped. The long sleeves proved useful at disguising her movements as she checked for messages. There was one new text.

'Urgent. Ring Dr Todd' and a UK mobile number.

Her mother's GP. Justine felt a wave of sickness rush over her. She swayed. Plate and glass fell. A strong arm surrounded her shoulders and supported her weight.

'I am Tatsuo Kagura. I am chairman of Kagura Art. You are ill. Please let me help you.'

He escorted her to a side chamber, requested a chair and a glass of water, tipped ice from a bucket into a napkin and held it to the nape of her neck. Then he stood silently beside her as she dialled Dr Todd's number, listened, and wept.

I must leave now.

But her mother had been unable to wait and now Justine sat alone at the kitchen table. For three days the kettle had been forever warm as a trickle of neighbours, villagers and family arrived with cakes, pies and bunches of late, pinched-looking local daffodils and chemically bright hot-house tulips from Holland. But Justine had not yet reached the point where she couldn't face another mug of tea. Today, the house was quiet. Everyone had returned to their normal lives. She ran her hand across the oiled tablecloth. Not the original one from her child-hood which had been patterned with nodding yellow daffo-dils; this one was ten years old or so, dating back to when her mother hung new curtains. Blue curtains, so bluebells on the tablecloth. It was another piece of the practical oiled fabric cut from a roll at the local hardware shop and so retro now it was highly stylish down south. A fact that would have left her mother bemused.

Oh Mum.

So many things said which should have been unspoken, and other things not said for reasons of embarrassment, shame, guilt, forgetfulness or neglect. Justine would always have regrets about her mother. Their relationship had been complicated, conflict inevitable from the day when Justine, a toddler, discovered her own power. The battle centred on the white mush her mother fed to her spoonful by spoonful almost every mealtime at this table. Justine was too young to know the mush was boiled potato, mashed with butter and Wensleydale cheese. It wasn't the flavour she had disliked, it was the repetition. She learned the power of the word no.

Carrying her mug with her, she walked from room to room. In the parlour stood her mother's piano. She was eight when she worked out her mother wanted her to do all the things she had missed out on during her own wartime childhood. Piano practice, country dancing, violin lessons. Justine wanted to run along the beach, jump in puddles, play football and rounders and tag with the boys in the village, wear trousers and wellies not skirts. She didn't understand why these things were banned, but her mother demanded proper behaviour.

Having found a box of photo albums last night, Justine had sat up late turning page after page of black-and-white photographs of Victorian and Edwardian couples until she found a photo that explained her mother's obsession with rules. Lorna, her mum, looked about five, wearing a white frilled and flounced dress with a blue mop cap, white socks and T-bar sandals. She stood in front of her parents who sat on high-backed wooden chairs, chins high, backs ramrod-straight. A hand lay on Lorna's shoulder; perhaps a reminder from her mother to stand straight, silent, and not to fidget or the photograph would be blurred. Justine had never seen this photo before; in truth she had shown no interest in her family. Now she wished she had.

In the end her scratchy co-existence with her mother was saved by needlework, her mother's hobby, which Justine was determined to hate but grew to love. The very first sampler she sewed, a horse's head, was a kind of embroider-by-numbers kit she was given for her birthday. Cross-stitch. An apt word, she decided, for her mother who seemed to be cross a lot of the time. But when the embroidery silks were taken out, a mood of calm descended on Seaview Cottage. Justine discovered previously unappreciated depths of patience displayed by her mother; how to hold the needle, how to hold the cloth, how to thread the needle, how not to prick your finger, how to stitch in time with your breathing, how to tie off a loose end before it got too short. Those weekend hours, sitting at the kitchen table together, had seemed nothing special at the time. Now she wished she had appreciated them more and told her mother so.

I was an ungrateful wretch.

She walked up the stairs into her parents' bedroom. It was most definitely still theirs. Her father had died fifteen years ago but his presence was everywhere in Seaview Cottage. The wooden stair rail she had helped him remove, rub down with sandpaper and re-varnish in Old Oak shade, standing at the bottom of the stairs to support the weight of the long rail as he struggled to re-fix it to the wall. The day she had seen her father naked when the shower rail over the avocado bath collapsed on him as, his head covered in shampoo, the yellow bar of soap plopped out of his fingers, bounced off the tiled wall and skidded across the floor. Drawn by the shouting and swearing, Justine and her mother had arrived in time to see him in all his nakedness, head down in the bath. Justine had been banished downstairs, but not before she noticed the amazing hairiness of his back and legs and bottom. That evening, when brushing her teeth before bed, she had stood on the toilet seat and balanced, trying to see the reflection of her own bottom in the mirror, to check for the presence of hairs.

Her father was the balm preventing an irreversible falling-out between 'my two girls'. He was the inspiration for Justine's first success, 'The Direction and Intention of Birds'. It caught the eye of the critics, earned her some decent money, and brought a contract with her first agent. She was ashamed now that she used that series to have a go at her mum. If she was being charitable to herself she would say she hadn't meant to cause hurt, didn't think her mum really cared for her art. But if she was being honest, she knew she had done a despicable thing. She dedicated the series to Dad alone. The logic was that it was he who first encouraged her to observe and draw nature, particularly to draw an injured pigeon they rescued. Her mother had hated that bird and it never occurred to Justine to include her mother in her formal message of thanks; anyway, that's what she told her father when he chastised her thoughtlessness.

I was such a bitch. I thought truth was the most important thing, when a little lie would have been kinder.

She walked downstairs, her hand smoothing that Old Oak stair rail. Sitting in the worn wooden chair which had always been hers at the square kitchen table, her mother on her left and father on her right, she rubbed her hands with their prominent veins, long fingers and bumpy knuckles.

I have Mum's hands.

As the tears began to fall, she glimpsed what it was to be a mother. To challenge, to push, to accept the hugs and shouts and kicks and anger. To love, despite everything. She had no right to criticise her mother. Being a mother was hard, she could see that now. Perhaps her mother had simply done the best she could.

I have no right to expect more than that.

She emptied the dregs from the teapot into the sink, and then tipped the tea leaves on to the compost heap at the bottom of the garden, as her mother had always done. Tomorrow she would leave the empty house and hand the keys to the estate agent.

It was still dark the next morning as she pushed aside the front gate and walked along the clifftop path. She had set the alarm early, meaning to get ahead of traffic on the motorway and be in London by lunchtime, but was unable to resist one more walk along the cliffs. Standing motionless, she absorbed the open space around her. The pale of day crept up on her, grey sea to the east, grey sky above, and for a moment the sheer space seemed empty of everything, threatening to suck her in so she became a part of it. She checked her watch; almost forty-eight hours exactly since she had lain here before the funeral.

I should come back more often to just stand here and feel this space.

A stir of regret, touched with guilt. She felt their absence heavily this morning. No one expected their parents to die but the years had crept silently by and before she knew it, they had been transformed into frail sparrows, all pointy bones, grating joints and swollen knuckles. She was glad they died untroubled. That was her gift to them.

She turned back towards Seaview Cottage. At the stile she stooped to pick up a feather caught in the hedge, a habit ingrained by a lifetime's foraging for materials. The feather was pale, like the white ladies dancing on the tips of the biggest waves in Filey Bay during a storm, white deepening to celadon and dark grey at its tip. Not the pure white of a gannet or the scruffy black of a shag, then. This was the feather of a herring gull, the bully of the cliffs, like those wheeling above her head now, soaring on the wind, squealing and yelping.

The cliffs were deserted except for a young woman, hunched deep into the hood of her dark anorak. Her eyes were lowered to the excitable dog on the end of an extendable lead, its tail wagging ten to the dozen. Justine stood aside making room for the pair to pass, and then walked on. The briefest of nods were exchanged, in the local way.

Seaview Cottage stood alone at the highest point of the chalk cliffs between Flamborough Head and Bempton Cliffs, the right-hand of a pair of semi-detached farmworkers' cottages. The other had been empty for twenty years and was home to all manner of nesting birds and field mice. At the wooden gate Justine stooped to pick up another feather tangled in the thorns of the unpruned rose, her mother's favourite flower. This feather was black. A shag, or cormorant. She put it in her pocket.

Sitting at the kitchen table, listening to the kettle begin to roar as it worked up to boiling point, she allowed the memories in. After her father's death, Justine's mother had described the process of mourning, the disbelief, the distress, the anger, the loneliness, the sadness, the emptiness and powerlessness. How it was important to embrace each stage and not force its end, to stay with the familiar until the process was complete. And never, ever, make a major life decision until a year had passed. Justine sipped her tea, becoming aware of how the familiarity of place seemed to anchor her to the chair. All was quiet now and she could hear the faint breaking of waves on rocks below, a gentle susurration. Stay. Stay.

Though Flamborough Head, and the sweep of cliffs north around Filey Bay to the jagged finger of rocks jutting into the sea, known as the Brigg, was a dramatic coastline, Justine would never have called it pretty. Startling, brutal, remote, perhaps. In her youth she probably never considered it in its entirety, seeing only its isolated parts, the birds, the cliffs, her home, their garden, the neighbouring fields, school, the village. In her latter teenage years, she couldn't wait to escape its seediness, the static caravans, peeling paint, boarded-up seafood stalls, the village claustrophobia in which everyone knew your name, living in the glass jar of observation. She wanted to see the cities with art galleries, museums and concerts. London's anonymity appealed, the possibilities of it, the sheer difference from home; passing face after face and no one she knew or who knew her. But as her time away from the East Yorkshire coast lengthened, she began to realise it cut through to the very centre of her being. There was a local saying: 'You can take the girl out of Yorkshire, but you can't take Yorkshire out of the girl.' She was that girl. She had lived in London for more than thirty years but often felt a stranger. She missed the fertile smell of the earth after rain, the lulling, reliable rhythm of waves hitting the shore, and the songs sung by northerlies howling through the guttering. She even missed the cold.

Sometimes, when abroad, there was a jolt to her senses, a noise, a smell, and she would close her eyes and imagine herself standing on that windy clifftop. After this happened she would long to make the journey north to Seaview Cottage, to walk the cliff paths with her parents, stand again at the eastern edge of England, breathe in ozone and feel health seep into her tired flesh. But as her career took off, it became more difficult to plan the time for such visits. No matter how much art she sold, Justine still longed to retreat to a secret place, to be alone, working, walking. Nature was as natural to her as breathing. It was just there and, in the way every other child assumes all children live this exact way of life, she accepted the fields and hedges, gales and vertical rain as the norm. But her life, the world of art, was in London. Not at the eastern edge of the country where broadband operated on a piecemeal basis.

Birds, though, had always been special to her, and to her father. On a Saturday walk across the neighbouring fields when she was about ten, they found a wood pigeon. One wing drooped to the earth. They showed it to the farmer who had, like all who worked on the land, a respect for life. He bound the broken wing to the woodie's body and nestled it in a box filled with screwed-up newspaper and an old towel. Justine carried the box home, excitement bubbling beneath, and then waited outside while her father persuaded her mother to let the bird into the house.

'There's enough wildlife outside the door, without me having it in the house too,' was her mother's regular complaint as Justine arrived home with injured or abandoned animals. She never knew how her father won the argument that day but the pigeon was named Davy Jones, after the lead singer of The Monkees, and took up residence in its box in a warm spot on the floor next to the Rayburn. The following day they ate a Sunday dinner of pork chops and apple sauce which Justine helped her mother to prepare as a thank you for being allowed to keep Davy Jones.

After dinner her father produced a sketch pad and pencils and showed her how to draw the bird. She drew and re-drew the pigeon, in pencil, in charcoal, in crayon. She longed for oil paints but her father said best to learn to draw in pencil first.

When frustration got the better of her, he told her a story.

'Picasso is such a famous artist that it's not widely known his father José was an artist too. He was a professor of art at a local college. In the square in the Spanish town where they lived, pigeons would gather in the sycamore trees. As a small boy, Pablo was always drawing birds. When he was thirteen, his father found him painting over his own unfinished sketch of a pigeon. José realised Pablo's talent was greater than his own and he vowed to give up painting. The family moved house and Picasso passed the entrance exam for art college when he was still thirteen.'

'So it all started with a pigeon?'

Davy Jones soon recovered and was released on the clifftop, but it was the beginning of something. First pencil drawings, watercolours, acrylics, oils. After 'Loss and Loss and Loss Again' she started to collect feathers and stick them to her drawings. Later she learned to call these works her collages. And so the castaway things in her life began to play a role in her art. Feathers, leaves, flowers, berries, stones, pebbles.

Justine went out into the garden and removed the 'For Sale' sign.

4
LONDON, MAY 2010

Lap after lap she swam, eating up the lengths with her effortless crawl, enjoying the sensation of arms and legs working in coordination, feeling her mind awaken. It was six thirty when she stopped to catch her breath, the water running down her body as the rain outside ran down the window panes, distorting her view of the trees and bushes outside into the sort of finger patterns drawn by five-year olds.

Her body clock was still refusing to acknowledge the change of routine. Pre-breakfast swims were not a lifetime habit for freelance journalist Rose Haldane, pre-breakfast anything in fact. She had been an uncommitted jogger until she moved in with Nick Maddox in his riverside apartment, renting out her beloved Wimbledon flat; she was determined to keep a fingertip hold on her independence. She suspected Nick regarded the retention of her flat as a lack of long-term commitment; she knew he was hoping for lifetime love, babies, one, maybe two dogs, a home with garden and tree house. Rose was more of a cat person but Nick's pet hair allergy meant Brad, her tabby cat, now lived with her sister Lily.

She tumble-turned neatly and pushed on, relishing the burn in her shoulders, loving the luxury of having a private pool to herself and remembering when she had been the one outside looking in. Admittedly the jogging only became a late-night thing when she first met Nick and wanted to check out where he lived. Now she was living with him in the same building she had once watched at night, wondering which brightly lit window was his. The pool in the basement was convenient but a bit short, only five full strokes, but it eliminated her lack-of-time excuse.

I must choose a form of exercise which is not influenced in some way by Nick. I could do yoga again. Or Pilates. Or boxercise.

She quite liked the idea of punching the hell out of a big bag but not today; today she had to think about a new client. It was the third one this week. A business interview for a Sunday current affairs magazine with the incoming Danish CEO of an electric cycling company with plans to hire its bikes to Londoners. And a personality profile for a respected art website of an artist with a new exhibition at a central London gallery. Both clients promised regular commissions if the first article was successful. The third new commission was for research with a television documentary team. She hadn't known whether to jump for joy when she first read the email or send a polite reply saying it wasn't for her. The commission came from Adrian Boult who had been Crime Editor at the *London Herald* when Rose had worked there as a feature writer. Now he was a producer at Tough Talk Productions. His email had arrived out of the blue two days ago, since when she had been chewing it over.

Do I want to be a crime reporter?

It was a big chance, something new on her CV.

But am I brave enough?

Perhaps. Not really.

But Adrian knows me and he wouldn't have asked me if he thought I wasn't up to it.

And the fee was double her usual freelance rate.

Is that danger money?

She took her mug of instant latte to her desk and settled down to read the programme briefing sheet again.

Objective: to identify and provide background information on suspected bogus abortion clinics which draw in vulnerable women by offering them help to get an abortion, but with the secret purpose of frightening them into rejecting an abortion. Suspect funding by unidentified foreign pro-life group.

Desk research only.

Identify suspect clinics, directors, method of operation.

Definition of how pro-life and pro-choice clinics operate legally. Identify senior women in public life for attributable quotes, pro-life and pro-choice.

Identify case studies.

Is it fraud or deception? Citizens Advice Bureau, women's groups, Victim Support etc.

US connection: US pro-life extremists have murdered surgeons. Check police for harassment of doctors in UK.

Status: programme production pending research findings and approval by Director of Programming for London Compass TV.

Rose hesitated. She'd had time now to adjust to the discovery that she was adopted as a one-day-old baby; Nick had helped with that transition. The family secret had been hidden for more than thirty years and learning to trust again had been a step-by-step thing. Reading the clippings in this buff folder made her feel sick that vulnerable women were still being manipulated. Somewhere in London a young woman may be unsure, frightened and alone, knocking on the door of a clinic, hoping to find a kind welcome, help and honesty but finding lies, misinformation and denial of her right to choose. Rose thought about Adrian Boult's job offer. Could she be objective, given her past, given her birth mother's attempted herbal abortion?

You can be objective for television.

She pulled a face, unsure. She believed every woman had the right to choose and didn't blame Kate for trying to abort her baby.

Me.

Just glad she hadn't. It wasn't something she often thought of now. Sufficient time had gone by to blunt the pain. She had no memory of her birth mother, Kate, and though feeling pity for the dilemma she faced, Rose felt inadequate to judge.

She read the list of suspected clinics. Aardvark. Aabbott Advice Centre. Achas Clinic. Abson House. Ardgay House for Women. Did these people really think that people chose a medical clinic based on alphabetical order?

Rose put the papers back into the buff folder. Should she do it?

She picked up her mobile to call Adrian and say, *yes please*.

5
LONDON, MAY 2010

On Saturday morning, Justine drew breath for the first time since leaving Seaview Cottage. She had stayed on a couple of extra days to re-organise. She cancelled the removals men, unpacked boxes and put everything back in its place, turned off the gas and electricity, and then returned to London. Each day since had been filled with phone calls to her mother's solicitor, accountant, the bank, utility and insurance companies. All the detritus of closing down a person's life. Paso a paso. One step at a time, as the Spanish said. Thankfully the will was simple, everything left to Justine. She instructed the solicitor to do what needed to be done to transfer Seaview Cottage into her name.

Looking at her diary, every day ahead was marked 'Green'. The launch of her new exhibition was rapidly approaching and there were no spare days to return to Yorkshire. She still had the last piece to make but hadn't entered her studio since her return, had set up her laptop at one end of the kitchen table, needing to complete her mother's affairs before she could even think about art again. She saw the irony of this. That the artist feted for dissecting her emotions for the world to see could not cope when real life happened to her. But she thought her mother would understand her need to compartmentalise. Justine told herself she was being organised and efficient.

Justine regretted she lived so far from Seaview Cottage. The house she co-owned in Kensington with Darya, her mentor, friend and sort of second mother, was large, comfortable, beautiful and a long way from home. But she had to be practical. Darya was almost eighty-six and seemed more fragile every day.

Paso a paso.

Today Justine would walk down the narrow passage from the kitchen to the extension at the back of the house where her studio was located. She would open the door and breathe in the stale air. Going back to work was a necessity; that was life. It didn't mean her grief was ended and her mother forgotten. She couldn't imagine a time when she would ever forget her mother, her father. With her hand on the door handle, she stopped.

Do I feel different, now I am an orphan?

She had never considered the meaning of that word before, though of course everyone was eventually orphaned in the natural way of things, if their parents died before they did. No, everything seemed the same, which was reassuring and a little baffling. Surely the world must move off its axis with her mother not in it. She opened the door to her studio and stepped in. Everything was as she had left it before flying to Tokyo. The air was musty so she took a wooden pole from its place behind the door and wedged open the long skylight above her head. It ran the length of the long room, like a spine. She cranked it open two notches and felt the cool air on her face. It reminded her of Flamborough Head except it smelt of London fumes, not brine. She walked from one end of the studio to the other, absorbing the quiet, pacing her territory, a lion in a cage. She could feel the rightness of the place.

The floor was scattered with discarded materials, blown about now by the gritty breeze. Although the studio was a scruffy place, always filled with work in progress, it was her own scruffiness. There was an order to it, not visible to anyone else. However, although the mess made her feel comfortable, dirt did not. So she took a broom and swept the worst of the mess away. With an old newspaper dampened under the tap, she wiped the large window overlooking the garden until the glass shone. This wave of housekeeping returned her mother to her, a memory of a gift, a set bought from the Betterware man who called at the door, a mini-kit of sweeping brush, dustpan and feather duster. She could not imagine a mother today buying such a gift for her daughter, but in the Sixties it was not considered odd.

Mum just wanted me to learn the practical skills. To be like her.

That sliver of realisation brought the tears again.

Justine had been offline since she'd got on the plane at Narita and was dreading an inbox filled with emails of condolence. It felt as if every tear she cried was a nugget of energy leaving her body. She decided to leave her emails until Monday. If she started early she would be able to clear them before her 10am planning meeting with Maud and the curator of her new exhibition.

A glance at her diary showed Monday was a wall of meetings. She hated these days when all she wanted to do was paint: the exhibition meeting, the PR meeting, an hour with her accountant which would no doubt last for two. Today she planned to ease herself back into art. Maud's nagging would have to wait. Yes, the launch at Barker Mews Gallery was not far off now. Yes, she would start work on 'Green 10', the only uncompleted piece.

She looked at the calendar hanging on the whitewashed wall above her desk. It was a Christmas gift from a canvas supplier; the same company sent her a calendar every year. An old-fashioned thing to do these days, but she liked it. She flipped over the page from April (Barbara Hepworth) to May (David Nash). Red ink circled the day of her press preview. The advertisement for her opening at Barker Mews had been published in the current editions of Frieze and Artforum magazines. The invitations had gone out. Justine still wasn't sure about the exhibition's title, 'The Unbearable Greenness of Green'. It was a bit twee for her liking but they'd been up against a deadline and had to choose something. Hopefully the press would think it meant something clever, they usually made up their own version of her truth.

From underneath her desk she pulled out a large box and tipped the contents on to her worktable, the folding sort used at bring-and-buy sales. With a pang, she tried to remember the last time she'd been to a boot fair or charity shop to forage for materials. Last spring, perhaps? Too long ago. It used to be a regular habit rather than a diary item. Vowing to forage more, she slowly sifted through the box. First she took the two feathers she had collected on the cliff; the white and grey feather was stored in an old shoebox labelled 'gulls', the black feather went into an old cereal packet marked 'shags & cormorants'. Next she up-ended a large brown envelope and a pile of used stamps fell on to the table, an impulse purchase on eBay. She sorted them into five piles – foreign, animals, footballers, people's heads and flowers – putting each grouping into its own small white envelope and labelling it. All five went into a large index box marked 'stamps'.

Work was soothing but it did not dispel her mother from her thoughts. It was she who first encouraged Justine to collect stamps. Under the fake silver Christmas tree one year was a thick pristine stamp album. Slipped inside it had been a Royal Mail collector's set of festive stamps – holly, ivy, poinsettia, hellebore and mistletoe. Justine stood at the filing cabinet and flicked through the envelopes until she found one marked 'Christmas' in her juvenile hand, loopy and serious. Out fell a mixture of Rudolph, nativity scenes and robins until, there they were, the original five Christmas florals.

She stood and stretched her shoulders, crossing her arms in a yoga pose she learned years ago and bastardised over the years into a regular mid-work relaxation technique. An hour had passed without her realising. Feeling chilly she closed the skylight, and then turned on the kettle, the portable gas heater and the CD player. The opening bars of Benjamin Britten's *Peter Grimes* filled the studio and she was transported back to that familiar clifftop where the waves crashed beneath. The kettle steamed and clicked. She made a pot of strong Yorkshire Tea and took a bar of Cadbury's Fruit & Nut from the plentiful supply in the fridge.

Mug in one hand and chocolate in the other, she crossed to the furthest end of the studio and sat in the armchair beside the window. With her eyes closed, she tried to meditate for ten minutes. Afterwards, as always, she was unsure whether she'd done it correctly but was encouraged that she felt a little soothed. Looking down at the garden, she noticed the solitary cedar, green and one hundred feet tall. It was subject to a tree preservation order, and, as Justine munched chocolate, she considered the people who decades ago, perhaps centuries ago, had sat near this tree while drinking tea. Trees symbolised life and death, longevity, solidity, permanence. She picked up her sketch pad and tin of pencils, and started to outline the cedar's skeleton. Her attempt was more like an LS Lowry man than a living thing; this wasn't going to be 'Green 10'. She dropped the pad on the floor and broke off another chunk of chocolate. Perhaps she should just fiddle and see if another idea arrived. The worst thing she could do was push it; it had to creep up on her. She walked to her shelves and assembled nature books, pots, boxes and brushes at random.

Two hours later, her hands resembled a snake part way through shedding its winter coat. She quite liked the process of rubbing and picking at the usual indefinable residue of glue/paint/dirt/stuff, though she never did it in front of anyone else, thinking it was a disgusting habit, like peeling sunburnt skin. She used a lot of bonding materials that were not visible on the surface of the finished piece, enjoying the knowledge that there was more going on than the eye could see, nature held together by hidden glue. Invisible guilt and secrets patched together with a smile. Her ideas often came together in bits and pieces connected by glue or fibreglass. She had been wanting for some time to experiment with Jesmonite to see if she could create a surface which could convincingly pass for bark. The process of fiddling, playing as she had when a child with cereal packets and toilet roll inners, called to something deep within and she lost track of place and time.

The doorbell rang and, as always, just for a moment the breath jumped into her lungs, tightening her chest and making her cough. It was an irrational reaction, after all these years. Hope mixed with anticipation. The doorbell rang again. Once, twice, again. Once more. Justine could imagine the finger pressing the button of the old-fashioned circular brass bell, which needed firm pressure for the bell to sound. It wouldn't be her, but if it was she imagined the finger would have an oval-shaped nail, neatly trimmed, healthy pink and flattish. It was a woman's finger, a woman's hand. The last time she had seen this hand it was a baby's, curled inside her fist like a comma. Secure. Trusting.

And then I betrayed her.

The five rings of the doorbell actually signified the arrival of her team, even though there was no meeting arranged. No one else rang the bell in the same staccato rhythm. They piled into the studio with their scarves and backpacks, their gym-style water bottles, MacBooks and phones, sipping coffee from pint-sized takeaway cups. Their smiles and chatter and hugs lit up the room and, despite her disorientation, Justine smiled too. Why were they here? They never had meetings on Saturdays. She couldn't knock their enthusiasm.

She accepted their hugs and condolences, a box of Maltesers and some kind of pot plant with white flowers.

'I don't know the right sort of words to say—'

'But you know we all love you and that's why we're here—'

'I'm really sorry, Justine, you poor thing. I wish—'

Their words circled her head like butterflies around a bloom and some of the deep chill left her bones; a coldness unrelated to the temperature of the room.

'Did you get our text? We've got a fab idea for a social media campaign. If you say yes, we can start work on it straight away. But if you want us to buzz off, we'll leave pronto.'

The space felt brighter for their presence. Justine quickly washed her hands and cleared the large table of the piles of books, their pages open at pictures of trees. Diagrams, photos, oil paintings. Art books, nature books, tree books, poetry books and biology. Cross-sections of leaves, tree rings, photos of Dalby Forest in North Yorkshire in its seasonal variations, dead trees, saplings, acorns. She stacked the books in three piles on the floor, turning their spines to the wall so they were unidentifiable.

Cal, Elena, Joy and Matthew were buzzing with gossip,

41

unpacking their bags, scrolling through updates and taking no notice of her for which she was profoundly grateful. If they saw her studying something they would ask excited questions and quickly it would become a tweet about her 'Forthcoming Works' without anything official being said. More often these days, this excitement made her feel weary. Perhaps her pace of work had slowed or it could be that she didn't know what she was doing and so avoided talking about uncertainties. She had learned to talk to them of her work only in the present tense. Sharing an idea when it was partly formed only lead to misunderstandings and misplaced enthusiasm for future promotion, which in turn made her anxious she might lose control of her story. If she controlled her public image, she could manage her own fear and regret in order to protect the ones she loved.

But that didn't mean she forgot. She had searched so many times she lost count. The first time was in 1987. She heard a woman call out in a shop. 'Jenny, where are you? Come back here this instant.' Justine went to her local social services where she was told there was no documentation about an adoption on 12 September 1983. Justine expected the answer but that hadn't prevented her hoping.

Another time she was walking along Marylebone High Street towards an interiors store, meaning to buy a vase for Darya's birthday. In a shop window was a child's name sign. 'Jenny'. Painted in rustic style, the letters were depicted as one continuous curving daisy chain. Changing the *y* to *i* was a thing of moments for Justine, but there was no bedroom door on which to hang it. That time she went to Somerset House to the office of the Registrar General of Births Marriages and Deaths. But in her heart she knew there would be no birth certificate for her daughter. And there wasn't.

6
LONDON, MAY 2010

Justine didn't return to her studio until Monday evening and she greeted her familiar space with a sigh of welcome. Today's meetings had been necessary business things, things which she felt would run just as well in her absence. Her presence enforced only by the disapproval tightening Maud's mouth when she broached the subject of her non-appearance. She had spent all yesterday dismantling and wrapping the nine finished 'Green' pieces, a job she would trust to no one. They were now lined up along the back wall of the studio, waiting for the arrival of the transport team to pack and deliver them to the gallery in St James. Justine had no creative idea whatsoever for 'Green 10' but she had vowed to make a start on it tonight so, before turning her mind to supper, she walked back and forth along the line, examining what she'd done in the hope that inspiration would strike.

'Green 1: Dorothy' was the largest piece on show. Standing tall, its central spine was blue. Dark blue with thin parallel stripes of white and red drawn with a fine paint brush, running vertically from the top of what was the prow of a boat.

The *Dorothy and Gordon Hardcastle* had been the lifeboat at Flamborough Head throughout Justine's childhood. Two years ago Justine had received a promotional email from The Yorkshire Coast Lifeboat Supporters' Society asking for funds to buy a new, high-speed, GPS-equipped inflatable boat which the RNLI proposed should replace *Dorothy* on the slip at North Landing. She wrote two cheques. One, a generous donation towards the new boat. The other in payment for the remnants of the decommissioned Dorothy that had been irrevocably damaged five miles off Bempton Cliffs in a rescue when it was blowing Gale Force 8 to Storm Force 10. Not for nothing was this stretch of Yorkshire coast known for shipwrecks. That night her crew saved seven Norwegian fishermen adrift in a rubber dinghy after their fishing vessel capsized in the heavy seas.

The locals mourned the loss of their boat, which had saved hundreds of lives since her launch in 1962. *Dorothy* was an Oakley-class lifeboat, built of African mahogany and designed not to capsize. She was an old lady when she was decommissioned. Justine was two years older than *Dorothy*, but their connection had started indirectly when Justine was seven and Justine remembered it clearly.

Death was an unfamiliar concept to Justine until she observed the last breaths of her friend's rabbit. After burying Floppy in a shoebox in Lucy's back garden, they had swapped theories about death. Justine believed Lucy, as owner of Floppy and daughter of the local Methodist minister, was bound to be an authority given that her father conducted funerals and the family lived in the manse next to the graveyard. The two girls spent many hours taking rubbings and copying into their notebooks the names and inscriptions on the gravestones, underlining the most-repeated local family names such as Stockdale and Tillett and Blownt. Top of their list were three people with unfamiliar surnames, who died at sea on the same day.

Joseph J Trilby, died January 16 1941. Age 30. Now thy earthly work is done.

Edward Gray Bartholomew, died January 16 1941. Age 50. Proud survivor of Dunkirk.

Paul Peter Prattlam, died January 16 1941. Age 17. Lost but never forgotten.

Lucy asked her father for help but in 1941 he'd been living in Africa. Justine's father couldn't help either; he'd been a soldier in the desert that year. Her mother clucked her tongue and said it wasn't a subject for seven-year-old girls. Lucy's mother said it all happened 'a long time ago.' And so Justine and Lucy agreed upon the bravest option open to them and walked down the cliff path to the lifeboat house at North Landing to ask Old Arthur who had been alive for 'a long time.'

He was at the slip, in his long wellington boots, washing down *Dorothy* where she stood on her trolley. Scrubbing brush in one hand, bucket at his feet, pipe in his mouth, he was singing 'For Those in Peril on the Sea', which Justine and Lucy both knew from school assembly. The three finished singing the song together, and then Old Arthur put down his brush and sat beside the two girls on the sea wall. Justine knew he was really old, she guessed at least fifty, her estimate being based on the condition of his hands: his pale skin was wrinkled by a life's worth of sea salt. She decided to save her pocket money and give him a tube of hand cream for Christmas.

There was a pause, as if they were waiting for something, and then he coughed deeply, so deep that he dislodged phlegm from his lungs. He spat and rasped and rasped and spat until the three sat surrounded by an arc of spittle at their feet. Justine thought she would be sick so she tried to hold her breath, knowing Old Arthur always did this before he was ready to tell a story. It was why Justine and Lucy had argued before coming here. The spitting was horrible. But, Justine insisted, although they hated Old Arthur's spitting, they didn't hate him. So if they could just look away during any spitting, he might tell them the story. He was to be relied upon to tell good stories, was Old Arthur, though sometimes they weren't sure if they were true or made up. They always started with 'I'll tell thee summat'.

They'd known him all their lives. He was the caretaker of the lifeboat house, and of *Dorothy* herself, but once had been a merchant seaman on a ship sailing to South Africa. Last term at primary school he talked to their class about the job of a seaman.

'Everyone who lives by the sea respects and loves it,' he said, and thirty-two heads nodded, 'but,' and there was a long pause as he stared from face to face, 'you should never forget the cold water'll freeze you in minutes, yon currents'll drag you under, even on a sunny day. It'll take you when you least expect it.'

He didn't mention January 16 1941 that day at school.

Justine showed him her notebook where the names on the gravestones were written out in best.

'Aye, those three, they died in the war.'

Justine knew only two things about The War. First, The War had taken all the country's money so now England was in debt to America and there was absolutely no money for treats. And two, the string of concrete bunkers along the clifftops, each a mile apart, had been built in The War to 'keep out Jerry'. Justine didn't know anyone called Jerry; the only Germans she'd read about were called Adolf and Hermann and Erwin. Expressly forbidden by her mother to go within six feet of a bunker – they were dirty and infested with rats, she said, and there may be unexploded ammunition inside – Justine and Lucy explored the one that was out of sight of Seaview Cottage. True, it was dirty. But there were no rats, only a very frightened field mouse and lots of spiders. They cleared out the rubbish, pulled up weeds and made a den.

'It wer' a German plane, flying home after bombing factories in Leeds.' Old Arthur's frown drew lines on his forehead. 'Any bombs they had left, they'd drop into t'sea.' At the same time, heading south for Hull and hugging the Yorkshire coastline, was a merchant ship full of food from America. It took a direct hit and started to sink. Notified by the coastguard, the *Lady Mary Fountwell*, *Dorothy*'s predecessor, did her duty and her crew fished some of the merchant seamen from the water but three drowned and were buried in the Flamborough graveyard. Old Arthur said that in Plymouth, where the sailors and the ship came from, there was a plaque thanking the Flamborough lifeboat and her brave crew for risking their lives.

Old Arthur, who confusingly must have been Young Arthur during the war, sailed on board *Lady Mary* that day and said he never forgot it.

'Every time I see summat green,' he said, 'I think on that sinking ship and those three dead sailors floating in engine oil.' He sighed.

The girls waited for him to go on, but he said no more.

'Why green?' Lucy prompted.

Because the food the ship was carrying was fresh vegetables. 'Ever since, the sight of that colour makes me feel sick.'

Without *Lady Mary* on whom to bestow her respect, awe, admiration and love, Justine transferred her fascination to *Dorothy* on that day.

Standing in her studio now, far from the sea, she wondered if it was obscure to use the blue prow for 'Green 1: Dorothy' when the piece was inspired by a different boat.

It's only a fib, no one will notice.

She was more exercised by what to do about 'Green 10' than about a colour swap. The last piece was usually the most difficult, least instinctive; mono-layered not multi-layered. She wished now she had chosen a different motif, a single colour was so restrictive. She pressed along the brow above her left eye, trying to free-associate on the nature of green, giving her imagination a loose rein to wander, aware of her skull tightening as if she were wearing a child-size rubber swimming cap.

Green woodpecker. Greenfinch. Goldfinch, no. Fields. Apples. Bowls. A football pitch. Wimbledon Centre Court. Lichen. New pastures. The flags of Pakistan and Saudi Arabia. Graham Greene. Green Park. Environmentalists. Verdigris. Lemons and limes. An emerald ring. Ecologically-friendly. Spanish. Verde, maduro*, ripe, unripe. Olives.*

To Justine, olives meant Spain, and the thought of Spain never failed to trigger the same memory. The one about loss and about consequences. The last time it happened was a year ago, at the supermarket, standing in the checkout queue watching a stranger's products pass by on the belt. Olives. Ham. Bread. Anchovies. Tomatoes. Apples. Bread. Lemons. She turned away from the olives and their memories, irritated with the woman in front who was taking an age to pack her purchases into her bags for life, when a child's voice called out.

'*Mamá! Mamá! Dónde estas?*'

Justine turned to call out 'I'm here' – then swallowed her words as she watched a dark-haired girl run to her stressed-looking, dark-haired mother.

Robbed of her breath, Justine's heart pounded. A box of eggs fell from her fingers. And again she regretted leaving, running away, a day before the deadline to register the birth.

It's as if she never existed. But I can't change the past.

It was a familiar thought, and what happened next was familiar too. By the time she got home that day a year ago, the migraine was pounding and pulverising her brain so it felt like a rejected pumpkin in the farmer's field; squashed, sliced and flattened by tractor and plough. Today, the memory of olives, combined with worry about 'Green 10', brought on another migraine. She retreated to the sofa, the light-white room blacked out by a tightly fitting eye mask. There was no escape from the incessant thrumming, drumming, buzzing in her ears as if full of electricity. Cup after cup of camomile tea, a cool compress on her brow, but still her head pulsed. Her veins, nerves and the crinkly nodes of her brain were independent forces, forcing their way through bone to fresh air as determined as the roots of an ash tree divining water through hard clay soil.

Her headaches followed a pattern. Sometimes, the network of knotted and gnarled muscles responded to the heat of an electric pad held against her neck and shoulders. Other times she sat, blanket-wrapped, the beat of every second taking an hour, wondering if her death would feel this violent and hoping for a silent slipping-away or the swift removal of her head. Hour after hour she waited, assessing any change for a sign of the migraine's retreat. Waiting for the moment when this pain would subside and allow her to sleep.

Today's pain was black. Black on black. White flashing lights, Titanium White? Justine stood with a microwave-heated wheat pad on her shoulders, a thick fleece hat pulled down over her ears and a ski neck-warmer snuggled up to her chin, wearing sunglasses despite the grey sky outside. She felt feverish and over-medicated, but over the worst.

Scooping a handful of glaziers' putty from the pot, she spread it thickly across the canvas to represent her skull.

Putty is bone-coloured.

Grey, cream, brain-coloured. Using a tablespoon, she scooped black oil paint from the pot on to the canvas, tipping it this way and that, and then lying it flat. She surveyed the result; the damp putty was slicked over by an oily black sludge. She balled her fist so the bones of her knuckles shone white through her parchment-pale skin, and then hit the canvas in time with the pounding in her head. The chemical smell of the paint made her head spin but it cleared a path through her sinuses and gave her brain a kick-start. After a break to retch in the sink, she added more putty, more black, more drips of Titanium White like splinters of light creeping round the edges of her sunglasses. She pressed the linseed oil putty now, massaging it as if to force the pain away, kneading it like bread dough. Her fingertips left a trail of grease across her temples.

Today's pain was black with grey.

Afterwards, she felt a kind of relief. As if a headache cleansed, bringing a new emptiness with which to face the day.

7
SPAIN, SEPTEMBER 1982

Her name was on the label above the desk. The workspace allocated to her was just one in a long line crammed along a long corridor. Justine had been at college for two weeks and already loved her studio. White walls, plain concrete floor splattered by the students who had each called this 'mine' before her. She liked this heritage of old paint. Her space had a particularly distinctive spillage in the shape of a cockerel, a similarity enhanced by one of her predecessors who had added a swoop of black tail feathers and red blob for the wattle. Desk, easel, small filing cabinet. Her space was separated from her neighbours either side by thin wooden partitions, nothing more than plywood which wobbled slightly as if alive in the light breeze from the open window.

She welcomed the afternoon silence. Except for these two hours every day, the space was full of industry and music. Her first few days here had been difficult. The Spanish students played pop songs so loudly and joyfully that Justine, struggling to concentrate, had resorted to ear plugs. But now, all was quiet. Everyone else had headed off for siesta. A sleep in the middle of the day didn't feel right. Given the solitude, she had hoped to have a half-finished canvas by now but her eyes were aching, her paintbrushes were dry and so was her throat. She lay down on the floor, relishing the cool of the tiles on her skin, her limbs stretching out in search of the coolest surface, and all the time thinking, thinking, and getting nowhere. The uniform off-white colour of the canvas she normally loved as the foundation for all her painting, which usually murmured a welcome to her, was silent and had been ever since Señor Romero handed out the assignment.

She'd stuck the worksheet to her wall. It said, 'Inside I am always a child.'

But I'm not.

She stood, sat, stood again, rummaging through her bag, fiddling with the heavy silver hoops which elongated her almost non-existent earlobes. Next she re-arranged her palette, paints and brushes. Spotting a stray spot of paint on the desktop, she wrapped a cloth round her index finger, dipped it in turps and dabbed at the stain. With everything spick and span, she stared at the sentence again and wondered what she had misunderstood.

I will not go home without doing something.

It was rare for Justine not to know where to start. She had felt uneasy about this class when she'd seen it described on the prospectus: 'The Role of Autobiography in Art'. The whole idea of autobiography intimidated her.

I haven't done anything in my life yet which is worth putting into art.

The beach. She spent half her childhood on the beach. Perhaps she could use that. But sand and sea were landscape, not autobiographical. She longed to walk miles along Málaga's beach again. It may not be Yorkshire's white cliffs but it was still beautiful, with those amazing mountains on one side and the emptiness of the Mediterranean on the other. She didn't want to follow an artificial project. Now she was here, she wanted to be free. As the sun progressed through the day the hills inland from Málaga went through the most amazing colour transformations, starting with a brown so dark it was almost black, to pink and yellow the colours of strawberry and lemon sorbets, and finally setting as a rich warm terracotta like the clay pots of geraniums that filled balconies everywhere in the city. She totally got why Monet painted his landscapes at precisely the same time of day to be sure his light effects were perfect.

I'm going to do the same, and I don't care if people think I'm copying his idea.

Every weekend she planned to work as Monet did. She

would go up into the mountains carrying with her the partially completed 11am, noon and 1pm canvases. Each would be placed strictly in its own unique position. Justine would wait for the allotted time to arrive upon which she'd leap into action, stopping and starting painting after one hour exactly as the weather conditions changed. Consistency of light was her aim. She had wanted to try this in London but the weather was too variable. Here each day so far had dawned the same. Her mind drifted, brooding on which views Monet would choose to paint if he were in Málaga, where he would set up his easel.

His easel.

She focussed again on the blank canvas in front of her. The sunlight had shifted and now fell brightly on the empty paper, shining, seeming to taunt her with its nothingness.

'Oh for goodness sake,' she said aloud, 'I'm not frightened of you, you know.' Then she checked left and right to make sure she was still alone. Her fear was of being found out, that her skill had no breadth, her technique shaky. She worried that her fate was to be a commercial artist who makes a living by producing endless variations of fluffy kittens for greetings cards.

But fluffy kittens do pay a salary.

She told herself to stop being dramatic. Painting fluffy kittens would be a perfectly respectable career; would pay the mortgage, provide a car, holidays, but it sounded repetitive and boring and she wanted more. Her painting was good, perhaps better than good, it just wasn't something she admitted. She squashed down a rising fear that her money was disappearing like water poured from a watering can on to the parched Spanish earth, and considered her easel again. She had experienced artist's block only once before, in the first term, first year, at RivesArt. Her solution then had been to walk away and come back later. Today she didn't dare leave behind a blank canvas, didn't want to admit defeat to the others in the class who she barely knew and who would return refreshed from their afternoon nap just as her energy was draining away. She stared at the clean brushes, waiting, hoping for an idea, a feeling, anything.

'Get real,' she said aloud. 'You cannot be afraid of a paintbrush. That is so pathetic. Be afraid of Ronald Reagan launching a nuclear missile at Russia. Be afraid of the Yorkshire Ripper. Not a paintbrush.'

She remembered the very first time art had felt difficult, long before RivesArt and Málaga, in class at secondary school. The theme was 'Death', but she had never known anyone who died. She excused herself on the basis that she had not lived her life yet, she was waiting for things to happen, and when they did she would become a great artist. But then she remembered Floppy, Lucy's grey rabbit, and painted a picture of swirling mist in shades of pale and dark grey. And when the theme was 'Anger' she thought regretfully of her red bicycle, stolen from outside their front door. Her parents couldn't afford to replace it and Justine resented the unfairness of a thief taking something which wasn't his. She covered her paper with thick circles of red paint, scoring criss-cross lines through it with a palette knife. Both pieces were in the portfolio that gained her admittance to RivesArt.

I'm over-thinking it.

She stood and walked slowly along the line of workspaces and peeped at her classmates' canvases one by one, feeling as if she was prying. One was completely covered in blue. Its neighbour; a dark brown pigment which, glancing at the palette beside the easel, was a blend of sepia and cobalt blue. The next student along the line had painted two circles, the outer blood red, the inner a palest baby pink. This last belonged to April Masterson, her flatmate. Stuck to the wall was a photo of a younger April and an older man who Justine assumed must be her father. April quoted her father a lot – he approved of this, he said that – and Justine was trying hard not to be irritated by this as she knew April's mother died when she was young and she only had her father.

Justine walked on to the next and the next. There were no amazing canvases here, nothing technically she couldn't have done herself. Not knowing the people, though, meant she had no idea of the meaning of their work which was, anyway, incomplete. Art was not just about technique, she was quickly learning. She stood in front of her own blank canvas again and turned it round – portrait, landscape, portrait – calmer now, waiting for inspiration rather than hunting it down. She picked up the paintbrush, running the sable tip through her fingers, as always loving its softness but feeling no colour. She put it down again, at a slightly different angle, and then sat down. In the top drawer of the filing cabinet was a jumble of papers, material for future collages, anything that caught her eye: coloured wrappers, bold typography from the newspaper, labels, postcards, bus tickets, paper doilies, corrugated card, the Spanish label off a tin of tomatoes rescued from the kitchen bin, and a brown paper bag from yesterday's breakfast.

Out of her jacket pocket she took an identical bag, slightly squashed, containing a bun she'd bought at the *panadería* this morning. Inside was a sugar-drenched, crescent-shaped pastry filled with eggy custard and apple. She didn't know its name but had bought it successfully by the simple method of pointing and smiling. She bit into it and waited for the sugar to hit her veins. This had become a daily ritual, a luxury costing a few pesetas. Her mother never bought shop-made cakes and consequently they held a mystery which Justine was determined to explore. A small kick of defiance as sharp as the toddler spitting out her mashed potato.

'Yes.' She jumped up. The off-white canvas was smiling at her now, she just had to work out how paint it.

'Inside I am always a child' by Justine King was the only piece from her intake chosen by a visiting professor who had exhibited in Madrid and New York. His selection of twenty student paintings from all Spain's art colleges formed an exhibit at Málaga's new shiny Tourist Information Centre near the port. The theme was 'Spanish sun and culture'. Justine, interviewed by the local newspaper, was relieved she wasn't asked how her painting fitted into the touristy sunshine theme. A photograph of her standing beside her canvas, smiling uncertainly, was printed on an inside page. It was her first press cutting.

No one but Justine knew her painting portrayed a sticky pastry. She hadn't told a lie, had she? It was just that no one had asked her to explain what it meant.

8
LONDON, MAY 2010

Thanks to her migraine, Justine lost a day's work. So on Wednesday, in need of fresh air and inspiration for 'Green 10', which remained un-started, she wandered eastwards across Kensington. She hadn't known where she was going until she stood on the doorstep of the Victoria & Albert Museum. This building was a womb for her; it comforted her when she felt vulnerable, inspired her when creativity ran dry. It was nurturing.

Justine stood in front of a display cabinet looking at four embroidery samplers made in 1913 for the museum by Louisa F Pesel. Inevitably, as always, they brought her mother close again and vertical tear tracks marked her cheeks. Without a tissue she gave an almighty sniff, thankful her mother was not here to see this disgusting behaviour. She breathed deeply, mopped her eyes with her sleeve and inspected her jumper for damage. Hardly a smudge; then she remembered it was a workday and therefore she was mascara-free. Her mother would have approved the lack of make-up, but disapproved the use of her sleeve. Justine would always regret not bringing her mother here to see this embroidery. It reminded her of sitting on the sofa side by side with her mother, learning to embroider, their knees toasty from the coal fire in the grate, a brass fireguard carefully placed between flames and flesh. It took her many weeks to finish her own sampler of stitches, unpicking and re-sewing. Rows upon rows of chain stitch, seeding, French knots and bullion knots, buttonhole, herring-bone and cross-stitch. Finally her mother had proclaimed it neat enough, framed it and hung it in the front room above the piano. But now her mother was gone and the sampler was in a box in Justine's study waiting to be unpacked. It was odd, seeing these things out of place, Yorkshire things in London, but then she was a Yorkshire thing in London too.

She meandered along the empty corridors, waiting for something to catch her eye. She stopped in front of a pile of wooden sticks seemingly at the point of collapse, but which according to the display card was actually a chair. Instantly she remembered Sam, a boyfriend at college. The relationship had lasted two months, his socialism made her feel naïve and 'country' and her constant messiness and collecting of rubbish was, as he described it, disorderly. But one of his many mantras had stayed with her.

'Things are never quite as they seem,' Sam, a journalism student from Rotherham, had said with a tone of superiority. 'People are full of contradictions. Think, say, feel, do, Justine. That's what journalists are trained to consider when they're interviewing someone. People don't always say what they really think, or do what they believe in.' It was the journalist's job, he said, to identify these contradictions and question deeper to reveal the truth.

Am I guilty of thinking one thing and doing another?

Was art a lie if the artist didn't believe in its message? And did it actually matter? To Justine it was about suspending reality, freeing the imagination; accepting trees made of stone, leaves made of painted metal and fabrics used to represent the sky. She disliked snobbery among the cliques who preferred sculpture to paintings, or acrylics to watercolours. She felt out of place. It reminded her of *The Frost Report* sketch about social class where John Cleese looked down on Ronnie Barker who looked up to Cleese and down on Ronnie Corbett, who knew his place. She knew her fondness for the sketch was evidence of the Yorkshire chip on her shoulder; it was still there, a bit soft round the edges now perhaps, but still there. It had been the common denominator with Sam. He worked at *The Guardian* now. She sometimes saw him across the room at openings. He had become a soft socialist with cashmere sweaters and a wine rack full of Rioja. Thirty years ago they had bonded over poverty and their struggle to fit in. Now both fitted in and had kept their accents. Justine smiled to herself, recognising a streak of her mother's Yorkshire patriotism in her own pride. She ran through her mental list of Yorkshire artists. David Hockney, Barbara Hepworth, Henry Moore.

Once 'Green' was launched and life returned to normal, she meant to return to Flamborough Head. She had an idea to turn Seaview Cottage into a studio, knocking down walls, putting in a picture window facing the sea. Until then she would have to make do. She would go to Tate Britain and stand in front of Hockney's *Bigger Trees near Warter* so she was ready for the next visit to Seaview Cottage when she could drive along Woldgate, stare across the rolling chalk hills at the tall stands of trees, and breathe deeply.

She thought again of the PS at the end of Maud's latest email. 'The gallery has had recent success with its other artists by selling studies, watercolours and preparatory sketches to complement a new series. Any chance you have a few which you can throw into the mix? Ciao.'

Sometimes Maud could be so crass, and therein lay their love/hate/appreciate relationship. Maud loved money, making more of it for Justine and therefore herself, and it had been her idea to raise Justine's profile. Justine protested, citing nerves, inability to express herself cogently and inability to control her undoubted skill at placing her foot in her mouth, but Maud ignored her, booked a media course and drew up a 'media personality plan'. Justine hated it all, it frightened her. Now 'Justine Tree the artist' was a means to an end, nothing to do with East Yorkshire girl Justine King. Even her name change was a calculated PR move. Now she approached a media interview or gallery appearance in the same way she guessed actors rehearsed before going on stage or politicians prepared before a news programme. She had learned the hard way how to make it work: a little research about the person asking the questions, rehearsal of her five key points, a review of her overall objective. Unable to explain her creative process adequately for

Maud, she had contrived an emotional network of motivations that explained her art, her life, her inner life. It was cobblers, of course, but the strategy was converting into sales.

But every time a new series was launched, Maud wanted more and Justine's fear kicked in. The trouble with lies was they seemed to mesh with the truth into one unified whole. Given the chance, she would rather live at Seaview Cottage, produce her art, put it on a truck to London and let Maud sell it all, her presence not required.

It wasn't that she had fallen out of love with art. That thing that made her go to Málaga still burnt within. She would still be doing it when her eyes were cloudy with cataracts. It was the heartbeat of her day. But when asked by a journalist to explain what her art was about, she could never answer. She had to admit, Maud's plan had helped with that. It always started a week or so before an exhibition. The media questions went round and round in her head and she tried to spot the trick questions, the ones that would dig out her secret. What is it about? Where did you get the idea? How different was the first version? Is there a hidden message? What are you trying to say? Why did you use that colour/timber/metal/leaves/rubbish/plastic? What does it symbolise? Why collage not oils? Why oils not acrylics or watercolours? What does it tell us about you? What part of you, of your life, is contained in your art?

It was the last couple of questions that frightened her and she would remain frightened, to some degree or other, until the whole process was over and she could retire again to her studio, free from the fear someone would expose her as a fraud. She wished she was brave enough to stand tall and say, 'I made this and it is what it is. Take it or leave it.' Her difficulty with watercolours was, she knew, about control. She envied artists who could exploit the fluidity of the form but distrusted the way it ran away from her. The liquid could run and run and when it did it took with it her vision of the finished effect.

I want the line to be where I have drawn it. To end where I want it to end.

It was why she preferred oils and collage. They were

malleable, correctable, exact. But she did want to master watercolours. She felt instinctively that they were the best way of capturing the changing sky at home, the waves, the wind in the trees. All liquid things.

She thought of 'Green'. It was acceptable, it would sell, it bulked out her body of work but the whole concept was static, predictable.

And is it me? I used to be brave and expressive.

She remembered the freedom with which she had created 'Inside I am a Child'.

From a custard pastry, for goodness sake.

She mourned the freedom of youth, without expectations or cares or regrets, just possibilities. She remembered her first trip to an art gallery. It was 1973, her second year at secondary school. It had been a flash of lightning in her insulated world.

The first thing she had noticed was the size and heft of the doors. They were as tall as two men, one standing on the shoulders of the other. Justine was not tall and the long brass handles were the length of her arm from shoulder to wrist. As she leant against the oak, using all her weight to push the door open, she memorised the moment for future recall.

My first time in a proper art gallery.

Not the little museum in the village with its photos of old fishermen and engravings of rows of women gutting herrings. Not the upstairs room in the library at Bridlington with its small collection of framed oil paintings of sea scenes, all dark brown and grey waves and clouds. So brown they looked dirty.

Her class had come by bus to Hull to the Ferens Art Gallery and her heart was bubbling with anticipation at seeing a Picasso in the flesh. Any museum which had the word 'art' in the title was bound to have something by Pablo Picasso. She was so excited at the thought of standing close to something he had actually touched, proof he started with a blank canvas, that she couldn't stop fidgeting. Of course she wouldn't be able to touch it, but she so wanted to. She had decided on the bus journey that, should she feel tempted, she would stand with her fists in her pockets. Standing in the wide tall foyer, waiting for the museum lady to finish talking, she realised there were no pockets in her school skirt.

I will fold my arms.

'Please, Miss.'

The museum education lady, who was not what Justine had expected from someone working in an art gallery, for she was dressed in an A-line tweed skirt which finished at mid-calf and a Fair Isle sweater over a cream blouse with daisies embroidered on the collar, stopped and turned.

'Yes, dear?'

'Can you tell me where the Picasso paintings are, please?'

'Picasso? Pablo Picasso? The Spanish artist? No, dear, we don't have a Picasso here. But we do have a painting by John Constable. He was English.'

No Picasso? It's not a proper museum if there's no Picasso.

Justine trailed from room to room without a glance at her questionnaire or her study partner Susan Pratt. Painting after painting, wall after wall, room by room, it all seemed the same to her. Just like those sea paintings in the library at Brid. Dark brown and grey. Ships tossing on the sea. Fishermen pulling in nets. Mariners shipwrecked. And then she turned a corner into another room. It was empty of people; just four paintings but dominated by the largest. At first it made her think of a tiger, with a large eye, and green-striped fur. Then she thought it was a paper cut-out of a tiger, laid flat, like the dresses you could cut out of *Twinkle* magazine with tabs to attach to the body of the paper girl. Then she wasn't sure at all what the painting was of, except that it definitely wasn't a shipwreck. She read the small plaque on the wall. It read: 'The Archer by Eileen Agar, 1967.' That was all.

I was seven when this was painted.

She took three paces backwards and, with her arms folded and fingers neatly tucked in, studied the painting. Then with her sketch pad and best HB pencil, specially sharpened last night, she sat on the polished floor opposite the painting, her back leaning against the wall. She thought there was probably a rule saying 'no sitting on floors' but had purposely avoided reading any signs so, if caught, she could honestly say she didn't know it wasn't allowed.

'The Archer' had two outlines, one inside the other, which she drew. Each had shapes that were a bit like legs, a head, a mane. The outer shape was solid black and was the shape she imagined an animal skin would be if it was cut off the animal and laid out flat like a rug. What a disgusting thought. Surely that couldn't be right. She concentrated on the inner shape. She sketched in the green tiger-patterned parts, though now she wondered if it was meant to be grass. At the top left, where the animal's eye should be, there was a daisy.

She stopped and examined what she had done.

That's not right.

She tore the page out of the pad, folded it into two once, again, and again, and then slotted it in at the back.

This time, she decided to really study the painting. To wait before drawing anything. To see what she could see.

She could see a tiger.

She tried scrunching up her eyes, to see if a different picture emerged. It worked with those dot pictures, where you only saw something if you looked through almost closed eyes.

She could still see a tiger.

Then she thought about the title. She remembered her father saying there was a star called The Archer, Orion-something. Or perhaps this was something to do with hunting. Or war. Didn't soldiers fight with bows and arrows at Agincourt? They had studied Henry V last term in history. Justine regularly got C's for her history essays.

When the loudspeaker announcement, 'the museum will close in ten minutes' was broadcast, Justine had completed two more unsatisfactory sketches. The last one was her own version of Eileen Agar's Archer. It was the first time she had used an existing painting and turned it into something of her own.

Two weeks later, when the library van parked at the side of the road, Justine spent half an hour sitting on the steps with the brick-like *The Encyclopaedia of Art* on her lap. There was a whole section devoted to Eileen Agar who had once visited the home in France where Picasso lived with Dora Maar. Finding 'The Archer' at the Ferens seemed pre-destined and so her vow to be an artist gained momentum.

9
LONDON, MAY 2010

An argument was ensuing behind closed doors at the Royal Academy of Arts. The meeting wasn't official; not diarised or minuted, more a conversation, a coming-together of unlike minds to discuss an election already made by Academician vote but awaiting the seal of approval by the Council. Tea, sandwiches and fruit cake were being consumed.

'Well I don't care for it. Bad decision, bad decision.' The speaker was a sculptor whose next birthday would see him attain the age of seventy-five, the age at which Academicians – that hallowed group of eighty artists who belonged to probably the best members' club in the art world – retired to become Senior Academicians. And so the way was opened for youth. Usually two places a year, sometimes three. That, and death, was the only way a slot became available for a new artist to be proposed, elected and anointed, signing the Role of Obligation previously signed by Reynolds, Stubbs, Turner, Constable and Landseer.

'She's blasphemous, her work is over-emotional, over-sexual, over-everything,' the sculptor harrumphed. 'I voted for the architect. He is not emotionally incontinent.'

There was some light mumbling around the table in a quiet corner of the Academicians' Room in the Keeper's House.

The newest Academician at the table kept his counsel. He had signed his name to the Roll of Obligation two years earlier, having practised his signature many times beforehand to ensure it would stand the test of time alongside the big names. He still wished he could cross it out and have another go. And he still felt he was a junior sitting at the prefects' dinner table. Generally he kept his mouth shut at these impromptu discussions that broke out over lunch among whichever RAs happened to be there at midday. But he didn't like the way the sculptor was steering the tone of the conversation. In fact it wasn't a conversation, it was one man expressing his opinion in an increasingly objectionable way. It was almost agitation. He wondered if he should interrupt, change the subject, talk about the weather. He glanced up at the tall windows as a sudden drumming sound proved the veracity of the prediction by this morning's BBC weathergirl.

'I voted for her,' said a red-haired freckly man sitting opposite. 'I think she's a breath of fresh air. Reminds me of Tracey Emin when she joined.'

'"Joined". It's not a tennis club. Hrrmph.'

The painter who had spoken dropped his eyes to his water glass, his thin lips pressed so tightly together they almost disappeared in a white line.

James Watercliff wondered why everyone, including himself, was so reluctant to speak. He disliked bullies.

'Her drawings are competent, more than competent. I don't care for her use of colour; dull, so much brown and green,' said the most senior artist present; a woman sculptor far more successful than the complainer who had slumped down into his high-backed mahogany chair.

James was sitting in a similar chair and he wondered idly if it was a Chippendale and if the bottoms of everyone round the table were as stiff as his. The carving on the shield back was rubbing uncomfortably against his spine so he adjusted his weight on to his left buttock, leant on the polished arm and then opened his mouth to speak. To ask what colours should be used to paint nature, if not brown and green.

'I find her work totally delightful,' said a pale-faced blond man James did not recognise. James closed his mouth and awaited another chance to speak. The man had a soft West Country accent. It was an attractive tone, well suited to the voiceover for a television ad for Cheddar cheese or Somerset cider. 'No one else out there doing what she does. It was a definite yes for me.'

There was a harrumphing from the sculptor. 'Yes, I'll give it to you, her technique is not to be challenged. It's her publicity I don't care for. She's always in the papers. I don't want to know what she eats for breakfast.'

The pale-faced man's voice grew firmer. 'Well, I found that feature in *Frieze* rather revealing. We are all driven, after all; just by different things. Mostly, I think, we all hide our basest motivations.'

'Her career path has certainly been unconventional, but that's not such a bad thing,' pointed out another artist, silent so far. 'It's not as if we are unaccustomed to unconventional artists. Remember Turner.'

'Not personally,' said the sculptor, and there was a faint chuckling in reply.

James finally found his voice. 'Well, it's a done deal. She's been nominated and has the required eight secondary signatures in the Nominations Book; it's a democratic process.' He stood and pushed his chair back. 'I'm new here. I hope you didn't all sit round and talk about me behind my back when I was elected.' The silence was prolonged.

'I would point out that she hasn't been formally admitted yet.' The sculptor was sitting taller, his voice firmer. 'She may have her letter of invitation, but I for one will be watching for any sign of disreputable behaviour upon which I will present a motion to withdraw her election before the meeting of Council in December.'

Afterwards as he walked across the courtyard, passing through the crowds gazing at Jeff Koons's living flower 'Puppy', and out on to Piccadilly, James Watercliff tried not to worry about that silence.

He decided to watch out for Justine Tree at the next RA drinks thing, and welcome her to the RA Outer Darkness Club.

10
SPAIN, SEPTEMBER 1982

September passed quickly and the weather in Málaga seemed to Justine hotter than any summer day at Flamborough. She had written a weekly expense budget to get through to Christmas but, having brought the wrong clothes from home, had already exceeded it to buy three t-shirts, a denim skirt and a pair of flip-flops. She was loving the heat, the smell of hot dust, the mid-afternoon shimmer on pavements and roads, followed by the cool breath of dusk. Places and people were beginning to attain familiarity and she no longer panicked about getting to class on time or boarding the wrong bus.

She had settled into a comfortable existence in the apartment with the other two girls. They were both doing fine art too and the three had most classes together, excepting their specialisms and personal tutorials. Justine had never met anyone quite like Maria Catalina Alba Roman or April Masterson. For the first week she had called Maria Catalina by her two Christian names until it was explained that every Spanish girl was baptised Maria something, after the Virgin Mary, and advised just to call her Catalina instead. Catalina's method of saving money involved eating eggs at every meal, broken together with whatever leftover bits of ham or vegetables she had saved from the weekly visit to her mother. April simply didn't eat, though, Justine guessed, not through lack of funds. She only ever nibbled and smoked. Justine's Yorkshire sense of thrift didn't seem to work in Spain. She could forage for art materials as easily as at home, but her idea of a cheap meal involved baked beans and toast. Lots of toast. She'd hunted high and low for baked beans in Málaga's markets without luck, only finding tins of beans with ham, which didn't look right at all. She couldn't find sliced bread either. The eating habits of the three flatmates meant that, as the first term progressed, Justine and April got thinner while Catalina became uncomfortably constipated. A chunk of Justine's grant cheque had already disappeared on mandatory books and art materials. Her pesetas seemed to buy little and her next grant would not be paid until January.

The girls found a flamenco club; cheap entrance, more expensive drinks. Its entrance was hidden up dark back stairs in the muddle of alleys surrounding the cathedral. The three flatmates found themselves in a room under the eaves that seemed to pulse with heat. With Catalina as their guide and interpreter, Justine and April were inducted into the fine art of flamenco appreciation. They ordered three glasses of fizzy water with lemon which they hoped would pass for vodka and tonic and which could be nursed all night. Catalina schooled them to curb their enthusiasm, not clicking their fingers along to the impossibly quick yet infectious rhythm of guitar and tapping heels. They wanted to join in but Catalina banned them from clapping their hands, which apparently marked them out as *turistas*. It came to be a weekly treat.

One night they went to see a celebrated local dancer who had just returned from Sevilla to great acclaim. Catalina had her sketch pad in front of her and Justine watched with envy as with minimal lines of her pencil Catalina caught the movement of Esperanza's skirt, her flying hair and clipping heels. April, who Justine suspected of ordering vodka and tonic without offering to share it, was smiling at the charcoal-eyed, jet-haired guitarist.

At 2am Inma, Justine's favourite singer, stepped on to the tiny platform that acted as a stage and stood within the semi-circle of guitarists, percussionists and backing singers. At the first pure note Justine closed her eyes and let herself fall into the music, leaving behind her worries about money, her outstanding essay on 'Van Gogh and Gauguin: Brothers or Rivals?' and her overdue preparatory sketches for the life class. The rasp of the woman's voice, at once so female, so full of life and loss, became at one with Justine's. Deep, grinding, irreversible, everywoman's regret and pain. The young voice, which was at the same time so old, vibrated through Justine's flesh so the two women and their cares became one.

The three girls left the club two hours later, Justine's ears ringing with another woman's troubles. Her own concerns faded with the protection of darkness. They walked down the alley leading from the club to the wider Calle Cister away from port and the bars, when a rasp of protest made Justine stop and turn. In a dark side passage Inma stood with her back against a brick wall, trapped there by a man, her hands reaching above her head as if hailing the Madonna. One hand was moving beneath her skirt, the other round her throat.

'*No más, más, más, querido. Ahora!*' said the singer.

Justine turned to Catalina. 'What's she saying?'

April gave a snort. 'What do you think she's saying?'

Justine shook Catalina's arm. 'But we should help her. She's saying no.'

'*No.*' Catalina's voice was sharp, her arm shot out in front of Justine to block her way. '*No, guapita, no.* That is her husband. They are enjoying the *privado.*' And she caught April's eye and they smiled.

The sound of the couple's quiet murmurs banished from Justine's head that lingering voice of regret and pain, and in a flash she felt cheated. She turned away.

Of course it's a lie. She's performing.

Justine felt tired, naïve, and a very long way from home.

As the three girls turned right along Calle San Agustin towards their apartment, looking east towards the new sun, Justine found herself walking a step behind the others.

11
SPAIN, OCTOBER 1982

October in Málaga was like no October Justine had experienced before. At home, the sky was winter grey, the sea winter
grey, everybody's mood winter grey. The northerly wind blew
straight through you as if you were made of paper. The sun, on
its rare appearances, was the palest wash of jaundiced yellow.
Here, the blue sky went on forever. It felt as she imagined it
would feel to be on a package holiday, having never been on
one.

She chose this particular café so she could listen to the
gipsy playing guitar on the street corner. She had seen him
play here before. She returned once a week as much to gaze
at him as to listen to his music. His face was carved from teak
and his voice full of Andalucían stones. His guitar may have
been made of leather rather than wood, burnished brown by
the oil of his skin, his fingers following the notes of an ancient
unwritten song. When he finished, she wished he would sing
for longer. Then there came a gentle chink of coins and he
stood at her elbow with a wide smile and a small velvet bag
in his outstretched hand. She had some pesetas in her pocket,
put there in preparation after observing on previous visits how
much he received from the locals. The custom was to hand
over the tiny coins, the ones the shops never charged you for
because they were too small to be bothered with. It was one
of the things she loved about the Spanish, this rounding up or
down to avoid pennies.

More or less, más o menos. *It matters not.*

The café was at the foot of the cathedral steps and was
probably the most touristy café in town. She could find a coffee

for half the price in a café in one of the dark back streets, sitting at the bar on a high stool, the crumbs and discarded paper napkins of breakfast at her feet. She'd discovered it was cheaper to drink inside and order in Spanish, rather than sit at a table outside and point at a picture on a menu. But the downside was a lack of drawing inspiration. So to justify the expense of sitting outside at this café, with its regular parade of new faces to draw, she invented a rule: one cup of coffee equalled two sketches for her portfolio. Her sketch pad was filling: faces, sparrows, the blue and white curlicues on the ceramic tiles edging the steps, the guitarist's hands, his full almost swollen lips, the tall iron railings surrounding the cathedral.

A waiter appeared to clear her glass. It was her custom to alternate coffee with water. Speaking quietly and clearly, she asked, '*Cafelito, por favor.*'

'*Sí, señorita.*' The waiter dipped his head and smiled.

It was rare for a waiter to answer her in Spanish; her attempts at the language were stuttering and shy. She hated being rumbled as a *guiri,* a foreigner, though she could pass for Spanish until she opened her mouth. Even Catalina said so. Her dark hair and strong eyebrows were the mirror of everyone on the street. No, according to Catalina the thing that marked her out as non-Spanish was her haircut. Spanish women simply didn't wear their hair short. Even post-Franco, they wore their hair long until it turned grey, when they wore it up. The shops sold only one colour of hair dye, black. She'd looked. No henna streaks or bleached highlights here, no Body Shop wash-in wash-out blackberry colourant like the one she'd used during the summer holiday.

The coffee when it arrived was the wrong sort. Again. She wanted an ordinary coffee with milk. The Spanish drank it only short, black and bitter with spoonfuls of sugar. This time she was served with a small glass cup containing warm milk with just a speck of coffee. She'd asked Catalina what she should ask for, and practised saying '*cafelito*'.

Perhaps I'm pronouncing it wrong.

She took a sip and screwed up her mouth at the pallid

flavour. Spanish long-life milk did not enhance the taste. Fresh milk did not seem to exist here. Two sachets of sugar made it drinkable, sugary milk. Then, with the cup halfway to her mouth and in a moment of clear connection with the world round her, she felt eyes upon her.

A boy was sitting on the steps of the cathedral, a book open in his hand. He smiled, a slow smile shaped by soft lips not yet thinned by age and life. He looked at her sketch pad then back at his own book and his smile widened. He had those soft liquid brown eyes possessed by all Spanish men what-ever their age. Justine had not yet stared deep into this national velvet; she was waiting for the right pair of eyes to present themselves. His eyes promised to be the type to cocoon her. He pointed at the spare chair next to her, and then lifted his hand to his mouth and mimed drinking. More shy smiles, and she nodded. She watched him approach. He wasn't tall. Slim, loose-limbed, he sat down lightly in the chair next to her. He smelt faintly of rosemary and chocolate.

Looking back afterwards Justine realised she never doubted he was Spanish. It wasn't just the eyes and the Spanish book in his hand, she could read the title, *El Genio de Gaudí*, there was a gentlemanly courtesy in his behaviour which reminded her of Granddad Bill, her father's father. Even though she had only known him as a child – Granddad died when she was at primary school – he always treated her as an adult. He ushered her through doorways first, pulled out the chair so she could sit, and showed her how to use a starched napkin in restaurants. Justine missed him.

'*Soy* Federico Gala.' The boy held out his hand in intro-duction. So formal.

Perhaps he's nervous too.

She was trembling all over.

'I'm, no.' She tried again. '*Soy* Justine King.'

'*Encantado.*'

They sat for what felt like hours staring at each other, smiling, though it can only have been seconds. There was a small scar on his top lip as if there was a tiny tuck in the skin;

it disappeared when he smiled, which he did a lot. His skin was a glorious caramel shade and his hair fell in a curtain of loose waves below his ears; a long fringe covered his eyebrows, below which his eyes cast warmth wherever they looked.

Federico turned out to be an architecture student and spoke enough English for them to have a conversation. The humanities faculty was based in a separate satellite building away from the main university, as was the arts department, which explained why she hadn't spotted him before. If she had, she would have remembered him. His classes were held in an old building near the dry riverbed, a former local Government office. Justine thought it sounded wonderful compared with the arts faculty, a concrete monstrosity squeezed between a second-hand car dealer and an electrical wholesaler on the outskirts of town.

They quickly found common ground. Both were suffering 'first-term pressure'; that nasty habit of lecturers to load on the work in an effort to weed out students lacking commitment. One of her current assignments was to analyse the works and influences of Velasquez, while he should be summarising the Bauhaus Movement. Listening to him talk in English, and wishing she had a cassette recorder so she could listen to his voice later, Justine knew she would miss her deadline. Even if he walked away now, this instant, leaving the rest of the day free for study, her thoughts would not be of Velasquez.

When he asked if she was hungry, she realised she had eaten nothing since a breakfast of bread and apricot jam. They shared a dish of tiny whole fried fish which other diners were eating but she had been too intimidated to try. She had never seen fish so small except those caught for bait by the fishermen on the wharf at Bridlington harbour.

'It is children fish, small and very good. You try.'

He held out a fish to her in his fingers, and tiny specks of batter fell off on to the table revealing a pink speckled skin. To Justine, who had always eaten fish using cutlery, this seemed an incredibly intimate and messy thing to do but she noticed an elderly couple at a nearby table eating similar fried fish with their fingers. So she opened her mouth and, for a reason she didn't know, closed her eyes. The hot fish touched her tongue and the flavour of the sea filled her mouth, a tang of salt. She swallowed and licked her lips where a dusting of salt lingered. It was better than Brid's best haddock and chips. Pink-skinned, not grey, and served on a plate, not wrapped in newspaper.

'Mmm.' She opened her eyes to see Federico looking at her expectantly.

Embarrassed she felt her face, hot from the sun, grow hotter.

'Is good, *sí?*'

'*Sí.*'

One by one, Federico pointed to the tiny fish and announced it. All small, all different shapes. *Boquerones,* which she thought was the same as the whitebait you could eat in English pubs, served in a small wicker basket with chips. *Salmonetas,* the ones with the pretty pink skin. Justine did not recognise *lenguaditos;* they were the biggest in the bowl and most obviously fish-shaped. Federico said the last two indefinable shapes were *puntillas* and c*hipirones,* types of tiny squid. Their tentacles were crunchy and delicious. To Justine, raised as she was on large white fish from the North Sea and the icy waters of Iceland and Norway, it felt like eating fish for the first time. Incredibly exotic. In a small eating ceremony, Federico sprinkled each fish with lemon juice then dipped it in mayonnaise so each had a white head. Going with the flow, she copied him.

'These are good,' he shrugged carelessly as he offered her the last fish in the dish, 'but not good as my mother make.'

Justine smiled. 'All boys think their mother is a great cook.' She'd only spoken to her own mother once since arriving in Málaga, which wasn't enough. She would telephone tonight.

'*Mi madre* make the best *pescado frito.* It is special dish for all of Cádiz. Best of Andalucía. Should make with correct oil and correct…' He hesitated. 'Correct *harina.* Made of the wheat.'

'Flour?' She smiled as she watched him talk earnestly

about the batter his mother made with water and special flour and the exact temperature for frying.

'Now *café*,' and he turned to wave at the waiter. '*Hombre, dos café solo.*'

Justine seized the opportunity, putting a hand on his arm then removing it quickly, afraid her hand might stick there forever. She looked at her hand, pink from the sun, and his Caramac arm.

'*Quieres otro tipo de café, guapa?*'

He's asking what I want.

Two emotions flooded through her at once. Pride that she understood his question, butterflies in her tummy that he called her *guapa*. Catalina had called her this, saying it was a term of affection.

'Tea please.'

'*No quieres café?*' He looked at her as if she had asked for champagne.

Quickly Justine explained the difficulty she had ordering coffee, and then waited as Federico and the waiter exchanged a rapid dialogue interspersed with lots of *sí*'s and *no*'s and much gesturing.

Finally Federico nodded. '*Sí, vale.*'

The waiter soon returned carrying a tray with six cups on it. Nodding first at Federico then at Justine, he retreated to the restaurant door beneath the shade cast by a large eucalyptus tree and watched.

Federico arranged the cups in a line, with the darkest brew on the left and the palest on the right.

'You know how the waiter he know *una persona* is tourist?'

She shook her head.

'A tourist is a '*café con leche*' because he no know how order *café*.'

'Yes,' she said and the blush edged her sun-reddened face a shade nearer to deep Cadmium Red. 'That's what the waiters give me.'

Tomorrow I will read my phrase book and learn to speak Spanish properly.

He pointed to the cup at the opposite end of the line, a tiny cup with about half an inch of black coffee inside.

'*Café solo*. We drink it with *azucár*.'

He stirred in two heaped spoonfuls of white sugar and passed it to her. She sipped and pursed her lips at the bitter black taste. She put it back in line and wished she hadn't agreed to the test.

He passed her a tall glass mug filled with black coffee.

'*Café largo*. Is same as *solo* but *con agua caliente*. Try.'

Before the mug reached her mouth, her lips were pursing in anticipation of bitterness.

'No.'

Next to the *café largo* was a medium-sized cup.

'*Café cortado*.' Federico handed her the cup. '*Cortado* it mean cut. Not strong.'

She dutifully sipped, then shook her head. This was getting embarrassing.

'*Nube* is cloud,' he waved at the sky, which was one hundred per cent blue, and then at the next cup. '*Pequenito* coffee *y leche*,' and he held up two fingers, pinched together.

This time she smiled, and took a second sip.

Federico nodded.

'*Sí*. My sister, my little lioness, she has nine years and this *cafelito* she drink.'

Justine's heart sank. Was her sense of taste so immature she was drinking coffee made for Spanish children? She considered the cup of *café solo* and wondered if she could acquire the taste. Federico was watching her patiently.

It's what he drinks.

Federico passed her another glass. 'This is *sombra*. It is more milk. Creamy.'

Justine expected to hate the *sombra* but with her first sip she was at home in the kitchen at Seaview Cottage, sitting at the table doing her homework, a mug of milky Nescafé and the biscuit tin at her elbow. Garibaldis, shortbread, custard creams, those odd milk biscuits with the pictures of sportsmen made of dots. Comfort food.

'I like this one.'

And I like you too, she wanted to add, but her courage failed her. Federico made her feel shy and bold, all at once.

12
LONDON, MAY 2010

Justine and Darya stood shoulder to shoulder in front of Eileen Agar's 'Marine Object'. Justine wished she were at the Ferens in Hull standing in front of 'The Archer', to see if the truth of the painting lived up to her memory of the green tiger. 'Marine Object' was familiar. They saw it once a week at Tate Modern, it was one of Darya's favourites and she never tired of looking at it. Justine smiled as she took her friend's arm. They had met twenty-seven years ago and shared a house all that time. The loss of her mother made Justine conscious of the fragility of the old lady's arm and she felt a premature sense of loss. She valued these trips to Tate Modern together, determined to continue them for as long as possible.

I will go again to the Ferens, one day, but I think I will be going alone.

In the last year, Darya had aged like a film on fast forward. Their outings to art galleries were becoming shorter in duration, their conversations circular.

'I meet Eileen one time. We talk about Russia. She go, you know.' Darya sighed, as she often did when talking about her homeland. Her fluency always improved when talking from distant memory and with a pinprick of fear, Justine realised she talked easier about Russia than she did about lunch. They had this same conversation last week.

'You knew her?' Justine worked at putting enquiry into her voice, although she knew the answers.

'We agree to meet for coffee, but she die.'

Together they leant forwards to read the display caption.

'... she brings together part of a Greek amphora that she

retrieved from a fisherman's net in the south of France with crustaceans and flotsam gathered on a beach two years earlier, and a ram's horn from Cumberland.'

Justine studied the sculpture. The organic nature of the work – the crustaceans, the flotsam and jetsam – reminded her of Gaudí. But the ram's horn seemed a step too far. Perhaps that was the difference between them, as artists. Eileen Agar took a stride further with found objects. Justine would have stopped with the amphora.

She is more adventurous than me. That's why museums select her pieces more than mine. I don't let myself go over the edge.

With that thought, there was only one room left to visit. The room Justine was most nervous of being in. She never stood in front of 'Storm 3' without a shiver of excitement and fear. Excitement that she made it into Tate Modern in its inaugural year and was still on display and not consigned to a temperature-controlled storeroom. Fear that she would never make another piece worthy of the Tate. Anxious that an anonymous visitor would stand next to her and say, 'What rubbish, what's it made of? Bubble wrap?'

There was bubble wrap in it, below the surface, simply to add texture and volume. She used bubble wrap a lot, and the kind of corrugated card used to package online purchases. Layer on layer, adding and subtracting, cutting, gluing, painting, wiping clean and painting again. Always the bubble wrap was concealed; she couldn't reveal the cheapo insides when pieces sold for six and seven figures, but if she didn't use bubble wrap there would be a vacuum.

Would I feel guilty about listing 'air' on the display caption?

She justified her bubble wrap on the basis that the value of art was not the sum of a piece's constituent components. Perhaps her use of bubble wrap would be discovered long after she was dead, as with Degas. His wax sculptures, made into bronzes only after his death, were now known to have been bulked out with wine corks, old floorboards, paintbrushes and even a salt cellar. A matter of saving money, Justine wondered, or artistic choice?

But if it's good enough for Degas...

She wondered how he would feel, knowing his cheap insides had been discovered, and decided he wouldn't care. Creating a piece of art was, to her, a journey to an unknown destination; like flying to Africa but not knowing which country you were going to until the plane landed. She admired this freedom about the Impressionists; they were about a particular moment in time, not about legacy. She studied 'Storm 3' again, trying to be impartial.

So if Eileen Agar had created this, what would she have done differently?

Once, she would have discussed this with Darya. But not now. Darya was looking at 'Storm 3' with her mouth curved with a hint of a smile. She was peaceful and Justine would not disturb her. She shifted on the hard seat. The wooden bench they were sitting on had such presence; it was made from such a beautiful hunk of timber that it too could be an installation. The wood felt warm to her touch and its oiliness made her want to sculpt with timber more than ever.

'I wish I could work with wood, elm ideally, but there's so little of it available now.'

'Hush, darling.' Darya gestured to a smart elderly couple who stood in front of 'Storm 3'. 'Hush. I want to hear.'

Justine didn't. She wanted to shout, to sing 'la la, ho hum, la la la, ho hum' with her fingers in her ears. It reminded her of receiving class feedback of her work at college. Ultimately she had learned to endure the comments of her fellow students, adopting a welcoming facial expression while singing silently in her head. Her tutor's final assessment had included the phrase 'must develop an open-minded attitude to critical feedback and view it as a positive.'

He'd say the same thing about me now.

The memory of that hateful man sent a shiver down her spine, a shiver which she knew could not be banished until she found the answer.

A loud male voice broke into her memories of Spain.

'He's really got the movement of the sea, hasn't he?'

The man stepped backwards, the better to survey 'Storm 3', until he stood directly in front of where Darya and Justine were sitting. His broad backside in yellow cord trousers now blocked their view.

'You can almost see the power of the waves, hear them crashing.'

'It's a she, dear.' His wife had put on her glasses to read the display caption.

'The colours are so stormy, he must have used so many shades of grey to achieve the final effect. Clever chap.'

'The artist is a woman, dear.' She smiled apologetically at Darya and Justine, and nudged him aside. 'Come on, you're blocking the view of these ladies.' She took her husband's arm and led him towards the neighbouring Míro.

Darya exploded with laughter. Exploded was the only word. The man with the cord trousers and his wife stared. Justine steered her down the escalators and up the ramp of the Turbine Hall, and all the time Darya laughed.

It wasn't that funny.

A knot of fear was growing in Justine's stomach. Darya had no family and when Justine dared to imagine the future, it frightened her. When she needed to galvanise herself, she remembered her mother.

I wasn't there for Mum. I will not abandon Darya who was there for me in ways my parents could not be.

13
LONDON, MAY 2010

They ate Heinz tomato soup with thick slices of bread and butter. Within recent months, Darya had forgotten her hatred of tinned soup and would happily eat the same thing at every meal if Justine didn't vary the menu. After they finished eating, Justine supervised Darya into and out of a bath scented with valerian and hops, into a floral-sprigged nightdress and pale cream cashmere bed socks, finally settling her sitting up in bed to watch *An Affair to Remember* on the large screen television at the foot of her bed. Grateful for the quiet night hours that lay ahead, Justine retreated to the studio, pulling down the blinds and turning the gas heater on full.

Tonight she would finish sorting the leaves she had abandoned. Her preferred method of sorting leaves was by shape. Old cardboard shoeboxes were her favourite storage containers for the simple oak, elm and hornbeam leaves; they lay between tissue paper that had originally cocooned her new scarlet Converse plimsolls. Only whole perfect leaves were saved, and a high percentage turned to powder at her touch. Saving leaves was a triumph of love over practicality, probably ninety per cent never survived the process to become part of her art, but the sorting was soothing. She had done this many times, had learnt the best method. Some would be used, splintered and broken, to symbolise vulnerability and change. The perfect ones; some she would coat in varnish, others she may paint.

She tipped the leaves on to a clean sheet laid across the floor, and knelt in the centre like a deciduous tree in October surrounded by autumnal loss. The compound leaves must be sorted into piles of horse chestnut, rowan, mountain ash. She had never lost the wonder she felt that first time she made a leaf picture at primary school: their delicacy, their muted colours, the fact that they were produced by nature, fed by rain and sun, untouched by human hand until she picked them off the ground. It had felt like magic then and it still did. Leaves freshly fallen felt soft and smooth, almost waxy, not sad dry brittle things. But alive. She had no concept then that she could make a career of something she loved. She mourned the loss of that picture.

Tonight two thin plastic carrier bags remained to be sorted. Stuffed with footpath pickings, they were all that was left of a walk through the village last autumn with her mother. Leaves, and the memory of their last walk together. Lombardy poplar, willow, walnut, the reds of copper beech and acer. Each leaf had its own scent, its own texture. She picked up a large padded envelope stuffed with fall leaves from Vermont; she'd arranged the swap with an American fellow collagist for a bag of typical English leaves. Out fell washed-out golds and reds, yellows and bronzes of pin cherry, basswood, American beech, red maple, alder and aspen from New England. Nearer brown than gold. She wished she knew how to stop the colour leaching from their vein-covered fragility, as delicate as Japanese hand-made paper. She stretched her neck, tipping her chin forwards and back, welcoming the sharp pain followed by relief as the muscle eased. Her worry was circular; a spiralling, re-visiting; returning to bad places which still looked bad even when viewed from a different angle. Had she lost that childish wonder at the fresh greenness of leaves? A childish wonder she now saw in Darya's eyes each morning as she spotted her jigsaw waiting on the table.

When the heat flooded through her arms and shoulders, back and neck and scalp, she knew she had done too much bending forwards. This searing pain was the signal she should have stopped an hour ago. She walked into the sitting room, sat gingerly on the sofa, and surrendered to the pain which was creeping up her neck and encircling her skull like a medieval torture helmet.

Scalding, burning; white with touches of yellow and pulsating; a yellow dwarf, the sun, ten suns. White flecks floated across her retinas, dazzling her, making a mockery of her eye mask. Justine tore it off her head and blinked quickly as if facing car headlights on an unlit country road in the black of night. A sliver of white moonlight peeped through the curtains and blurred every object until her eyes slowly adjusted and shapes gradually came into focus. She was in the sitting room. The armchair opposite with its blue embroidered cushion, the outline of the black marble mantelpiece, the gilt frame of Darya's favourite painting, 'A Girl from Pereslavl' by her friend Evgenia Antipova. Everything was surrounded by a white corona. She moved her head tentatively from side to side, the pulsing pain of earlier dulled into a bruised ache.

She walked out to the garage, not focussing clearly, knocking into door frames, the banister, the grandfather clock in the hallway which chimed three as she passed. She searched the store cupboards at the back of the dark garage for the stuff left over from the last time the house was decorated. Her fingertips found a wallpaper paste brush, an enormous thing heavy in her hand, six inches wide with a cheap plastic handle. It felt solid to hold. A tin of Brilliant White gloss paint.

In her studio, she turned on the desk light and adjusted the dimmer to its lowest setting, then unrolled a wide canvas across the floor. At each corner she placed a brick. Two full arm spans wide, long enough for her to lie down on end-to-end. Splash, splash, white paint on off-white canvas; white paint on the floor didn't matter, wrinkles in the canvas didn't matter, loose hairs off the brush didn't matter. Migraine did not know accuracy. With her largest palette knife she scored deep channels through the squidgy Brilliant White paint. Pressing down to the threads of canvas, she rubbed and sawed so they frayed, like her skull splintering under the pressure of her brain fighting to escape the imprisonment of bone. In an effort to find a yellow she knocked over her trusty old metal toolbox; tubes and tubes scattered over the floor resembling a fallen tower of

Jenga. Unable to focus on the tiny lettering of the paint labels, she picked selected colours at random and squeezed great globs of paint into the jagged clefts scored among the whorls of Brilliant White. A nebulous mass of white scored by hot yellow spikes of pain.

Pain is white. Pain is yellow.

The knowledge that she produced her most honest art after intense pain did not help her fear of being found out. After every headache session, she put the canvases at the back of her store room and told no one. In a way she did not understand, the pain unlocked her vulnerability, stripping away her carefully constructed layers of untruths. She was terrified that if someone saw a headache painting, they would guess the real story. That one lie, the one in the beginning, had doubled and tripled and quadrupled so now she did not know what in the tangle of her life was true and what had been fabricated to hide what she had done.

14
LONDON, MAY 2010

Two days after the migraine three women stood in a row, hands on hips, lips pursed. Every now and then, a head would tilt forwards a touch, a neck stretched as if to focus closer. The mirroring was unconscious. It was not an exercise in theatrical art, but the process of final approval of the layout of Justine's exhibition at the Barker Mews Gallery. Tomorrow the cleaners would arrive. Monday was Preview Day comprising VIPs, important collectors and invited press. On Tuesday, the exhibition opened to the public. This was the last chance to change things.

Maud at Justine's right was nodding, occasionally writing a note in a tiny turquoise leather notebook with a slim black pen. The only one talking was Zuzannah, the gallery's curator who was justifying her decision to arrange the pieces out of number order. Each woman was holding a copy of the glossy catalogue that was for sale. Justine stood in the middle, her position signifying her importance in this triptych, her hands still spattered white with gloss paint, her mind still fogged from the migraine. These were getting more intense, more immobilising, and her usual tricks had stopped working. She hated green because it symbolised Darya's frailty and decline but when painting was still simple, it had been her favourite colour. She remembered her first paintbox, the memory as clear as if it had happened yesterday.

It was 1971, her eleventh birthday. From her parents she received a large bar of Cadbury's chocolate and a paintbox. A slim rectangular white tin, it held twelve small pans of watercolour paint and had a clever hinged lid which could be used as a palette for mixing colours. She recited the names of the colours as a mantra. Lemon Yellow, Cadmium Yellow, Cadmium Red, Permanent Rose, Ultramarine, Prussian Blue, Emerald Green, Permanent Sap Green, Yellow Ochre, Indian Red, Burnt Umber, Lamp Black. Roses were not red, they were Cadmium Red. The hedge was Permanent Sap Green. Her bike was painted Ultramarine. There were nowhere near enough greens in the box for her liking.

Three days later she learned there were more colours. Her mother produced the Grattan catalogue from which she had ordered the paintbox and showed Justine the full selection. She lay on her bed for a whole afternoon, turning the pages slowly, backwards and forwards, absorbing all the Winsor & Newton colours, the paintbrushes and papers, mysterious bottles of liquid. There were over one hundred colours of oil paint including, she didn't understand why, nine whites. Surely if she wanted white, she simply left that bit of the paper unpainted? She marked with an X the items she longed to have and hoped her mother would take note at Christmas. Just in case she didn't, she started to collect all her pocket money in an old screw-top jar which used to be full of her mother's blackcurrant jam. Her collection of greens grew; those bought, and those she learned to mix herself.

Winsor & Newton was a mysterious world and she wanted to be part of it. She wrote a letter to the company. It was the third attempt which was posted; the previous two were dismissed for smudges, and once, a spelling mistake. She wrote about her new paintbox and how she wanted to learn how colours were made. Three weeks later, she got home from school, feeling sour after a fractious afternoon of spelling and arithmetic tests, to find a large box sitting next to the brown-and-black patterned Heirloom Hornsea Pottery milk jug in the centre of the kitchen table. Justine had never received a box in the post before.

Her fingers tingling, she carried it upstairs and sat on the floor of her bedroom and slowly, savouring every moment, unpacked it. It was better than Christmas. Once the box was emptied she sat surrounded by treasures she hadn't known existed. Two thick pads of watercolour paper, one just the right size to fit in her pocket, the other as big as her school exercise books when opened out wide. Special paper, for painting! She usually drew on the paper her father gave her, on the back of leftover things from work he didn't need, old cardboard display boards, old price lists, product cards. Some of the paper was shiny and no good for painting, but it seemed ungrateful to tell him. He sold carpets and had boxes of product information leaflets he gave out to clients; when his company discontinued a carpet, he gave the leftover leaflets to Justine for drawing. Enclosed in tubes of corrugated cardboard were two squat bottles, shaped like a bottle of Quink. The first was labelled 'Masking Fluid', the second, 'Granulation Medium'. Her favourite things, wrapped individually in fine blue tissue paper, were paintbrushes especially for watercolour painting. Two large brushes, exotically called Mop and Wash – the names were written on the handle in gold lettering – were made from hair as soft as the very tip of a cat's tail. The next two she unwrapped had flat blunt ends, half an inch and an inch wide. Each was labelled One Stroke, which she guessed meant they put lots of paint on the paper in one stroke. She would try them for skies and sea. The last brush was called a rigger; it had long bristles and a tip as delicate as an eyelash. Excellent for painting the twigs of a tree, she thought. She was a little disappointed that none of her brushes were made of sable. She wasn't sure what it was, but sable brushes were the most expensive in her mother's catalogue. And she liked the *ssss* sound of the word, like the waves breaking on the rocks below. Breaking, smashing, crashing, pounding.

Crasssssh. A banging of metal buckets and general clatter announced the arrival of the cleaners and the bubble of memory popped. Justine blinked at the gallery, at her exhibition, back in the present where green represented something different.

The D-word. Dementia.

The exhibition was named for a day one year ago. They had been driving along the M3 and the fresh leaves were bursting open in the woodlands lining the road. Green everywhere, the promise of spring. It was mid-May and the verges were speckled with the white and pink blossom of hawthorn and wild roses. They lunched at a country pub with Darya's oldest friend, the watercolourist Bogdana Balas, but the amiable reunion evolved into distress. Darya had struggled to hold her cutlery, as if the knife and fork were alien objects, and had become unusually tearful. Justine asked for the bill before dessert menus were offered. They drove home in silence. Darya sleeping, Justine afraid. A week later, a consultant uttered the D-word for the first time. Darya had nodded and seemed not to retain the diagnosis, Justine had retreated to her studio and did what she always did in times of distress. She painted, she created, she mixed and muddled, and out of it was born 'The Unbearable Greenness of Green.'

'So what do you think, Justine?'

She blinked quickly, several times. Maud and Zuzannah were watching her expectantly.

'I was just saying,' Zuzannah said slowly, 'that this might be best positioned over there by the door.'

Justine tried to focus on whether positioning 'Green 7: Anxiety' before 'Green 5: Roots' would really pose a problem for the appreciation of the exhibition. 'Green 7: Anxiety' was one of the later pieces which had taken a long time to resolve. 'Green 5: Roots', however, she was proud of. After the disturbed nights, she longed for sleep but knew she must get this right.

'They have to go in order, Zuzannah. That's how I planned it.'

Both women nodded and Justine was both relieved and surprised at the ease with which they accepted her pronouncement. She was weary, the long days spent supervising the hanging of her work would have floored an ox. The sheer physicality of the work was draining; although the porters did the heavy work, Justine liked to get involved, pushing pieces an inch here then there so they were exactly positioned, crossing fingers and hoping there would be no breakages, gradually transforming the gallery from a blank space full of wooden crates into an elegant exhibition space full of creativity. Without fail she found the roller-coaster process painful, exhausting and exhilarating. Without fail, halfway through she always wanted to run away.

And now only one piece remained to be put in position. 'Green 10: Decline and Fall' had been so difficult to finish and, for this reason, Justine's gut instinct told her it was a piece too far. She was also ashamed of the price tag affixed to it by Maud. It was a cubic assemblage, one metre square, in an acrylic case. She had reverted to her safe materials, trees and leaves, as a representation of life and death, of time passing, of the inevitability of one's lifespan, but had then distorted the perspective by chopping, tearing, ripping, cutting and then re-assembling bark with leaves, sycamore with oak, oddly-matched pieces attached with decorator's masking tape or secured in place with long running stitches in dark red wool. At its centre was a tree trunk made of Jesmonite, its bark flaking, peeling, detached. It was an attempt to show how dementia dissected one's perception of everything. Nature distorted. Past, present, future. But now that she stood in the physical space where the piece was to go, she knew Maud had been right: there would be a gaping hole without it.

Justine's mouth was dry. She was in need of a cup of tea and perhaps two more painkillers. She turned to look for Zuzannah's assistant to ask for tea and her eyes swept across the display as if seeing it for the first time. She made a small private intake of breath. Zuzannah had done well. Perhaps the fears of her migraine were unfounded. The dark of the night hours and pain could do that; skew facts, inflate fears, confuse memories, indulge paranoia. Maud tended to err on the cautious side when forecasting sales but purchasers were already expressing interest in the first three pieces. Experience had taught Justine that the first pieces made of any new work were the ones that flowed. Ten was her absolute limit for a series, which was why this gallery was so suited to her output. Any more and Maud would have to find another location. The request for watercolours, which had caused Justine such grief on Saturday morning, had been forgotten in the tension of the last couple of days much to Justine's relief. She wished the media interviews would disappear as easily.

The room was quiet except for the gentle rumble of rain drumming on the glass roof above their heads, the glass roof designed to let natural light flow in to illuminate the gallery, but at the moment the spotlights were illuminating the grey sky. Almost everything was decided. Justine vetoed the suggestion of green carpeting while Maud reined in Zuzannah's green-themed food and drink proposal which featured avocados, lettuce and absinthe. However both approved of a single coloured accent in the white gallery space: a waist-high bowl made from a single piece of polished burr maple, piled high with shiny Granny Smiths. The bowl, on loan from the Victoria & Albert Museum, was by Mark Lindquist. Justine loved it, had specifically requested it, and was pleased with its effect.

She glanced round for Darya who was sitting at a table in the corner, turning the pages of a large book, an illustrated guide to Van Gogh. Justine noted the pages were turning quickly and Darya was not actually looking at the photographs. She had seemed agitated earlier and Justine sat with her, talking repetitively about how green was her favourite colour, particularly the fresh spring leaves. The repetition had soothed Darya and Justine had left her with Vincent.

Now the three women began to discuss the relative merits of no backing sound, a wind-effects CD or Michael Nyman, when two things happening at once broke the chapel-like hush. An invisible door, artfully disguised as a panel in the plain white wall, opened to admit Zuzannah's assistant. She was carrying a tea tray. Earl Grey, shortbread biscuits. Always the same. Justine liked that. Before they had settled on Barker Mews three years ago, she and Maud had visited another much-lauded gallery with a Mayfair postcode. The curator had mentioned five times that she'd worked at Tate St Ives and longed to move to MoMA, and then served stewed lapsang souchong with rice milk, and Jammie Dodger biscuits. The whole experience was surreal.

Before Justine could move towards the tea tray, the double doors at the rear of the large open space banged open to reveal a line of five porters carrying large wooden frames. 'Green 10: Decline and Fall' had arrived. It was in separate pieces that sat in a tower to form a cube. Justine had brought her installation kit which covered most eventualities – paints, rags, glue, Blu Tack, pins, assorted brushes, bubble wrap, knives and scissors. She would have preferred to unpack her work herself but the gallery's insurance prohibited this. Knowing she should allow the porters to do their job, she took a biscuit. A shortbread fan, her favourite. She preferred the thin crispiness of the fan to the chunkier bite of a finger. She chewed and thought of her mother for whom a packet of shortbread re-arranged in her beloved 1953 Coronation biscuit tin was a Christmas ritual as ingrained as turkey and stuffing. Justine recalled one particular Christmas. It was a clear memory for it was the first time she drew a blackbird with which she was even partially satisfied. Which means she must have been about eight. She wondered now how many of her memories were tied to drawing.

It was Christmas Eve and her mum had been cooking all day. Justine helped make the sausage and bacon rolls, arranging them carefully, lined up in rows like sleeping soldiers. The tray was in the pantry now, covered by a cloth and awaiting the oven tomorrow. The turkey was dressed and in the pantry too. Justine sat at the table, surrounded by a halo of crayons, drawing blackbirds. A male, black with an orange-yellow beak; a female, not black at all but brown and slightly speckled. The scent of stewing apples filled the kitchen, destined to be made into apple sauce and served with the roast pork and crackling on Boxing Day. The joint of pork was wrapped and stored in the garden shed, cool and out of the way.

'Justine, will you come and help me, please? We're going to sort the biscuit tins.'

'Really? Are there chocolate fingers? And teacakes? Can I keep the silver paper?'

'You'll have to come and see for yourself.'

The same three biscuit tins were used every Christmas for biscuits. At the beginning of November her mother bought a packet of 'special' biscuits a week, the treats, the favourites, saved for Christmas. Once the tins were filled they would live on the sideboard in the front room, easily accessible to everyone until emptied. Then they would be washed, aired so they were completely dry, and stacked on the highest shelf again. Life at Seaview Cottage was cyclical and reliable.

The Coronation biscuit tin was filled only with shortbread. Chocolate biscuits went into the deep round lilac Quality Street tin. Penguins, Club and other wrapped biscuits were stored in a battered oblong tin with a picture of the *Queen Mary* ocean liner on the lid. This tin had been sent to Justine's mother by her eldest brother Geoffrey. He ran away to sea when he was fourteen and worked as a steward on the ship's maiden voyage to New York in 1936 but was killed during fighting in Italy in the Second World War.

Mother and daughter spent a happy hour together at the kitchen table. Justine sorted the packets of biscuits into three piles, one for each tin, and then organised each individual pile of biscuits according to shape and colour of wrapping. She took special care arranging the chocolate biscuits, her favourites, and the shortbread, her mother's.

When they were finished, her mother gave her a hug.

'One day you will teach your own son or daughter to sort biscuits into these tins at Christmas.'

Justine nibbled a chocolate finger but could not imagine a day when she would be a mother like her mum.

She swallowed the last bite of shortbread fan and reached for another. Zuzannah could not be accused of being mean with the biscuits. Justine could not abide meanness. She had brought her mother's biscuit tins back to London with her; they were sitting on her desk back at the studio at this very moment, empty. She planned to fill the Coronation tin with shortbread and keep it next to her kettle as an alternative to chocolate.

By the time she'd eaten her second biscuit, 'Green 10: Decline and Fall' was in place. She circled it, checking, running her fingers gently over its surfaces. It had travelled well and required only a fleck of Prussian Green on one corner, smudged and blended. The particular rag in her kit today had once been a white t-shirt and, as she dabbed, she remembered a three-way argument in Málaga with April and Catalina about what type of cloth constituted the best rag. April said it was an old tea towel, one of the white ones with a blue stripe which your granny used for polishing glasses. For Catalina, a neatly hemmed square cut from an old brushed cotton bed sheet. The pattern and colour didn't matter, she insisted. *No pasa nada.* Justine argued that any type of rag should do the job and she still thought so. Three decades had passed since that discussion and she was ashamed to say she had no idea where Catalina was now. April was running an art website called *Gallery*** and seemed to flit round Europe's most stylish destinations. They were nodding acquaintances and for that Justine was grateful; April knew more of her secret than anyone else alive, not much, but more. When they were students, they sat late into the summer nights on that tiny balcony in Málaga, enjoying the cooling of the night air as Spaniards do, living their lives outside at night like bats. The three girls imagined their future art careers, discussed endlessly the merits of Miró versus Picasso versus Dalí versus Velazquez. They argued about the point at which they would justifiably be able to call themselves 'artist' – selling their first piece, being interviewed for *Artforum*, showing at the Biennale, being made a Royal Academician, making their first million, seeing their work on permanent display at the Tate or the Metropolitan in New York.

Justine circled 'Green 10: Decline and Fall', rag in hand, dusting, polishing; not essential but grateful for having something practical to do which excused her from the small talk. Zuzannah and Maud's heads were bent together like two saplings curved by a prevailing wind.

Justine closed her eyes. Tonight she would cook spaghetti bolognese for supper and let Darya choose a DVD they could watch together. Tomorrow was her last free day. She was not needed at the gallery so she planned to potter in her studio, pack away her 'Green' materials and lay all her work surfaces bare. Perhaps if she had the energy she would attempt to remove the worst of the Brilliant White spillage from her studio floor. She would dust the shelves and if the day was fine she would wash the windows and throw them open to let in the daylight. She licked her lips and removed every trace of shortbread biscuit. Tomorrow, she would fill her mother's tin.

15
LONDON, MAY 2010

They went their separate ways from Barker Mews that afternoon. Justine put Darya into a cab to be taken first to the Royal Academy on Piccadilly and then home. She had a thing for Jeff Koons. His living flower 'Puppy' was erected in the RA courtyard and she had visited it four times already since the show opened two weeks ago. Justine got into another cab headed for Wigmore Street to Margaret Howell in search of something black to wear for the preview.

Justine was later home than she expected, having detoured to Selfridges. She dumped her bags in the hall, called upstairs to Darya, and went into the kitchen to start dinner.

The sauce was in the microwave re-heating and she was weighing the pasta, six ounces for the two of them, when the phone rang.

Darya was at the London Hospital. Which was nowhere near the Royal Academy.

How on earth did she get there?

There had been an accident. The caller, Sophia Something-or-other, said Mrs Kushkupola was a little bruised and shaken. Because of her age she was being kept in overnight for her concussion to be monitored.

'We do not admit emergencies here, but given the lady's age and condition, we have made an exception.'

They were a little concerned, she added, about some disorientation in the patient. And about payment.

Justine had run outside and flagged down a cab, not thinking to take a coat, a nightdress for Darya, carrying nothing except her handbag.

Gaining admittance to Darya's room was not straightforward.

'No,' Justine repeated to the receptionist, struggling to imbue her voice with patience. 'I am not Mrs Kushkupola's daughter or her sister or her granddaughter or her housekeeper. She has no living relations. I am her friend, we live together.'

She noted the pursing of the receptionist's lips. 'She is my best friend.' The words caught in her throat. She was ready to argue, to fight, to gain admittance through a loading bay, break through a fire door or climb down a lift shaft to find Darya's room.

'She is my – my godmother. And you called me, remember.' This, and her credit card, were finally sufficient to gain her entry.

Darya was sleeping in a high metal-framed bed. The blood of a fresh bruise was spreading below the skin of her jaw line, and there was a neat criss-cross of stitches on her right eyebrow. Mum would have been proud of those stitches, thought Justine, and then felt ashamed of such a trivial thought. Darya's left wrist was in plaster. An oxygen cylinder stood nearby but was disconnected. A cannula led from her right arm to a bag of clear liquid suspended on high from a metal stand next to the bed. It dripped slowly, like a leaking tap. Saline, Justine assumed, or glucose. The injection site was bruised. Several attempts had been made to find a vein, according to a nurse who wheeled in the drugs trolley.

'She needs a good rest. We gave her a shot to put her out all night, so if I were you I'd go home to sleep while you can.'

'While you can.' Her implication, thought Justine, is that tomorrow will be worse.

Well, it's nothing that I haven't already considered.

The nurse returned the clipboard to its place on the metal bar at the foot of the bed and turned to leave.

'Do you know what happened?' Justine was alarmed at the note of desperate appeal in her voice. She was finding the not knowing difficult to deal with. 'I don't understand what she's doing here, she was supposed to be in Piccadilly.'

The nurse turned round and picked up the notes again. 'It says here…' She ran her finger down the paper, turned over a leaf. 'Here we are. She was brought in by a passer-by, a Mrs Broom who works at the laser eye surgery place round the corner, who found her confused on the street outside. She'd obviously had a fall, you can see the bruising and there was some blood. Her clothes are there.' She pointed to a cupboard in the corner of the room. 'But no one saw what happened. In fact we didn't know who to contact until we found her art card in her bag.' She smiled at Justine, a smile full of sympathy for the future. 'The membership secretary at the Tate recognised the name and gave us your number. There was no other identification. Nothing, in fact, except a £20 note, tissues and peppermints. It might be an idea to put a postcard in her bag, with your contact numbers, just in case.'

Justine swallowed. Just in case.

I should have thought of this.

Lately Darya had been mislaying everything: her purse, her glasses, her credit cards. Found by Justine in odd places which were rapidly becoming regular hiding places. In the bottom kitchen drawer beneath the pile of clean folded tea towels. Tangled in dirty clothes in the laundry basket. In her underwear drawer where Justine had to stifle a smile when she found four unopened boxes of Mr Kipling Bakewell tarts.

God forgive me, but I get irritated with her.

She took a deep mental in-breath, and got out her notebook and pen from her own handbag and leant on her lap to write. 'Put note in Darya's bag with full name, address and my contact details in case of emergency,' she wrote in wobbly letters. When she looked up, the nurse was regarding her with eyes full of understanding.

'Take it one step at a time, that's best, dear.' She patted Justine's arm, and left.

Just at that moment Justine felt incapable of standing up, let alone taking a step on her own.

For the first time she wondered if she was being overly ambitious. 'Green,' Darya and searching again. All at the same time.

In the time capsule of Darya's hospital room, Justine existed as if she inhabited some kind of parallel universe, standing alone at the centre of one of those time-lapse scenes in films where cars and people buzz around a city, hours pass, lights go on and turn off, car headlights and tail lights blur into lines of red and white. Unreal. So used to living and planning her life by the clock, and losing sight of morning/afternoon, day/night, Justine waited. She stretched out her hand and touched Darya's bed. The linen felt cool to the touch, tightly tucked in, with an acrylic waffle blanket folded across her feet.

This is happening, this is a hospital.

She opened the tall cupboard at the side of the bed. Inside were Darya's clothes. Her best blue wool coat with the integral scarf, her Astrakhan hat, the old lady's black leather shoes which fastened with Velcro straps. Justine smoothed a hand over the coat remembering the way Darya used to wear it, standing tall and shoulders square as if she were a Russian countess. Now it might belong to the Lady in the Van. There were spots of blood and mud down the sleeve. It would have to be dry cleaned. Any tears could be invisibly mended. She turned off the bright ceiling light but the room dimmed only a fraction, illuminated by the hospital's energy output which was considerable; fluorescent tubes in the corridor, red standby dots on television and telephone, flickering yellow street lamps outside, all overlaid by pearly moonlight. She stood at the window, taking comfort from the sound of Darya's snuffling snores which made her sleep sound normal rather than drug-induced.

I never waited like this beside Mum's bedside.

The thought flew into her head from nowhere.

I wish I had, horrible though it is. Better to be here and know. Being on that plane flying back from Japan and not knowing, that was the worst. If I know, I can deal with it.

Outside, a nightingale sang, a reminder of life's sweetness in the dark hours of life.

But this is not the end. Darya is not about to die.

Not tonight, at least, not quite yet. Until then they would live with the condition every day, every hour, no escape, no remittance. Justine knew what she would be told tomorrow. Last year, after the cutlery incident, she had trawled the internet. The signs of confusion were common ones. Like complaining she was hungry when they had eaten an hour earlier. Like starting a sentence and stopping mid-phrase, then starting a new sentence only to stop short again. Like tears, without provocation. A dribble of incidents at first, increasing in occurrence, forgetting what happened five minutes ago but remembering intimate details about her childhood. About Masha her pet rabbit. About her mother's beautiful singing voice. Sometimes speaking in Russian, sometimes in French or English.

Justine had done the reading, bought the books, read the blogs. She thought she was prepared. How wrong she had been, how arrogant, how unthinking. To see her best friend, her mentor, her cheerleader become this frail old lady, lying in the hard hospital bed, pinned so tightly in position by the white sheets that she looked unable to turn over.

'Sasha.'

The voice from the bed was but a whisper, hoarse, almost pleading. Darya's eyes were closed, she hadn't moved.

'Sasha. *Chéri*?'

Sasha, Darya had confided to Justine one night not long after they first met so many years ago, had been her one and only love, and how in the war she waited for him to return to her, to rescue her.

It was Darya who rescued me, in more ways than she knew. She gave me a place to live and the emotional support to pick myself up and start again, without ever intruding on my grief.

Justine had never explained to Darya how she'd come to be so desperate on the day they'd met. Now she wished she had been braver and told her friend when she was still able to understand.

'Sasha.' Darya's uninjured arm pushed at the tight sheet and her eyelids opened the tiniest of slits. Her voice was yearning.

Justine leant forwards, pulled at the sheets to free the hand and folded it in both hers. It felt as if she were cradling a dead butterfly.

'Shush, Darya, sleep, honey. Everything's fine.'

Soon Darya was snuffling and snoring, sounding normal again and Justine tried to take comfort from the familiar. She stroked Darya's hand absently, tracing the raised veins and knuckles, feeling the resemblance to the bark on a tree centuries old.

She looked at Darya's face, etched with the soft frown, and wished she had asked her more. Perhaps there would still be time, perhaps it would be her childhood and youth that Darya would be able to talk about, how she left Russia in the war and met a man in Paris, the man who married her and rescued her. But not art. Oh how Justine had loved discussing art with Darya; the prizes, the reviews, the gossip, the up-and-coming students to watch, to invest in. But truth was, they hadn't talked about art in that way for months.

No, longer than that.

Justine shook her head briefly and the light of the room cleared away the darkness of the unknown.

'Stay positive,' she said aloud. 'Think of something else.'

The nightingale was still singing outside. She closed her eyes and tried to relax into its trilling scales, up and down, faster and faster, and then a pause before the scales started at the bottom again. A master of rhythm. Her breathing fell into time with his song and her head gently nodded on to her chest.

She sat up straight with a start, her head flicking backwards as if propelled by a rubber band. Where was she? In hospital, sitting in a royal blue chair. Darya was still sleeping, her delicate eyelids fluttering. It was one of those straight-backed, colour co-ordinated armchairs, upholstered in wipe-clean plastic found in hospitals and public buildings. Their cushions were stuffed with concrete. She shifted her bottom and the blood flowed back into the muscles. Slowly she turned her chin left and right, hearing the grinding of bone in her head between skull and vertebrae, stretching the muscles in her neck, easing the tension. But the source of Justine's tension was outside her body, and in this room, lying in the high metal bed; a frail elderly sparrow. Defenceless, and relying on her.

On me.

The bands of pain tightened round her head.

'Not now,' she said aloud. 'I have enough pain already.'

This migraine was a monochrome experience. She was trapped within a vortex of pain, lines spiralling like a child's kaleidoscope, colour but not colour. Bands of pain pulsed around her skull, tightening, vice-like; she felt sightless but could see colours dwindling to a black dot. Perspective was upside down and inside out. Colour was black and white.

Was there really a black hole in her head? Space where there was no space? The black dot became a butterfly, approaching and receding, squeezing and squashing her skull. Wave on wave, pain on pain. No catharsis.

When she woke, her head ached but her eyes were clear. She knew the meaning of the pain.

'Pain' is the first syllable of 'painting'.

It was early morning but the hospital stirred with movement, illness was never silent. The sounds amplified in Justine's sensitised head so every beep was a boom. A night nurse arrived to check on Darya, and Justine requested an eye mask. She was given a thin hand towel which she folded over her eyes before settling back in the royal blue armchair, and slept again. The next time she opened her eyes, she felt better; not right, but better than before. Her head was spinning, as if she'd drunk four double espressos, and everything was slightly fuzzy at the edges.

Later, when she no longer needed to wear sunglasses indoors to blunt the pain of sunlight, she finally understood why she dressed in monotones and rejected bright colours in her art. Because vibrant tones made her think of Spain. Specifically, the Málaga sky at sunset, at the tipping point, seconds before the sunlight disappears in swirls of Indian Yellow, Cadmiums Orange and Scarlet, and at the top Scarlet Lake.

In my sub-conscious, pain is multi-coloured.

Sitting here in the bubble of illness, Justine felt a step removed from the world, from her world of art, and that distance brought clarity. Her headache paintings were special. She knew this because the doubts that attached themselves limpet-like to all her other work – was it good enough, was it finished, could she ever improve it enough to show it to someone else, should she start over and re-use the same canvas – were absent. Only within her headaches did her strength fracture, her resolve to forget falter, allowing in the memories of everyone she had loved and lost. Federico, her mother, her father. Her baby. And soon, Darya too. In waking hours she consigned every painful thought to the lock-up box in her mind, and painted and collaged, assembled; re-painting, re-forming, discarding and starting again. Only in her headaches did the loved and lost return to her. Federico, smelling of rosemary and chocolate, the warmth of the Málaga sun on her face. Mum and the scent of a freshly baked cake just taken from the oven. Dad taking her hand as they walked along the cliffs, testing her bird-spotting knowledge, taking it in turns to point at a bird and competing to be first with the correct answer. The feeling of a just-sharpened HB pencil. And every minute spent with her baby.

16
LONDON, MAY 2010

Darya was asleep, propped up against her pillows, a Sudoku book open on her lap. The blank squares of the grid, empty. Justine closed the door silently and tiptoed down the stairs to her studio. Today's page in her diary had one word scrawled across it in capital letters. 'Clean'. It was her end-of-creating process, a day devoted to drawing a line under the completed work, clearing a blank canvas in her mind, the studio and her diary, to make space for the next project. Usually she enjoyed the routine; today she felt as heavy as lead. This morning she had brought Darya home from hospital and safely installed her in bed.

She switched *Peter Grimes* on repeat, hoping the 'Sea Interludes' would transport her north to the Yorkshire coast. More and more she felt pulled to Seaview Cottage, but it was impossible. She wondered if her instinct was telling her to run away. But now more than ever Darya needed routine, consistency, familiarity. She did not need to be piled into a car with luggage and driven for six hours to a strange house where her bed was in an unfamiliar room. Life seemed simpler in Yorkshire, though Justine was not naïve enough to believe the illusion. It was grief talking, the pull of home.

Perhaps I can take my life with me, when Darya is better.

But she would never move Darya from her home.

With the high violin melody of 'Dawn' punctuated by darting viola arpeggios, she allowed her mind to leave London, Darya and 'Green' behind, until she stood at the edge of the cliff. Her mother was icing a cake in the kitchen, her father was polishing the car. The wind in her hair and the sound of waves, advancing and retreating, the twirling flight of gulls riding the gusts filled her head leaving no space for worry.

At first she dusted gently but her intensity grew with the rhythm of the music, so that when the CD reached the clashing cymbals and beating drums of 'Storm', waves crashing against the rocks, its French horns sweeping up and down the scales, she was sweeping furiously, her cheeks reddened with the effort. She was heading into a tempest but was unable to change direction.

'What harbour shelters peace, away from tidal waves, away from storms? What harbour can embrace terrors and tragedies?'

She should change the CD; it was too emotional, too tragic. But familiar. Familiarity won. She hummed as she washed windows, and still the music pulled her onwards. By late morning the last box was packed, labelled in red marker pen, and put away on a shelf. The morning sun disappeared and roiling dark clouds presaged rain. Summer was still more than a month away. Outside, the limbs of the biggest chestnut tree waved in the manner of a famous conductor instructing his symphony orchestra, while the giant cedar creaked and swayed in the wind and the musical waves crashed on the shore. She estimated the mess had been reduced by half.

She turned on her desk lamp and spent some time online, ordering a biography of Jacob Epstein and a new crime novel. With a ping, Maud's daily e-update arrived. 'Green 6: Not Forgotten' had been sold to a collector, a regular client who had been awarded a private sneak preview. The price was excellent, more than the sales forecast had predicted. Also attached was an interview schedule for tomorrow.

She turned her laptop off and waited to feel relaxed, expecting the sonorous French horns and the woodwind raindrops at the beginning of Act 2 to combine with the smell of Mr Sheen and work their usual magic. The tone had changed, the music was arresting now, not threatening. Cosy inside, with the afterglow that a hard session of cleaning brings, she made a pot of tea and carried it on a tray to the window. She ran a fingernail along the purple foil wrapper of a new bar of chocolate, and broke off a chunk.

Normally after a successful opening she would leave Maud to do her job and go travelling alone with nothing more than a rucksack, her art box, a couple of books and a change of clothes. The Black Isle, Grizedale Forest, Gower, the Calf of Man; her art owed a debt to each. Sometimes, the idea for her next series came to her during these days of walking alone, sitting, resting, being within nature, thinking. Above all thinking. But the next work would have to be created in London. She closed her eyes and pretended that the dull hum of traffic was really the waves breaking on the East Yorkshire shore, pretended she was walking Danes Dyke, the ancient defensive cutting that slashed across Flamborough Head almost severing it from the mainland in the shape of an unwanted nose. A Roman nose. Thin chalky soil beneath her feet, the scent of salt. She imagined the large sky above and the wide acres of ploughed fields stretching far beyond her sight.

Her mobile beeped. A text. It would be from Maud. Did she never stop working?

I should have emailed to say yes to those interview dates. She'll keep ringing and texting and emailing until I reply.

She replied with a one word text. 'Yes.'

The sun reappeared between a gap in the clouds and its rays fell across her chair. The music reached 'Moonlight' and the pace slowed; Justine's heart rate and breathing followed suit. Her thoughts gradually disconnected until she, like Darya upstairs, was asleep, absolved from having to do anything.

'What harbour shelters peace, away from tidal waves, away from storms? What harbour can embrace terrors and tragedies?'

The music played on and, as always, Peter Grimes died.

It was a dream which felt real. Waves crashed in a storm, the worst storm she could ever remember. Water everywhere, dripping, splashing, composing its own symphony. The wind was the percussion section. She pulled the collar of her thin jacket up to her neck but it made no difference. Her bare feet in summer sandals, soaking wet. She was in London, running through puddles, water lapping her bare toes. Not waves, dirty city rainwater lurking in gaps between broken paving stones.

'What harbour shelters peace, away from tidal waves, away from storms? What harbour can embrace terrors and tragedies?'

She crossed the road, ignoring beeping horns and squealing brakes, and still she ran, becoming more lost every moment, one memory swirling into another. Lost and alone, eight years old, in an unfamiliar department store at Christmas, looking for her mother's brown tweed coat and legs in her solid brown suede boots. She stood in a sea of anoraks, blue and brown and grey, children eating toffee apples, tall men in dark coats, surrounded by a forest of bodies so tall they reached up to heaven. She couldn't see where to go for help. Queues for the tills, for the toilets, queues to watch a lady with a hat of hard hair in a pink sweater with pointy boobs and a pearl necklace demonstrate how to slice a hard-boiled egg with a gadget made with thin wire.

'Ideal for festive nibbles,' the pink woman said, as the chorus of 'Rudolph the Red-Nosed Reindeer' played on repeat.

Justine woke with a start. The rain still poured down outside, *Peter Grimes* had finished. Her heart was pounding and she wanted to reach out to that lost child, to take her hand and help her find her parents. She felt lost and very alone without her mother, knowing they would never again arrange the Christmas shortbread in the Coronation tin. She picked up a detective novel and tried to lose herself.

From three floors above came the sound of a bell tinkling.

17
LONDON, MAY 2010

At 2am there was a bump and a bang outside her bedroom door. Justine found Darya on the landing, walking back and forth, talking aloud.

'And I said it to her, darling, I said it to her and she said it also. But that was very good, very good.'

Justine stood quietly, not wanting to disturb her, assessing the situation. On Darya's release the hospital had issued guidelines for after-care which included possible disturbed sleep, possible headaches, possible confusion, possible temper tantrums. Nothing about night-time wandering.

The bump and bang seemed to have caused no injury. Darya looked calm, normal, except she was talking to herself as if it was the middle of the day rather than before dawn. A thick ceramic vase had fallen from a table on the landing and rolled against the skirting board, unbroken.

Making a mental note to move the vase and the table in the morning, she took Darya gently by the arm, and whispered softly and gently.

'Yes, that's very good. Here we are, let's get back into bed.'

She rolled back the duvet and helped Darya to lie down, and then lay down beside her. It was incredibly hot beneath Darya's duck down duvet, but she didn't dare leave her. Long after Darya's breathing slowed to a light snore, Justine lay awake, considering. Perhaps a toddler gate at the top of the stairs would prevent the worst accident.

It felt as if she had just fallen asleep when there was another bump and a bang. She sat up with a jump. The bedroom door was open and Darya was pacing again. It was a long night. In total, she slept for two hours before her alarm went off.

As she swirled mouthwash, Justine wondered idly whether Calpol might make Darya drowsy enough to stop the night-walking. She must ask the doctor. Thankful she had organised for a private nurse to stay with Darya today, so she wouldn't have to worry about daytime wanderings, falling down stairs, knife cuts, kettle scalds or burns on the gas hob. For the foreseeable future, the hospital had made clear, Darya should not be left alone in the house.

She freshened her face with a wipe then re-arranged her flattened hair with gel, and tried to remember if Maud had said anything about photographers. Today was Preview Day at Barker Mews, the 'Soft' Opening, Press and Guests Only. General Public from Tomorrow. The capital letters were Maud's; Maud spoke in lots of capitals. Certainly Barker Mews would want to take their own photos. Another glance at the clock: she was really late, later than was fashionable for an artist. She had to leave. Now. No time for deodorant, no time to work out how to detach Maud's interview schedule from the email in order to print it out. She thanked God for well-cut clothes. From her wardrobe she pulled a pair of black skinny jeans, shoe boots, the soft white blouse bought at Margaret Howell and a French grey asymmetrical jacket she'd bought in Paris and always wore when she didn't know what to put on for an interview that may involve photos.

She clumped noisily down the stairs from the kitchen mezzanine, cursing the boots that she persevered with because of the extra height and elongating effect they gave her legs. Perhaps her neutral look would fit the label of 'troubled artist' or 'challenged artist' or whatever label the press wanted to attach to her after seeing the exhibition. Perhaps 'colour blind artist'. She had actually read that once. The truth was, she was too tired to care. Her eyes crinkled to a slit against the bright candelabra in the hall, and she flicked the off switch. Damn, she'd forgotten to take a painkiller and there were none in her bag with a whole day to get through. She'd get the cab to stop at the chemist's.

She forgot. Within an hour, the press and VIPs started to

arrive at Barker Mews for the breakfast-to-brunch preview. An hour later and every corner was crammed. There was no space to take a step back to consider without banging elbows or treading on toes and egos. Maud was working the room, doing her job, and Justine was grateful for that. After a double dose of ibuprofen on arrival scrounged from Zuzannah, combined with an avoidance of caffeine and alcohol and the consumption of one pint of water every hour, she felt better. She stood now, nursing a tall tumbler of tap water with a slice of lemon, watching the journalists mill round, clutching their press kits. Not one had left yet which was either a sign that the art was good, or the food.

'Christ, it's hot in here. I'm finished, are you?'

The voice came from Justine's right. She turned to identify the speaker. According to the name badge on her chest she was Maggie Hill and she was standing beside 'Green 5: Roots', looking bored. Her question was addressed to the woman by her side, slightly taller, slightly slimmer, with short curly dark hair and wearing a to-die-for pair of Pierre Hardy boots. Justine had to wait for the second woman to turn towards her friend before she could read her name badge. Rose Haldane.

Justine had met neither woman before and, as she knew all the influential art journalists in the UK and US, they must be non-specialists. During Maud's brief introduction on their arrival, she had greeted each guest with an automatic handshake and a 'Do let me know what you think'. This was one of her three proven phrases for such occasions, the other two being 'It's a lovely opportunity to mingle and talk about art; enjoy yourselves' and 'Please help yourself to a drink and a nibble, and let me know if you have any questions'. None of these statements was intended as an invitation for further communication.

The second journalist's face was now millimetres from the surface of 'Green 5: Roots', as if searching for flaws. Too close for Justine's comfort. The upright was bark, painted with a mixture of Olive Green and Indigo over Artex-textured powder applied thick with a spatula. The base was a stack of tree roots, bark scratched and torn. The effect was rough, jagged, raw. Justine remembered the day she had applied it, the day Darya tried to put her right shoe on her left foot and sat in tears, unable to Velcro the two straps together. Justine sat on the arm of Darya's chair and stroked her hair to calm her, breathing in the scent of the baby shampoo Darya's hairdresser used to keep her fine hair soft. And then Justine had been in tears too, the combination of baby scent and soft hair stabbing her heart with a blade.

I can't cry now.

Instead she busied herself, checking the interview list for this afternoon. 'Haldane, Rose: 6pm interview. The Boo Club, Whitechapel. Personality profile for *Gallery**.*'

That's April's website.

She remembered now, Maud had justified Rose Haldane's invitation by saying she was a freelancer with a good syndication record, her articles published round the world in a wide cross-section of titles from the Sundays to global business magazines to in-flight and hotel magazines. She wasn't an art expert, more a Jill-of-all-trades, a highly successful and effective Jill-of-all-trades if the original Pierre Hardy boots were anything to go by. And if she wasn't mistaken, that was a Givenchy bag. Justine preferred to avoid non-art journalists. In her experience they over-simplified everything.

The muscles wrapping her scalp started to tighten again. She sneaked through the service door and closed it behind her. She stood alone in the storeroom slash kitchenette slash office for a moment and breathed deeply, practising her neck stretches. She had taken so many painkillers in the last twenty-four hours she must be in danger of toxic-mixing so she poured a glass of orange juice and slipped it slowly, trying not to think about April. Or Darya. Instead it was the face of Andrés which flew into her head, all those glasses of *zumo de naranja* she drank. She dialled the nurse's mobile and was told Mrs Kushkupola was doing well this morning, not unsettled, and currently had a visitor. The mental impairment nurse was doing an assessment. Justine wished she were there, knew she should be there. Her muscles squeezed a little tighter across her scalp.

'Ah, there you are.' Maud stuck her head in the door, her eyebrows furrowed, but the frown quickly replaced by a wide smile. 'You must meet Johan.'

Back in the gallery, Justine smiled brightly as Maud introduced her to a bronzed curator responsible for managing two private American collections. No identities were revealed but Maud whispered the names of a pop singer with a curvaceous figure who lived in Miami, and a middle-aged CEO who dressed in t-shirt and jeans. Justine smiled while Johan talked at her, allowing him to ask her questions then answer them himself. He seemed to find this satisfying and really, given the circumstances, he was the ideal person for her to talk to. As long as Justine smiled and nodded, and allowed him to squeeze her elbow as they moved round the gallery, she was not expected to contribute anything coherent to the conversation. Much more preferable than talking to journalists where every word could be printed to haunt her forever. Though she could have done without the arm-holding. Unbidden, a memory of Andrés arrived, of his hand on her elbow when they were at the *peña*.

Finally Johan left to catch a private plane to somewhere glamorous. After spending twenty minutes with the man from The Woodland Foundation and, in her role as honorary patron, agreeing to chair a round-table discussion at a conference about the decline of ancient tree species, Justine found herself alone. She took a deep breath and tried to empty her mind.

'It's about birth and death, don't you think?'

Justine turned slowly. Standing nearby were the two journalists she'd overheard earlier. They were now considering 'Green 4: Fading', one of the two pieces bought by Johan.

The smaller woman leant forwards to read the display caption. '"2010. Wire, plaster, oil paint, found objects, leaves." Well, that's helpful. Not an effing word about what the effing thing is about.'

'Maggie, ssh.' Rose turned, as if checking for eavesdroppers.

Just in time, Justine stepped sideways behind the Japanese correspondent for *Artforum* magazine who was conveniently standing nearby and was conveniently as tall as a basketball player. She had to admit, Maggie Thing was right. She must say something to Maud, get something done about the display captions.

The two women stood shoulder to shoulder now, looking directly at the piece. Justine stood behind them and looked too.

'Well I still think it's about birth and death. And grief. And loss. And pain.'

Justine turned away, not wanting to hear any more.

Is it that obvious?

Their voices, raised, followed her towards the drinks table.

'Rose, you're seeing things that aren't there.'

'It's just that it – it reminds me of the loss in Kate's diary.'

The woman called Maggie made a noise a bit like *tch*.

'It does, Mags.'

'Everything in life is not about you and your family, Rose.'

Justine poured herself a cup of tea, added milk, stirred and took a leisurely sip. When she turned, they had gone but the woman's words rang round in her head.

And grief. And loss. And pain.

18
LONDON, MAY 2010

Rose was sipping her coffee when Adrian Boult arrived for the meeting at Café Pizzicato on Dover Street, round the corner from Barker Mews Gallery. He looked different. If she hadn't been expecting him, Rose might not have given him a second glace. She hadn't seen him since she left the *London Herald* to turn freelance. Adrian had left soon after. Their paths hadn't crossed naturally at the *Herald*, crime and health being odd bedfellows, but they had bonded when both were picked on by their bullying editor and had stayed in touch since via LinkedIn. Two earlier attempts to meet had foundered and Rose was gratified not to have lost the connection. They settled down with coffee, Rose; and mineral water, Adrian; and for five minutes caught up on gossip about their post-*Herald* lives and other newspaper colleagues. Rose's story was carefully edited, as she assumed Adrian's was. His changed appearance, it turned out, was due to a new interest in triathlons.

'I swim too, and run.' She sat up a little straighter in her chair, wishing she hadn't ordered vanilla syrup in her latte. An extra five lengths tomorrow.

Adrian nodded and smiled. It was the slightly condescending acknowledgement of a runner looking down on a jogger and reminded Rose of Nick when they were first dating. When she told him she went running, he had demonstrated eight essential stretches to do before setting out. Then, in the first flush of love, she had understood for the first time her mother's desire to do anything to keep her husband; a desire which had led to Rose's own messy adoption. Rose wasn't convinced she would do *anything* for love; most things, but not one thing in particular. She became aware that Adrian was talking with energy, about what she had no idea; so she concentrated on the present and things to be done.

'I've got a team of freelancers working on this, Rose, each with specific areas to target. I want you to research protests and violence targeted at medical professionals. UK only, not America. I'm talking to a CNN news editor there who reported on surgeons murdered by US pro-life extremists. You know the drill. Check police for harassment of medical personnel. The British Medical Association should be a good starting point. Also try the Royal Society of Medicine and the Royal College of Obstetricians and Gynaecologists.'

Rose was writing notes quickly, trying to keep up as Adrian ran through his requirements. It was a long list.

'What I really want is personal experience, how it affects the doctors doing their work, how patients are referred to them, what precautions they take to protect themselves and their patients, have they considered whether to stop performing abortions.'

'When will it be broadcast?'

'Not sure yet. My job is to deliver the programme proposal to Compass. If they green-light it, it will be filmed quickly. We need all our ducks in a row with this one. I want you to put everything else aside while you work on this.'

Rose was too late at hiding the look of dismay which flooded her face.

'I know, I know. You're a freelance and you have other jobs. I can't give you orders. Sorry. But I do need you to prioritise it.'

She nodded, playing with her coffee m ug, t wisting and turning it in her hand.

'I've got a profile to write for a new client, but it's quite straightforward. In fact I'm doing the interview after this so it should be written and filed by the end of tomorrow latest.'

A little manipulation of the truth doesn't hurt.

Adrian nodded with satisfaction and closed his A4 moleskin notebook.

'Let's get on with it, shall we? If you do this first job well, I have another one lined up for you.'

By 3pm, Justine's headache had returned. A taxi was called to take her home. Everything that happened at the preview that day was forgotten, as if the pain had activated the erase button in her memory.

Just as dementia was pushing the erase button in Darya's brain.

Rose and Adrian exchanged a hug before turning in opposite directions. Rose was headed east for Whitechapel, the Boo Club.

She stood at the bus stop and reached into her handbag, popping a contraceptive pill out of its foil sleeve and swallowing it dry. Only one left on the strip; better extract the box from its hiding place tonight.

Longing to start Adrian's research straight away, art seemed frivolous in comparison. She checked her mobile. A list of new emails. Only one text.

'Apologies. Justine Tree interview cancelled. Please call to rearrange. Maud Nettles.'

Art was forgotten and Rose's head filled with obstetricians, gynaecologists, harassment and possibly murder.

19
SPAIN, OCTOBER 1982

Justine was sitting on the terrace outside the student cafeteria. The chill in her bones had nothing to do with the weather. Somehow the warmth of the sun wasn't reaching her skin. Someone, it could only be another student, had stolen from her.

I should have gone to Leeds. I'm so far from help here.

Her grant was already spent. It hadn't been much in the first place, awarded on the assumption that her parents would top it up. But they had been unable to send her any extra money and now her holiday savings were gone too. But when the cash from her purse was taken, things got serious.

I wish I'd never heard of Picasso's bloody dove.

She knew what her mother would say.

'Stop feeling sorry for yourself and do something about it.'

So after class broke up, she reported the theft to her tutor.

'Perhaps you've learned your lesson now, and won't be so careless with your purse.' Paul Willow smiled ruefully. 'Everyone finds it difficult to get by, Justine. You'll find a way. The first term is so difficult because everything is strange. What are you going to do when you leave college? You need a plan to manage money, because pure artists rarely make enough to live on.'

'They don't?'

'Come to lunch and we can have a chat. My treat.'

Afterwards she knew it was daft to have gone. She was careful not to choose the most expensive thing on the menu but ate three courses, plus bread and olives, until she was crammed. She needn't have worried about being tongue-tied. Willow talked about his own art, his previous jobs, his ambitions for his career, his dislike of the heat in the Spanish summer, the irritating *mañana* habit that meant things took ages to get done, and his longing for a pint of English beer. For the first time she noticed his habit of running his fingers through his long pale hair, drawing attention to it with a teenage toss of the head.

After forty minutes, he hit on her. She managed not to recoil from him with a shudder. His class represented a quarter of her assessment.

'Think about it,' he said as he waved to the waiter and ordered an extra dish of potatoes. Justine looked at them, swimming in oil with fried ham on top. Her stomach churned.

He leant forwards, his leonine fringe falling over his brow. 'I can help you, if you help me on occasion.'

Is he saying what I think he's saying?

With hundreds of responses running through her head, she took a dry bread stick from the basket and bit into it. A hard lump stuck in her throat. She forced it down with a swig of beer, trying to drink without spluttering, not meeting his eyes.

He handed her a thin paper napkin from the dispenser.

'Come on, Justine, you know what I mean.'

Then he smiled at her, a charming crinkly smile. An arrogant smile, designed to be irresistible, confident in its success. She wondered if she had imagined the threat.

Of course she knew what he meant. Of course she said no thank you, she'd be fine, would work something out. She stood to leave and he said the offer of a loan was always there, she only had to ask. He would charge no interest. At the door of the restaurant, she peeked back. He was watching her with a look of irritation on his face.

20
SPAIN, OCTOBER 1982

She stood in front of her easel. It was Saturday morning and college was empty, which suited her. She would prefer no witnesses to what she was about to do. She'd hardly slept last night, worrying about money and Paul Willow's snide invitation. She got up much earlier than usual, ready to get stuck into her plan of action. She would sell pictures to tourists. It was such an obvious scheme she felt stupid for not starting sooner. Really, it was no different from music students busking on the Underground at home.

Having decided to use Picasso as her Málaga theme, she carefully painted three canvases with Pablo-esque interpretations of the sun, a wave and a seabird. When, at the end of the afternoon, she stood back and surveyed her work, she knew she should have stopped earlier. She was in fact quite pleased with the red canvas, circle upon circle in an ever-decreasing spiral, each shade slightly different from its neighbour. The blue canvas was the same idea except with horizontal lines, therefore a bit derivative. The grey and white canvas had a black beady eye in the centre.

Are the tourists really going to get that this is a seabird deconstructed?

She took the canvas and started to rip it in two.

It's impossible, painting for people who don't understand art.

She stopped when the tear was two inches long. She meant to set up her easel in time for the early evening crowd, so there was no time left to paint anything new. If she ripped them up she would have wasted the whole day. She knew what was guaranteed to sell, because she walked past them every day on the way to and from her bus stop. But she hadn't been able to do it.

I will not sell out and paint fluffy kittens and pots of geraniums.

She packed the three canvases into her folder and headed out.

She didn't sell one picture. Too big, too expensive, too arty. She wasn't sure which, maybe all.

She wandered along the beach, finally settling in a comfortable spot where she could look out to sea, towards the horizon, and imagine she was somewhere else. Anywhere. As the tide crept up the sand towards her, she wondered what would have happened if she had said yes to Willow. She watched a dot approaching along the beach, a wobbling dot that slowly came into focus as a cyclist. Pedalling heavily against the wind, the cyclist was loaded down by a huge box fixed to the handlebars. It was the fruit seller who plied her trade up and down the beach selling to thirsty tourists, doggedly soaking up the weakening rays in shorts while the locals wore jumpers and jeans.

Justine was thirsty, made thirstier by the fact that she couldn't afford to buy a slice of watermelon. If she was really thirsty she could drink water for free at any water fountain, one of which Málaga seemed to have on every street corner. It was something about every citizen's right of access to the water seeping down from the rainy Andalucían mountains into the reservoirs along the dry coastline.

She shook her head regretfully at the girl. *'No, gracias.'* She opened her purse and turned it upside down. *'No tengo dinero.'*

The girl smiled. *'No pasa nada, guapa. Tómalo!'* She offered Justine a slice of watermelon in her outstretched hand, palm flat as if she were feeding a timid horse.

'Inglesa, sí?'

'Sí. Gracias.'

The girl turned and pushed her bike through the deep sand, heading south towards a circle of sunbeds and more tourists.

Justine licked her fingers, took a bite and spat out the black seeds in an arc round her; positioned as the *cantante* at the *peña,* at the centre of her circle. And then she became aware of something stuck to the underside of the melon. A small white card.

'Puerta Abierta: la agencia de acompañantes bienvenido'.

Out of her bag she pulled her pocket dictionary. She knew *puerta* meant door and *bienvenido* was welcome. *Acompañantes* meant 'escorts'.

Justine pulled her cardigan round her shoulders and shoved the card into her pocket. She turned into the wind and started the long trudge towards home.

21
SPAIN, NOVEMBER 1982

Istán was at the end of the line for Bus 722. A village high in the mountains, Federico told her, with a lake surrounded by slopes of pine trees. He promised so much beauty, there would be too much for her to paint. Justine had woken early the following Saturday to find Málaga swamped by a haze which behaved as a Yorkshire sea fret, foreshortening the horizon, blurring the lines. It had been chilly first thing, almost shivery, but now the sun was burning through the mist and it wasn't even ten o'clock. Her t-shirt was dark with sweat from the walk to the bus stop and she'd already drained half the water in her flask. The thought of the lake sustained her but the sight of Federico waiting for her at the bus stop did the job just as well as paddling in cold water.

After an hour on the bus sitting side by side on the narrow seat, they caught their first glimpse of the lake, only for it to disappear behind a hill as the bus groaned and twisted up the road, another rock face, another stand of pine trees, another precipitous drop, another view to paint. Federico, keen she appreciate the beauty of Andalucía, proved an enthusiastic guide. She was torn between paying attention to his monologue and concentrating on the touch of his brown arm, which lay parallel to hers, smooth, soft, the fine dark hairs tickling her skin in the most delightful fashion.

The road seemed to twist in on itself in a multi-layered figure of eight. She could ride the 722 every Sunday of her study time in Málaga, and produce new art each time. This nature was different from anything she had experienced before. Bright sun casting white light and deep shadow across the terracotta-coloured earth, jagged rock faces in cream and yellow that looked millions of years old, dried grasses shimmering a gold so pale it was almost white. Istán was so far from Justine's idea of home that she might have travelled to the Mojave Desert.

There were three other passengers, plus the driver. Two old men sat together on the front seat in such an atmosphere of possession that Justine suspected they had shared the same seat since their first day at school. Brothers, perhaps. Their heads bent together as they spoke, almost touching. On the back seat of the bus sat a thin boy, about twelve or thirteen she guessed. His eyes were dark and his brow furrowed, his hands smoothing down the creases in his trousers. Perhaps on his weekly trip to see his grandmother, perhaps to visit a girl. Justine smiled at him, but he seemed embarrassed and turned away. Her ears popped twice as the bus climbed, finally stopping in the shade of a wide spreading tree in the centre of Istán. The small square was empty of people. There was a church, and opposite, a building that may be the town hall. Doorways stood open and the ubiquitous multi-coloured strings of fly curtains shifted idly in the warm breath of the morning breeze.

Federico went in through one door and returned moments later with a loaf of bread, two apples, and a paper bag full of huge tomatoes, the smell of which made her think of her father's sandwiches. Crusty white bread sliced thickly, salted butter, slices of home-grown tomato with a sprinkle of sugar. She could taste it now.

Dad would love Spanish tomatoes.

The 722 would return to Málaga in five hours. The bus was parked beneath the tree and the driver disappeared through another set of fluttering door ribbons, while the three passengers melted away behind closed doors. Justine and Federico re-filled their flasks with the ice-cold spring water from the drinking fountain beside the church.

'We go here,' Federico pointed. He picked up her rucksack and she followed him along the deserted street, turning off the road and along a dusty path. When she had first conceived her plan of going wild, she was on her own and the aim was to walk until she found a place that felt right. She was confident she would know it when she found it. She wasn't sure, now, how this was going to work with Federico here too, but when she had said she was coming here he had offered to be her guide.

After only thirty minutes walking along a rough path, she found her place, a lay-by where one herd of goats could pass another.

'*Sí,* is *cabra* here.' Federico pointed to the dusty hoofprints and scattered droppings the size of tiny marbles.

They sat in the shade with their backs against the bare rock face, surveying the lake hundreds of feet below. The water was dark, almost black. Another time she would get off the bus lower down the mountain and find her way to the shore-line. The view seemed full of earth and sky; the sheer space in the countryside took her breath away. It was so wild, so untouched, not a sign of human interference, though so near to the city and beaches.

It's exactly what I wanted.

'Thank you. *Gracias.*'

Federico smiled.

He seems happy because I'm happy.

This was a new sense of awareness for her. He picked up a book, something he had to read by Tuesday, and she turned her mind to art. Directly in front of her was a thin line of blue sea, on her right was the mountain with a summit shaped like a pert breast. She reached for her rucksack, unpacked her kit, unrolled a sheet of tough paper and weighted each corner with a pile of small pebbles. What she really needed was some sort of portable folding board; perhaps she could ask her father to make one for her. But, for now, she liked her current arrange-ment; when they left, these tiny cairns would remain. A kind of stone 'I was here'.

She sat back to consider the land surrounding her. She squeezed her eyes almost shut and squinted, the layers of coloured rock and line of blue sky forming into clear colour zones. At the bottom was the darkest band of colour represented by the lake. She opened her eyes a bit wider and let in the bright blobs of colour, random dots of yellow flowers and white cloud and the dark green foliage of umbrella-shaped pine trees. Everything shimmered in the heat. Suddenly across her vision swept five or six exotically coloured birds in blue and bronze; twirling and diving, as if dancing especially for her. She sat entranced until the colours and shapes were burnt on her mind, and then she began to collage. She'd forgotten how free it felt to work outdoors; the last time had been on the cliffs at home and she'd had to abandon it halfway through because of rain. Quickly she applied the initial bands of colour; and then examined the plants nearby. She found a pretty patch of daisies and scattered their yellow petals across the paper, followed by small, toothed leaves from a kind of wild rose. Finally, after a bit of a search during which she slipped twice and scraped her ankle, she found exactly what she was missing: a thigh-high weed with delicate white star-shaped flowers, like the demure lace caps of Victorian maids. After an intense period involving copious amounts of glue and even the bronze-coloured dust on which she sat, she was satisfied. This was for her, not for tourists, not for college. Her patience with sightseers was running thin. It wasn't her fault if they didn't understand her paintings.

She had been so consumed that she hadn't noticed Federico was also busy. With a penknife he'd constructed chunky bocadillos. They sat in the shade, side by side, eating.

As good as Dad's tomato sandwiches. Just different.

She wished the lake were near enough to swim in but blushed inside at the thought of taking off her clothes in front of Federico, wanting to, but terrified of doing it all the same. She wondered what he would do if she suggested now that they go for a swim. She stood up, looking for a path but could see no steps downwards. Then his warm hand was in hers and he pulled her down to sit beside him.

'Tell to me what you are.'

Justine studied her hand in his as she tried to work out what to say. She wanted to sketch his hands, his fingers.

'Justina?'

125

She didn't know what to say. She was thinking about his hands and how it might feel to be caressed by them. So brown, so smooth. And then she remembered the eggs.

'Okay, there is one story. It's sort of funny.' She took a breath and prepared herself to remember.

'It was Christmas morning. I must have been about ten.'

Following a conversation with the library van lady, Justine had seen a picture of a painting by Velázquez of an old woman cooking eggs, and had learned how the great masters perfected their craft by painting still lifes. Everyday objects, ordinary things. And so she decided to do the same thing, to learn her craft. She drew studies of fruit and vegetables, a table lamp, a brass horseshoe, the milk jug, the teapot, the log basket, a knife fork and spoon, and her mother's knitting needles stuck into a ball of wool.

But no eggs. Their hens had stopped laying; her mother said probably because they were getting on a bit. Then Mrs Gill, their nearest neighbour, had yesterday given Justine three eggs warm from her own henhouse. Justine remembered Mrs Gill's generous smile and decided to draw that too. She hadn't drawn mouths or lips or teeth before.

'Here you are, chick. I know your hens aren't laying at the moment. One each for your breakfast tomorrow morning. Happy Christmas to you all.'

Justine bypassed the kitchen and took the eggs straight to her bedroom. It was a bare space warmed only by rising heat from the fire downstairs, which meant that for most of a normal day her room was freezing. But from Christmas Eve the front room fire was lit after breakfast and the whole wall radiated heat. So she sat on the floor with her back against the bed and her feet flat against the warm wall, and drew. Her first attempt was a simple sketch but one she was intensely pleased with. Two eggs were brown, the colour of conkers, and one pure white; she set them gently rolling and drew them where they rested naturally. She would draw them again tomorrow after opening her presents.

She was up first on Christmas morning and beneath the silver tree with its cracked, inherited glass decorations, found three presents addressed to her. She shook them, smelt them, felt the shapes and bumps and identified the possible contents. An embroidery kit from her parents, a pound note from Granny Stannard, and a selection box from Grandma Jean and Granddad Bill. Allowed to open one present before her mum and dad were awake, she opened the latter.

She put a match to the ready-laid fire and watched the Cadmium Yellow flames lick round the balled newspaper and twigs. Soon it was roaring. She threw on a hefty log and settled down on the floor to explore the selection box. Crunchy, Curly Wurly, Milky Way, Caramac, Chocolate Buttons and a bar of Fruit and Nut. Knowing she shouldn't eat before breakfast, she unwrapped a Milky Way, not her favourite so she preferred to eat it first and get it out of the way. The Fruit and Nut bar would be saved until last. She threw the wrapper on the fire and watched it ignite in a flicker of blue then disappear. The chocolate disappeared quickly too. Her parents were up now, kissing and hugging her; a wink from her father made her think he'd noticed the opened chocolate.

When I'm a successful artist, I'll invite my parents to my modern home for Christmas lunch. I'll serve shop-bought mince pies and shop-bought Christmas cake so Mum won't have to do a thing.

Her toes nicely toasted, she moved her feet away from the fire and reached for her small sketch pad and pencil case. She could hear her mother's laughter as she prepared breakfast, the deeper murmur of her father's voice.

'Here we are dears, a treat. Three eggs from Amy Gill. Isn't she a treasure? I found them in your room, Justine, I don't know what you were thinking. Eggs are too precious to play with.'

Her mother laid three plates of fried egg, grilled tomatoes and bacon out for breakfast that Christmas morning.

'So you eat egg you want to draw?' Federico smiled and, although the memory cut, even now, Justine smiled too.

I had to try very hard not to hate Mum for taking my eggs and not telling me, but I can't tell Federico that. Things are so black and white at that age and hate is a very strong word.

'Your friend who give you egg, she call you *gallina* – chicken? Yes?' His brows were furrowed.

'Sort of, little chicken.' Justine smiled. It was almost worth saying something especially to provoke this brooding quizzicality.

'Now it's your turn. Who are you?'

'Is simple. I want to be *arquitecto* since I am small.' He held his hand up at about knee height. 'That is story of me.'

'There must be more,' she protested.

'We return now,' Federico pointed to the sun, 'or bus he go without us.' He stood and hoisted his rucksack on to his back.

Justine quickly packed her things, rolling the collages loosely – she had made three – and carrying them tenderly under her arm. With the pert breast mountain on their left now, they followed the path to the square. The bus was waiting, its engine running, the same three passengers seated on board. She climbed aboard, said gracias to the bus driver and was gratified to receive a nod in return. They sat in the same seat as during the uphill journey.

That evening, she realised the significance of the day. She had spent the whole day totally and exclusively in Federico's company. And it had been so easy.

She laid out the three pieces on her bedroom floor and signed each in the right-hand bottom corner 'JK'. On the back she wrote lightly in pencil 'Istán/1', 'Istán/2' and 'Istán/3'.

22
LONDON, MAY 2010

Rose was experiencing déjà vu as she stood in front of a pile of earth, grass and refuse, trying to understand its hidden meaning. Her interview with Justine Tree, cancelled last week, was finally happening today after much to-ing and fro-ing with Justine's agent. Rose was yet to receive any direct communication from the artist herself but the postponement had given her time to concentrate on the medical research for Adrian, for which she was grateful. Now she must switch hats again.

She leant forwards to read the name label. 'Green 2: Infinity.' Beside the typed name and date was a red dot. She circled round, looking at the rest of the gallery. There were red dots alongside every piece in the show but she couldn't grasp what made this work so desirable. She doubted her chances of writing a feature worthy of scoring ten out of ten. A Tenner. After all these years, Rose was still driven to write the perfect feature for the buzz of achievement that came with feedback from readers. She knew she was making it unnecessarily complicated; she was writing a personality piece not an art essay.

But I want to understand it.

And that need had drawn her back to the Barker Mews Gallery again. 'Green 2: Infinity' was about six feet long and five feet high and filled the wide lobby area between the two main exhibition spaces. It consisted of four horizontal layers. On top was a wide band of real grass, above an almost invisible line of brown earth. Rose hesitated to touch, anticipating a buzzer. It looked real enough. The widest strip was next, white flaky bits. She peered closer; possibly a combination of broken sticks of teacher's chalk with white flakes of paint left over from stripping woodwork, with white paint sloshed over the top. The last layer was stones, stones of all shapes, sizes; white and grey. Rubbish was strewn at the base: rusty half-squashed drinks cans, screwed-up scraps of paper, plastic milk bottles, bits of netting and two non-matching flip-flops. Floating above the assemblage – it was important to get the terminology right, she told herself – was a semi-circular wire from which hung a moon. The moon was made from, she leant a little closer, a white stone with a hole in the middle like a doughnut. Out of the hole peeped an electric bulb, unlit. She followed the wire to the wall where it was plugged into the sort of timer switch she had used for her cat Brad's timed feeder dish. Light on, light off, symbolising night and day, she supposed. To Brad it symbolised Whiskas.

The whole effect reminded her of a cross-section from a geology book. It was a cliff, Rose decided, but she was at a loss to explain its meaning or execution or venture an opinion. Heartily wishing she hadn't delayed reading the pile of research on Justine Tree last week, she sat on a white cube stool and opened the press pack. She read: "Green 2: Infinity' 2010. Grass, earth, stone, light bulb, wire, timer switch, found materials, preservative."

Found materials, she knew, meant materials that had been found by the artist, found as in picked up off the ground. Scrounged, liberated, foraged. Free.

She read on. 'A political statement challenging the disposal of waste at sea from ships and its damage to the environment. It is estimated that every square mile of ocean contains 46,000 floating pieces of plastic. Some of this rubbish is washed ashore on the twelve mile coastline between Flamborough Head and Filey Brigg in East Yorkshire. Every tide brings more, polluting the beach and endangering the lives of wild-life in the sea and onshore. Plastic debris causes the death of more than a million seabirds and 100,000 mammals per year. Syringes, toothbrushes and cigarette lighters have been found inside dead seabirds which eat them, mistaking them for food.

Plastic supermarkets bags have been found in the stomachs of whales. To register your concern at the way our oceans are being used as a rubbish dump, sign the petition at Save Our Coastlines.'

Ah. Rose looked at 'Green 2: Infinity' again. She'd noticed the individual elements of the piece but not the whole. Now she got it. She remembered the biography sent to her by Tree's PR which explained how she changed her name from King to Tree to publicise man's abuse of forests.

So it's about how man's obsession with stuff is destroying the planet.

Trying not to draw attention to herself, she quietly slipped the half-drunk plastic bottle of French mineral water into her coat pocket.

23
LONDON, MAY 2010

An hour later Rose was standing on the doorstep of 23 Hill Court Road, Kensington, ringing the bell. Justine Tree opened the door and showed no recognition that they'd met before. She resembled a youngish Joan Jett or an older Kristen Stewart. The fresh-faced Justine Tree was wearing skinny grey jeans, frayed and splattered with paint, a black t-shirt with a skull design on the front, and a long black cardigan which reached her knees. Her dark hair was rumpled, her fringe soft and flopping over her brow. Not the manicured and coiffured artist Rose had failed to shake hands with last week. Rose followed her into a cool, cream, tiled hallway, making mental notes as she went: double-height ceilings, ornate white plaster cornice, pale grey walls and shiny metal Indian console table. No pictures, no art. Which was a bit odd. Why wouldn't an artist have her own paintings on the walls of her home? Perhaps it was a statement about the nature of art, like that French play about the totally white canvas. Or perhaps it was a bit too 'me, me, me' for an artist to hang their own pictures at home. She realised Justine had paused to look back over her shoulder and wondered if she'd missed a question.

'You have a lovely home.' She winced at the blandness of the statement.

A bell rang faintly in the distance, the tinkling of fairy bells or wind chimes. After a quick apology drifting over her shoulder and an instruction to 'follow the corridor as far as it will go and you'll come to my studio, please make yourself a coffee,' Justine disappeared and Rose was left alone.

The corridor seemed to go on forever. Finally a closed

door. She knocked, because it felt wrong not to, then entered. The space was vast, at least six double garages big. It was clean, sterile; a smell of bleach lingered. The room was long and rectangular with a high glass roof; the light was natural, tinted with green. It was cold. The colourless room was dominated by a huge canvas covered with red and black shiny paint which stood on an easel pushed into a corner. Something in it drew Rose towards it; its intensity, the texture which seemed to move. Her fingers reached out and gently touched the surface, knowing she shouldn't but curious all the same. She expected it to be tacky but it was hard, almost rough.

I was right about the pain.

Wanting to use the advantage given to her, of being there alone, she walked to the enormous picture window at the far end of the room and looked out over a walled garden.

So that's where the green light comes from.

The boundaries of the garden were invisible. She recognised a copper beech hedge, similar to the one at her father's house in Richmond, some large shrubs and a huge cedar tree. She pulled a notebook and pen out of her handbag. Information such as this could enrich the feature, vital if she was to squeeze out an extra couple of hundred words. She wrote.

'Studio: metal industrial shelving along one wall stuffed with a jumble of shoeboxes and huge plastic crates. Labels say "driftwood", "wool/fabric/blue", "nails", "earth." Shoved into the gaps are bits of wooden fencing, branch of a tree, blue plastic bucket the shape of a sand castle. Books, magazines, catalogues everywhere, no order. Black box files stood in a row, as neat as if they belonged in an accountant's office. An old sewing machine, the kind with a shaped wooden cover. Desk piled with papers, old computer, indigestion tablets, and a microwaveable pad which was brown at one edge and smelt of burnt wheat. A glory row of framed photographs; the artist with other artists, shaking hands with politicians, planting trees. All official PR photos, posed, lots of bright white teeth. A small painting of olives, ham and bread. Black CD player & stack of CDs. Elgar. Britten. The Runaways. Kate Bush. Suzi

Quatro. No vase of flowers, no trendy pen, no family pictures, no mobile or tablet. A battered oblong tin with a picture of an old ocean liner on the lid. Small table, underneath is a row of new red bricks, a metal toolbox'.

Is she about to build a wall?

She wrote on.

'On the opposite wall is a kitchenette plus double sink in which a large piece of paper is floating in a sludgy blue liquid with an oily sheen. Across the width of the room hangs a plastic washing line; on it hang three similar pieces of paper, pegged and drip-drying. All blue, various mottled effects.

'In the centre of the room is a huge table made of a sheet of wood screwed to old kitchen cupboards, a smaller folding picnic table, more crates stored underneath containing torn plastic fishing net, used drinks cans, flip-flops, squashed plastic food trays, torn pieces of polystyrene, plastic shampoo bottles.'

No wonder the place smells of bleach. Did she wash them all?

Tapping the camera app on her phone, Rose turned in a circle, taking photos carefully one by one so she could print them out later and build them into a large picture of the studio. A door banged somewhere in the house. Rose shoved her phone into her bag.

Good, now we can get on with it.

The door opened and Joan Jett came in. She had aged ten years in ten minutes, her face showing what Rose's mother Diana used to call worry lines.

'I am so sorry I had to leave you. Have you, oh yes, good, you've made yourself at home. Shall we sit here?' She gestured towards the two armchairs by the window.

Rose noticed with interest Justine's quick glance towards the table with the bricks before she covered the lot with an old bed sheet, swamping it as completely as velvet tablecloths had covered Victorian dining tables and their seductive legs.

'Sssh.'

Is she shushing me, or the bricks?

Justine turned to Rose and smiled.

'Coffee or tea?'

What was that about?

'Tea, please.'

Justine walked to the kitchenette as if nothing odd had happened. She turned on the kettle, then popped two tablets out of a silver sleeve and chewed. Rose stayed silent, not wanting to break the moment. Justine carried on with what was obviously a well-honed routine with tea leaves, teapot, kettle and mugs. She lit the portable gas fire and steered it to the chairs then sat down, her hands arranged on her lap in a relaxed pose, her smile a little tight.

'Well, where shall we start? Ask me anything.'

In Rose's experience, anyone who said 'ask me anything' usually gave few answers.

Best stick with open questions then.

'Do you remember the first thing you made?'

In the distance, the tinkling wind chime rang. Justine stood up.

'I am so sorry. I'll only be a moment. Please, drink tea. Eat chocolate, help yourself from the fridge.'

The door banged behind her, and all fell silent.

Justine was out of breath by the time she got upstairs.

'Where is Masha?'

Justine bit her tongue. Darya was looking at her with such hope in her eyes, such trust, that Justine didn't know whether to say Masha was asleep in his hutch in the garden or tell her again that he was dead. The rabbit had been dead for almost eighty years. Lying was not one of Justine's talents despite having done it practically every day for twenty-seven years.

This is different. It is not about me. If the truth frightens Darya, I will lie.

Lying would be quickest too, so she could go back downstairs. But as she was turning over the options, there was a flash of lucidity in Darya's eyes. This happened on a daily basis; sometimes it lasted for a moment, other days for hours. Those days were the happiest.

So she took the small bell from Darya's hand and put it on the mantelpiece.

'I've got to go back downstairs for a while, honey, there's a journalist waiting in the studio to interview me. You will be all right here for a while, won't you? Do you think you can sit quietly for a while without ringing the bell?'

Darya nodded, not just once but tapping out such a fast rhythm Justine feared her head would drop off her neck and roll across the floor. She put her hand on Darya's shoulder.

The nodding stopped.

'Oh yes, oh yes, darling, you go and do what you need do, need to do, I'm fine here, fine here.'

Darya gestured toward the room, waving her arm in ballet style, drawing her hand as if through water, leaving a soft rippling trail from wrist to fingertips, her little finger held slightly apart in the Russian tradition.

Justine knew the first rule was to keep Darya happy in her own bubble, not to contradict or correct her when words came out in the wrong order, and most definitely never to finish her sentences. Often that was difficult.

Her hand was cool on Justine's wrist.

'Your mouth, I like you to smile.'

Justine caught her own irritation, annoyed at being so transparent, and vowed to smile whenever she was with Darya. Fear made her tense. Tense with Darya, who had done nothing wrong, tense about the journalist downstairs who had no idea of the fear she generated in Justine's heart.

She made a huge effort and smiled.

Darya clapped her hands in delight.

'You are pretty when your mouth smiles, so pretty.'

Unable to ignore her curiosity, Rose looked beneath the velvet tablecloth. In the toolbox was a pair of pliers, a hammer, assorted screwdrivers with red handles, screws, wall plugs and a chisel. Each brick was painted with one word in white: Lost. Found. Death. Renewal. Birth. Re-birth. Lost. Found. Forever.

Rose covered it up again, wishing she hadn't pried.

Curiouser and curiouser.

Her stomach rumbled. Rose investigated the contents of the fridge. Squatting on her haunches she blinked, unsure if she was seeing clearly. Was the fridge another work of art? Each of the three shelves was crammed with at least fifty bars of Cadbury's Fruit & Nut. In order to prove to herself later that she hadn't imagined it, she took a photo on her phone. She had found the first paragraph to her article.

Where is she, for goodness sake? I haven't got all day.

Tempted to walk out of the door, Rose remembered the prospect of more work from a new client, and knew she had to stay.

But I don't have to sit here like a ninny.

After this interview Rose was due at the Tough Talk production office in Shepherd's Bush by four. Her initial research for Adrian had been straightforward and Rose had been quick to ask how else she could help. He tasked her with finding eyewitness victim reports. It was imperative, he explained over the telephone, that the women explain their own experiences in witness statements. Without them, he feared the programme's claims would sound unrealistic, even fantastical. She hoped he'd be pleased with what she'd found.

She didn't need to re-read the witness statements, she could remember every word, but was drawn to them just the same. The document on her iPad was titled 'Testimonies'. It contained the most heartbreaking interviews Rose had ever conducted. The women ranged in age from almost sixty to sixteen. Each had attended a women's advice clinic in the last thirty years, seeking information and abortion advice. Each clinic initially offered a reassuring welcome and impartial support. But after the pregnant woman stepped through the door, the mood changed to threats and intimidation. Accusations of murder. She had spoken to more than forty women. Six gave sworn testimonies, ten provided anonymous statements and the others asked her to respect their privacy and leave them alone. Which she did.

'I saw a nurse called Karen,' said Georgia Lowett. In her mid-twenties now, she was nineteen when she went to the Gaia Erinall Clinic for Women. 'She was lovely, a sort of mother figure, kind and comforting. Reassuring, you know. She said there was no rush to make a decision, I could have time to make up my mind. But when I said I didn't need time, I wanted to go ahead with it and when would I be able to meet the doctor, well, then Karen changed. It was like in a horror film. She called me horrible, horrible names. She said if I went ahead and had the abortion, I would be a murderer and the clinic would tell everyone. My mum, my dad, everyone would know. I would be so ashamed. I was so desperate. In the end I lied. I said I had decided to keep my baby after all and thanked them for helping me. They let me go. I went straight home and told my parents and my dad took me to the police. Mum and Dad were fantastic through the whole nightmare. The police went to the office where I had met Karen and the other nurses but there was no one there. They'd done a bunk. They must have been suspicious of me.'

As Rose had listened to the women talk about their experiences, as she wrote up their statements at home later, as she read and re-read them, she got angry.

She saved the document. She would be able to recite the statements to Adrian without need of her iPad.

I have to harness the anger. I have to use it, not let it run away with me.

She was in danger, she knew, of losing her objectivity.

This is not about Kate. Or me.

But it felt personal.

She looked at Justine's studio, trying to get her mind back on track. Art not abortion. Art not adoption. But her head filled with her birth mother, imagining Kate's pain, alone and pregnant; tasting the foul herbs she'd drunk, pity for her isolation in a military-style mother-and-baby-home, sorrow for the removal of her one-day old baby, anger at everyone who failed to notice her pain, grief for her death of an accidental overdose a mere four months later. Pity for all young women seeking help and finding lies.

Eyes stinging, Rose fumbled in her bag then walked unsteadily to Justine's desk in search of a box of tissues. Nowhere. Searching beneath papers, lifting a white stone paperweight from a pile of paper on the bookshelf. Her eyes filling, her sight blurring, papers fell to the floor, and heavier things banged and clattered on the wooden boards. Amid the mess was a blue box of tissues. Sniffing and choking, she perched on the edge of the desk and let the wave of sobs overtake her. She was on her fifth tissue when she realised how odd this behaviour would seem if Justine walked back in.

I must put everything back.

She stood up with the stone paperweight in her hand, twisting round, trying to remember where she had found it.

The door opened and Justine walked in, her eyes fixed on the white stone in Rose's hand.

Justine wanted to remove the chalk paperweight from the journalist and remove the journalist from her house.

'I'm sorry, I was looking for tissues.'

That was when Justine noticed her cheeks were a curtain of tears, and her anger reduced a notch.

What has happened to her? I've only been gone five minutes.

'Here,' she took the box of tissues from the floor and gave it to the woman.

'I didn't touch anything else.' Rose sniffed. 'Sorry about this, I'll be okay in a minute. Just being silly. Here.' She handed over the stone.

Justine tried not to grab her paperweight. She slipped it into the pocket of her cardigan, feeling the heft of its weight sink into the wool, not caring about the subsequent stretching.

'Take your time.' She heard her mother's voice, 'Don't stare, Justine. It's rude.' She made herself busy at her desk, keeping her eyes averted, giving Rose the sort of space she would want if she were doing the crying.

Justine glanced nervously at the cloth covering the table of bricks. It appeared untouched and she breathed a little easier. She sneaked a glance at Rose who was blowing her nose.

Here I am fixated on my problems and Rose has problems of her own.

'Is there anything I can get you? Did something here upset you?'

She took Rose by the arm and led her to the chairs by the window. They both sat for a moment and looked out at the garden. There was that twilight tone of darkness, Justine observed, shadow cast by clouds.

'I'm so sorry, what must you think of me?' The tissue was crumpled in Rose's hands as she kneaded it into a ball. 'You're being very kind, thank you. No, it's nothing to do with you. It's me, or rather it's my mother.' And on the last word, the tears started again.

Justine waited a moment as Rose's breathing slowed to a more regular pace.

'Is she ill?' She hoped she would say no. Justine couldn't cope with any more illness and death.

Rose shook her head.

'No, not ill. She's dead. They're both dead.'

Justine's stomach twisted.

'Both?'

Justine made a fresh pot of tea and they ate a whole block of Cadbury's between them. Out of habit, Justine carefully extracted the chocolate from its wrapping and smoothed the crinkles from the foil. She looked up and Rose was watching her.

'I save everything.' She flattened each purple wrinkle, pressing with her fingertips, careful not to tear it.

Rose shrugged. 'Sure, but what is it about chocolate? I just need to think about chocolate and I put on two pounds, but you,' she waved at Justine, 'you're beautiful and you eat loads of chocolate.' She laughed. 'Some things are just not fair.'

Justine was taken aback. No one had ever called her beautiful, except Federico.

'No, life isn't fair.' She hesitated. 'Will you tell me now why you were crying?'

Rose sighed. 'While you were upstairs, I read some papers

for a meeting I'm going to later. I'm doing research for a television programme.'

'Television?' Justine tried to keep her voice calm.

She knows. Any minute she's going to ask me.

Rose nodded. 'It's a big chance for me. I haven't done TV before. It's an investigative programme about abortion and, for me to do my job properly, I have to be objective about the subject. I thought I could, but I can't.'

'Why, if you don't mind me asking?'

'I'm adopted and I know my birth mother tried a herbal abortion. She died soon after I was born so I've never been able to talk to her about it.'

Birth mother? Abortion?

Over the next half an hour, Rose told her story and Justine listened. How her mother died when Rose was thirty-five and that's when she found out she was adopted. How she investigated her records and discovered the woman she thought of as her mother was actually her aunt. Rose's whole family had kept the secret.

Justine worked hard not to cry, worried that if she succumbed her own story would come bubbling out with her tears. When Rose finally fell silent, a clock somewhere in the house chimed four.

When Justine closed the door behind Rose, she sank to the floor, the spikes of the hairy doormat sticking through her jeans.

Is that how she *feels?*

It was only as Rose rushed down the escalators at the Tube station, late now for her meeting, that she realised Justine never explained the source of the tinkling bell.

24
SPAIN, NOVEMBER 1982

It was lunchtime. El Paseo del Parque, the walkway through the linear park which reached alongside the port to the foot of the tenth century castle of Gibralfaro, was lined with tall palms offering welcome shelter from the sun. A heavy perfume hung in the November air, with not a breath of a breeze to stir the leaves. They were sitting on a bench beside El Jazminero, the sculpture of the jasmine-seller, eating bread and olives, chewing, licking oil off their fingers, and unable to take their eyes off each other, unable to stop smiling.

When I'm old, I want to remember this.

'Here, *querida*. Eat.'

Federico held an olive to her lips and, feeling she was in a DH Lawrence novel, she opened her mouth and let him pop the olive inside. They now ate lunch together every college day, sitting on a bench, their thighs lightly side by side in delighted recognition of their growing mutual attraction. Federico's coyness was attractive, a refreshing change for Justine from the Yorkshire boys who after a week would be pressing her to indulge in a bout of hip-grinding. She liked the old-fashioned flirting. It was sensual, the first time she truly understood its meaning.

They had sort of fallen into food roles. Justine provided the bread, bought from the *panadería* opposite her flat, a different shaped loaf every day. *Pan pueblo*, a long oval big enough to feed a hungry family. *Pan Andaluz,* smaller, with a diamond design on top. Justine's favourite so far was the creamy *Mollete,* flat oval bread rolls from Antequera in the hills north of Málaga, often eaten for breakfast; toasted and sprinkled with olive oil, chopped tomatoes and salt. Every day Federico arrived with a tasty accompaniment to go with the *pan*. Yesterday, slices of *jamón* so thin they were almost transparent, the wine-coloured ham marbled with white swirls of fat. Before that it was salted almonds and triangles of hard cheese the colour of Indian Yellow, drizzled with oil. Today, a jar of home-cured olives.

Justine had never tasted an olive before she arrived in Málaga.

'My first time was at a welcome party for foreign students. I went with April, my flatmate.' She spoke slowly, catching his eye to confirm he understood.

He nodded.

'Anyway, I'm not good at parties. I don't know how to talk to someone I've never met.' She paused, remembering how they had met. 'A dish of olives was passed round and I did what the others did, I took one and put it in my mouth.'

She grimaced. 'It was bitter.' She looked at him and he smiled.

'*Sí, amarga.*'

'And it had a stone in it.'

'*Sí, hueso.*'

Her mother would have been delighted with her behaviour: she hadn't grimaced or coughed but continued to smile at a tall blond Norwegian student who had introduced himself in perfect English and was now outlining how he intended to be the new Munch. Wanting to challenge his pretentiousness, wanting to spit out the bitter object into a small paper napkin, instead she had nodded politely and swallowed it, stone and all. The next time the small dish did the rounds, she politely refused.

Remember the coffee, Justine. And the fish. They turned out to be lovely.

And so she took one from Federico's jar, chewed and swallowed. No stone. She gestured to the olives.

'*Bueno.*'

Federico smiled that wide smile which made the tiny scar on his top lip disappear.

'Ah *sí,* these olive *mi madre* makes. '

Justine had known it. Yesterday's *jamón* was from one of his parents' pigs, the *almendras* the day before came from his grandparents' orchard.

'They are very, *dulce.* Esweet, yes?'

'*Sí,* sweet. '

'Esweet.'

She loved the way he said his *s*'s. And Justine realised as she said the word that, yes, these olives were really sweet. She could taste, she concentrated, lemon, rosemary and something aniseedy. They sat peaceably together, tearing chunks of bread and eating it dry, without butter, in the Spanish way. She was actually starting to prefer it that way. Butter suddenly seemed rich. She chewed slowly, and examined El Jazminero.

'He is here for to remember all men who sell...' A pause while he searched for the correct word. 'It is flower, white, we say *jazmín.*'

Justine nodded. 'Yes, jasmine.'

She looked more closely at the statue, a man with a broad tray slung round his neck and yes, there were flowers in his tray. And then she smelt it, the heavy scent in the air was coming from the bushes in the shrubby border behind their bench, the tiny white star-shaped flowers living only a day before shrivelling at nightfall. She got up to read the small sign, a wooden label stuck in the earth. '*Jazmín Común*'. Tomorrow there would be new flowers here, new scent, new lovers.

Is that what we are? Lovers? But he hasn't kissed me on the lips yet.

She didn't want to move, wanted to claim this bench as their own, mark it in some way like those she sometimes sat on at home in sheltered spots on the clifftop. The benches with the plaques were always the ones with the best views of the sea.

'Federico and Justine fell in love here,' their plaque would say.

His voice broke into her reverie.

'*Mañana mediodía* I see you here? I want to show you El Cenachero.' He waved towards another statue, a hundred yards

144

away, of a man carrying a basket hung from a yoke over his shoulders. 'He is man with fish.'

'*Sí,*' she smiled. '*Mañana mediodía.* El Cenachero.'

If a boy at home asked to meet her for lunch beside the statue of a fisherman, she would have said no.

25
SPAIN, NOVEMBER 1982

When she got home, the till receipt was stuck to the fridge with a piece of sticky tape. It fluttered in the breeze from the open window. To Justine, it was a red cape being waved at a bull. When she'd left for college this morning, she'd known the receipt would be there when she got home. Today was shopping day and, according to their rota, Catalina's responsibility. Justine was due to sweep and mop all floors, April would clean the kitchen and bathroom. She avoided direct eye contact with the receipt and looked round the tiny apartment which was laid out like a wheel with every door leading off from the study room. April's bedroom door was shut as usual but Catalina's was wide open. There was the sound of running water from the bathroom, Catalina's voice singing sweetly, the lyrics incomprehensible.

It'll be about love.

Catalina had met a boy too. She sang all the time and drew pictures, of mouths, lips, one mouth in particular. Justine knew how she felt. With a sigh, she dumped her bag on the floor, went straight to the kitchen sink, poured a glass of water and downed it in one. The sink was clean, so April had already done her jobs. Justine kept her back to the fridge but somehow the fluttering paper filled the room. She couldn't pay her share of the communal shopping bill although the amount wouldn't be huge; it only covered household essentials such as milk, loo rolls and washing-up liquid. Each girl paid for her own food. She went to her room and checked the pockets of her jeans and jacket. Nothing. She searched systematically through her drawers for spare pesetas, not expecting to find any, having conducted the same search last week on shopping day. Justine still owed April for that, and she owed Catalina who had paid her own and Justine's share of the cost for the *fontanero de emergencía* to unblock the toilet. Neither girl was pressing her for money, but Justine felt uncomfortable.

I have to sell some paintings. I have to.

The original sun, wave and seabird paintings were still unsold despite Justine cutting her prices in half. Displayed alongside were three new paintings, half the size, lower prices. Studies of variations of the beach: golden sand, two-toned pebbles, dark grit. Not one person had stopped. She didn't want to reduce her prices further. She had done her sums. She would have to sell hundreds at the lower price to make enough money to settle her debts. Priced higher, the sale of three paintings would put her even until the end of the month.

She wanted to shout out, 'I'll be famous one day and this painting will be worth millions', but dared not. She could hear her mother tutting. Changing her manner hadn't helped encourage passers-by to stop and step forwards to take a second look. Making eye contact and smiling didn't work. Nor did sitting on the wall and pretending indifference.

From her pocket she removed the melon-seller's card.

The address was not far from Plaza de la Merced. She had expected some kind of office, but the address on the white card was a *panadería*. Its door was locked for siesta. The wide wooden shelves were empty of bread. Justine double-checked the name of the street. This was the right place. Then she saw what she had missed. A small bell by the door frame with Salón 21 hand-painted in neat numerals on the brick. She pressed the bell and stood back to wait, hoping no one she knew would see her.

Do not think of Federico now.

She did as her mother had taught her to do when she couldn't sleep for worries about exams. She imagined a strong box with a key. She lifted the lid and dropped inside her thoughts of Federico, his face, his eyes on hers, his smile. Then she firmly closed the lid, locking it and pocketing the key.

With a bang the roller blind on the inside of the glass door shot up, making Justine start. Staring out was a woman who did not look as if she baked bread for a living.

26
SPAIN, NOVEMBER 1982

Bernadita conducted Justine's interview in an upstairs apartment which also functioned as a beauty salon. She was not the melon-seller from the beach but, as she explained to Justine, was the owner of a hairdressing business as well as the escort agency. She made the job sound easy. According to her, it was a simple matter of putting on a nice dress, smiling, and being a charming companion for a few hours.

'Many estudents they work for me. It is easy way to make money while you estudy. You want work tonight?'

Justine glanced at her watch in the gloom of the *peña*. She thought it said ten to two. She swallowed a sigh. It had been a long day. After saying yes this afternoon, she hadn't expected to start work so quickly. Bernadita had offered her a free haircut, shampoo and blow dry, after which Justine felt more polished. Her fingernails were also filed and coated with a clear coat of varnish. With an advance on tonight's fee, she had gone to a shop recommended by Bernadita and bought a cotton dress, knee-length; dark blue with a paler blue floral trim at the hem. Not her usual sort of thing but its sweetheart neckline and fitted waist made it seem more suitable for a formal evening with a businessman.

The pressure of her client's arm was heavy against hers. They'd been to two bars before this and, after doggedly attempting conversation, he finally gave in. Inevitable, she thought, as his level of English was on a par with her Spanish. He seemed nice enough but, despite Bernadita's assurances that clients wouldn't expect her to speak Spanish, she now realised how wretched it was to spend time with someone with whom you could not communicate beyond three-word phrases from her phrase book and the pointing of her index finger. She had waited for Andrés – was that even his real name? – at ten o'clock, seated on a bench outside the Iglesia Santiago. He knew her as Sarah. He pronounced it Esara.

She found it surprisingly difficult to smile when there was nothing to smile about. Andrés took her to a busy bar where, sitting at an upturned barrel used as a table, he ordered wine, olives and a plate of thinly sliced stringy ham. He touched her only the once, cupping her elbow with his palm to guide her through the crush to the exit, and for this she was relieved.

Bernadita said he was a gentleman.

The evening was endless and Justine suspected he was taking his time, stopping to talk with people, as if wanting to be seen with her. Next another bar, this time with a proper table and menu. For thirty minutes he pointed out things on the menu, and then pointed to the décor. She smiled and nodded. Along one long wall was a row of huge barrels, each one marked with a different signature. He talked expressively about this, with much gesturing and slight spitting. Justine deciphered the words *Franco* and *vino* out of the melee.

She said *sí* a lot.

She would have been happy to stay at the second bar but he wanted to move on. When he led her up the dark stairs to the *peña,* she didn't know what to do. This was their club, hers and Catalina's and April's.

Please let them not be here tonight.

The *peña* was dark and loud inside which forced him to stop talking, for which she was relieved. Instead he greeted other people. He seemed to know everyone and they greeted him with smiles and slaps on the back.

Is he important in Málaga?

She tried to look at him without his catching her. Good-looking, she supposed, in that small, swarthy Spanish way. She wasn't tall but she was at least two inches taller than him. Justine kept her eyes on the table when Andrés spoke to someone but he always tried to draw her into the conversation. She allowed her cheeks to be double-kissed by strangers, and could hear her mother tutting loudly.

She shifted in her seat, moving her arm away from his, but he followed her movement so now his elbow pressed her ribs. She did not like being used as a trophy; she did not like his proprietorial possession of her arm; though to be fair he still had not touched her in any other way. Playing arm waltzing with him was tiring and she longed to go home. But he had paid for four hours. The last hour dragged, not because she didn't enjoy flamenco but because she hadn't chosen to be at the *peña* tonight.

I'll insist that my next client, if there is one, takes me somewhere of my choice.

There would be another client. Her left hand went to the wad of folded pesetas in her pocket. She had been pleasantly surprised when he insisted on paying her at the beginning of the evening. She thought briefly of what to do with the cash. Pay April and Catalina first. Bernadita for the dress. Then food. Then, and only then, some new tubes of oil paint. She could maybe afford three. She was out of Cadmium Red and needed it to finish her submission for Paul Willow, which was due at tomorrow's class. She glanced at her watch again. Today's class.

Andrés put another glass of *zumo de naranja* in front of her and nodded kindly. Justine had drunk so much juice she felt she would turn into an orange. She wondered what Andrés was doing here. He seemed a nice man, not pushy compared with the students who had been her only previous dating experiences. Immediately her mouth filled with the taste of Federico's olives and bread and fried fish.

Forget about him.

She took a gulp of juice, then another.

Andrés smiled. So many white teeth. Justine wondered why he didn't have a wife. He was much older than her, certainly the age you would expect a businessman to be married. And that is how Bernadita had described him. 'He has company,

151

he sell and repair *coches*.' Justine had expected a middle-aged man with grimy fingernails who ran a garage.

Perhaps he's just lonely.

The other side of the room had been totally dark while the performers were on stage but now, in the changeover of dancers for the final set, the glare from a spotlight picked out one pale face at the other side of the room. April. Who had said she was going to work late in the sculpture room at college.

What on earth is she doing here?

As the new dancer stepped into the centre of the room, resplendent in red and white spots, frills and flounces, the arc of the spotlight widened to shine on the audience. Justine saw the answer to her question. Sitting beside April was an old man, at least fifty, wearing a white shirt and a scarf tied at his neck as a cravat. Dapper, her mother would have described him. Justine remembered the photograph above April's easel at college, and knew the man with her tonight was not her father. The light passed on, the dancer's heels began to click, and the faces of April and her companion were hidden again in darkness.

When the lights came on twenty minutes later, it was as if April had never been there.

27
SPAIN, NOVEMBER 1982

Midday the next day, Justine stood beside El Cenachero waiting for Federico. The statue was in the full sun and, after ten minutes, the heat defeated her so she returned to the shady bench by El Jazminero. She had a clear view of the path where she expected to see him approaching. No sign of him yet though, and he was ten minutes late. He had never been late before.

Her portfolio was laid carefully on her lap, her painting in its protective cradle. 'Winter Landscape in the Style of Constable' was still wet. She had finished painting an hour ago. She dared to think it her best assignment yet. Today Willow would talk about portraits, a discipline she found intimidating. The twin challenge of portraits and oil paints, which she had never attempted seriously until she came to Málaga, was the biggest challenge she had faced. It gave her a real buzz. So while she waited for Federico, she studied the face of the jasmine-seller.

If I had to paint him, how would I do it? Profile or full-face? In a cloud of white stars?

In the background she could somehow hint at the bubble of optimism in Spain now, but with what? Could flowers be optimistic? Last month's election victory by the socialist party had been welcomed with fiestas throughout the streets of Málaga. There was an underlying buzz of expectation because Spain was no longer suspended in transitional political limbo after decades of the Francoist dictatorship; it was a democratic state for the first time since 1936. Justine tried to imagine herself into the head of Elizabethan portrait painter Marcus Gheeraerts the Younger – who painted 'The Ditchley portrait' of Queen Elizabeth I – and considered painting the jasmine-seller with layers of modern political symbolism. Sunshine, a ballot box, cranes and building blocks, cars and aeroplanes, olives and oranges. She studied the face of the statue. Without doubt his most arresting feature was his bone structure. She could highlight his cheekbones and so hint at his character. Noble. Loyal. Hard-working. Beloved. It was all a lie, of course; she could never know his character. But all art was a personal interpretation. The statue itself was the sculptor's version of a person, a person who, she suddenly realised, may not be real. But art was not a photograph; a photo could capture every shadow, every blemish. Art could embellish, shorten a nose, deepen blue eyes, make blonde hair golden, make thin lips fuller.

If I wanted to show the truth, I would have become a photographer.

She looked at the face again, trying to see his skull. It was important to understand what lay beneath. Portrait painters studied bone structure and muscles; Michelangelo and Leonardo da Vinci dissected human remains. Degas studied horses galloping and pigeons flying.

If I wanted to study muscles, I would have become a doctor or a vet.

Perhaps the most striking thing about El Jazminero was really his eyes. Could she emphasise them as Vermeer did with 'The Girl with the Pearl Earring'? His use of white to highlight the collar of her blouse, the pearl of the earring, her wide young eyes and a single brushstroke to show the lusciousness of her bottom lip. All finished with the shock of lapis lazuli used for the blue headscarf. She didn't want to copy the idea and didn't know the colour of the jasmine-seller's eyes, but perhaps she could invent it. Or perhaps she could be braver, be like Modigliani and elongate the face, add angles, black lines for emphasis.

She jotted down a few notes in her sketchbook then crossed them out, scoring out her writing so the words could not be read. She didn't want to imitate someone else. She wanted to do her own thing. The only problem was, she hadn't a clue what her thing was. She looked in the direction from which Federico would arrive. Her eyes were tired and itchy. She'd finally left Andrés and got home by three, then was up early to buy the tube of Cadmium Red, working without breakfast to finish her winter landscape. Her subject was the hedge that ran on the left of the lane between home and the bus stop. She enjoyed the process of painting it, the memories of Flamborough Head and the change from summer to autumn, the new chill to the breeze which smelt of the ocean, the scattering of golden and bronze leaves, the deep fertile brown of the ploughed fields. In Málaga, summer and autumn seemed largely indistinguishable except that early mornings and late evenings demanded a jumper and jeans, shorts at midday. It had been worth waiting for the new tube of Cadmium Red; the painting would be anaemic without it. It had three horizontal bands. At the top, a line of pale grey sky heavy with snow; at the bottom, a line of white snow on the ground; and from left to right across the middle of the picture, a band of red berries. Cotoneaster, pyracantha, hips and haws, holly. With just the odd dash of green and brown to represent leaves and earth. Not exactly 'winter landscape in the style of Constable' which had been the brief, but it represented what winter meant to her. Except that someone looking at it who didn't know it portrayed the countryside might think the red was a swipe of blood. Had she overdone it? Perhaps there would be time before class to tone down the red; the paint was still tacky. Maybe she could add something to indicate nature. A tree. A bird.

Less red.

She checked her watch. Federico was twenty minutes late now. She stood and turned towards the *plaza* where the buses arrived and departed, hoping to see him in the distance. And walking towards her with a broad smile on his face and a bunch of red flowers in his arms, was Federico.

'Hola, querida. Lo siento que llego tarde.'

The red carnations were the exact same colour as the slash of berries across her painting. Crushed between their chests as they hugged, the flowers released a spicy scent reminding her of clove oil, her mother's preferred cure for mouth ulcers. The flowers were unexpected. She had never been given flowers by a boy and felt embarrassed saying thank you, embarrassed to have no gift for him.

They sat side by side on the bench and quickly ate all the *ensaladilla rusa* in the plastic box, which Federico produced from his rucksack. He had been home to Cádiz last weekend and was still producing home-made food for their lunch. In her painting frenzy this morning, Justine had forgotten to buy bread, but it didn't matter as he had brought enough food for four people. She wolfed down half of everything. The *ensaladilla rusa* reminded her of the tinned potato salad her mother served for Sunday tea, but it tasted a hundred times better eaten in the Spanish sunshine. They drank water from the public drinking fountain which stood in the shade of a tall eucalyptus tree, halfway between El Jazminero and El Cenachero. For pudding, Federico bought a paper bag of hot roasted chestnuts from the vendor across the street. And as she ate, his good humour spread over her like a warm blanket. Laughing, blowing on to the hot chestnuts and their burnt fingers, he told her about his morning class.

'We talk about an *arquitecto famoso. En* Barcelona. *Se llama* Gaudí. He make beautiful buildings. You visit Barcelona?'

'No, but I have heard of Gaudí. Isn't there a cathedral that's unfinished?'

'*Sí, tienes razón.* But I think of you this morning *porque el maestro, perdona,* the teacher, he tell us that Gaudí, he estudy nature,' he took her hand in his, 'and I think of you. He make the Sagrada Familia. It is, *como se dice,* it is a *bosque.* Trees.' He looked up at her, questioning.

'A forest?'

'*Sí, sí,* a forest. The *maestro* say this and I think of you because you love the nature, yes? You draw tree and *hojas y muchas flores.*'

He pointed to her sketchbook, which had fallen open at

a study of the jacaranda trees that grew near her apartment in Plaza de la Merced.

'These *flores,* they are beautiful.' He hesitated. 'You are beautiful painter, Justina, beautiful person.'

Three beautifuls. No one had ever said that to her and it brought a lump to her throat.

On the left page, a pencil sketch of the flat oval seed pods and the light feathery seeds; on the right page, a monotone blue study in pastel of two large panicles of flowers.

'And did Gaudí paint flowers?'

'He estudy rock and insect and the *arboles de olivos y los usa* for the *arquitectura.* For the *construcción* and *diseño.'*

'Yes,' she said eagerly, 'I've seen photographs. There are paving slabs on one of his buildings decorated with octopus, starfish and tortoises.' One glance at Federico's face showed he didn't understand.

'*Animales,*' she said hesitantly.

'*Sí, sí, y pescados*. For *decoración.*'

'*Pescados?'* She pointed at the statue of the fisherman.

'Is different,' Federico laughed. 'El Cenachero he sell fish for eating.'

He dug into the paper bag and brought out the last two nuts, juggling them from palm to palm, blowing on them.

Justine looked at his pursed lips, and imagined them kissing her collar bone, her nipples.

She took the nut he offered to her and popped it in her mouth. It had a deliciously smoky taste, woody. It reminded her of lapsang souchong tea.

Federico was waiting, expectantly. '*Dime,* now what you do?'

'I'm sorry, I know you've just got here and the food was really *bonita,* but I have to go. I'll be late for my class.' She glanced at her watch. '*Tarde.*'

'Aah.' Federico leapt to his feet. '*Yo voy también.* I have *cita* with *Maestro Dominguez.* Here; is for you, for if I late another day.'

He pressed into her hand a folded slip of paper, his telephone number, and she wrote hers on the front of his folder. They kissed. Justine knew she should leave but didn't want to let him go; so she stood, cradling the carnations in her arms, as Federico retrieved his bike from where it was chained to the railings. Then, holding hands for as long as possible, they turned in opposite directions, until only the tips of their fingertips touched.

Justine saw her bus approaching and let go. 'Bye-bye,' she called over her shoulder as she ran.

'Justina! *Momento,* Justina!'

She stopped and turned. Federico was standing with his hand still outstretched towards her.

'We meet here tonight? El Jazminero?' He seemed suddenly nervous. 'Please, is *importante* for me.'

'*Sí,*' she called back to him. '*Sí,* tonight.' She called out so loud that the driver of the bus, the passengers and the entire population of Málaga could hear her, and she didn't care. She was being carried along on a wave of emotion over which she had no control, and it did not frighten her one little bit. She kept her hand in her pocket, clasping the folded slip of paper.

She arrived early at their bench that evening. Content to wait, indulging in the glow of knowing he would arrive soon, she soaked up the Spanish twilight. The sun was preparing to set, turning the sky the palest of pastel pinks tinged with raspberry, and she was musing about their relationship. Just forming the word 'relationship' made her shiver. When did a 'thing' become a relationship? It was a subconscious sort of musing; she didn't think 'I wonder who has the power'. Instead she wondered if she cared more because she arrived on time twice in a row, or whether Federico was being clever by making her wait for him. Thanks to her mother's almost Victorian dislike of improper conduct, Justine was incapable of being late for anything. As a teenager she had tried to be late, feeling the need to be early for every appointment was a sign of being desperate for approval. But it didn't feel right. Whether this was self-approval or approval from her mother, or God, she wasn't sure. She just knew she felt uptight and English compared to Federico. She wouldn't be without her alarm clock and diary.

The jasmine-seller's statue cast a shadow across the wide path in front of her, almost stretching to the bed opposite which spilled full of red and yellow starry lantana flowers. She preferred the plant's common name; El Bandolero, the Spanish Flag. She examined El Jazminero from every angle, to capture his cheekbones, his nose, to cast shadows and track the light. She should take photos of him from every angle but didn't have a camera. Perhaps April would have one she could borrow. April had everything.

April had said nothing about last night at the flamenco club and neither had Justine. She handed in her winter landscape to Paul Willow without amendment. Painting over the Cadmium Red would have made her night with Andrés a waste. Her skin prickled at the thought of his hand on her elbow, escorting her up steps and down steps, through crowds in bars. She was surprised at the strength of her reaction as he had treated her with courtesy and, though old and rather formal for her taste, was not unattractive.

He's harmless and the money is a saviour.

The early evening crowds strolled through the *parque,* a continuous stream of people: strings of teenage girls, giggling arm in arm; young men, all swaying hips and jutting chins; grandmothers, mothers and daughters, heads bent in conversation and slow smiles; and couples walking side by side, still dressed in their formal work attire. Most of the men were wearing suits, most were not as attractive as Andrés. She shivered again, suddenly feeling cold as the raspberry sky turned to Purple Madder and the first evening breeze blew in from the chilly sea and brushed her arm. She pulled her jacket over her shoulders, and shifted along the bench into the sun. El Jazminero's shadow now filled the pavement in front of her and cast the lantana's flowers into shadow.

Do I feel this way about Andrés because of Andrés himself, or because of Federico?

She had told Federico nothing of her financial troubles,

nothing of the *peña,* nothing of Andrés and the agency. She worried her silence was a betrayal of their relationship, though it seemed way too early for confessions and commitment. Only six weeks. Too soon.

Should I tell him everything about me?

The thought made her stop.

Has he told me everything?

She had his phone number but not his address. They spoke different languages and though his English was amazing, their conversation was conducted in pidgin English.

But I should at least tell him I have no money.

It was getting colder and she worried about paying the winter heating bill. She prayed for warm weather but accepted that if there was a cold spell the others would turn up the heating. She had been amazed to find the Levante, a wind which blew west across the Mediterranean to Málaga, promised to be just as strong as the gales that blew across the North Sea to Flamborough Head.

Something touched her foot and made her start out of her reverie. A yellow football rolled away across the footpath, chased by two small boys who were followed by a harassed-looking woman who had to be their mother.

'*Lo siento,*' said the woman.

'*De nada.*' Justine repeated the phrase Catalina had taught her. 'It's nothing.'

Federico has helped me too. I feel less of a stranger here now.

She was grateful for this, and for his approval of her portfolio. He seemed to be impressed by her work, and she felt more comfortable at college because of that. Was it something to do with approval by a stranger being more worthy than approval by a friend? He was still something of a mystery, which of course piqued her interest even more. She didn't think he was being mysterious on purpose, just different. He was curiously formal, which she wasn't sure was a Spanish thing or a Federico thing. Each encounter had ended with a Spanish kiss – cheek to cheek, left then right. Her lips ached. Thinking of the weight of Federico's hands on her shoulders as he kissed her farewell – and she could remember each of the kisses, the when, the where, the kiss – she thought of his lips, and the softness as they brushed her skin. He had such a glorious mouth, lips like bruised fruit against his brown skin. Impatient for his arrival, she glanced at her watch.

If he's late for the second time in one day, does it mean I'm not important to him?

At lunchtime he had said it was '*importante*' to meet her tonight. What kind of important? Kissing important? Cuddling important? Meeting his parents important?

The thought of more made her shiver, a shiver nothing to do with a new, chiller edge to the evening breeze.

'Justina.' He was there, leaning over the back of the bench, whispering her name into the soft baby hair at the nape of her neck, his warm breath sending shivers down her spine. Her face flushed as he sat down and kissed her, cheek to cheek, left to right.

'You are *muy tranquila. Qué piensas?'*

Justine shook her head helplessly, her brain stopped working, her mind focussed on her neck, her cheek, his breath.

I can't possibly tell him what I'm thinking.

'So, what is this important thing you talked about this morning?'

Her lips were suddenly dry. She licked them, and then Federico leant forwards, shyly touched his lips to hers and didn't remove them. Justine was sure that when she was older she would still remember their first real kiss that evening. With the benefit of years of love and sex, she would look back and recognise the accumulation of anticipation, the inevitability.

When they surfaced, breathing was difficult.

He read a poem to her, in Spanish, there in the garden heavy with the evening oily scent of the box hedges surrounding them. About love. She lay with her head in his lap, and vowed to remember this moment all her life, the strength of his thighs beneath denim, the blue ceiling above with static stars and the moving lights which were planes, the smell of a city winding down after a long day, most of all his voice.

'It is about two people who want…' He hesitated, searching for a word in English. 'They love.'

As he read from a book held in his right hand, his left arm lay heavy on her shoulder. Justine could feel every inch of contact. At that moment it felt as if the connection was permanent, that they would live their lives together as twins. With that thought came a flicker of fear, and of excitement. Was she too young to think 'forever'?

No. I am old enough to face what life brings and it has brought me Federico.

As Federico read, his breath touched the hairs on the top of her head and re-arranged them. To start with she concentrated on his words, but recognising about one in twenty she stopped trying to understand and listened instead to the silky tone of his voice. She always felt in a spin, rushing, impatient, impetuous even, whereas he was so at peace with himself and with time. She let his spirit soothe hers.

Tú justificas mi existencia:
si no te conozco, no he vivido;
si muero sin conocerte, no muero, porque no he vivido.

He closed the book, then gently kissed the end of her nose. 'A man *que se llama* Louis Cernuda, this he write since many years.'

'It's beautiful. What does it mean?'

He paused a moment.

'Mmm, is difficult. He says,' taking her hand in his, 'he says, if I not know you I am dead. If I die *sin,* hmm, without I know you, I am not dead because I not alive.' He took a deep breath.

'Justina, I know you *unas semanas* but I like you *mucho*. Excuse my English.'

He paused and Justine leant towards him, trying to be patient, hoping he couldn't hear the blood rushing through her veins.

'When we drink coffee together, I not know you. Now I know you more and you are beautiful person.' He held her hand as she was shaking her head. 'Yes, you are beautiful because you not know it. You work hard, you are kind and,' he turned her hand in his and gently drew circles on her palm with his thumb, 'your skin is so white and, *como se dice?*' He stopped, shook his head impatiently.

'*Aquí.*' He closed the tattered paperback and handed it to her. '*Un regalito.*'

Now she did rise from her prone position, shyness forgotten, kneeling up on the bench at his side and kissing him hard on the lips. She put into her kiss all the words she couldn't find to speak, hoping he would understand. That she felt overwhelmed by his friendship, the miracle that he was interested in her, the pale rather intense English girl, and that she liked him too, so much.

They strolled far and wide that long evening as autumn closed and winter opened, along the passages of the Old Town, stopping in front of the cathedral with its elaborate Baroque façade.

'Is highest *catedrál* in Andalucía after La Giralda in Sevilla. Is beautiful, no?'

'But what happened to the other tower?' Justine pointed at the unfinished spire.

He shrugged. 'She is called La Manquita, which mean lady with one arm.'

As they walked she sneaked glances at him as he talked, noticing the light in his eyes as he explained the structural details of buildings, the materials, the Spanish words for architectural styles.

I look at him too much. I mustn't let him catch me doing it, it's too obvious.

As they walked up the hill to the fortress-like Alcabaza, she pointed out to sea and asked about the geography of Spain, where was north and where was south, and was that really Africa on the horizon.

Anything to let me watch him while he's distracted.

At the top they turned round and walked down again to the port where silent fishing boats gently rocked at the turn of the tide, and then back through the Paseo del Parque, past El Jazminero and El Cenachero, stopping beside the nymph with the pitcher and the nymph with the seashell. They circled the narrow walkways of the *parque* and then returned to the jasmine-seller because he was their first. At midnight, they walked along the wide pavement away from town, past the bullring and out to a wide stretch of beach Justine had never seen before. Together, in a sheltered private place on La Malagueta beach, they lay under blankets Federico produced from his rucksack and where the chill of the night did not reach them.

Afterwards, they lay like spoons beneath the blankets. Somewhere, a clock struck two. From the rucksack Federico produced a candle and an empty wine bottle, and made an impromptu candlestick. By the flickering light, he selected a pebble from the beach, just big enough to fit snugly into his palm. With his penknife he scratched an 'F' on to the stone. He kissed it softly and put it into her outstretched hand. With her heart pounding, Justine selected her own pebble from the high tide mark, taking more time than he had in her selection process. Shape, colour, weight. Borrowing his penknife she scratched her mark, taking care, wanting it to be right. Then she too kissed her pebble and gave it to him.

28
LONDON, MAY 2010

It was still dark outside when Rose's mobile rang. She was on her third mug of black coffee and halfway through a Digestive biscuit, the half-eaten packet beside her mouse mat. This combination had been her father's remedy for early morning starts when the eyes were open but the brain was absent. She was trying to read the British Medical Association website.

Without understanding how, she knew it was Justine calling.

'Rose, there's something I want to tell you. Will you meet me at the V&A when it opens at ten?'

The halls were quiet and empty when Rose arrived, and had more of that quasi-religious feeling than when she normally visited. She had never been here at opening time. Tiptoeing, grimacing every time the soles of her shoes squeaked on the highly polished floor, Rose made her way to their agreed meeting point in the Medieval and Renaissance Gallery. Justine had said it was her favourite place in the museum and Rose was curious to see it. Justine was the only one there, a small body, almost girl-like, sitting on a wooden bench which ran along the curved brick wall of this oddly shaped gallery. It was as if she was insubstantial, almost disappearing into the background.

Justine didn't acknowledge Rose's presence; she was gazing straight ahead at a wooden staircase fixed on the wall opposite, an island of her own.

Rose sat down beside her, not wanting to break the spell. She studied the staircase, trying to see what Justine was seeing, wondering if artists had a vision different to ordinary people.

It was an odd exhibit, like a heart or a liver surgically removed during an autopsy and displayed in isolation, removed from everything which gave it life and meaning. Was the rest of the sixteenth century French house still standing? Perhaps in its place stood an executive family home with cream walls and curtains and a tree house in the garden.

'If a person is separated from her family before her memories began, do you think her soul knows what she has lost?' As she spoke, Justine's eyes never left the staircase but her hand lifted, rested lightly on Rose's wrist then away again.

Rose hesitated. 'I think it must be different for each person. I always knew I was different from my family.' She tried to remember a specific thing that had given her, as a child, such a strong conviction that she didn't belong to her mother as her younger sister Lily did. 'I have no memory of Kate, my birth mother, no fleeting glimpse or smell which made me wonder. But I did wonder all the same.'

Justine was nodding intently and Rose had to work hard not to look at her knees again. She would not be a coward.

I have to explain it right.

'With the hindsight of years, I have sympathy for both my mothers. They took the decisions which at the time seemed right for them. It's easy to sit here and criticise something I can never fully understand.'

Justine was gazing at her with a flicker in her eyes as if she was deciding whether to speak. Rose paused, waiting as she had countless times in interviews, allowing the interviewee space in which to find the words to tell their story. The only sound in the gallery was a magpie on the glass roof, searching through the leaf debris and moss for insects. As Rose watched, the blue patch on its wing caught the winter sunlight and flashed as bright as a high-powered torch with a new battery.

'I gave my baby away.' Justine's voice, when it came, was a whisper.

Rose leant forwards to hear better, cursing herself for not bringing her digital recorder and then hating herself for even thinking that.

'I gave my baby away.' Quietly, haltingly, Justine started to tell a story of a student who went to Málaga to study art and found love instead.

Why? Why is she telling me this? Why me? Because I'm a stranger.

Rose remembered how it had been easiest to talk to an adoption counsellor during those first days after discovering she was adopted.

She's telling me because I know how it is to be in her child's position. She's seeking my understanding for what she did, seeking forgiveness.

Rose listened as Justine talked of the thrill and fear of studying abroad, the foreignness of it all, the dark liquid eyes of her boyfriend, the instant connection which breached the language barrier, the doubts about whether it had been real love or a crush, the fear of shaming her parents. As Justine talked, her voice quickening, her eyes brighter, Rose remembered that drive to tell your story once you've started. Less like confessing, more like the body's over-riding need to vomit after eating something bad, the need to expel followed by exhaustion.

Justine fell silent and Rose watched as her head dropped, chin to chest, eyes closed. She waited what felt a respectful time, enough for Justine to gather strength, before speaking quietly. The hush in her voice was not for the silence of the vast empty vault in which they sat, but for what Justine had lived through.

'Why do you want to find your baby now, after all these years?'

Justine straightened up with a sigh. 'Because my mother has died and now I feel free.'

'Your mother never knew she had a grandchild?'

'No, I never told anyone. I could never have brought that shame down on my parents. It would have killed my mother. She raised me properly, as she was raised. There was no room in our family for an unmarried mother.' Her voice was tight now. 'It would have been easier to fly to Mars.'

Rose nodded. 'There were a lot of secrets in my family too.'

The difference is that my parents lied to me, but Justine lied to hers.

It had been a while since Rose's head had been so full of her adoption.

'I have tried, on and off, over the years to find her. I called her Jenni. I wasn't good at searching and, I realise now, I didn't try very hard. I let myself be beaten.'

Rose had no words of wisdom to offer. Her experience was finding her birth mother, not a missing daughter. She remembered her counsellor's advice when she was searching for her own birth parents. Bella said that barging in without forethought could cause irreparable damage. Some birth mothers may have kept the secret all their lives. But here was Justine, a birth mother, needing to find her daughter.

Lucky Jenni.

'I'm terrified she'll resent me because I gave her away. Is that how you felt?'

Rose was silent. She had buried these feelings deep for a reason.

Doesn't she realise how painful it is to think of these things?

'Did you hate your birth parents when you first found out you were adopted?'

She made an effort not to shout out, 'Don't you know this hurts?'

Calm, Rose, be calm.

'I don't think I'm qualified to advise you, Justine, sorry. Both my mothers are dead so I never got the chance to talk to them about it, which means I don't know how they would react to me finding out the truth.'

'You found your birth father though, didn't you?'

Rose thought of her father John, who today was working on the deli counter at EasySave.

My dad.

'Yes.'

'And you don't hate him.'

No. Yes. A bit.

'No, I don't hate him, but some days I remember the lies he told and I don't like him very much. But that passes. He is my dad, he raised me. I've never known another father. I had three parents and he's the only one I have left. I have to make the best of our time together while I can. He was seriously ill a few years ago and I realised I don't want to lose him too.'

To soften her words, Rose took Justine's cold hand and warmed it in hers. Justine didn't react; Rose might as well be holding the hand of one of The Three Graces upstairs.

'Every situation is different, Justine. You have to make your own decision, no one can predict how a stranger will react.'

'I know. I am realistic, you know."

Rose smiled ruefully. In trying to be cautious, to protect Justine from pain, she hadn't meant to sound so discouraging.

'If it helps, the truth hurts less than the lies. It sounds a bit trite, but that's how it was for me.'

'Believe me, I know all about truth and lies.'

Justine's face was turned towards Rose who saw no disguise there now. Then the penny dropped and Rose understood.

I've been so dense not to see it earlier. This is why all her work is about loss.

A light had turned on. She wished she could go back to the exhibition at Barker Mews Gallery and look again at all those pieces of 'Green' to examine them through the prism of loss. And after the flash of excitement when a great idea arrived in her head, a piece of inspiration, a knotty problem solved, came the realisation.

I can't write about this.

She thought of her own adoption story and how she would feel if their roles were reversed, if she were asking advice from Justine the journalist.

Okay, so it's off the record until, unless, she says otherwise.

Once she had thought that, Rose felt easier.

It was she who broke the silence. 'Before you do anything,

I think you need to think very carefully why you want to find her.'

'Isn't it obvious?'

'What I mean is, are you searching for yourself or for her?'

Oh Rose, shut up, don't start this.

Justine's brow crinkled. 'For myself?'

'Do you really need to find her, to meet her, to be a part of her life? Is it a need like breathing and eating? Or is it enough to know how she is doing?'

Justine stared at her. To Rose, it felt as if she was being looked at by a stranger.

Justine found it exhausting, pretending to be someone she wasn't. Twenty-seven years of it. Press receptions where the sweat bubbled from her skin with the relentlessness of rainwater forcing its way from a drain cover during a downpour, waiting for the journalist's question, the one someone always asks. 'It's so dedicated of you, to focus on your career rather than have a baby. Do you think your art would be different if you were a mother?'

Such an intrusive question. Do they ask Rachel Whiteread, Maggi Hambling or Fiona Banner about babies? Did they ask Graham Sutherland or Paul Nash? She didn't know if they were parents or not and didn't care. So she learned to smile and say something bland, so bland it wouldn't be quoted. She didn't say what she wanted to say.

Because the Unique Selling Point of her art was her emotions, she laid bare her emotions for everyone to see. It was her public image. Like Tracey Emin, except Tracey was telling the truth. Justine was often mentioned in the same paragraph of press articles as Tracey. They were often lumped together as 'hysterical single female artists', except Tracey's success was a mountain next to Justine's hill.

Critics moaned about the impossibility in getting beneath the surface of Justine Tree. 'Impenetrable', the kinder ones said. 'Inaccessible'. As if she were a difficult-to-find-building in a maze of one-way streets. Others said there was nothing else to find. The word 'superficial' was used a lot. 'Emotionally incontinent' too.

But it's not really me.

That's what she wanted to shout, but didn't. She simply couldn't bear to see pain engraved on her parents' faces and know she put it there. She couldn't tell the museums and curators and art investors who supported her work, bought it, commissioned it, that it was all based on a lie. She couldn't tell Darya the truth about the desperate art student she took into her home on 12 September 1983.

If I continue with the lies, I will never find her. If I tell the truth, I will lose my art.

Now, she was terrified.

Rose tried to watch Justine without seeming to stare. Her brow was furrowed with deep lines that seemed permanently etched. Her voice, when she finally spoke, was ancient.

'I don't know, I haven't thought about it that way.'

'Well, perhaps you should.' Rose's words were harsher than she intended.

Justine rubbed her eyes, smudging her mascara. It made her look her age.

'You're right. I am being selfish.'

'If you're just curious about her, there are ways of finding information without doing damage.'

'Can you do that for me?'

No, definitely no.

'No, Justine. You need a specialist. If you want to know she's safe, happy, you can do that without making contact with her. Then leave her alone. She may try to find you. Anytime. In thirty years' time. But if you actively want to be a part of her life now and are prepared to tell her the truth, including all the ugly stuff, then you have to take the consequences.'

'Rejection.' There was no questioning tone in Justine's voice.

'Yes, possibly.'

I've said too much.

Rose felt uncomfortably hot and wished she weren't wearing a chunky sweater. It prickled her neck and she longed to scratch.

Rose stood up. 'Do you mind if we walk for a bit? Perhaps find a coffee.'

So they walked slowly through the halls, heading in the general direction of the main entrance. Justine seemed occupied with her own thoughts, for which Rose was grateful as realisation after realisation was pinging in her head like incoming messages on her mobile.

Birth. Death. Loss. Betrayal. Rejection.

The same words were painted on those bricks in Justine's studio. The public thought they were getting Justine's real emotions, but Rose wondered if 'Justine Tree' was a persona for public consumption just as Beyoncé turned into Sasha Fierce on stage. If Justine King's story went public, it would send Justine Tree's prices rocketing. Her work would be printed on postcards, biographies would be written. A retrospective. A television documentary. Her hashtag would trend. She wanted publicity for trees, well she would get it. Except the amount of newsprint used to tell her scandalous story would chop trees down, not plant them. But Rose had interviewed enough famous people to know Justine did not seek notoriety.

She just wants to find her daughter.

Justine seemed to be walking in a daze and Rose followed her lead, unsure which way to take to find the café. Then they turned a corner and directly in front of them was a sandstone Buddha on a plinth. Justine stopped so suddenly, Rose bumped into her. With an intake of breath she watched as Justine stretched out a hand to the stone, her fingers lingering without touching, then retreating. Finally she stood with her hands in her pockets.

She turned to Rose and smiled and her face looked calmer. 'I imagine the stone would feel warm. I've never touched it, though I long to know how it feels. Stone is nature at its most solid, after all.'

'Would you ever sculpt in stone?'

Justine shook her head.

'The café's this way,' she pointed and they walked on. 'No, but I want to work with wood. Raw wood. I'm trying to work out how.'

She pointed to an empty display cabinet. Inside a label said 'On Loan'.

'It's the bowl at the show, the one with the apples in it. The V&A loaned it to me. It's Mark Lindquist's 'So Long Frank Lloyd Wright' bowl and I wish I had made it.'

Rose remembered the elegant bowl, marvelling that it was possible to borrow an exhibit from the V&A.

'If you love wood, stone and metal so much, why do you bother with collage and paint? Why not just get stuck in?'

Justine sighed. 'I wish it was that simple, but the technique is beyond me. The ultimate would be to work in bronze. Just think of the greats. Giacometti. Rodin. Brancusi. The legacy of the Bronze Age, the beginning of civilisation. That's more than three thousand years BC. A few years ago, only in the Nineties, some fishermen near Sicily found a fourth century BC bronze figure of a dancing satyr. Beautiful. So old, but so modern. It is such sophisticated art but I find it rather intimidating. Henry Moore, Barbara Hepworth, Elizabeth Frink, Eduardo Paolozzi. I can't match that.'

She stared at the empty space where the Lindquist bowl should be. 'Maybe I should start by learning how to carve a small piece of wood and then work up to a tree.'

They walked past the Great Bed of Ware and Justine halted again, standing so close to a display cabinet her nose almost pressed against the glass. Inside was a tiny beaded christening basket. Rose read the display caption. It was made in 1659 and survived intact.

Justine spoke without moving her head. 'I don't know what my daughter is called now.'

Rose stood next to her, close so their shoulders touched. The proximity was comforting, and she hoped Justine could feel the warmth too.

'My birth mother called me Alanna,' murmured Rose.

'That's such a pretty name.'

Tears were running down Justine's cheeks now. Then without warning she clasped Rose's forearm, her fingers digging so deep into the muscle it made Rose gasp.

'My parents are gone now where my truth can't hurt them. Please help me to find my daughter.'

Not for the first time, time seemed to concertina together when they talked. The morning had disappeared. It was a dark afternoon, the sky grey and lowering, threatening rain, thunder, as Justine watched Rose walk away along Cromwell Road.

And so it begins.

She walked home because it would take longer, because it would give her time to practise the story she would have to tell. Tomorrow, some day soon. It shouldn't be difficult; she'd been telling stories most of her life. This would be the last one. She was drawn west by something deep in her core, the same primeval urge that leads birds in migration and guides an injured animal to its burrow. Inside her head all sorts of stuff was swirling round. Memories mixed up with faces: Darya's, her mother's, her father's. And Málaga.

Justine felt drained of energy after talking to Rose, avoiding the holes in her story as carefully as a child dancing along a pavement singing 'Step on a crack and break your mother's back'. She had expected to feel good, expected that empowering Rose to search would go some way to righting her old mistakes. But asking the question had felt different. Scary, like walking along an endless dark tunnel at the end of which may be a locked door. She longed for Federico's approval. To see the gentle smile in those velvet eyes. To hear his voice say '*Tranquila,* Justina. *Todo bien,* you have this *niña* to find.'

'But,' she forced the words out between her teeth, 'but she may not be your daughter.' This was her worst fear. She wanted him to be the father, but wanting did not make it true.

29
LONDON, MAY 2010

She shivered as she climbed the stairs to Darya's room. The heating was on full and the house was sub-tropical. Darya was sitting in her black velvet-upholstered armchair beside a roaring fire, playing Junior Scrabble with Mrs Purvis. It was the first day without the nurse and so far everything was working well. Justine suspected Mrs P was showing her own early signs of dementia. Perhaps the shared feeling of plunging into the unknown helped make Darya and Mrs P regular afternoon companions.

'Tea, ladies?'

Two bright-eyed, pink-cheeked faces smiled up at her.

'Ooh yes please,' said Mrs P, before nudging Darya and whispering loudly, 'they do look after us so well here, don't they? Lovely cake.'

Justine smiled, as she did every time Mrs P said this, trying not to feel hurt but hurting all the same. She feared the day when Darya stopped recognising her as Justine and instead saw a stranger. She had been aware of an odd flash of anger in Darya's eyes, specifically when Justine was in a rush and was hurrying Darya to do something she didn't particularly want to do. For example, taking her tablets with a biscuit and a cup of tea mid-morning and once when a stand-in chiropodist arrived to replace gentle Mr Small who flirted with Darya and made her giggle.

Once the old ladies were settled again with tea, cake and the Scrabble board, Justine made sure the little brass bell Darya called Tinkerbell was within reach, and retreated downstairs to her studio. She sat by the window. It was getting dark and London's lights were turning on.

I didn't beg, did I? I couldn't bear it if she thought I was begging.

She replayed that final scene with Rose again and again in her head. It hadn't gone right.

She was trying to leave and so I had to say it.

She had been working up the courage to ask Rose to do it since the moment they met in the Medieval Gallery.

What have I started?

A bang outside and a scattering of coloured lights lit the roofs away to Justine's left. Fireworks. Another bang; more lights, red this time and in the shape of a heart. The next, a yellow star. A third, red lips.

How do they do that?

She rubbed her left temple where the tiny muscles had tightened at the first flash and flicker. She made a pot of camomile tea from a packet of teabags kept especially for warding away migraines. Then she took a box from beneath the large table and settled to the soothing job of sorting and sifting a batch of used and special edition stamps she was collecting with a specific future project in mind. Miniature in scale. It was a fancy she had, nothing definite, but if she played, a plan may formulate. She organised them by colour. Bluebirds from America with blue caps and wings and blush breasts, pale blue and white Wedgwood vases, grey and blue classic locomotives, various British bridges set against summer cobalt skies, the English Lakes, and a wide variety of national flags featuring all shades of blue. The repetition of the task calmed her, though inside her head fireworks were still bursting into sparkling hearts and stars in silver and blue, gold, purple and red. A headache followed the flickering and flashing.

Justine's head was so full of red hot pain and every shade of red was there.

Cochineal, crimson, carmine.

Scarlet, vermilion, madder, magenta.

Blood red, fresh and dried. Cherry Coke. London bus red. Chanel Rouge red. English postbox red.

Cadmium Red.

When she woke, she was sitting in the dark beside the studio window. A scattering of blue postage stamps lay in her lap. Her headache was gone. Outside, the London sky was dense black, the fireworks had finished and clouds were hiding the stars.

Upstairs, Tinkerbell rang.

30
SPAIN, DECEMBER 1982

Justine continued to juggle her parallel lives as winter arrived and Christmas approached, but was finding it increasingly difficult to keep track of the fibs. To Federico, about being broke; to April and Catalina, about why she was getting dressed up to go out in the evening; to her mother, in her occasional phone calls home; to the friends of her various clients, who assumed she was a new girlfriend. Remembering what she had said to whom was a challenge and the creeping shame was relentless. She wasn't sure if she was more embarrassed at being poor, or at taking money for pretending to be some bloke's girlfriend.

She had completed four more appointments for Bernadita, four boring business dinners, and currently had the equivalent of twelve pounds in her purse. But the rent was due on Monday and she was worried the debt cycle would start again. When Bernadita called to say there was a new client for her to see, she felt relieved. Relieved, but guilty. She told herself to get on with it, to not be so hard on herself. She now had two regulars plus Andrés.

It's not as if I'm sleeping with them for money.

Every time she allowed herself to think about it, she wanted to tell Federico, ask for his help. But she loathed the thought of seeming needy and didn't want to admit she had secrets from him. Her lock-up box had come in for a lot of use lately. Then three nights ago, he told a story about stealing a chocolate bar from the local shop and she almost confessed.

'I understand, it is horrible not having money,' she said at the end of his story, and then hesitated.

He interrupted. 'No, is when I have eight years and it was,

como se dice, it was game with boys. I am unhappy. Stealing is bad. *Mal, mal.*'

Justine had never stolen but her lies felt just as bad.

Her art was unaffected. Her marks for portraiture and sculpture were better than she dared hope and she loved the new abstract classes. Best of everything was Federico. She wanted to tell him he was special without actually scaring him away, but didn't know how to say any of it in Spanish. So before she set out to meet him on their last evening together before the holidays, she searched her phrase book. It had sections for Arriving at Your Hotel, In the Restaurant, and Hiring a Car, but nothing about Holiday Romance.

Is that what this is?

The thought made her stop. It didn't feel temporary, as if it might fizzle out, but perhaps it was for him. She wasn't entirely sure why he liked her, but didn't dare ask him in case it brought attention to her not-so-attractive points. Perhaps it would be better to say nothing. On the other hand, nothing ventured nothing gained. So she asked Catalina to help.

Catalina had giggled. '*Realmente*?'

'Yes, really.'

'So then you say this.' She whispered in Justine's ear. 'And then you say also *cada día, cada noche.*' Another giggle. 'He will understand.' She wrote it all down on a piece of paper and Justine studied it before folding it up tight and putting it in her pocket. All evening at the cinema with Federico and in the bar afterwards while they ate tapas and drank beer, and after midnight sitting beside El Jazminero, holding hands and talking about art, Justine sensed the presence of the note and what was to come.

If I am brave enough.

They walked up the winding path that led up the hill to the Alcazaba, beneath the dark pine trees, their scent deepened by the day's winter sun so it reminded her of a Badedas bath. At the top, they sat on a stone wall and gazed at the stars.

'There,' Federico pointed skywards, 'he is Orion.'

Justine looked up at the Archer and just said it. '*Te quiero.*'

And he laughed out loud. Actually laughed. There was one second when she didn't know what to think, and then he was hugging and kissing her and they were both laughing.

'*Yo tambien, te quiero.*'

'Did I say it right?' She whispered as he kissed the nape of her neck.

'Yes, yes, *correcto. Te quiero, cada día cada noche.*'

Christmas was coming and tomorrow he was going home to Càdiz.

'*Lo siento*,' he said. 'I want here with you, *pero* is not possible. *Siempre te quiero.*'

She woke early the next morning, her head singing with their words of love last night. It was the first time she had said that to anyone. The first time anyone had said it to her. It felt huge, she wanted to burst with happiness, wanted to be with Federico and just look at him. She simply had to see him again before he left. There was a family party tomorrow for his parents' wedding anniversary, which he said was *imposible* to miss, then Christmas and New Year. Straight after Epiphany, the architecture department was going to Valencia for a study trip; so Justine wouldn't see him again until the second week of January. She rang the telephone for his apartment and one of his flatmates answered. Federico had left for the bus, he said. And so Justine ran, quicker and with more energy than any of her PE teachers at school would have recognised. There were three buses waiting, a line of people snaking towards each one. At the furthest one, she saw him, climbing the steps, loaded with parcels and bags. As she had sensed him watching her, that day at the café when they first met, now he swivelled and raised his eyes to hers, then waved. The queue parted to applause and smiles as he climbed down the stairs and put his parcels on the ground.

'I had to see you again, to tell you that *te quiero. Realmente. Totalmente.*'

'I love you,' he smiled. 'Really. Totally.'

As the bus pulled on to the road and drove away, she felt a small cut to her heart.

The rest of the day fell rather flat and Justine filled the time writing an essay. The Christmas holiday stretched ahead of her and she decided to make the most of it. In truth, Federico going away solved a dilemma. She was drawn to him as metal filings to a magnet, at the expense of everything and everyone else. But she was addicted to art too. Both demanded attention, each interfered with the other. She was alone in the apartment; April had flown to Paris to meet her father, Catalina had been swept away by Juan Antonio for a mysterious weekend. Justine had a plan; to paint every day.

Her eyes were heavy, the cost of a late night with one of Bernadita's clients. It had been her third appointment with Diego, a teacher of history, the second family party she had attended with him. She suspected he may be gay and her attendance was a ploy to silence his relatives' questions about girlfriends and marriage. The party finished as the sun was rising.

Picasso painted without sleep. Rembrandt painted without sleep. I can too.

And so she made a jug of coffee. Her abstracts excited her and terrified her in equal measures but, after a morning's work getting her head round the theory rather than guessing at the process, the terror faded. She spent the afternoon with her sketch pad playing with ideas. The step-by-step method of breaking up objects and re-assembling them seemed to her oddly liberating. Breaking the rules: a horizontal tree trunk, a majestic oak, its twisted branches isolated vertically beside it, leaves and acorns floating as if they were snowflakes, the blue sky at the bottom of the picture became water, the dark brown earth moved to the top replacing clouds full of snow and cold. She was itching to try the same process for a collage. Perhaps she would do that next.

She hardly noticed Christmas pass. She learned that, for the Spanish, the celebration of Epiphany on January sixth was more important. In Yorkshire, her mother told her during their Christmas Day telephone call, it was snowing. Then in those meandering days between Christmas and New Year, Bernadita called. So after a morning of tackling a portrait of El Jazminero, Justine found herself sitting on the low wall that separated the road from La Malagueta's dark sandy beach, thinking about Federico but waiting for another man. She closed her eyes to the sun. The lapping of the waves, the screeching of the gulls, the Spanish music; it could be summer in December.

'Esara. Esara.'

There was the roar of an engine and she turned. Andrés was calling from a car, stopped at the side of the road and blocking traffic heading east. She got into the car and Andrés greeted her with a Spanish kiss – left, right, cheek-to-cheek – and steered back on to the road without a glance in his mirror. Justine flinched but didn't dare look back at the squeal of braking tyres. They headed away from town; the sea on her right was the exact same shade as Matisse's 'Blue Nude'. She glanced at Andrés. He was driving with the window wound down, left elbow resting on the sill in the sunshine. He was wearing a smart dark blue shirt under a bright aquamarine V-neck sweater, black trousers with a crease, and black shiny shoes. She felt scruffy and much younger than him. To outsiders they must seem father and daughter.

Sod it. He knows I'm a student.

Surely he wouldn't take her somewhere with a dress code.

No, he doesn't want to see me because of my dress sense.

That thought made her feel slightly sick. He didn't want to see her for her conversation either. Today, as at every other meeting, his behaviour was polite. His interest in her made her anxious but also grateful for the money. And guilty about Federico.

Oh hell. Just get on with it, Justine. He's a polite man, not a white slave trader or a rapist or a murderer.

The traffic slowed as the road narrowed, passing house after house jumbled together seemingly without recourse to town planning, piled so precariously on top of each other up the hillside it might be a child's Lego game. The walls dripped with pink bougainvillea, balconies crammed with pots spilling out flowers with abandon – red, orange, pink, like an artistic mix of the fruit-flavoured jelly cubes used by her mother to make a trifle for tea on Sunday. At home, the trees would be leafless. The sudden thought of her mother, at this very moment snoozing in front of the fire after a big lunch of roast lamb and mint sauce, rising in an hour or so to whip cream to put on top of the trifle for tea, made her want to be home.

They didn't go to a bar or a hotel. He squeezed the car into a parking space which looked far too small. Justine got out of the car, wondering what on earth she was doing: meeting a strange man, getting into a car with him at a time only months after the Yorkshire Ripper was convicted of killing women left, right and centre. She had come out today without telling anyone where she was going or who with.

Am I utterly stupid?

Andrés took her arm as they crossed the narrow street, despite the absence of traffic, and lead her down a narrow passage between some of the Lego houses until in front of them the sky and sea opened up into a sheet of unified blue.

'Here is El Palo.' He waved his arm left and right, taking in the narrow promenade and the row of cafés packed side by side crowded with people sitting beneath awnings. Everyone was eating and drinking, and there was the smell of frying fish. 'Here, Spanish make *fiesta.*'

It was an awkward lunch. Andrés didn't seem to mind her silence. Justine often felt his eyes on her when she was concentrating on her plate. He ordered for them and while they waited they sat mostly in silence. It was uncomfortable. Justine made herself smile. When the first platter arrived, she decided there must be some dastardly irony at work. The restaurant's speciality was fish, nothing else. *Boquerones,* tiny fried anchovies. Next, pink-skinned *salmonetas. Lenguaditos,* baby sole so small that the fishermen back home threw them back as being not worth the bother of cooking. *Chipirones,* tiny squid. Finally *rosada a la plancha,* a type of grilled fish served with salad. To start with she nibbled only bread sticks but in the end gave in to hunger. All of it was delicious, sprinkled with a squeeze of lemon and a dusting of salt and, despite hating herself, she ate it all. She remembered the children fish and every mouthful tasted of betrayal.

I do not deserve Federico.

Three hours later, Andrés said farewell to her with another Spanish kiss – left, right, cheek-to-cheek – and a rolled wad of pesetas. She watched him drive away, unsure if it was her imagination but his kisses had seemed to linger longer on her cheek this time.

She walked home slowly, worrying about the payback Andrés was expecting, running through the possible scenarios.

He was married and wanted to divorce his wife, and was waiting for her to catch him with another woman.

Me.

He was unhappily married, couldn't divorce his wife but longed for female company.

Me.

He preferred men but needed to be seen about town with a woman.

Me.

He preferred a companion who would not demand emotional involvement, would not ask too many questions.

I didn't ask one question.

He was too shy to ask a girl on a date.

Stop complaining and be grateful for the money.

Her right hand covered the buckle of her bag, shielding the precious cash inside. There was enough to pay the rent on the first day of January. The cost of next term's tuition was paid directly by her UK grant so her biggest outstanding debt was the cost of the trip to Madrid at Easter. The Prado. All students were expected to pay their own way and absence not tolerated. This seemed at once hugely unfair to Justine, though she would have died rather than be the only student not to go. When she had finally plucked up the courage before Christmas to tell her tutor she could not go, he offered her a loan. And a little extra to tide her by.

'No hurry,' Willow had said with a wink. 'I've told you

184

before, there's no need for you to struggle. You can pay me back when you're ready.'

The wink still worried her.

In the summer term they would visit Barcelona. She couldn't miss that chance to see the work of Gaudí. Federico talked, lived and slept Gaudí. The Barcelona trip had to be paid for in February. She was determined not to borrow from Willow again.

She hoped Andrés would want another date before then. Maybe two.

That night she dreamed she was floating above the cranes and spires of the *Sagrada Família,* trying to reach Federico who was operating one of the cranes. But she drifted this way and that, and he was just out of reach. Baby fish floated in the sky, live and wriggling, as if swimming though air. But when she looked closer she saw they were not fish but peseta notes, swirling in the breeze. And sitting in the clouds above them, scattering the money at his feet, was Andrés. He was laughing.

When she woke up she did some arithmetic. One pound was worth about two hundred pesetas. She had sold the grand total of two pictures. Five hundred pesetas. Less the cost of paint and canvas for the two sold and the thirty-four unsold. It didn't add up when she could earn five thousand pesetas for drinking orange juice with Andrés.

31
SPAIN, JANUARY 1983

It was all wrong. It shouldn't be this hot in January. It was the first day of the new term and she had walked to college. Her feet hurt; both heels had blistered yesterday so today she was wearing flip-flops ill-equipped for uneven pavements in winter. Justine shut out of her mind her mother's voice drilling her about appropriate footwear. Her mother had never walked miles a day to college and back, had never put her bus fare pesetas into a jar designated 'food money'. Her mother had never been to college, or her father. Nor visited a foreign country, let alone lived abroad. Justine didn't feel superior, just different.

A mile to go. The bypass was in sight. The Escuela de Bellas Artes was a modest building, hidden behind a scattering of cranes and construction sites, a sign of new hope in Málaga though at the moment the pavements everywhere were blocked by dust and rubble. If she could just get to the junction, she could rest in the shade for a moment. The earth was as hard as concrete, no rain since a spitter-spatter in October, no downpour since February last year according to Catalina. Dust and rubbish filled the gutters. Her feet were black, the thin rubber-soled flip-flops no longer azure. Her shoulder ached, her portfolio weighing heavier with each step. One hundred yards to the roundabout and she could sit, and rub her feet.

She didn't see the rock that tripped her until she was falling, a partially-buried rock masquerading as dust. The blue thong of her flip-flop snapped as if it were a liquorice lace. She fell, recognising pain a second before it hit. Double pain. Her shoe flew through the air, her shoulder bag twisted round her neck and her portfolio burst open, the sketches scattered like dried-up leaves and acorns, once living things but now rubbish in the gutter. She took the brunt of her weight on her hands, her palms bloodied and studded with gravel. She tried to sit up. Dirt was everywhere. There had been no time to stop her fall but all the time in the world to feel the pain. She imagined it must be similar if jumping into a river on a hot day, waiting for the impact of the water, seeing it approach, knowing it would be freezing cold. Inevitability.

She wasn't walking because she wanted to. It had taken all her spare cash to pay Willow for the Prado trip but there had been no calls from Bernadita and as soon as one debt was paid another appeared. Even the stream of tourists was thinner this week. No sales so far. She sat in the gutter beside a parked lorry which, high on its roof, supported an advertising hoarding designed to appeal to drivers on the flyover above her head. It was promoting a brothel; the illustration showed a topless woman with a red heart covering her crotch. Justine felt bruised and battered, as if she had rolled down a hill from top to bottom.

Two egrets flew by, a slash of white in a true blue sky above the grey concrete. To Justine at this precise moment, everything had become the colour of dirt. Her wounded hands, her broken shoes, the knees and seat of her jeans, her scattered sketches. The birds turned seawards, as if the land had nothing to interest them. Justine sat in the dust and watched them until they disappeared. She was so relieved Federico wasn't witnessing this. Her tears turned to anger. Anger at the driver of the car which drove slowly past where she sat in the gutter, staring but not stopping. Anger at the skinny dog which sniffed at her feet then burrowed into her bag which lay just out of her reach. Its sharp eyes never left hers while it pulled out her lunch. A bread roll and one tomato.

'Shoo, get away.'

The dog stood still, its head cocked to one side, watching her. She didn't move. It wolfed down the bread roll in two gulps and limped away. The tomato lay smashed on the tarmac, as red as the blood on her palms. She put her remaining flip-flop on straight, collected her dusty belongings and carefully wrapped the tomato flesh in a handkerchief. The right lens of her sunglasses had popped from its frame and was run over by a passing car. All that remained was an oval mosaic of shattered plastic.

She limped the rest of the way to college, rinsed the squashed tomato at the drinking fountain in the courtyard at the side of the college entrance, and then ate the remains washed down with gulps of cold water. She repaired her appearance in the ladies' loo, washing her hands and feet awkwardly in the sink and stuffing her shoes into her bag. She walked into class barefoot. Going unshod at art college was not weird enough to attract comment; it might even earn her a few brownie points, proof that she suffered for her art. It was a new term and eagerness filled the studio.

The drawing maestro, Señor Gonzalez, instructed them in the beauty of Leonardo da Vinci's art. Justine spent two hours in intense concentration, attempting to replicate the intricate detail of da Vinci's studies of hands. Fists, palms, fingers, wrists, hands praying, beseeching, fingers interlinking, fists threatening, children's hands. The process of losing herself in her task dulled the pain in her palms and heels, and she was feeling better. Remembering that Picasso too had sketched and painted hands reminded her of what had led her to Málaga in the first place. She knew he had faced and overcome obstacles in the pursuit of his art; he had always found a way.

And so will I.

After college she did some research; she spent an hour sitting and watching tourists meander past the pavement sellers on the Calle Cister, noticing which they ignored and which were the busiest. She knew what she had been doing wrong. The tourists didn't want art. They wanted a memory of their holiday. Something which fitted easily into a handbag or pocket and wasn't expensive. Something they could put in a clip-frame and hang in the hallway so when their neighbour asked 'where did you go' they could point to the portrait of Málaga. She would need to give some thought to the price. Not cheap-cheap, low enough to be affordable but not so low as to imply the painting was poor quality. Emboldened and energised by her summary, she went home to paint.

In her bedroom she feverishly cobbled together six collages on plywood using materials pulled from her foraging box underneath her bed. Nothing else mattered. The image of each was the same – the Alcazaba at sunset. They were average, she had rarely created worse, though it felt as if her stiffened fingers were blunt instruments using wide wallpaper brushes. She saved them from mediocrity by using a roll of sandpaper, found under the kitchen sink, tearing a horizontal strip to represent the jagged teeth of the castle walls. She sloshed a layer of quick-drying varnish over the lot. While they dried, she wrote up a price list in her best calligraphy. After ten minutes spent caring for her feet, more washing, gentle application of antiseptic cream, plasters, socks and her plimsolls loosely tied, she grabbed her sunhat and rucksack and walked through the Old Town.

She set up her easel close to the place where all the buses stopped, near the newspaper stall outside the Iglesia Santa Maria de Jovenes. The shadows of evening crept across the cobbles towards her feet. Panic, she found, made her feet ache less and she vowed to stand there until the night was black if only she could sell something. Even one picture would be a triumph. The sun was starting to lie down upon the sea's horizon. She leant against the church's iron railings and admired the warm light of dusk, beneath an orange and banana-coloured sunset. As the queue shortened and other painters left, she shifted her pitch closer to the bus stop.

Finally, she sold two to a tourist she suspected of being drunk. He spoke with an American accent and was wearing shorts the size of a sack that flapped round his white knees, so she guessed he was a day tripper from the cruise ship docked in port.

She didn't care if his purchase was fuelled by beer. It was

the first time she sold two pieces to one person and she longed to tell someone.

This small triumph created a swell of pride that carried her through the following time, counting off the days until Federico would return from Valencia. There was a new project in Tuesday's sculpture class, one which was to occupy the entire term. Public Art. The brief was to create a sculpture to celebrate the planned restoration of the port, according to a brief submitted by Málaga's town council, the Ayuntamiento. The brief was ten pages long, covering the history of the port, dimensions, budget, and the intended message of the sculpture.

'This is not a theoretical exercise,' Paul Willow explained. 'The Ayuntamiento wants to commission a sculpture, and,' he held up a copy of the brief, 'it has offered the college the opportunity to pitch ideas. So, get to it.'

While she read, she could feel his eyes on her. And later, when he circulated past each student in turn, he stood behind her without speaking for as long as it took her to do some complicated mathematical calculations to confirm the weight and volume of her idea of a giant seashell. When she turned to look at him, he leant forwards and whispered in her ear.

'Please see me in my office after classes finish, Justine.'

For the rest of the class, her sums didn't add up and the scale of her shell was wrong.

As she waited outside Willow's office for his private study tutorial to end, she examined her own hands, softly pressing her flesh bruised by yesterday's fall, running a finger over her skinned knuckles, feeling the sharp bones, the ripples of torn flesh now pink and puffy.

'Come in.'

Shaken from her thoughts, she picked up the bag and portfolio and followed him, sitting on one of the six wobbly wooden chairs set in a circle and reserved for students. The seat was still warm from its previous occupant.

He stood beside his desk, looking down at her, and didn't speak for a moment. Justine wasn't sure if he was waiting for her to say something. She quickly reviewed their conversations. She'd paid him for the Prado trip and the next money wasn't owed until the end of the month, she was sure, unless she'd added it up wrong. Or perhaps he was going to hit on her again. She'd already decided she wouldn't go out for lunch with him again, no matter what.

'I need the next money urgently, for reasons I am not going into here. Suffice to say, if you don't pay up I will get you thrown out of college for debt, perhaps even prostitution.'

Oh God, has he seen me with Andrés? Deny, deny.

'What? But I haven't – I can't. Please.'

She was talking to emptiness: Willow had left the room.

What have I done to make him hate me?

She knew the answer to that. She'd said no.

Sitting and worrying did not make a problem go away. If she paid him he would go away, she reasoned. The comment about prostitution, she chose to decide, was his stab in the dark. If he knew something, surely he would be explicit. So governed by her experience of what sold, she decreased the sizes and increased the prices and switched to paintings. As well as the Alcazaba at sunset, she widened her subjects to include the bullring at sunset and the roof of the cathedral set against a pure blue sky. She also painted cheaper postcard-sizes of the sunset over the sea, using up every colour paint she possessed. By Wednesday morning, her bedroom floor was transformed into a production line, a mosaic of tiny sunsets, each no bigger than a brown five thousand peseta note, the one bearing the face of King Juan Carlos I.

While she painted, she drank tap water with no lemon, no money for anything but bread, and ate artichokes from a tin found at the back of a cupboard. She didn't like artichokes but was so hungry she greedily swallowed every last drop of oil from the tin so it dripped down her chin and smudged her black t-shirt.

Her sunsets were yellow first, then orange, pink, purple and, as her tubes were used up, they became less naturalistic

– turquoise, blue, grey and brown. The most frustrating time was waiting for the paint to dry. Wasted time. She hesitated before signing each piece; this was not how she had imagined it would be. But with a shrug, in the bottom left-hand corner of each piece she painted a tiny 'JK' worked patiently with her calligraphy brush.

She set aside one painting, different from the others. A small still life of olives, ham and bread. It was for Federico. She planned to give it to him tomorrow; a belated gift for Epiphany, in the Spanish way.

32
SPAIN, JANUARY 1983

Sales were poor on Wednesday. No cruise ship had docked and she'd sold only one sunset, but she didn't care because Federico was arriving tonight. She hung on in desperation for another sale until it was too late to go home and take a quick bath. She dumped her art gear on a bench in the garden opposite the bus stops for trans-Spain destinations. The bus from Valencia via Granada was due in fifteen minutes. She sniffed her armpits. Not good. She looked round; there was a pharmacy two blocks away. She walked quickly. There was a haphazard queue with no visible order; three elderly ladies sat on chairs inside the door, chatting, watching; a teenager hovered near the stand of sunglasses; a middle-aged man by the door. It was one of those Spanish queues where each person seemed to know their turn. Everyone looked up when she walked in. She nodded, saying '*Buenas tardes*' and receiving a nod and a '*Buenas tardes*' in return, and walked confidently up to a perfume dispenser, making a show of sniffing them and checking the prices. She sprayed a generous waft across her hair and neck, wrinkled her nose as if unsure whether she liked it, and exited.

She waited, and time played its cruel trick. Every minute lasted two, the clock passed ten o'clock, the bus from Valencia arrived and Federico was not on it. She checked her bag; Federico's still life was there, folded neatly in a square of white tissue paper. She waited, feeling increasingly sick. Had she got the time wrong, was he coming home tomorrow, was he on the next bus? Half past ten passed and she grew less certain that the right thing to do was wait. What if she left and he finally turned up, his bus delayed? He would think she didn't care. What if he'd got an earlier bus and was waiting for her now, at El Jazminero? They were birds, flitting backwards and forwards, missing each other in the open air. She went into a bar and phoned his apartment, longing to hear his voice and hear him call her *guapita*. It rang and rang, then came an answerphone message she didn't understand, and then the phone went dead. His flatmates were a mystery to her; she had met Adrián and Alejandro only once and they were warm and welcoming, but she wasn't sure now if she would recognise them if they passed by in the street. That was when she realised she didn't know where he lived, not exactly, just that it was somewhere north of Plaza de la Merced, uphill past the dried-up riverbed.

How could she love someone so completely that she got goosebumps when he said her name, but had never been to his home?

Or he to mine.

With hindsight it seemed remiss. They had known each other for three months and fallen easily into the habit of meeting at El Jazminero and finding solitude together on the beach. It was convenient and halfway between their respective apartments. This seemed pretty normal to Justine where teenagers at home also retreated to the beach or bus shelter to be together in private, so avoiding awkward questions from parents.

She shivered. Winter was here and it would be too cold for beach-side lovemaking tonight. The thought of cuddling with Federico in a cosy bed warmed her insides.

But I don't know what he eats for breakfast, or the name of his sister.

Was he sub-consciously isolating her from the rest of his life? Did he have secrets he didn't want her to know? What did she know about him?

He studies architecture, I know he does, I've seen his books and met his friends. That's it. I'll find one of his friends in a bar.

She walked for ten minutes through the Old Town, slowly, looking in the open doors of bars where light and noise spilt on to the cobbled pavements. She found herself down an alley she didn't know and stopped, needing a plan.

If he arrives late and I'm nowhere to be seen, what he will do?

She wandered on from bar to bar, drawn in by the warm fug of bright lights and music, cigarette smoke and talk, searching for the texture of Federico's black hair and the way it curled over the collar of his shirt, the particular lilt of his head as he laughed.

Then in one noisy bar, full of chatter and laughter, she spotted him across the room.

'Federico.'

Her words were lost in the noise but her heart leapt and she pushed through the throng to get to him. Trying not to wonder what he was doing here and why he hadn't come to look for her, she tripped and fell. The strong arm that helped her to her feet again belonged to a man with hair the same colour as Federico's, and he was the same height, but his eyes were not Federico's, his smile wasn't Federico's. She was invited to stay, to have a beer, but she thanked them and left, choking back tears.

One alley morphed into another, narrow and dark, and she went in bits of the Old Town new to her. She didn't know where she was, her mouth was sour and the blisters on her heels were bleeding again.

The flat was empty when she opened the door. Cold. Its silence, an accusation; she should have continued searching. On the hall table, beside the telephone, was a note.

He called.

She grabbed it. In April's handwriting was written 'Willow called.'

Justine sank to the floor, cold, sweaty, and feeling more alone than she ever had before. She longed for her parents to hug her, hold her, tell her she was safe, tell her what to do. They would be asleep now in their narrow double bed under the draughty eaves of the small cliff-top cottage. Outside the black sea would be churning and swirling as the tide breathed in and out, stirring the bones and booty and detritus of ships lost to the rocks centuries before, still there as evidence should someone dive down to locate the wreckage. Sometimes the secrets revealed themselves after years of hiding, brought up from the seabed by strong currents and winter storms, washed up on the tide and left as a string of rubbish at the top of the beach. Justine preferred her secrets to stay hidden.

She took a deep breath, then another, and leant back against the wall. She did not need her parents.

Willow can't get me here. I'm safe.

The terracotta floor tiles chilled her feverish skin slowly, limb by limb. Another deep breath and with it, she hoped, would come cool logic.

Think. Think about one thing at a time.

Federico missed the bus. A family matter to delay his return. Maybe his mother was sick. He might be on tomorrow's bus. A glance at her watch showed it was now today's bus.

I will see him later today. I will.

With that thought a muscle in her jaw unclenched and then re-clenched.

Next, money. She would never sell enough paintings to tourists to pay off her debts but she had to keep going, even though she hated it, even though it made her art feel dirty. She would not think of her tourist pictures as 'art'. They were just a part-time job she did to help pay her way. Yes, that felt better. Her pictures paid for food. The big debts still remained. Surely a teacher should not exploit a student in his care, but she didn't have the slightest idea how to complain about Willow. Best to pay him, make him go away. She had borrowed the money from him, she was ashamed of that.

I do owe him.

When the telephone rang the noise seemed loud enough to wake up the whole of Málaga. Using energy she did not know she possessed, she jumped to her feet.

'Justina?'

'Oh. *Hola,* Bernadita.'

'You want work tonight?'

'Now?' Justine was conscious of her scabby knees, the dirt on her t-shirt. 'I don't think so, no.'

'Justina. It is Andrés. He ask to esee you.'

'Oh.'

'He want esee you very much, Justina. He is client *importante* for us. If you will not esay yes to him tonight, then I must ask other girl who will esay yes. You must, please.'

'Oh, but it's so late.'

'Late? No, no is late and he will pay more. Twice times.'

A moment's pause. 'Justina, you understand*? Agradecimiento.'*

Justine so wanted to sleep now, but Andrés was a generous tipper and always such a gentleman. It would be good money just for sitting with him in a dark bar for a couple of hours. Hastily she ran her feet under the tap, the lukewarm water sluicing away the flaky trails of dried blood. She ran a hairbrush through her hair and changed her top. A spray of April's 'Charlie' and she left the flat.

They were in his car, driving up the hill behind the bullring, claustrophobic white walls penning in each side of the car. He drove slowly, a slight turn of his head to the right. Justine knew he was looking at her. She kept her eyes pinned on the tarmac ahead.

Agradecimiento. Of course that's what Bernadita meant.

Gratitude. She'd heard sex referred to in many ways, not this. Rising fear was making her legs feel weak.

I had sex that one time with Joe when I didn't really want to, just after Sam and I finished, and it was okay, manageable. And Andrés is not a stranger. He's a gentleman with nice manners and a smart car. He even asked for sex in a courteous way.

But no man who used an intermediary to arrange sex for him was courteous. Why didn't he ask her himself? That was the normal way of doing things. But he was not her boyfriend. She had a boyfriend.

Oh Federico. She bit her lip.

The car wound slowly up the hill. Below, the lights of the town passed fleetingly in and out of view in the black space between houses.

Where are we going?

In an almost hysterical flash of humour, she wondered which scared her the most: going somewhere in a car with a strange man at the risk of attack, or having sex with a strange man to earn money. She knew what her mother would say to that. Tart. And not an apple one, either.

I will be strong.

Not for one moment had Andrés made her feel afraid of him.

It will be over quickly. I will tell no one, take the money, pay Willow, and never do it again.

The car pulled into the driveway of a large white house. Black iron gates opened and closed automatically behind the car.

She kept her eyes closed throughout. Truth was, in the end it wasn't so horrible. It felt like punishment and it felt deserved. Andrés was polite throughout and his body was quite nice, given that he was so much older than her. He did not try to kiss her and, when she peeped at his face, his eyes seemed glazed as if he were somewhere else and didn't want to look her directly in the eyes either. In the end, it was a transaction. He was discreet, placing the money on the table at her side of the bed and then leaving the room. She pulled her clothes on roughly and followed. He had turned on the lights. On the wall at the top of the stairs hung a large photograph, in pride of place, asking to be noticed. It showed a young Andrés wearing a dark suit and a proud smile, holding the arm of a beautiful woman with black hair down to her waist. The white of her dress was made brilliant by the bleak black wooden frame, its draping of black lace. Things started to fall into place.

Afterwards, he gave her a lift down the hill into town. Once home she set the shower to run hot and while she was waiting she filled a glass with hot tap water and drank, filled again and

198

drank until her throat was scalded. Next she stood under the shower until her skin was pink. She got into bed, naked and damp, and closed her eyes. But the last time she'd been in bed with her eyes closed, she'd been paying her debts. She did not sleep. And she did not open the lid of the lock-up box.

33
LONDON, MAY 2010

When the alarm clock went off at 6am the next morning, Rose was already sitting at her laptop working on the article for *Gallery***. She had decided in the middle of the night not to start investigating the lost daughter until this feature was written and submitted. Her mobile rang, and caller ID identified it as *Gallery***. The editor chasing the feature.

Rose silenced the call and attempted the first paragraph: 'With a fridge full of Cadburys' Fruit & Nut chocolate bars, Justine Tree's studio in Kensington is re-stocked in preparation for work to start on her next series. True to her environmental credentials, Tree saves the purple foil chocolate wrappers for use in her future artwork. Perhaps 'The Unbearable Greenness of Green' will be followed by 'Purple Days'.'

Did it sound too facetious? The brief requested a review of the exhibition, financial data and personal colour. It was essentially a personality profile, not an art review. Her mobile rang again. April Masterson, the editor of *Gallery***, was not to be ignored. They had never met. The commission had arrived by email but Rose knew of Masterson by reputation. She was said to be a stickler for getting the art detail right. Rose's source was Maggie who had freelanced for *Gallery*** for a year before landing her current job as news editor at *The Scene*.

'She's a stuck-up cow,' Maggie reported when Rose rang her with the news of her surprise commission. 'But the website's got a good reputation; accurate, informed, respected. Rumour is Daddy owns it, not her. If she likes you you'll write for her regularly. It's a good name to have on your CV. My style was too informal for her taste, I think. She does have a real chip on her shoulder.'

'What sort of chip?'

'The if-you-can't-do-it, write-about-it chip. It makes her demanding.'

'Ah.'

Rose answered the call.

'So,' said April Masterson. 'How's the Justine Tree piece coming along?'

No preliminaries, no getting-to-know-you pleasantries.

'I'm working on it now. She was ill last week so the interview was postponed. I've got some good stuff.' She hoped April wouldn't ask for detail.

'Written the intro yet?'

'Just polishing it.'

'Read it out then.'

Rose hesitated. She'd never been asked this before.

'Just read it out, Rose. If it doesn't grab me, it won't grab our readers and readers on websites have twitchy index fingers, you know.'

So Rose read it, somehow pronouncing the words and holding her breath at the same time.

'I like it.'

The knot of tension in Rose's stomach released.

'Get it to me tomorrow, yes?'

'Er.'

'And Rose, make sure you talk about light. The light in Yorkshire, the light in London, in Spain, and how her handling of light has evolved.'

'Right, sure.' April had hung up before Rose said the second word.

Light; right. I'll have to read up on that.

The onions had been cooking for a while in butter in the frying pan over a low heat and were beginning to turn a golden caramel. With a wooden spatula Justine stirred the onions in a rhythmical fashion. In truth the pan required no input but she found the movement soothing. It had been a long day and if given a choice she would lie down on her bed with the curtains drawn. Playing lightly in the background was Beethoven's 'Cello Sonata No 3', her go-to relax album. She had her back to Darya, but could hear her. She was sitting at the kitchen table, her sleeves rolled to her elbows, and with a wooden rolling pin was systematically flattening a piece of pastry before kneading it into a ball and starting again. Justine knew the pastry would be grey by the time it was fitted into the flan tin and topped with the onions. But it would make a tasty enough supper once she had added beaten eggs and a few pieces of leftover smoked salmon. It was Friday night and this was their accustomed Friday night meal. Darya would eat smoked salmon at every meal if Justine didn't vary her diet. Rolling out pastry was a useful distraction that Darya never tired of and one drawer of the freezer cabinet was kept full of supermarket packets. Justine understood the fascination. She could recall the satisfyingly sticky texture of Play-Doh and made a note to buy some for Darya.

She put the tart in the oven, poured herself a glass of wine and leant back against the fridge, watching Darya who was now crayoning a picture of a tiger in a large colouring book. The kitchen was her favourite room in the house.

Can it really be nearly twenty-seven years since I first sat at this table?

She swallowed once, twice, her throat drying at the memory of how vital Darya had been that day.

When did I last thank her for saving me?

Darya was slowly colouring a black stripe along the tiger's hind leg, being careful to stay within the lines. Justine noticed she was completing each colour before moving on to another crayon. Methodical, even now. Justine reached out to still her hand.

'I can't remember the last time I thanked you. But I have not said it often enough.'

Darya shook her head. 'Not needed.'

'Thank you.'

As on that first night, they sat across from each other at

the long wooden table, each looking deep inside the other. To Justine, the memory of meeting Darya was as clear as yesterday. When she had first walked into this kitchen in 1983, the cupboard doors were golden oak with cathedral sculpting. Now they were glossy duck-egg blue. There was still no blind or curtain at the tall sash window, privacy sacrificed so the fine proportions of the original woodwork were visible. The floor was the same too, bare oak planks. The seamlessly fitted golden oak kitchen with its large American fridge and double sink had seemed so fine to Justine, so elegant, so spacious. She stayed, but had felt like a visitor, a lodger, until one day they had sat down and talked about the future, two single successful women, both financially independent, and agreed to share the house. Papers were signed, money exchanged, wills amended so Justine left the house to Darya and vice-versa and it became their joint home. Each had a self-contained floor for privacy when desired, leaving the downstairs rooms for joint use and Justine's studio in the extension at the back. The kitchen was their home, though; that's where they spent most of their time together. A proposal and plans lay in Justine's inbox from a kitchen designer. It was time for a refresh. The drawer runners were sticking and the door to the pan cupboard would not open at all. The composite stone work surface had absorbed myriad wine stains, and the whole thing would benefit from a fresh coat of paint. But the designs for a replacement remained unstudied. Justine didn't want to change a room so central to Darya's life. She needed familiarity.

One wall was covered in a mosaic of small frames, Darya's treasured collection of Russian *lubki* prints; simple graphics and narratives based on popular tales. In the centre was Justine's favourite *lubok*, 'A Monster from Hell', a hand-coloured creature, part dinosaur part dragon. The chair in which Darya sat now had always been 'her' chair, a sack-back Windsor carver with elegant sweeping arms burnished by years of contact with her arms. The refectory table was satisfyingly bashed, burnt and generally mistreated, needing only a treatment once a year involving a rub down with sandpaper and a coat of oil to look glorious again. If she sat in her chair, opposite Darya, Justine's fingers could stretch forwards to find the striations made by a mishandled carving knife, and follow the indentation burnt by a straight-from-the-oven casserole dish full of piping hot coq au vin. Like the wrinkles on their faces, these marks on the table were proof of time passing. The day was approaching when the annual sand-down and oiling treatment was due, and as usual Justine would undertake both procedures. Time could not be stopped. It was the only dependable thing in life.

When Rose arrived and was shown into Justine's kitchen, she didn't expect to be invited to supper. Darya and Rose were formally introduced and shook hands. Darya said something in French, returned to her tiger and did not speak again.

'I've come to say I'll do it.'

'Good.'

Rose was aware of a small nod from the elderly lady seemingly busy with her colouring book. She sat down at the old wooden dining table. Darya pushed towards her a fluffy pencil case full of crayons. Darya coloured and Justine busied herself with boiling salad potatoes and mixing salad dressing. Rose took a thick piece of cream paper and drew a cat. Disappointed with the effect, she turned the paper over and attempted a house. A straight garden path to a picket fence, adding a curly hedge and bare tree trunk for a garden, and two red chimney pots with twists of smoke that merged into the clouds above. Quietly she studied her surroundings, gratified to be there. It was the sort of kitchen she coveted, just the right side of new but worn, cabinets of a beautiful pale blue colour, lived in, warm and loved.

Nick was at that minute at home preparing pissaladière. Rose hoped it would keep. The contract was in her bag. A fee had not been agreed yet, but she had pencilled in a daily rate plus expenses allowance. It was on the upper side, something Nick had insisted on. As was a research fee for her sister Lily who had agreed to trace records and certificates, confirming the old research done by Justine.

'Always add the extras in before, it's awkward to ask for more later. Fees are easier to negotiate down than up,' he insisted last night. 'People with money never worry about the little costs. Trust me, she'll sign it.'

And when Rose produced the contract after the meal, Justine signed it without a question.

34
LONDON, MAY 2010

Rose scribbled the six headings from Rudyard Kipling's poem on a notepad, then put down her pencil and stared at them.

I keep six honest serving-men
(They taught me all I knew);
Their names are What and Why and When
And How and Where and Who.

The 'Who' was Justine and her daughter. She sighed and sipped the coffee Nick had put on her desk just before he left for work. She'd been up before him again, it was getting to be a habit. The coffee was cold.

She could do 'When' too. Justine had run home from Málaga in 1983. She gave birth in London, so that was the 'Where'.

Or did I just assume it?

She made a note on her pad. Identifying the facts for a news story was one thing, but facts to do with Justine seemed elastic. She had given Rose a letter last night, sealed, for safe keeping. 'I wrote it for her, after I – after I left her. I am terrified of losing it.'

Rose worked her way through Kipling again, looking for black and white answers, writing a list of questions. There was one glaring thing she didn't know: the birth father's name. She wrote 'Federico?' She pondered on that question mark. Thinking was making her hungry. She struggled to get the top off a new jar of strawberry jam. The scent filled the galley kitchen and Rose remembered her grandmother Bizzie, a consummate jam-maker. It was a year since Bizzie had died; a heart attack when she was walking among her roses. Rose had often thought it was a lovely way for Bizzie to go, surrounded by the flowers she loved, and if she could have chosen the means of Bizzie's passing this would have been at the top of her list.

What would Bizzie say I should do?

She heard her grandmother's voice as clear as a bell. 'Justine was a young woman who made a mistake. We all make mistakes, Rose. How would you like it if in fifty years your son or daughter dug into your secrets without you knowing? Just ask her. She wants you to help her, after all. So, so.'

Rose ate her toast and drank two mugs of tea then rang Justine to request an information-gathering meeting. Justine was rather tetchy with her and somehow Rose rung off without an agreement to meet. So instead she wrote a list of questions and emailed it.

Justine knew she should call Rose to apologise. She had no excuse other than that her head was full of the smell of oranges. Which meant memories of Málaga where the pavements were lined with orange trees, the air scented with their blossom. Which brought a wave of memories of Federico. Which meant grief. All because she'd opened a jar of chunky marmalade.

She sat in the kitchen armchair, resting her head against the wing back. It was an old-fashioned 'granny-tipper' chair bought for Darya, the type with a mechanism that raised the seat so it was easier to get out of, though Justine was the one who sat in it most often.

Rose is doing the job I asked her to do, the job I'm paying her to do. I can't blame her for ringing at a bad time.

Today was May 25, Federico's birthday. She sighed. It was going to be a sighing day. This was the only day in the year that she allowed herself to remember him, because if she thought of him every day she would never put a foot out of bed. Every jar of marmalade held memories for her because of the first jar he gave to her.

Justine cleared away her uneaten toast.

It's so long ago it doesn't matter.

She'd been telling herself this for twenty-seven years and it still wasn't true. She screwed the lid on the marmalade jar and put it back in the fridge, and then returned to her study and her emails. She read Rose's list of questions, then typed out a list of facts she thought might be useful. Her own date of birth and home address. Email address, Twitter, Facebook and website urls. Dates when she started and graduated from college. Maud's contact details. And Málaga: date arrived, address, courses studied, address of college, the date she ran away, the date Jenni was born.

There, that'll keep her going.

She emailed the list, attached a Personality Profile written by Maud's PR assistant, and logged off. Then she made herself a mug of tea, sat beside the huge glass window in her studio and looked out at the garden. Her thoughts were thousands of miles away. She wanted to be with Federico today, eating *mermelada*. Instead she had to go to a drinks thing tonight at the Royal Academy and dare not miss it, given the delicate state of her nomination as Academician. Depending on who she talked to, her election was either a sure thing or hanging in the balance. She wanted to believe the first but feared the second; and so, despite hating professional socialising, she would go.

I will smile, shake hands and say intelligent things and they will love me.

At eleven, the front doorbell rang, as she expected. It was the usual delivery by the florist. Twice a year – today and September 12 – a simple bunch of red carnations. She arranged the flowers in a vase and set the vase in the middle of the kitchen table. Then she returned to her chair, covered her face with a silk scarf, and closed her eyes.

It took Rose precisely one minute to open Justine's email attachment and scan the answers to her questions. The excitement at seeing the message in her inbox evaporated. Justine hadn't answered anything. It was a list of unrelated dates and names, disconnected from Rose's questions. It was the sort of list provided by an ex-employer about an employee they sacked. Nothing Rose hadn't already googled.

Perhaps she's having second thoughts but is too polite to tell me.

Justine stirred and saw the world through a prism of multi-coloured light. She had fallen asleep with her face covered by Darya's paisley scarf. Interested in the play of light and shadow, colours morphing together as if inside a child's kalei-doscope, she looked carefully from left to right as the shadowy forms of the room became recognisable. She removed the scarf from her eyes, smelt the marmalade on her fingers.

Him. And her. Impossible to disconnect them.

My daughter.

She knew in her heart she had no right to say those words aloud, perhaps no right even to think them. She was not a real mother. She was a 'biological mother'. She had done the deed with the seed, had pushed and strained and ejected, but hadn't been up to doing the whole life care thing. She was a non-mother, a failed mother, a mother without child. And no one must know.

So why did I employ someone? I'll end up as a hashtag on Twitter.

Her cry of frustration was loud enough to stir the neigh-bours but was also a relief, so she did it again, each cry more subdued than its predecessor. It helped, the crying, acknowl-edging the feeling rather than ignoring it; a bit like removing a splinter from your finger and pressing the wound afterwards for that pleasing, clean kind of pain.

That is Rose's job; she has to pull the splinter. Because I want to know. I need to know. Where she is. How she is.

She smoothed the silk square, folding it in half and half again.

And I don't need to tell Rose everything.

Later the same evening, James Watercliff walked into the private drinks party at the Royal Academy of Arts on Piccadilly and recognised no one except the barman who had performed the same role at the last drinks thing he'd attended here six months ago. He asked for a large glass of Shiraz, took a gulp, allowed the barman to top up his glass and then waited for the welcome kick of wine to hit his bloodstream. He shook hands with a woman who was writing a biography of Mary Moser and Angelica Kaufmann, the only two women among the thirty-six founding members of the RA in 1768. James nodded and smiled as the author talked; interested despite his distraction, all the time casting his gaze around the room in search of Justine Tree. It wasn't definite she would be here, but as a nominated artist she would be stupid to miss it. He had heard further bitchiness about her nomination; nothing odd in that, he doubted any RA gained one hundred per cent approval. In his book, life was too short to hold out for universal liking. This was a gossipy, cliquey world, but sometimes the gossip could edge into nastiness. He couldn't work out what Justine Tree had done to upset people. He didn't much care for her large installations but her collages were insightful and whether her artistic style was emotionally incontinent was a matter for her and her team, and no one else.

And there she was, standing with her back to the wall, straight and tense as if trying to push every vertebra into contact with the wall. She had no drink in her hand, so he made his apologies to the author, selected a cocktail from the tray of a passing waiter and negotiated the circuit of bodies.

'I thought you looked in need of one of these.' He offered the cocktail to her, which she accepted rather, he felt, as if he had offered her a live lobster.

'Ah. You don't drink?'

'Not much. I get frightful headaches so no alcohol, no caffeine, no cheese. I'm afraid I'm not much fun.'

'I'm sure that's not true. I'm sorry, how rude of me. I haven't introduced myself. I'm James Watercliff.'

'RA?'

'Yes. Two years ago, and I still feel like a junior sent with a message into the prefects' common room.'

She smiled and, he thought, relaxed a little which had been his intention. She seemed to be standing a little less upright now.

'I'm Justine Tree, almost RA.'

He thought she sounded like a first-timer standing up at an Alcoholics Anonymous meeting.

'I have this theory,' he smiled. 'There are two sorts of artist. The butterfly that likes sunshine and bright colours. It is a social being that flits from one flower to the next in search of the tastiest morsel; it has a short attention span and is easily diverted. And then there is the toad that prefers cool, shady places away from the sun. It retreats beneath foliage, always watching for the choicest things to eat; it keeps still to avoid drawing attention to itself.'

She took a tiny sip of her cocktail. 'So, you're comparing me to a toad?'

'Yes, I am.' And he waved his arm at the room. 'Here, we have excellent examples of both species. The common or garden butterfly of an average size, will live for up to one month. The common toad, however, can survive for fifty years.'

'I'm fifty next year so I must be a toad.'

He hid his surprise. If he had guessed her age, he would have thought seven or eight years younger. They clinked their glasses. 'To toads everywhere.'

There was a silence, which James felt compelled to fill.

'I confess that is all guesswork. Some butterflies live for a week and others hibernate or migrate, so really it's a lesson that we shouldn't generalise.'

She nodded and smiled and there then followed that type of silence that occurs between two people who have just met, who have identified one subject in common but, on exhausting that subject, are left without a topic for discussion. James felt momentarily uninspired and, as Justine had fallen silent, he resorted to tradition.

'Have you had the tour?'

She shook her head.

'In that case, if you allow me, I will be your behind-the-scenes guide. You cannot leave here tonight without having seen the Nominations Book and the famous Francis Bacon page.'

He stowed their glasses on a convenient table and then took her elbow and ushered her through the crowd. James, who had arrived with no other plan than to be welcoming to Justine Tree, now found himself her mentor. He introduced her to his agent who was hovering beside a potential new client, and to two people he had met that day in the Academician's Room when the sculptor had been so obnoxious – the red-haired painter, and the pale-faced man with the Cheddar cheese accent. Justine smiled and shook hands with them but had little to say. She simply seemed shy; a quality which James found difficult to reconcile with her heart-on-sleeve public image. Was it simply public relations, he wondered, or a case of geographical snobbery? Surely the days had passed when a northern accent was too brusque for London tastes. And so, as they walked along the corridor, their shoes squeaking in time on the parquet flooring, he talked to fill the silence. He told her about that conversation in the Academician's Room.

She stopped dead. 'But I don't know any of these people.'

'The nomination process entails people you don't know voting for you.'

She nodded, and walked on. 'I don't see what I can do to change their minds. I've never been any good at lobbying or selling.'

This time he stopped. 'I can see that, but, if you don't mind me being frank, you seem very different from your public persona.'

She smiled. 'It's just PR, you know. The real me is very boring and not worthy of column inches. If I could I would paint every minute of every day. Given the choice, I would run away from London tomorrow and not speak to the press or collectors or curators. But those are not helpful feelings for any artist to act upon.'

He found himself liking her honesty. And so he told her about the obnoxious sculptor's parting threat, to block her nomination if there was any sign from her of 'disreputable behaviour'.

'That's a bit rich,' he added. 'Artists have always been disreputable, nothing's changed there.' He thought this would make her smile but her face blanched of colour. He wondered if she was feeling ill and regretted pressing the cocktail on her when she was clearly teetotal.

First he showed her the wooden Ballot Box and the old marbles once used by RAs to vote on nominations, and then the Nominations Book. He leafed back through the pages to 1950 and the entry for Francis Bacon with the notorious hand-written note at the top of the page, 'Nomination declined – by implication – through failure to reply to three letters'.

'No other artist was nominated in 1950 so I suppose they must have really wanted Bacon.'

He flicked forwards to his own page and then to the current page. Beneath Justine's name were the signatures of the eight supporting RAs who formalised her candidature. He watched her face, wondering at the thoughts flickering behind that immobile expression. She was amazingly difficult to read. Perhaps it was the lack of alcohol that rendered her so opaque; he was frustrated by the lack of insight available to him but admired her rejection of the social more to drink. As she held the base of her hand to her forehead, pressing hard, he wondered if she was in pain.

'Come on, I'll call you a cab.'

Justine didn't look back as the taxi pulled away from Burlington House and turned west along Piccadilly. The eight signatures below her name in the Nominations Book were reassuring, and James Watercliff had been charming. Perhaps there *would* be enough support from artists if the truth about Jenni came out.

I can't be the only artist who's told lies. If they use things like that as membership criteria they'd probably have to chuck out half the RAs.

And that thought made her hopeful. It was late, and only two hours remained of Federico's birthday, so Justine closed her eyes and allowed the memories in. The trouble was she couldn't remember to order, and sometimes an unwanted image returned.

35
SPAIN, JANUARY 1983

She woke with a start. Someone was singing. Justine had no recollection of going to sleep, of dream or wakefulness, only of lying in her bed all night with her eyes closed. She was frightened that when she opened them, she would be in bed with Andrés again. But she recognised the singing voice, a voice she heard every day and it made her feel safe. Her eyelids were crusted together, her skin felt dry and tight. The thought of Federico got her out of bed.

Today I will see him and it will all be a misunderstanding.

Catalina was singing in the shower, something in Spanish about love. Justine sat on the edge of her bed and waited for Catalina to leave.

When did I last speak to the girls?

She couldn't remember. One day was merging with another and when she was in the flat she was either avoiding the girls, unable to face the concern on their faces, or they weren't there. She put her ear to the door now and could hear Catalina moving about. Justine was desperate to be clean again, even though her skin still smelt of lavender from last night's hot shower. She would never buy anything lavender-scented again. The door of the flat banged shut, footsteps tapped downstairs. Justine sat still, listening. The rest of the flat was silent. April must have left already. Justine tiptoed to the window and peeked out. Catalina was walking across the *plaza*, her college bag swinging at her side.

The water ran cool from the hot tap so Justine boiled the kettle and poured the water into the washbasin in the bathroom, mixing it with cold to a bearable temperature. As she scrubbed herself with a soapy flannel, the hot tears arrived, burning lines down her cheeks until she was sobbing with a violence she couldn't remember ever doing before.

Justine wrapped herself in a towel, dried and dressed, then phoned Federico's apartment. Still no answer; she was beginning to wonder if the number was correct. She decided to go first to college to pay Willow; after that she would find Federico.

The money earned last night was safe in her purse. But crossing the Plaza de la Merced she found herself deviating from her normal path, drawn to Picasso's childhood home. Its windows were boarded up, the paint peeling. How desperate was she, to hope for answers from the man who had experienced everything life threw at him and then put it into his art. For half an hour she sat on the bench opposite his house, deep in thought, but Picasso had no advice. A stout woman stopped beside her, sprigs of flowers in her hand. She pushed them under Justine's nose, her other hand held out flat. Dried lavender and rosemary.

'*Por favor?*'

The heavy scent of lavender made Justine's head swim with memories of last night. Her face burnt, the backs of her knees, her ear lobes and armpits, elsewhere. All the places Andrés had touched. Burning as if on fire. Internal shame. Eternal shame. Perfection spoiled.

Federico, I have wrecked everything.

She stood too quickly and stumbled, knocking her bag off the bench. She knelt and faltered again. A strong hand under her elbow; the woman was at her side, helping her to sit again. Justine felt ill, stupid, vulnerable. Mostly she was thirsty. She gathered her things together and went to the water fountain to drink, splashing her face, her wrists.

Only at the bus stop did she realise her purse was missing.

The walk to college seemed endless. She sat on the back row of the lecture theatre, her notepad open in front of her, not listening to the simultaneous translation through her headphones as a guest speaker spoke for two hours about 'Kurt Schwitters: Merz or Mess?'

216

She'd highlighted this on the lecture list on her first day at college when she read the course content documents. That was a long time ago now, and it had been a different Justine doing the reading. Schwitters was renowned for his collages and assemblages and she had longed to see one in the flesh and not a reproduction in a book. But when the lecture ended, she had written only three lines. All related to Federico. She would find him, tell him she loved him, and tell him she was poor. If he did not love her after that, then he was not worth it. She could hear her mother's voice in her thoughts.

Her head was aching again and she knew she must drink water. The spring sun was low in the sky and the Spanish girls were wrapped up in jumpers, jeans and knee-high black leather boots, but to Justine it felt like high summer at Flamborough Head. She stood patiently in the queue for the water fountain. Just as she bent to drink she was aware of a presence at her elbow.

Please, not Willow.

Her hand went instinctively to her bag but the money earned with such pain last night really was gone.

No matter how many pictures she painted and sold by Saturday, it wouldn't be enough. *Damn that woman.*

It was Willow. She stood straight and wiped the water from her chin with the back of her hand. Her plan to tell him he was an exploitative, blackmailing fraudster who should be sacked and never allowed to teach again vanished as her parched tongue swelled to fill her mouth. She felt as if she'd eaten three cream crackers, as if saliva did not exist.

His right eyebrow rose so high it disappeared below his floppy fringe. She'd never noticed before, but he had a very weak chin, a thin jaw. She couldn't believe she'd thought him quite attractive at her first tutorial. In fact he had a weasel face, pinched, with small dark eyes. He bent towards her, grasping her elbow as she tried to step back. The result was an ungainly tussle. Other students were watching and he seemed to notice this too because he released her arm. She rubbed the flesh, not because it hurt from his touch but because it felt branded.

He whispered, 'Pay me today, or I'll make sure you're thrown out.'

'But – but you said I had until Saturday.'

He shrugged. 'I can make sure you never work as an artist.' *Can he?*

'If you don't pay up today, I will add interest each day. Have you got that?' His hand grasped her elbow again and she tried to pull away.

'Why do you hate me?'

'You students are all the same, you think you can spend, spend, spend, no responsibility at all for real life. Well, debts have to be paid.'

He leant so close his lips brushed her earlobe and his whispered words smelt of coffee. She coughed.

'There is a very easy way to wipe the slate clean, as you very well know. I have offered you this option before. You have been incredibly stupid. Do not be stupid again.'

She tried to shake her arm free. 'Get lost.'

Willow swore and caught her wrist, pinching so tightly it felt as if his fingers would touch the bone.

'You're coming with me.'

Without Federico's address there was only one place left for her to go to find him or someone who knew where he was. The architecture department. She'd been there once before with Federico but had walked there from the city. She had never gone there from the arts building and was unsure which way to take. She concentrated on putting one foot in front of the other. Shutting her mind to everything except Federico. It took her ages. She got lost twice, although the second time she asked for directions and actually understood part of the answer. She walked through the north side of town, a part she had never been to, the part without bars. Finally she arrived at a tall building with classic white columns. Grand, compared with the art department. The corridors were quiet, everyone was in class.

When she did see someone, she forced herself to concentrate and asked in her halting Spanish.

'*Conoce a Federico Gala?*'

She hoped she was saying it right. People just shook their heads or shrugged.

'*No.*'

'*No.*'

There was no sign of Adrián or Alejandro either. Finally, in the tiny bookshop, a blond boy, German she guessed rather than Spanish, smiled at her. '*Ja.* I know him. But he is not here.' He was holding a huge hardback titled *Bauhaus: The House of Walter Gropius.*

'I know he went on the department trip to Valencia but I thought he would be back last night.'

The German boy shrugged and said Federico hadn't been in their early lecture that morning. 'It is surprise for me because today is time for our Gaudí work.'

'And he loves Gaudí. Yes.' Justine nodded. Nothing would stop Federico from handing in his precious Gaudí project, nothing except something really serious.

'*Gracias*. Err, *danke*.'

The boy smiled and turned back to the shelves.

She went to the student information office and asked for Federico's address. She used her phrasebook and tried to speak clearly, she thought she'd done it right but couldn't understand the replies. This was not going right. All the replies were negative; she got that much by the amount of head shaking.

Then one lady smiled apologetically.

'This information we not give. *Privado. Lo siento.*' She spoke slowly. Justine knew she meant well, but the sympathy made her feel worse.

She walked outside and screamed. Once, twice, again, until she felt she could breathe again. She sat on a wall, remembering the last time she saw Federico. How he looked. His smile. The flicker in his jaw when he was worried about something. His lips. His words. The solid warmth of his body. Remembering how he looked the last time they met. It was as if he had walked onto the bus and into nothingness.

36
SPAIN, JANUARY – FEBRUARY 1983

She got home feeling more weary than she knew it was possible to be. The first thing she saw when she pushed open the front door of the apartment, was a note on the floor.

Federico. At last.

Hands trembling, she unfolded the crisp white sheet of paper. There was an address and five words. 'I will not forget this.' It was not Federico's handwriting. It was Willow's. The fact that he knew where she lived frightened her. She crumpled the note in a ball and threw it out of the window but missed. The paper ball bounced off the wall and rolled to a stop to her feet. She kicked it away, not caring where it went.

She carried a hard wooden dining chair out on to the tiny balcony. Her eyes were open but her mind was blank, as if she had followed Federico into nothingness. She felt able to do nothing more than sit here and wish for him to be with her. A rim of pink and orange along the rooftops opposite shimmered as the sun fell through the sky. And then, like a shutter coming down, all was dark. The house at the end of the terrace sat in shadow. How many hours it seemed since she sat on that bench, asking Picasso for help.

What did I think was going to happen?

A rattle, a key in the lock, the creak as the door opened, the creak they had meant to fix but for the lack of an oil can. Creaks seemed pretty small beer at the moment.

'*Hola*? Justine? *Estas aquí*?' Catalina's voice was so quiet that for the first time Justine felt frightened. She tried to stand up.

'I'm out here, on the balcony.' Her words came out in a whisper.

For a moment there was a pause, like the breath between rolls of thunder before the rain starts. Then, through the lace curtains that hung still in the night air, came Catalina. Her tanned face had a grey tinge.

'Something has happened.'

'Yes.' Catalina held Justine's hand firmly in hers. 'Juan he tell me, the *maestro de arquitectura* talk to estudents at end of lecture. At Año Nuevo, the *abuelito* of Federico is ill.' She patted her chest. '*Un infarto.* Federico and his mother go in car to hospital in Càdiz and there is accident.'

Justine opened her mouth but could not speak.

Catalina nodded. *'Sí. Muerto.'*

A cry echoed round the Plaza de la Merced. To Justine it was a fox at home, rutting in the hedgerow. She did not recognise her own voice.

She felt as if she had been beaten and left to die. Sometimes, she wished she were dead. She lost count of the days, when was day and when was night. Catalina and April did their best to care for her, tempting her with a sunny seat, a glass of freshly squeezed orange juice, and she tried to find the energy to please them. After a couple of days of lying on her bed she moved to a chair at the window. She could hear life going on outside, but did not feel a part of it. One day April sat her at the table with her paintbox, some cleaning cloths and a bowl of soapy water. Justine emptied it, sorting and re-filling, wiping away the smears. She sharpened pencils but did not pick up a brush. Another morning, April suggested she sort her collage box so Justine emptied the contents on to the cool ceramic tiled floor of her bedroom and sorted everything into piles. At the end of the day she put it all back. So this was what stasis felt like.

The nights were endless. Hour after hour staring at the pattern on the ceiling made by light from the lamp post outside, the cracks in the plaster, the tiny puncture marks on the walls where drawing pins had once been, the dark outlines of long-vanished posters of previous occupants. She imagined the faces. Sid Vicious. John Lennon. Bob Marley. Federico. Gone. Her alarm clock stopped for want of winding.

Eating a mouthful of toast at breakfast to please April, feeling sick at the taste of the marmalade because marmalade meant Federico. Refusing coffee, because coffee meant Federico. She drank tea without milk. Snapped at April for nagging her. Lacking the energy to work out what Catalina was trying to say, not wanting to upset her.

Three letters arrived, one for each of the girls. From the accommodation office. An increase in rent. Justine opened the envelope and the room began to spin. She was the maypole; her arms were pale ghostly ribbons flying around. Her sharp collarbones fluttered as delicately as a baby bird's wing.

On Day Eight, she wrote a letter. Catalina had come home with Federico's address and telephone number in Cádiz. It seemed the college felt no need to protect his privacy now he was dead. It took her a whole day to write three lines. In English. To say sorry. But how do you comfort a man who has lost his wife and son, a girl who has lost mother and brother? And a grandfather dead too. Catalina wrote a translation, Justine folded the two pieces of paper into an envelope. She walked to the letterbox, her arm looped through April's, and was amazed that she welcomed the support of a strong arm.

Letter posted, they sat together on Picasso's bench. A pause. She wondered how she had been a girl, so in love with the idea of a dead man that she talked to a building as if he still lived there. But he hadn't sat beside her, his warm thigh next to hers, and spoken of art and architecture. Justine couldn't believe she had been so obsessed by the Spanish artist. It felt like someone else's life.

Writing the letter was a catalyst. After it, her body moved less stiffly. She returned every morning to Picasso's bench and sat, expecting nothing. April encouraged her to walk further, but

Justine dared not, afraid of what she might see and feel, afraid a dam might burst. The other girls returned to college but Justine ignored their hints and suggestions that she join them. Then one day she remembered Picasso had lost too. His sister died when he was small, and soon afterward the family moved to Barcelona. And he had lost in love, too; Eva, the woman in many of his cubist pictures. Justine couldn't remember if that was her real name or not but she had a book about cubism. Without realising it she was on her feet and walking, wanting the book, needing it with an urgency she hadn't felt since that last night when the thought of Federico dead had not entered her mind. She dodged the traffic as she crossed the road, running through the open front door and upstairs to their apartment. It was obvious, she had to strip everything down to its basic shape and reassemble it in a simple form.

There were more notes from Willow, more telephone messages. The notes were thrown in the bin, and she deleted the messages from the tiny answerphone cassettes each night before the others got home from college.

She retreated to her collage box again and again, sorting and sifting, losing herself in the repetition. One day, she stopped putting things into piles and started to mix things together. Juxtaposing unusual partners. She felt rusty, needing encouragement like a stuck chain on an ignored bicycle. She had no idea of theme, no title, and the choice of material was random. The piece had nothing to do with her coursework, but she didn't care. College didn't matter. The end result didn't matter. The form and colours didn't matter. The process was everything and the process came from Federico, from his goodness, from his love for her and hers for him.

Sitting on the floor, surrounded by the contents of boxes, she sat back on her heels and remembered their conversations about Gaudí and Picasso, fish and birds. She picked up a pencil, her stiff fingers feeling numb, and started to sketch *puntillas* and *chipirones*.

She watched on the balcony as two sparrows danced with each other, to and fro, waltz, tango, quickstep; the darker male fluttering delicately towards his beau who retreated. A bird kiss-chase. She was transfixed by their courtship. Then one morning, the male stood guard over a broken drainpipe at the corner of the building. Each time the female returned with a single piece of dried grass, a dead leaf, a single flower petal, held out to him as a gift, he accepted the material from her beak and placed it neatly in their new nest. Justine found her paintbox, poured water into the chipped glass she used for mixing, and selected a fine brush. It seemed fitting that her first subject should be courting sparrows. The first line she painted felt freeing.

A letter arrived. Confirmation of examination dates, course-work deadlines. She slipped the folded paper back into the envelope, tore it in half and threw it in the kitchen bin. Then she lay again on her bed, curled in on herself like a sleeping child.

I didn't know grief meant emptiness.

She had expected it to be tears and screams but it was nothing. He had been taken from her and she was powerless to change it. She could change nothing, do nothing. She knew she should tell someone about Willow, stop him blackmailing someone else. But telling someone would make it real and, in the big scheme of things, Willow was a flea. She sipped water, with a slice of lemon, from the jug left for her in the fridge by April.

Andalucía Day, February 28, was the first day for seven weeks she hadn't felt ill.

Is that it, then? Is this the end of mourning? Has the pain gone?

She felt short-changed. Federico was the love of her life and she expected her grief to last for years. Not seven weeks.

Was our love that shallow?

She told April first.

'Oh.' April's hand flew to her mouth. 'I mean, actually it's rather wonderful, isn't it? Federico lives on.'

April and Catalina were well meaning but clucking companions and Justine longed to get away. They thought her problem was a matter of logistics, food, grief.

She knew two things. She could not stay in Málaga, and she could not go home pregnant to her parents. She would not worry them, shame them; she feared their disappointment and silent censure.

But I have to do something.

Instead of going to college, she started to paint tourist pictures again. She knew she was treading water, except that each kick underwater was a tiny step closer to her decision. And that she must make her mind up soon. She stayed inside, painting, building up a stockpile.

When Bernadita rang, Justine agreed to attend a business dinner with 'Fernando' who requested someone to stand at his elbow, smile, say nothing, and wear a ring on her engagement finger. At first she refused the ring, thinking that would be a betrayal of Federico, but Fernando insisted and so she got through the night by imagining her ring finger had been severed from her hand. Neither Justine nor Bernadita mentioned Andrés. Fernando took the ring back from her afterwards. She did not speculate about the nature of his lies, she was telling enough of her own.

There was only one thing to do.

37
SPAIN AND LONDON, MARCH 1983

It was a long journey from Málaga to London Victoria coach station. Three days sitting in the same seat with not enough stops for the loo. Justine sat with her jeans unzipped and her t-shirt pulled down. She listened to Duran Duran sing 'Rio' on the Walkman April pressed into her hands on that last morning in the apartment on the Plaza de la Merced. Justine knew she would never return.

She spent the journey dozing. Simon le Bon was hungry like a wolf and for thousands of miles he sang the background track to her dreams. It was easier than thinking, but it wasn't 'Cherry Bomb.'

She woke with a start. The bus had stopped and there was some sort of kerfuffle going on. It was pitch dark outside, and all the other passengers seemed to be asleep. Outside there was the murmuring of voices and the banging of doors. A road sign said 'Aéroport de Toulouse'. She closed her eyes, reaching for the dream disturbed.

Hours later she opened her eyes and saw wide open fields, sunshine, the road lined with tall ranks of trees lined up like soldiers. She sensed a presence next to her. A stout woman sat beside her, holding open a large paper bag that smelt of France. Pastries, bread buns, croissants. She said something in French and smiled, shaking the bag at Justine who nodded and took a croissant.

The first mouthful was buttery and flaky, so good, as if it were the first food she had ever tasted. She ate a second, and a third.

The woman mumbled again in French.

They sat companionably, eating in silence. It was the first time Justine had felt comfortable in silence with someone else since Federico. Nameless, they munched and watched Napoleon's tree-lined roads pass by.

Justine felt hungry for the first time in months. She'd forgotten the feeling. She licked flecks of butter-rich pastry off her fingers, savouring the sweetness of the croissants, the faint sour-milk flavour of the bread.

When the bag was empty, the woman screwed it into a ball and put it into an enormous handbag that she cradled on her knees. She was the size of a rugby player and, with her bag, filled the whole space of the seat.

She pointed at herself. 'Ginette.'

'Hi Ginette, I'm Justine. *Merci*,' and she held up the last croissant.

The Frenchwoman nodded, then settled into her seat and closed her eyes. It was a companionable journey. Justine felt a moment of ease, relaxing into the limbo between countries, between decisions. When the coach drew into Victoria Coach Station, it was dawn, cold and raining. Justine hitched her rucksack on to her back, picked up a bag in each hand, and began to walk.

She walked until the straps of her rucksack were chafing her shoulders and her feet ached from treading the wet streets. Her cheap Spanish espadrilles were not made for rain. It felt unreal. She sheltered beneath a tree in a scruffy children's play park, three rusty swings hanging forlorn in the rain. None of this was supposed to happen. To beat away the self-pity, she gave herself what her mother referred to as 'a good talking-to'.

Well, it has happened, so deal with it. Instead of fannying round here, work out what to do.

That sounded easy, but she didn't know where to start.

I made my plan in Málaga, I just have to make it happen.

But having a plan wasn't the same as executing it. And since when had London been so freezing? She shivered and checked for the umpteenth time that her cotton jacket was zipped up.

It was. That her collar was turned up at the nape of her neck. It was. But it didn't stop the cold seeping down her spine, it didn't stop the drip of rain dribbling down to her bottom. For a moment she was tempted: she could be at Seaview Cottage in three, maybe four hours. Warm in front of the fire, warm in her bed looking at the familiar faded wallpaper patterned with tiny rosebuds. But she knew she couldn't go home. Her mother, her father. Just one glance at her face, Justine knew, and her mother would know. It wasn't the consequent shouting that frightened her, the row, the anger, perhaps even tears. It was the disappointment. And the worry. She knew her parents worried about her, only child and all. She didn't want to see disappointment and anxiety etched in the lines of her mother's brow, and know she put it there. Seeing her father would be worse. He wouldn't shout but his silent concern would douse her with ice colder than Yorkshire rain. She would protect them from regret.

Focussed now, she started to search the places where such things were bought and sold. Telephone boxes. She counted seven pubs in a couple of miles, walking out in a spiral working south from the river. She passed loads of stuff to forage but didn't have the heart to collect it, couldn't imagine collaging again, and that frightened her. Her espadrilles were so sodden she was walking in bare feet, very Joan Jett and Cherie Currie. After the thirty-third phone box she decided to try one more and if it didn't have what she was hoping for, she would squat on the floor and try to sleep.

In the thirty-fourth phone box she found a white card. The black type was surrounded by a frame of vine leaves.

In trouble? We can help you. You need not be alone.

38
LONDON, MAY 2010

The notepad in front of Rose remained stubbornly empty. Her major difficulty was a lack of trust in Justine's memory. How accurate could someone's recall be about events of almost thirty years ago? She started to doodle, drawing circles on the blank page, pondering the nature of memory, and one of her mother's favourite songs started to play in her head. She knew that while she remembered an incident from her childhood as clearly as the day it happened, Lily remembered the same incident, but differently. With a Lily-ish twist.

Am I right? Is she? Or are we both wrong?

She hummed. The song was from a film from her childhood, she couldn't place the title. Maurice Chevalier? Louis Jordan? And who was the woman? English, not French, correcting her lover's well-intentioned but incorrect memory of the day they met.

We met at nine, we met at eight, I was on time, no, you were late
Ah, yes, I remember it well
We dined with friends, we dined alone, a tenor sang, a baritone
Ah, yes, I remember it well.

She hummed as she thought of the information she wanted from Justine, wondering if it were unrealistic to expect all the facts, all correct. Was it inevitable that the truth became blurred with time, even more so if that truth were difficult to face?

That dazzling April moon, there was none that night
And the month was June, that's right, that's right
Ah, yes, I remember it well.

Perhaps Justine may prove to be an unreliable witness. Rose realised she had been naïve to assume her search would be made easier with Justine to refer to. Documents would always be more reliable than memory. She wished Lily would ring with some answers.

Gigi, *the film is* Gigi.

And with that thought, her mobile rang.

It was Lily. 'Just a quick call to tell you I've found nothing so far. There's no birth certificate in 1983 for Jenni King. Or death certificate.'

Rose couldn't help grimacing, but it had to be checked.

'I still have to try the alternative names you gave me.'

Rose had suggested Lily try some variations and misspellings.

'I haven't found a baptismal record yet but I've just started looking for that. Then I'll check the newspaper Birth Marriage and Death columns. Do you want me to try for a gravestone inscription?'

'No, don't worry about that.'

She knew Justine had done the first stage research herself, tracing the accessible documents, but Rose wanted it done again. Systematically, her way. Justine didn't strike her as a systematic sort of person.

'Do you need anything else? I've just got some new freelance work and I'm going to be really busy.' Lily always spoke as if she'd taken a gulp of laughing gas, no time to breathe in between sentences.

'That's great. What is it?'

'One of my neighbours has asked me to help her arrange things. Take in deliveries, dog walk, book flights. That sort of thing.'

'So, you're going to be a life manager.'

There was a slight pause as Lily digested this, and then she laughed.

'Is that even a proper job title?'

'Of course it is. I do have more research for you, if you want?'

Rose's list was long, some of it factual, some of it hopeful. Justine's addresses throughout her life. Name of social services office where the adoption might have been processed. Names. Dates. Places. Facts. Any official document related to Justine Tree or Justine King. And Darya Kushkupola.

She rang off, promising to email the list to Lily. She pondered the last item on her list.

How was Darya relevant?

Rose was still unclear about the role played by Justine's Russian benefactor. She seemed to represent an alternative mother figure for Justine, though she was also referred to as the artist's best friend. Where did she figure in this story; was she the reason Justine didn't go home to her parents when she was pregnant? Wasn't it the natural thing, to go home to your own mother in those circumstances? And then Rose remembered her own birth mother. Kate had not gone home to her parents for help because of a row with her father. Not all families were happy or transparent.

There are things she's not telling me.

What actual proof was there that Justine King ever had a baby? What if she didn't?

What if it's a publicity stunt, or some kind of installation art?

Rose was uncomfortable with modern art, afraid her lack of understanding was an intellectual weakness. Perhaps when she paid her account, Justine would ask for all the research material Rose had gathered for the case. Perhaps it would be set in acrylic and put on display at Tate Modern, like Damien Hirst's thing with flies and a cow's head. Or was it a sheep's head? It would be called 'Study: Self-Obfuscation' or 'Memory + Lie = Truth'. She'd noticed that the titles of many modern art works included plus and equals signs. Her mind ran over the documentation she'd gathered to date, mentally sorting it, tidying, discarding the chaff. Sanitising. Cleansing. Adapting. Files to delete. Paper to shred.

It was time to finish, pour a glass of wine, relax. Nick would be home soon. At that thought, Rose realised how unfair she was being to Justine.

Don't we all tell lies?

She wrote a second email to Justine, friendly, open, polishing it to ensure it was non-threatening, asking, 'Tell me the story of what happened.'

Justine tried at first to type her story on the computer, but after deleting her first paragraph for the fifth time, she wondered if pencil and paper might be better. It wasn't. It was almost as if there were an invisible valve inside her head which opened and closed to allow memories in and out, but was now stuck on shut. She had no doubt that Rose would find her daughter without her input. Her track record was good. Justine had asked around. She was respected, described as honest and determined. She would not stop, Justine was sure about that.

Unless I stop her. Should I?

No. She owed it to her daughter to face up to what she had done, to be there, if she wanted, for the rest of her life. Or leave her alone. Whatever she wanted, whatever the consequences, the tears, the arguments.

She could see the newspaper headlines now.

'Justine Tree's love child found after 27 years.'

'Abandoned child reunited with celebrity mother.'

'Mother and daughter reunion.'

Agh, be realistic. She's got a mother. One who didn't disappear; who was there every day, who plaited her hair and helped with homework. She won't want me. She won't remember me. I have to stop thinking of her as a baby. She might be married with children of her own.

That hadn't occurred to her before.

I might be a grandmother.

She put down her pencil and went upstairs to Darya, knowing she would be doing a jigsaw, attracted by the repetitive sorting. Soon they were sitting knee-to-knee across a small table. There was way too much blue sky for Justine's liking. She hated jigsaws with that three-inch band of blue at the top of the picture. Justine's view of the picture was upside-down. Beside them on a small brass trolley was tea for two in china cups delicately sprigged with ivy and edged in gold, and a large plate of biscuits. Ginger Nuts for Darya, chocolate Hobnobs for Justine. Jigsaws of the Old Masters had been a favourite pastime for Darya for years; they used to absorb her for hours on a wet winter afternoon, reconstructing a piece of art she loved. Her favourite colour was blue and so she'd arranged all the blue sky pieces at her side of the large wooden tray. She seemed content to have them all in one place.

It was a while since she had given Justine the correct jigsaw piece to fit a space. The deterioration since her fall was dramatic. Justine persisted with the jigsaw because it made Darya smile, which these days was Justine's biggest daily priority. Today's Old Master was 'The Hay Wain'. That was the box Darya had pointed to, so that was the box Justine opened. As Justine's mind settled to her task, her fingertips too began to shift jigsaw pieces round the table at random, sliding them in smooth slow circles, making a pleasing swooshing sound on the table top.

Darya fell asleep in front of her nightly helping of *East-Enders*. She loved it as much as Justine hated it, the principal reason being that it was a benchmark for Darya's deterioration. She had watched it from the first episode, through Den and Angie, Ian Beale, Grant and Sharon, the burning of the Queen Vic, the re-building of the Queen Vic. Justine had missed many episodes, Darya watched every one. Now she didn't know the characters' names. Except Ian Beale who she greeted with 'Hello Ian, you're a bastard' every time he came on screen which, when the storyline centred on him, could be a bit wearing. A recent development since her return from hospital was that Darya talked to the television as if the characters were in the room with her. If someone asked a question of another character – 'Has So-and-So been in?' 'Where's Thingummybob? –

Darya would answer, often with a swear word. That was new too.

So Justine was relieved when Darya fell asleep and she

could turn over to a Sky Arts programme about Georgia O'Keefe. The commentator was analysing one of the flower paintings. Red, with petals folding in and out, curving, suggestive. A lily? Justine tutted; why did they see sex in everything? And now the flower was moving, fluttering in a breeze, breathing as if it were alive, and then something metal and shiny appeared from nowhere and stabbed the lily. Red, everywhere was red.

Justine woke with a start. The memory was as clear as if it was a film she'd just watched on the evening news, not something from almost thirty years ago.

She wanted to run away from the bloody lily, away from the people who showed her the bloody lily. She cried out.

Then there was a hand on her arm, a soothing voice. Patting, gentle rubs, a soft shushing noise, as if a distraught baby were being calmed.

'It's all right, dear, all right.' The voice was sing-song, the hand stroking her arm familiar, its pale loose skin gathered in folds, soft pleats that smelt of lily-of-the-valley.

'You're here, dear, and I'm here.'

Sitting opposite her was an old woman, bones ghosting beneath the transparent skin, large freckles the size of thumbprints. Between them was a discarded jigsaw with plain blue pieces that didn't seem to fit. And Justine knew she was safe from the memories now, until she slept again, until tomorrow when Rose would ask more questions which she must try to answer.

39
LONDON, MAY 2010

The riverside path was empty but not silent, as Rose jogged slowly home. The river was never silent even at night. Water slapped against stones as a police launch went upriver. Two seagulls sat on adjacent telegraph poles and shouted at each other. And over Battersea Bridge a steady stream of black cabs, red buses and white vans passed in parallel, north to south, south to north. The colour of each vehicle was made invisible by the dark of the night except when passing beneath a street lamp, creating a multi-coloured line of white headlights, red brakes and rainbow-coloured metallic paint finishes. Rose liked this time of night. In her previous life, pre-Nick, she had jogged at night. Those times when she was unable to sleep, when she faced a brick wall in the search for her birth parents, jogging had got the neurons in her brain moving again. The longing for quiet, the fresh air, well, fresh for London, but mostly it was the emptiness that made her pull on her trainers. She'd run along this path a few times in those days, actually, when she'd first met Nick and had sort-of stalked him, running past his apartment, gazing up at the balconies and wondering which was his. She'd never told him. Was that a lie? Or a simple omission; like her failure to tell him she didn't want a baby, words unspoken because she didn't want to disappoint him, because the time for saying them was long passed. She stopped running at night once he found out. Unsafe, he'd said. She missed it. Suffice to say, Nick was in Scotland tonight in a hotel, ready for an early morning meeting at his factory to talk face creams.

She ignored the lift and climbed the stairs to their top

floor apartment. It was his home really, not hers, though she never would have admitted that, not wanting to upset him and his delicate need for her to need him. Except she didn't need him. She liked him, wanted him, loved him. But perhaps she'd lived on her own too long to actually need anyone. On nights like this, when she was alone, she longed for her small flat in Wimbledon; but it was currently occupied by a newly qualified dentist and a marketing assistant. No pets. No children. Twelve-month lease. The renewal date was looming again and a big part of Rose wanted to snatch her flat back, to make it hers again. But there was Nick.

She settled at her laptop again, a steaming mug of tea in the one o'clock position beside her mouse. That was another thing she could only do when Nick was away: night-time working. Although he worked hard, he worked in his office and when he left it for the night he was pretty strict about leaving stuff behind. As a freelance, she was based at home and did what needed doing when it needed doing. There had been a couple of talks recently about the work thing that had ended in an uneasy agreement to try to be more accommodating of the other's needs. Nothing really had changed. So she relished the chance to sit at her computer without the tut of disapproval.

Tonight her brain revolved, considering Justine, waiting for answers. When she couldn't see the wood for the trees she found it helped to put a project aside for an hour and concentrate on something completely different. So she clicked on the Word folder marked 'Kate'. The last-modified date was nine months ago. How had so much time passed since she'd researched her birth mother? It felt like a betrayal, like promising to telephone your mum every Sunday night and then not bothering.

The documents listed were familiar from her early research but now felt so distant. Not that long ago, these documents had been open on her screen in multiple windows, closed only with resentment when paying work had called. The project was to find information about Kate which would re-create the real person rather than an avatar; My Birth Mother. She had stories of Kate growing up, but Rose was desperate for stories about

Kate the actress. She opened a new Excel sheet and started to input a timetable of the plays Kate featured in, the theatres/towns she played in, her co-actors and production companies. From this she hoped to find people still alive. She would give anything to breathe life into the hippy girl in her treasured black-and-white photo.

Is this how Justine's daughter is feeling right now?

Next she tried to log on to a website she had used before to access Kate's mother-and-baby home records, but the access code given to her ages ago by her social worker did not work. She typed a quick email and got an automatic response: 'Eileen Greenaway has left Enfield Social Services. For all matters concerning adoption services in the Borough of Enfield, please contact Kelly Kazlauskas.' Rose felt a small loss. It was schoolmistressy Mrs Greenaway who had told Rose the name of her birth mother and, in Rose's head, seemed to represent a connection to Kate. Mrs Greenaway who, despite seeing practically every possible adoption story possible, had sympathy and support for baby Alanna.

For me.

Rose sighed, wishing she could ask for advice about Justine. The birth father was a mystery, unless it were Federico, but Justine seemed reluctant to talk about him which indicated to Rose it must be someone else. If Justine had put herself about in Málaga, it was probable there were so many boyfriends it would be impossible to trace the biological father. The child could be anywhere. The only concrete thing Rose knew was the gender.

She typed a quick email to Kelly Kazlauskas. She had hoped to track down two girls who gave birth at the mother-and-baby home at the same time as Kate. They might have shared a room with her, or mealtimes; have memories. She went back to her original research notes. Yes, there they were. Cherry Fawcett. Twins, father an unknown serviceman. And Joan, Joan Mary Mellor, she had a little boy. The father was Joan's uncle. Rose wondered at Joan's bravery in committing that nasty family secret to black and white.

Where were Cherry and Joan now? She wondered whether to ask Lily to do this. She picked up the phone and dialled. No answer. She glanced at her watch. It was gone ten. As a single mum to two-year-old Kathie, Lily's late nights were usually spent at home watching box sets with Rose's cat Brad curled up on her lap.

Rose sighed. She really must try to get some sleep. Tomorrow she had an early meeting with Adrian at Tough Talk. She had confirmed two more witness statements which, and she thought this was key, both came from the same clinic. The details tallied with two of the interviews in her first report for Adrian. The clinic had traded in London in the Seventies and Eighties and claimed to be a charity, although the Charities Commission knew nothing about it. To Rose it was a sinister 1970s version of the American Pro-Life Movement which had, it was assumed, never made it across the Atlantic. Tomorrow Rose would present her case to Adrian: discard all other research and focus on the Astraea Clinic.

She'd checked out the name, a classical, mytholog-ical, innocent-sounding name for a place that manipulated, exploited and traumatised vulnerable young women. Astraea was the daughter of Zeus and Themis – she was the Greek goddess of justice, a symbol of innocence and purity. Rose hated the people who ran the Astraea.

40
LONDON, MAY 2010

Next day, the meeting at Tough Talk's offices was an hour old and the coffee jug had already been refilled. Rose was regretting the Americano she'd grabbed to drink on the Tube. She was pleased, though, with her contribution and Adrian's reaction to it. The team had agreed to focus on Manchester Women's Choice, Harper House and the Astraea Clinic. Rose didn't know what her next contribution might be but had decided to say yes to whatever research Adrian asked her for. He was currently in a huddle with the art editor discussing visuals, so Rose took the chance to leaf through the deep blue manila folder she had been given that contained the team's consolidated research for the project. She flicked past page after page; financial reports, lists of directors, screengrabs of web pages, pages of lists and photos. And then something caught her eye and she stopped.

The last time she read an official document and saw a name she didn't expect was when she read her own original birth details. But the name on this list wasn't Katherine Ingram. It was Justine King. The date was March 1983.

41
LONDON, MARCH 1983

After asking her name, they took her in. Justine was so tired, so grateful, so disbelieving of her luck in finding a welcoming place that wouldn't judge her.

'Eat. Sleep. Rest. We can talk tomorrow.'

And they smiled. There were so many smiles at the Astraea Clinic, a pat on her arm, a steaming mug of hot cocoa with whipped cream and a melting chocolate flake on top. She slept in a bunk bed in an empty dormitory, twelve neat crease-free beds.

Glad to be alone, to be doing something, she slept deeply. The next morning she woke ready to face what she thought of as 'the process.' It was her way of shielding herself from what was about to happen. Physical pain she could deal with. The process, she didn't want to think about.

After eating a breakfast of scrambled eggs, toast, orange juice and coffee, she was shown through a door. Expecting a consulting room, and a morning involving an interview and questionnaire, followed by a hospital room, a high examination bed, stirrups, a speculum, the reassuring smell of antiseptic and an examination, she walked into a room empty except for a high-backed armchair, a television and video player.

Everything turned black. Black with red streaks, a sunset in hell. Her own personal 'Scream'.

She ran through the rain, cold rain, running she knew not where, only that she had to get as far away as possible from that horrible, horrible place. Running so hard she tripped herself up, over-striding like an athlete stretching for the winning tape, splashing through deep puddles that drenched her bare legs with dirty rainwater, her cheesecloth skirt sodden to her thighs. She slowed to walking pace, turning left through a gateway and finding a small park. She was alone. The rain ceased to matter; she couldn't get any wetter.

Her brain didn't know how to process what she had been made to watch. She felt knifed in the belly. They had been kind to her, promised to help, assured her she would not be left alone, that they would support her decision to end her pregnancy. And then they forced her to take the decision they wanted. Smiling, all the time.

Shivering, she buttoned her thin jacket and walked with her chin to her chest. When the American man who introduced himself as Doctor Franks left the room to fetch tea and biscuits, Justine ran. She had kept her rucksack with her, her money, her passport, but did not dare risk retrieving her bags from the bunk bed. Away from the tall house built of solid-looking Victorian red brick she ran. Away from the house of lies. It hadn't said that on the card with the vine leaves. Her belly ached; from hunger, from the emotional punch, the kick from the video. Her hand cupped her flat stomach.

What sort of people show a film like that to an obviously vulnerable young woman?

She closed her eyes but that didn't shut out the soundtrack. Some doctor explaining the step-by-step procedure. Death. Murder.

As the numbness dissolved, anger roared in to replace it.

I believed them because of their smiles, the warm bed and food. Does being pregnant kill your brain cells?

For the third time she completed a circle of the park. As her legs tired the steps faltered, her feet clumsy, and she stumbled until, feeling tired as if she had been awake all her life, she sank to her knees and felt the grit press into her flesh and the dirty water bathe her skin.

Do something.

She sneezed, an inelegant explosion which she had no hankie to quell. How her mother would tut. And with the thought of her mother came flooding back all the Yorkshire common sense she had inherited.

I have to look after myself now, it's not just about me.

So she did the obvious thing.

42
LONDON, MAY 2010

It was five hours since she'd left the meeting at Tough Talk Productions and Rose could think of nothing else. She had been tasked with coordinating the Astraea interviewees and preparing the women to talk to camera. She said nothing about the true identity of Justine King. A researcher in the USA was to investigate the clinic's business background. It operated online now, using social media to encourage vulnerable women to sign up for a confidential consultation with a local doctor where, it was promised, the abortion options would be outlined and every support given while a decision was made. In the blue manila folder were transcripts of interviews with 'Anna' and 'Regina', both false names, who had talked to other journalists on the team. Rose read each twice through and the descriptions tallied with her own witnesses. Her head was full of Kate and Justine and who knew how many other women who could see no other option but abortion.

She poured herself a glass of sauvignon blanc and opened the doors to the slim balcony. Below, the river flowed downstream, disappearing over the horizon with the reliability of nature.

She wondered how Justine had escaped from the clinic.

How do I find the words to ask her about it?

There was the bang of a door behind her and then Nick's hands rested gently on her shoulders, his lips caressing the nape of her neck. Rose tried not to tense up. She would shed her mood. Tonight was Friday, their date night. That's when she realised she'd bought no food; the shopping list for the agreed menu – risotto and chocolate mousse – was untouched in her purse.

'Sorry, honey, I forgot the food.'

'I know.' He kissed her left ear, something she tolerated. In her book, tongues and ears were on different parts of the head for a reason. 'I know.'

'How?'

'Superior detective work.'

She shivered and he wrapped her in his arms.

'Come on, tell me how you know I forgot the food?'

'No carrier bags in the kitchen.'

'Well done, Hercule Poirot.'

They undressed and stood under the large monsoon shower while the hot water washed away Rose's anger and Nick's stress, during which they agreed to eat out. An hour later they were in a cab going to Nobu. Nick wore an understated linen jacket and jeans with an exquisite silk shirt that looked plain but did not have a plain price tag. Rose blow-dried her hair, applied mascara and a touch of lipstick, and then pulled on a red shirtdress, brushing away the longing for a box set and a cuddle on the sofa.

It was some time before she realised that Nick was out of sorts too. He wasn't talking about work. Normally the sound of his voice soothed her, and she'd loved it in their early days together when they'd curled up together in bed, propped against a pile of pillows, and he'd read to her. Nothing cultural or romantic, just whatever he was reading at the time. Ian McEwan, William Boyd, John Grisham. She couldn't remember the last time they'd done that but knew he cottoned on to the idea after she first mentioned longing to fall asleep while being told a story. It was a silly thing to say, a memory of childhood, of her mother Diana reading *Little Women*, and it was a memory connected to her sadness about not appreciating Diana while she was there. Then Nick caught her in tears one evening, she explained why and so the habit with John Grisham et al. had started.

She worried he had fallen in love with her at a time when she wasn't herself, during her Weak Rose year. She had been racked by anger, betrayal and uncertainty and he had been so supportive during her search for her birth parents. But that time was long gone and she was Strong Rose again.

Tonight she let him order for both of them. Tempura for him and black miso cod for her. She had said once it was her favourite and it didn't seem to occur to him that she might want to eat something different.

I like the black miso cod. Don't be difficult.

'So what did you do today?' Her voice was bright and perky and she hated it. To her ears it sounded so artificial; a plastic rose in a vase on a restaurant table, so obviously not the real thing.

His face darkened and she wished she'd said something about sushi.

'That Spanish villain has a two-page feature in *Global Beauty* today and a four-minute interview on their YouTube channel. It's a clear case of passing-off; I wish I could prove he bought jars of Night-Renew cream and copied the labels.'

'What does your lawyer say?'

'Nothing. Their copyright expert has been on paternity leave, then sick. I'm not paying their fees to pay someone who can't come to work for six weeks.'

This discussion had a familiar cycle. Nick complained, Rose attempted to soothe him but inadvertently made him more irritable. It was as if he wanted to be bad tempered though Rose couldn't see how complaining about something actually changed anything. Every time she felt this way, she reminded herself how Nick had always been there for her.

It felt as if they were still trying each other on for size, though she had expected they would have this sorted out by living together. But perhaps you never did, perhaps that's what a long-term relationship was: a constant re-adjustment. This was the longest relationship Rose had ever had and she hadn't quite appreciated that it was a matter of constant evolution, constant shifting. She loved Nick, and he was the first man she'd loved who was a powerful personality. Her previous boyfriends were weaker, weaker in terms of emotional strength and intellect. She had met her match in Nick as he had with her. Which meant both had to make adjustments.

Later, after making love slowly and voluptuously, Nick was sleeping heavily as if knocked out by a falling coconut. Rose went into the bathroom. Silently she slipped a tiny contraceptive pill from the packet she kept at the bottom of her tampon box and swallowed it with a handful of cold water from the tap. She extracted a new silver strip of pills to transfer into her handbag, her insurance against getting caught out.

I will not make the same mistake as those women who went to the Astraea.

The door opened behind her.

'Sorry, love, I need to pee.'

She stood on tiptoe to kiss him on the cheek and moved her hand, holding the pills, behind her back. The blush ran up her cheeks to her forehead, not in the gradual way the sun rises but the speeded-up film of a car crashing. Boom. One moment, nothing, and then there it was, written on her face for all to see. Her face seemed to be saying, 'I just lied'. Rose had learned long ago that she could not lie and get away with it, so in most situations she told the truth. Now, she lied with silence.

She lay in bed waiting for Nick to return. The strip of pills was safely hidden in her handbag in the wardrobe. He came back to bed and was asleep again in two minutes but Rose lay awake, wondering how Justine lied so convincingly to everyone for twenty-seven years, jealous she couldn't lie as well as Justine obviously could.

43
LONDON, MAY 2010

South of the River Thames, Justine also went out for dinner that night. As she got out of her cab, the door opened by a concierge in Jupiter Tower livery, two very slim women wearing form-fitting dresses de-taxied next to her. The non-eye-contact was made on the street in that way only Londoners and New Yorkers seem capable of. Justine hoped to leave them behind but they followed her into the lift. She was heading to Orion, the top floor bar, for drinks before dinner at Mercury. It seemed the women were heading to the same place. Their not-quite-hushed conversation continued about a feature in tomorrow's Sunday newspaper, on sale on the London streets late Saturday evening, in which an artist had been photographed in a black t-shirt and black jeans. It was a 'What I would tell my student self' feature. Justine knew they were talking about her, and they knew she was the subject of the feature, but all three studied the lift floor.

According to the taller of the two women 'she' was wearing the wrong colours for her skin tone, given her dyed black hair. Black clothing was so draining for a woman of her age, she said in a loud whisper to her nodding friend, and that she must be well into her sixties.

For the record, Justine was almost fifty, her hair colour was natural, her skin and bones were her own, her teeth their original colour.

Is the world really so callous now?

At no time did either woman make eye contact with her, directing their eyes away from the mirrored walls of the lift to the floor and the flickering red numeral which, for Justine's liking, was not changing quickly enough. Although she had become hardened to overhearing people like this talk about her and her art as if she were public property, deaf, or devoid of sensitivity and unable to be upset or offended, it still stung.

She could trace the start of this trend to her first magazine profiles and television interviews at the time of the 'Sensation' exhibition at the Royal Academy. She had been one of the less flamboyant artists there, no messy bed, no gloss paint, no dead animals. Justine's fame arrived long after diamond-studded skulls and quilts made headlines. When going out, she had recently taken to wearing earbuds connected to one of those mini iPods as big as a matchbox, listening to something soothing and classical. It proved as good a disguise as a wig or baseball cap. David Bowie walked the streets of New York unchallenged because he was carrying a Polish language newspaper, and somehow the Tube travellers who did recognise Justine discounted her as a lookalike because of her iPod.

The women had moved on from Justine's appearance to her accent; 'northern' and 'regional'. The latter comment was the first spoken contribution of the silent woman who, Justine noticed, was wearing matching nail polish and lipstick of the Mary Quant variety which Justine remembered longing for in her teens. Perhaps 1970s fashions were coming back in. Justine held no truck with fashion per se, she simply knew what was comfortable and what suited her. She was indeed wearing a black tailored shirt and narrow black wool trousers, her ankle boots were charcoal leather with metal studs and her cashmere jacket was slate grey. She felt good, she thought she looked good, and she didn't care a fig whether other people approved of her clothing.

'Of course it's all imagined, her famous emotional intensity. It's made up.'

The fuchsia-lipstick woman asked how her friend could possibly know this.

'If she's not a mother, Eva, she cannot possibly be connected with the centre of her soul.'

'You mean she's a fake.'

At that precise moment, the lift doors opened and the top floor restaurant with views across the city's rooftops was announced over the tannoy as in an old-fashioned department store.

'Floor Fifty-Two. Orion.'

She's right.

Justine was shown to a table and served with a glass of champagne. She sipped it then put it aside, wondering how long Maud would be. The reservation at Mercury was for nine thirty. This was a celebration. 'Green' had sold out and Maud's spoken and emailed vocabulary every day of the exhibition so far was liberally laced with capitals. Including her analysis of add-ons, the sales of limited edition prints, licensing contracts for prints and posters, stationery, tote bags, t-shirts and books.

Ambitious. Bigger. Better. Authenticity. Rarity. Body of Work. Artist Integrity.

But I am a fake.

44
LONDON, MAY 2010

In Kensington, the large bell in the church tower at the end of the road tolled on the hour, half-hour and quarter-hour. Inside, Justine didn't hear it. Resenting the way last night's celebration with Maud had swallowed up time, she awoke early and started work on a new piece provisionally entitled 'Justine's Box'. It was the first small-scale collage she had started for years; a scattering of bits and pieces, arranged and stuck down onto a flat surface. A stand-alone piece. Everything recently had been An Assemblage, A Collection, A Series; Maud's capitals, because collections of a minimum of ten pieces were more lucrative, easier to sell and easier to promote. Justine's problem was that her ideas didn't come sized large in convenient blocks of ten.

'Justine's Box' was the real her. It was a long time since a project had come together so quickly. It flowed from the moment she turned on her studio light in the heavy grey of early morning, her fingers reaching into the storage boxes on the shelves as a robot picked an order in a giant warehouse. Layering memory on memory, symbol on symbol, building up a picture of her truth. She would wear her real heart on her sleeve. That thought jarred as she recalled the women in the lift.

Breaking for more tea, she turned on her mobile which beeped with a string of messages and incoming texts. Ten missed calls. From Rose, who had yet more questions. Justine squashed down her irritation.

She's only trying to do her job, a job I am paying her for.
The front door bell rang.

Damn.

'Justine's Box' tugged her towards it; it was hers, it came from within her. The bell rang again, held down now continuously with the aggression that heralds a visitor who will not go away. Justine knew Rose would not go away, not unless Justine cancelled their contract.

They stood in the chilly studio, Justine not wanting to sit as it seemed an invitation to stay and she wanted to get back to the Box.

'Why are there no people in your art?'

'There are.'

'Not many.'

Silence. Justine met Rose's gaze and waited for the next question.

'Have you ever painted a portrait?'

'Yes.' The word was blurted out, defensively.

She remembered it as if it were yesterday. She had been in the apartment alone; April and Catalina were sitting exams where she should also be. The pencil felt at one with her hand, the graphite at one with the paper. She could feel Federico's eyes on her, warm, as warm as the touch of his fingers. She blinked, slowly, feeling the faint pressure as eyelids moved across the corneal globes; a moment, a pause, a relief from the intensity of his gaze. When her eyes focussed again on the paper, she concentrated on the fine dark line that defined his lashes. But when she looked up, she was alone and Federico was dead. She tried to concentrate on the paper but pressed so hard the pencil's point splintered, piercing the paper. It was a black smudged mess.

Justine seemed lost in another world and Rose was wary of startling her. Just as she was wondering whether to clear her throat, or clatter the tea mugs, Justine spoke.

'It feels too personal, you see, as if I'm invading their privacy, which I would have to do to paint a good portrait.'

'And you would hate to be the subject of a portrait yourself?'

'I can't think of anything more detestable.'

A bell rang and Justine disappeared; upstairs to Darya, Rose assumed. She was difficult to warm to, Justine; a bit like trying to hug a hedgehog. But her devotion to Darya was warming and Rose's eyes prickled, not for the memory of her two mothers but for Grandma Bizzie. She could hear Bizzie's voice telling her, 'Don't be so soft, you should be thinking about those who are living, those you love,' and her mind flew instead to her grumpy farewell with Nick this morning.

'You're working, on a Saturday?' His words were full of disappointment, his tone had a little more steel. He stood in the kitchen door, his feet planted wide jamb to jamb, his hands on his hips, making himself too big for her to squeeze past. Rose avoided confrontations and had made a promise to herself last night as she'd lain awake after the pill incident. She would compromise more, be less snippy with him, try to see things from his point of view. So this morning she made a big effort not to snap back. She bit her tongue, resisting the urge to point out he had worked the previous two weekends and she had neither complained nor sulked. So she smiled and took his arm, suggesting they go to the cinema this evening. A date night. This had appeased him. Were these compromises a sign of a maturing relationship, or a dying one? She remembered Lily saying that with hindsight she should have known William was having an affair when he played golf more often. Nick wasn't big on golf, he went running instead.

Not wanting to think about Nick, she perused Justine's shelves. Art magazines and exhibition catalogues, books on Bourgeois, Kiefer, Hopper, Rauschenberg, Wood. Remembering the fashion designer she once interviewed and how she'd found a way into his personal obsessions by spotting his magazines – his desk had been piled high with copies of *Vogue*, fashion show catalogues, Net-a-Porter catalogues, and *Family History Monthly* magazine – she examined Justine's bookshelves more closely. *Artforum, Frieze, Art Monthly, Art Review, Flash Art, Blueprint, Design* and *BBC Wildlife Magazine*.

She was looking at photos of cheetahs when Justine returned.

'How about a fry-up? I'm starving and there's a great Turkish café round the corner.'

They ran through the rain into the warm fug of Tariq's. The windows were steamed up, making the small room seem cosy and separate from the real world. Justine was right; the Royal Saturday Breakfast was just what was required. Perhaps the cholesterol count would give her courage to ask the dangerous question that seemed to hang over their heads in a silent speech bubble. Between a hash brown and a charred grilled tomato, Rose talked about the Astraea and the list she had found.

Justine's face paled and she put down her knife and fork.

'Yes, I went to an abortion clinic. It was a horrible place. A nightmare. I paint about it sometimes.'

Seeing the expression on Rose's face, she added, 'Not for public view, more as therapy really. To try and exorcise the ghost. Except I've been painting these pictures for nearly thirty years and I still have the nightmares. Clearly, my home-made therapy isn't working.' She laid her knife and fork neatly side by side on her plate then swigged the dregs from her mug. 'Do you want another tea?'

Rose wasn't sure if she was belittling the experience in order to forget it, or discourage more questions.

But Justine seemed to know what Rose was thinking. 'Don't mind me, it's a survival mechanism. On the nights when I can't shut out the memories of the film they showed me, I am a wreck. My migraine pictures – that's what I call them because the stress always gives me a blinding headache – are the opposite of 'Green'. They just happen. I splash paint here, there and everywhere. There's no plan, no examination, no intention. For God's sake don't mention them to Maud, she'll try to build them into a series.'

Rose watched her, fascinated. If it was a performance, she was quite convincing. Then as loudly as it had started, it stopped. Rose pushed aside the rest of her breakfast. It was too much and too greasy after all. She realised Justine was waiting for her to speak.

'I saw an excerpt of the Astraea film yesterday.' She was watching Justine's face closely. It was blank.

'I'm doing some research for a TV production team about illegal abortion clinics. I didn't set out to research you. Honestly.' It was important to Rose that Justine understood this was a separate job, that she hadn't set out to pry into her secrets.

'Tariq!' Justine waved her mug at the man behind the counter. 'Can we have two more teas, please?' Then she looked at Rose again. It was full-on, eye-to-eye, it said: 'I trust you'.

'I can't think of the right words to describe the Astraea. I can't believe that place is still operating. If it's the same set-up, they are villains dressed up as doctors and nurses. Actually I'm glad you've found out. I knew I had to tell you. I didn't want to, but it is a part of my story. I don't know whether I'll be able to tell my daughter though. It's not the sort of thing you should admit to your child.'

And Rose immediately thought of Kate.

How would I feel if she was alive now and told me that she tried to abort me?

She was a bit taken aback at Justine's openness. Getting information out of her was akin to opening an oyster shell and finding it empty. She wondered now at the easy confession.

'Can you get it? The clinic? Legally, I mean. Surely it must be breaking a hundred laws?'

'We hope so,' Rose said. The documentary team planned to hand a file to the Director of Public Prosecutions before the programme was broadcast. The allegations were exploitation of women, tax fraud, charity misrepresentation.

'I know you'll think this is odd, but I'm grateful to them.' Justine was sitting with her elbows on the scrubbed Formica-topped table, both hands cradling a new red mug full of steaming hot tea. She wasn't looking at Rose, though; her eyes seemed fixed on the wall opposite where a calendar of Istanbul was turned to August 2009.

She's done it again, sucked the breath from my lungs.

'Why?'

'Because, without them, without that disgusting film, I would never have understood what my baby really meant to me. I came home from Spain and the only thing to do seemed to be get rid of it. I just couldn't see what to do. If – if they had been professional at the Astraea I don't think I would have run away.'

Her eyes were clouded, her brows scrunched in two dark zigzags.

'My baby. She deserved a chance at life.' Her voice cracked.

She gripped Rose's arm so tight her fingernails snagged on the fabric of Rose's sleeve. 'Please. You have to find her for me. I don't know how much longer I can stand not knowing.' She dragged in a breath as if she were desperate for a cigarette. 'I was so worried I'd made a mistake, I almost sacked you. But now I know you have to go on.'

The original video Justine was forced to watch in that clinic lasted thirty minutes, but it took her only fifteen minutes to re-live it as she told Rose. It was odd how time, condensed over the years, made emotions stronger. Aware of Rose's eyes on her, she was determined not to show weakness but couldn't stop herself. She closed her nostrils to the smell which swept up her nose, although the blood was only ever on the television, in her imagination, not in the room with her. That's how this video was supposed to work: imagination. You thought the worst and made a snap decision. Old blood, dried, clotted, dark, almost black. Flies buzzing.

Some days she could smell it everywhere. In her perfume as it warmed on her skin, in the sizzling of Darya's favourite pork chops under the grill, in public buildings where carpets were dense with old dust. She knew it was shame that distorted the memory, shame she had thought something so extreme would solve things, shame at her capitulation, her desperation, her lack of fight. The sensation of being beaten by her circumstances, so desperate, was still so immediate it made her catch her breath with regret. She was ashamed she had not fought as her parents had taught her to, as Federico would have wanted her to, expected her to do.

To her credit, Rose sat and listened and waited. No questions, no gasps or intakes of breath. Her eyes did not lose contact with Justine's own. And Justine respected her for that.

Am I starting to like her?

As Justine knew it would, the pain started to circle her head. In loose spirals at first, looping round in the way of those floppy plaited ties she fastened her ponytail with at secondary school, tied in a red bow, the long ends dangling to her shoulders. Amazing, to think she'd ever had a ponytail. As her words dried up and the red cord pulled tight across her skull, the knot tightening, her eyes became blurry. She could see Rose's mouth moving as if under water, with bubbles instead of sound.

She closed her eyes and was living the video again.

Rose could only sit and watch as Justine's eyes glazed with pain. She was pressing her left brow bone, dot-dot-dot, left to right, right to left, back and forth, a path worn bare by a trapped animal pacing along a fence. The headache seemed to have come from nowhere and Rose, wondering if it was stress-related, suggested they walk back to the studio. Justine shook her head and rummaged through her handbag for a painkiller which she swallowed with a glass of water and a digestive biscuit offered by Tariq. And now they sat, waiting for the medicine to work. Justine said it would be a while, that she would be fine on her own and Rose could go. But Rose had one more awkward question to ask and couldn't leave without asking it. Adrian wanted Justine to be interviewed on camera and was pressing for an answer. He had marked Justine's name in the 'yes' column despite Rose's protestations. Her real identity was still a secret but they were struggling for first-hand accounts of these clinics, how it felt, what was said, and Rose had made the mistake of saying she knew someone on the list. But, looking at Justine who was resting her head back against the cool café wall, her eyes closed, Rose knew she couldn't ask now. Another day. Maybe. Maybe never.

They sat like that for an hour and Rose found it soothing. She closed her eyes too and allowed her mind to drift. It was as soothing as the first dab of antiseptic cream on a fresh graze, a bleeding knee, the shushing of Grandma Bizzie as she applied that peculiar greasy pink cream from the small yellow tin. She wondered if Justine knew the same antiseptic from her own childhood. She sneaked a glance. Justine's eyes were closed.

We must make an odd couple.

Rose didn't care. It was the sort of things friends did; supported each other, didn't walk away.

Are we becoming friends?

'Well, now you know that you might as well know the rest.'

Rose thought Justine's eyes seemed brighter. Her brow was less furrowed.

'It's not a happy story. I don't come out of it well, at all. But you need to know if you're to find Jenni.'

Rose felt a flutter of anticipation in her right hand, the impulse to pick up her pen. But she resisted.

Just let her talk.

'She had the most amazing little fingers, miniature, so delicate. How could I ever have thought of getting rid of her? But the clinic won, didn't it?'

Justine nodded at Tariq as yet another mug of tea was placed in front of her. She reached for her purse but he waved her money away.

So what went wrong?

'My parents were so proud of me, of my success at college. It was more than they'd ever dreamed of and I just couldn't tell them that I failed them. They gave up so much for me. Dad did overtime, Mum took in dressmaking. All those hours of extra work and economies, sacrifices, selflessness. What did I do? I wasted it.'

Justine paused to take a gulp of tea.

Rose hesitated before speaking. 'But I don't understand. Why couldn't you tell them?'

Justine stared at her as if they had never met. 'The Eighties weren't really liberated, you know. Perhaps on the surface but not in my bit of Yorkshire and not my family. No, I couldn't.'

It was a sharp answer which brooked no query.

'So you didn't see your parents at all?'

'Oh yes, I went back to Yorkshire.'

'You did?' Rose knew her astonishment showed in the tone of her voice.

I must try to be neutral. She went back and didn't tell them?

'Yes, I wasn't showing and the sickness had passed.'

'But weren't you tempted to tell your mum?'

'Of course I was, but that would have been selfish. That would have been for me. A moment to make me feel better would cause them a lifetime of pain. I stayed for a month. I felt the best I had in a year. Mum's home cooking I guess. I did some painting, worked in the local café and earned some cash. And I researched what to do, made some telephone calls. A friend from school helped me and I am so grateful to her.'

'Where did you go?'

'London. I felt I could be anonymous there. I registered at the doctor's with a made-up name.' She smiled ruefully. 'No computer records, remember.'

Rose hadn't expected that. So that was why the paper trail was impossible to follow. Still, something still didn't seem right.

'But why didn't you keep her?'

Justine breathed deeply and stretched. Rose could see the pain had aged her ten years.

'I tried to. But then everything went wrong. So I left her on a doorstep. I walked away.' She breathed deeply, as if steeling herself, then added, 'I walked away and a bit of me felt relieved.'

Rose looked into Justine's eyes and there was truth there.

Why didn't she tell me this at the beginning?

Rose mentally reviewed her notes to see if there had been any hint of abandonment. She watched as Tariq stretched up the wall behind the till to remove the chalkboard with the breakfast listing and hang the lunch menu in its place. Chicken tikka masala, pork chop and roast potatoes with two veggies, or ham and egg salad.

A foundling. Abandoned. No name. No documents. Confidential fostering. Closed records. I will never find her.

'She depended on me, and I abandoned her. What kind of mother was I? No kind.' Justine's head was bent over the table now and she was crying quietly into her hands.

Rose could feel it, hanging in the air. There was more to come. It was an instinct honed through years of interviews.

'What is it, Justine? Is there something else?'

Justine raised her head. Rose was shocked; her eyes were veiled, as if they had stared at death.

'How can I face her now and tell her I walked away from her? Ran away?'

'Perhaps you don't tell her,' Rose said gently. She wondered how she would react if she were Jenni. 'Complete honesty is not always the answer.'

'Some days, I think it would be better if I was dead.'

'Better for who? For you? Or her?'

'For both of us.'

Rose wanted to slap her now.

'So why do you want to find her, Justine? Why put yourself through this agony?' She knew her voice sounded firmer and expected a reaction. 'Forget about finding her and get on with your life.'

Shock was written across Justine's face. 'Of course I want to find her. How could I not?'

Tariq did not ask them to vacate their table; instead he brought more tea and a plate of biscuits. Lunch was served. To Rose, the bustle and noise of office workers was white noise. The smell of curry made her nauseous. She sat, her hand resting on Justine's arm, knowing she could not walk away but not knowing what to say.

And all the time, in Rose's head, circulated thoughts she tried to quash. Knowing they were ungenerous, knowing they were selfish and totally unrelated to Justine's dilemma.

You are lucky, your daughter is alive. You can find her, talk to her. My mum is dead.

But she said nothing because she was not Jenni and Justine was not her birth mother.

What I think doesn't matter.

Justine looked at the plate and wondered which biscuit was Jenni's favourite, wishing she knew, feeling sad that she didn't. The choice was fig rolls, shortbread fingers or chocolate chip cookies. No choice. She took a shortbread. One mouthful of the buttery crumbliness, savouring the gritty dusting of granulated sugar on top, and for an infinitesimal moment she was back in the cosy kitchen at Seaview Cottage helping her mother at Christmas. She would always have regrets about her mother.

Which biscuit would Rose choose?

A fig roll.

Really?

She chewed, feeling a bit better. Perhaps it was the sugar, perhaps it was telling the truth.

I did it. I said the words aloud. I left my baby on a doorstep and walked away.

It felt, not good exactly, but, she struggled for the words, it felt freeing. She licked her fingertip and pressed it round the plate, picking up every last crumb of shortbread. It had been her mother's favourite biscuit and so Justine, seeing how her mother's eyes drooped after a long day sewing and having just watched her father eat three shortbread biscuits one after the other, said she preferred the chocolate ones. It was worth it to watch her mother smile her gentle smile as she bit into the extra golden finger. She had been told never to fib but had decided that, occasionally, one was justified.

Remembering her mother's face the last time she saw her alive, Justine couldn't imagine her mother telling a lie to anyone.

It just wasn't in Mum's DNA.

Rose popped a large chunk of fig roll in her mouth, chewed, working out what to say.

'Life is too short, too short to allow shame and lies to mess up your family relationships. Everyone makes mistakes, after all.'

Am I still making them?

Justine studied her. 'Did you hate your mother?'

'I decided not to hate any of them. It was a positive decision. I hoped that if I ever did something bad, I would be forgiven too.'

Justine crossed her fingers beneath the table.

'I hope Jenni will forgive me.'

I remember the upward tilt of her top lip, almost a pout, irresistible. I have missed twenty-seven years of scraped knees, school Nativity plays, dental appointments, teenage tantrums, exam revision. She faced all of these with another mother. Does she know she has two? I am the Other Mother.

45
LONDON, MAY 2010

A gale blew for the rest of the weekend, gusting so hard that Nick and Rose carried in the furniture and pot plants from their riverside balcony. Unseasonal rain drummed against the floor-to-ceiling window and the pealing of Sunday morning bells at St Mary's were whipped away by the wind. Rose's mind felt whipped up too, unable to eject Justine from her brain. She and Nick spent Sunday tiptoeing round each other. She suggested they watch football on television, he proposed going for her favourite walk in Battersea Park.

In the end, he went jogging and Rose drove to Richmond. To ask Bella for advice on what to do next, what to say next, and whether to tell Justine she could go no further with the job. The two women had become close after the search for Rose's birth mother and especially so afterwards, when Bella and John, Rose's dad, started dating.

'I want to help but I don't know how. Everything is a dead end. No names. No dates. Her story is pitiful. And I pity her.'

Now, Bella frowned. 'It's not your job to help, Rose, it's your job to do the research. You have to disengage from the personal stuff. Remember how I used to talk to you, when you were searching for your birth mum?'

Rose did remember. She'd been thinking about that all weekend, re-running her last conversation with Justine and replacing herself with Bella. She couldn't forget the notion that Bella was better equipped to be doing this job than she was.

'I told you this when you first talked about becoming an identity detective. You are qualified to do the research, but not to offer counselling.'

'I'm not, offering it that is.'

'But you seem to be doing it.'

Rose nodded reluctantly. 'Not on purpose.'

'Well then, you either have to get yourself qualified or employ someone who is.'

'Okay. I'll stick to research and document chasing. Facts. Is that acceptable?' As she said it, she knew it wouldn't work.

Bella nodded. 'You're a journalist, keep your conversations with Justine on that formal interview basis and you'll be fine. If you need help, just call.'

Rose went to bed early that evening. At the back of her bathroom cabinet she found an old packet of herbal sleeping tablets, out of date and not touched since her days at the *London Herald*. She swallowed one and gratefully surrendered to blankness. The bliss of not thinking.

Darya's chin nodded forwards, resting comfortably on her chest. Justine watched her, noting the new creases in the soft skin at the corner of her eyes, the light catching a silver hair sprouting from a mole on her chin. They were sitting side by side in the studio armchairs, facing the garden, with the French windows thrown open and the soft spring air turning the pages of the Sunday newspapers on the coffee table. Darya would sleep for an hour, tucked up beneath a woollen rug, full of tea and Mr Kipling cake, exhausted by the last ten minutes spent pushing the pieces of a Matisse jigsaw this way and that. 'Snow Flowers 1951': eight panels of unidentifiable flowers in orange, pink, white and green. A little like seaweed. Impossible to complete but Darya, who loved the colours, collected all the orange pieces.

Justine could not imagine how Darya must feel, knowing her mind was fading, knowing her memories were slipping away and unable to stop them. If someone was to custom-design a torture process, this would be it. She rose, brushing the wispy silver halo of Darya's hair as she passed, almost a non-existent touch but enough for Justine to feel connected with her. She knew these times were precious, and limited, and she felt overwhelming fondness for her friend.

There were no meetings scheduled, nothing pressing required by the gallery or Maud, no requests from Rose. It was time gained. She went to the shelves and one by one pulled out what she thought of as her headache paintings. Canvas after canvas, blood red, crimson, carmine, magenta and white, sometimes lemon and an orange the deep colour of Spanish clementines. She lined them up along the wall, gliding over the floor in stocking feet, moving the canvases as quietly as if a fractious baby had just fallen asleep. Darya slept irregular hours now, fitfully, as if disturbed by memories of life her conscious mind could not remember, as if unable to recognise daytime from night.

The paintings surprised her, the grouping making an impression where a single piece had failed. She turned some around, having painted on the back of some canvases – a habit learned in Málaga to save money – and curious about others that had been painted over rejected paintings.

These are really rather good.

They had a spontaneity that had been missing since her early collages. She considered each canvas, wanting to place them in a logical order. She saw a sharp, honest pain. Like a paper cut on a fingertip; invisible but deeply painful. When she was happy with the sequence, she sat on the floor with a pencil and notebook in hand to work out titles, dates and back story. There were fifteen canvases. Two were unusable, one possibly adaptable though she was loath to amend it now and lose the raw spontaneity.

She wasn't sure of Maud's response because, although Maud was always asking for smaller works to sell she preferred them to lock on to one of the big series. Maud talked about the building blocks of Justine's body of work. But these stood alone. She decided to call them 'Pain/Truth'.

46
LONDON, MAY 2010

Rose had never been good at waiting for someone else to respond – call back, email, send copies of reports by post – and was often tempted to go and do it herself. But years of journalism had taught her more could be achieved with a smidgen of patience. So on Monday morning, instead of nagging Lily, she worked her way through Kate's tiny diary. Leather-bound, black, small enough to fit in the back pocket of her jeans, with a slim pencil which slipped into the spine. Rose painstakingly checked each name in the Address section, searching online, cross-checking it with her list of the theatre productions Kate had appeared in. The first two numbers she rang were unobtainable. The next person on the list had died only weeks previously and so she made profuse apologies to the widow for being a nuisance. Finally, finally, she spoke to Madeleine Noach, who had acted with Kate in rep and was amazingly still living in the same first floor flat in Hampstead with the same telephone number.

The discussion was not as she expected. Madeleine, who seemed to be going deaf, kept asking who Rose was.

'I'm Kath Ingram's daughter. That was her stage name. Perhaps you knew her as Kate? She had your telephone number in her little black book.'

'Little black book? Those stories about Frederick Bell and me in 1963 were totally false. I won that part totally on merit. I acted with Olivier, you know. Twice. I was in *The Devil's Disciple*, dreadful costume, you'd think his films would have bigger budgets, and then something at the National. Was that *The Recruiting Officer?*' Her voice hesitated, and Rose could almost hear her brain ticking with the effort of remembering. 'I never lay on the casting couch, though I know many actresses who did. With some film directors it was the only way to get a tiny part. I could tell you some stories. One of them is famous now. A Dame.'

'Did Kath?'

'Kath who?'

'Kath Ingram. My mother.'

'Who are you again?'

And so the circle was completed only to start again. Rose asked about the wages, explaining that Kate had struggled for money and lived in a squat.

'Well, it was the Sixties,' replied Madeleine. 'Are you sure she didn't live in a squat to be trendy? Or to make a political statement? Lots of people did, you know. The money was bad, it is true, but I hear it still is. I was lucky, my grandmother left me a legacy which subsidised the meagre wages. No one could survive solely by acting in rep, you had to consider it as apprenticeship and learn everything. I knew one actress who dined out very well after performances. A different man every night. Good-looking ones too. She paid in another way, of course. One always pays in one way or another.'

Yes, there's always a price.

Madeleine was talking now about Vivien Leigh. It was clear to Rose that Madeleine neither knew who she was talking to on the telephone, nor if she had ever appeared on stage with a Kath Ingram. She thanked Madeleine and crossed her name off the list.

With her sixth call, Rose was luckier. Jeremy Bottle was set designer at the Crucible in Sheffield, where Kate had acted in the Sixties. Jeremy was too young to have known Kate but, when in desperation she called HR at the Crucible, they had transferred her call to him. He liked to talk, did Jeremy. About his current production, which was two weeks into a three-month run – a revival of Alan Ayckbourn's *Relatively Speaking* – the bitchy female lead, his last theatre, his big rival Gilly Something. Trying to get the conversation back under control and the subject back to the theatre, she asked where he had studied theatre design, hoping he'd perhaps understudied a senior set designer who would remember Kate.

'You're Rose Haldane the journalist, aren't you? I've just read your *Gallery*** interview. I studied fine art with Justy, dear, at RivesArt. Or course she was King in those days. I went to Amsterdam for my year out. Justy went to Málaga. That's where she met April who owns *Gallery***, as you know. Málaga is wonderful now, but it was very different in those days apparently, quite seedy. Nowadays there's a new museum opening each year, can't think where the money is coming from. Russian mafia, probably.'

Justy? April and Justine know each other?

Rose thought back over her dealings with April, and the commission for Gallery** that had introduced her to Justine in the first place. At no point had either April or Justine hinted they knew each other.

More secrets.

Jeremy was still talking, oblivious to the silence from Rose's end of the telephone. 'Rumour was she shagged her tutor in Málaga and got sent home early. She took some time out, no one was told why, but she came back late and passed with honours. Of course she did. She was, she is brilliant. That's why she's got work in the Tate and I'm a set designer.' He giggled. 'I met someone years later who told me Justine and April had both been shagging the same bloke in Málaga.'

Rose was gob-smacked. 'Err, Jeremy, is that all true?'

'Don't know, darling, but that's what everyone said at the time. There was another rumour about an escort agency, but I only ever heard that story once so it's probably rubbish.' And he giggled again, as if he were on a sugar high.

Is Justine still keeping secrets? I thought we'd turned a corner at Tariq's.

When was a lie well-meant and when was it damaging? She thought of Nick and wondered what he was lying to her about. She had decided not to be too hard on herself, and to trust Nick. So, by rights, maybe she should apply the same standards to Justine and cut her a bit of slack. But that went against all her journalistic instincts.

I can't back off. I have to ask the questions or I'm not doing my job properly.

Her ears were ringing with Jeremy's scuttlebutt, her head pounding with his giggles. She took a note of his mobile number and asked if she could ring him again if she had more questions.

'Delighted, darling. Absolutely delighted. Oh, and say hello from me to Justy when you see her next. *Arrividerci, bellissima.*'

Rose closed her eyes and recapped Justine's story, probing, testing. She grabbed her bag. She had some questions for April and needed to see her face when she answered.

'So,' said Rose.

'So?' April raised her right eyebrow in the sardonic way that Rose envied but never achieved. She didn't know what to say next, didn't know how to form her question casually. Her mind had emptied as if a tap was turned on and her intelligence flowed out with the water.

She's using the silent technique on me, damn her.

She wondered if April could feel the elephant in the room.

'Okay. I'm doing more research about Justine Tree and I'm checking up on her time in Málaga. I have some information that she, that you, both...' A pause. 'That she slept with her tutor in Málaga and got sent home.'

April swallowed a laugh. Rose hadn't expected that.

'Can I ask who told you this?'

'I don't reveal my sources. I'm asking you for confirmation.'

'Well no, it's not true. Not totally. Your information is partly true.'

'Partly?'

'Well, she didn't sleep with her tutor, not to my knowledge anyway, and she wasn't sent home from Málaga. She left of her own accord.'

'I was told that the two of you shagged the same man, that you had a massive falling-out and she went home to England.'

April screwed up her mouth. 'You've got a lot of twisted information.'

'Explain it to me then?'

April's story was tantalising but frustratingly light on facts. She had put the pregnant Justine on a bus from Málaga to London but didn't see her again for five years.

'We weren't at the same college, I was at Putney, and I didn't see her for years and years. Then one night I was out for dinner and she came in with a huge group. Damien Hirst, Gavin Turk, Gary Hume. Not her sort of crowd, I wouldn't have thought. Anyway I never saw her with a baby or talked with her about the pregnancy. I felt uncomfortable raising the subject with her.'

Rose was on the train home, reviewing her notes and thinking of the questions she should have asked. The train went into a tunnel and the lights flickered. Rose felt weary. April had given her confirmation of what she already knew, but no new leads.

Not even a sniff of a lead? There must be something.

She re-read her notes again, slowly. April had worked for an escort agency – why, Rose couldn't establish, she suspected April wanted to try being a rebel – and one night she saw Justine with a client she had also dated. And when pressed if she and Justine had shagged the same man, April had said, 'If you come back to me with a name, I'll try and help.' She hadn't denied the two women had been with the same man and probably argued about it.

Classic avoidance technique. In one of Rose's favourite films, *All the President's Men* about the Watergate scandal, *Washington Post* editor Ben Bradlee reads White House statements and describes them to reporters Bernstein and Woodward as 'non-denial denials'. In other words, a statement made to sound like a denial without actually being one.

Inspired by her two heroes, Rose decided to bluff it.

Rose's finger was millimetres from pressing the doorbell when Justine's front door opened and she appeared with a tiny lady with a cloud of dyed black hair. Rose stood aside to let them pass. A car drew up at the kerb, as if by prior arrangement, and a young man in a neat white nurse's uniform emerged. He took the cloud lady by the arm and manoeuvred her gently into the back seat.

Justine and Rose stood side by side and watched the car disappear round the corner before either spoke.

'That was Mrs Purvis. She used to live next door but now she lives with her son in Hammersmith. She still comes most afternoons to play Junior Scrabble with Darya. To be honest, neither can spell these days but they enjoy moving the tiles about and making patterns on the board.'

Justine smiled. Rose thought she looked exhausted.

'Did we have a meeting arranged? I'm sorry, I've forgotten it.'

'No, but I have some questions to ask.'

Justine nodded and turned back into the house. Rose followed, shutting the heavy door behind her. Along the corridor leading to the studio, she pressed her back against the wall to make space as three women and a young man passed out, calling farewells to Justine, juggling rucksacks and boxes. Neither woman spoke until they were seated in Justine's studio, which seemed to have been the location of a long meeting. The large rectangular table in the middle of the room was covered with a debris of paper, eight place settings with used water tumblers, discarded plates, vol-au-vents and sausage rolls. Rose had wondered about Justine's team, realising she couldn't run what was effectively a multi-million-pound business on her own. She must have a personal assistant, PR, marketing, sales, finance people and so on. Until today they had seemed invisible.

She turned back to Justine and found the artist watching her, as if she knew what Rose had been thinking.

That all this time I've underestimated her. Perhaps, I've even been quite condescending to her.

She felt ashamed. Her mother had a trick of knowing a Bible verse to suit any occasion and Rose was sure there was one which would fit this moment. Something about not judging other people without judging yourself.

'My team is rather messy but we had a lot to plan today. Eighteen months of exhibition commitments, promoting the current exhibition, planning the next series, a product licensing offer, PR requests, an invitation from a gallery in Brazil. I hate these kinds of days. All I want to do is paint, but I can't. I have to see the accountant and my lawyer and my agent.' She ran a tired hand across her forehead. 'You said you have some questions?'

'Yes.'

Deep breath, Rose.

'Why didn't you tell me you know April Masterson?'

'How is that relevant to your contract? We shared an apartment, that's all.'

'She's my boss.'

'I know.'

A pause followed while Rose reassessed, knowing she had started in the wrong place, her tone too aggressive, accusing. She tried again.

'I know from other sources that you worked for an escort agency when you lived in Málaga, going out on dates with men, escorting them to restaurants, official engagements, business dinners and such. I have a list of the agency's customers and I need you to tell me which ones to focus on.'

Silence.

She's not going to challenge my bluff.

She sought eye contact, a key element of any bullshit strategy, but Justine was staring at the floor.

'I'm not passing judgement. What you did was up to you, and I am not going to tell anyone else about it.' Then, remembering her realisation yesterday, she added, 'But if I am going to find your daughter, it would speed things up if I knew who her father is.' She looked directly at Justine now. 'So I need the truth. No more lying by omission. Could it be one of these businessmen?'

Justine's eyes continued to focus on the floor. 'I don't know how you know, I don't want to know who you've been speaking to. But how can you believe something a stranger's told you, how can you be sure they're telling you the truth?'

'Oh come on.' Rose let her anger show. 'Perhaps you should ask yourself why I should believe you? How can I be sure that what you tell me is the truth? You've lied to everyone, your parents, the media, for years. Your whole life is a lie and I think you're still lying to me or at least not telling me stuff. Is it such an ingrained habit that you're incapable of seeing where the line is between covering up your big lie, and telling an everyday untruth? There is not some big plot out there to unveil the truth of your life, *Panorama* and *The Sunday Times* are not running investigations. People don't care. It is your life, you do with it as you want. But you've asked me to find your daughter. If I'm going to be successful, you have to start telling me the truth. Otherwise I'm out of that door now and you will never see me again.'

Rose hadn't planned to say all that.

'I'll leave you to think about it.'

She took a step backwards towards the door and paused, hoping. If Justine was going to waver, she would say something now. Now. Now?

Nothing.

Her mobile beeped with an incoming email from Lily. It read: 'No docs found for birth in 1983 in UK of daughter Jenni to Justine Elizabeth King. Also checked Jenny, Jennifer, Jennie, Jeni, Jenifer, Jen, Jenefer, Genefer, Ginifer, Juniper, Ginevra and Jenniver. King, Kings, Kinge, le King, de King, Cing and Cyng. Sorry.'

Rose turned back to Justine, holding her mobile in the air.

'Is there something else you need to tell me, Justine? Why there is no record of Jenni's birth in 1983? Or have you conveniently forgotten that too?'

Justine's face was immobile.

Rose relished the bang of the door as she slammed it behind her.

Justine winced as the studio door closed and Rose's footsteps retreated along the corridor to the front door.

Rose's ultimatum and the bang of the door felt like a blow to her face. She rubbed her cheek as if it stung. She had grown to respect Rose, was beginning to feel she could become a friend, and now she wondered if Rose was right. Had she buried the truth so deep and covered it with layers of fiction so that even she didn't know which was which any more? Or was her brain forgetting the horrible stuff in an act of self-protection? Justine wasn't sure. What she did know was that she was tired of lying, or re-telling the same elaborately constructed stories that had come to be her truth.

Then tell her. All of it.

It would mean going back to that darkest place.

The memory never faded, the nightmare never dulled. Sometimes she hoped it was gone, but in the place where she was most truthful with herself she knew it would always come back. It always started the same way. A hand, her hand, reached out towards a large cardboard box on the outside of which was stencilled, 'Del Monte tinned peaches'. Her hand nudged open the overlapping flaps. Inside was a baby, frozen white. Its eyes wide open, staring, asking why.

Rose let herself out of the heavy front door and turned left towards the Tube station. It felt good to walk away, a relief. She would go home, type up her notes, send an invoice for work done and move the Justine Tree folder into 'Completed' on her Mac. Tomorrow she would send out some emails to editors with proposals for features. Flesh out a proposal for Tough Talk Productions. Real life. Working for Justine was surreal. Justine herself seemed to be the biggest obstacle to the truth and that was nuts. She turned the corner into Jermons Road and was thinking about a feature pitch for *Family History*

magazine, when she heard footsteps behind her. Heavy disconnected steps, uneven, someone running, but the sound was of
hard soles not trainers. Then she felt a hand on her shoulder,
heard deep breaths, smelt a familiar perfume. Shalimar. And
oil paint.

'Wait, please.' Justine gasped for breath. 'I'm sorry. I
haven't been fair.'

'No, you haven't.'

'I will tell you, if you want to listen.'

With mugs of tea in front of them, the two women sat
opposite each other across the wooden kitchen table. Rose
turned her eyes to Justine, afraid of missing the blink of an eye
or nervous gesture indicating the need for a huge pinch of salt.

'Did Jenni actually exist?'

Justine's mouth screwed up as if she was squeezing the
words out. 'Of course she did.'

'Then why is there no birth certificate?'

'Because I didn't register her birth. I meant to, but
somehow I never got round to it. And then I left her. I'm sorry,
I should have told you.'

'Yes, you should. It doesn't help me to trust you, Justine,
when you keep hiding things from me.'

'I'm not.'

'You are.' Rose knew she was on the verge of shouting.
She took a slow breath. 'You said you would tell me.'

There was a pause, probably only seconds.

'I don't know what to tell Jenni when you find her because
I don't know who her father is. I don't want her to think I was
a slut.'

Rose waited.

Be patient. Don't put words in her mouth.

Rose waited until it was plain Justine had no more to say.

'When you do meet her, if you meet her, you don't need to
tell her everything. Not if you don't want to. Take it one step
at a time.'

Justine nodded. '*Paso a paso.*'

'That's Spanish?'

Justine nodded. 'Federico used to say it.' A smile drifted

across her face, a warm smile Rose had not seen before. It made her seem years younger.

'Federico didn't know, I was too ashamed to tell him I was broke. Which I can see now is silly, but that's how I felt then. So I sold paintings to tourists.' She shrugged her shoulders. 'Not many, I was rubbish at it really. I earned the most money with an escort agency. It started out fine, I would go out with a man who wanted a partner for the evening. Usually it was a business event. And then, one time, I was offered extra money if the evening continued after the dinner.' The muscles tightened across her cheeks and her voice hardened.

'I hated it, but I did it. I paid my bills. The only person I hurt was myself. I have regretted it every day since. I told myself it was a necessity. That I could have done worse things, so I used the shame and put it into my art.' She took a long drink of tea.

Rose limited herself to a small nod, trying to repress her surprise.

'Most of them were one-offs, just evenings out. But Málaga was very different then. It was a small place and sometimes I'd see one of their faces across a room, but we never acknowledged each other. It was a decent escort agency, clean, safe. I didn't know their real names and they didn't know mine. I had one regular client, Andrés. He was – he was kind to me.'

She cradled the mug in her hands as if it were deep winter and her hands were frozen.

Rose waited but the silence dragged on until she thought Justine needed a nudge to continue.

'So, Andrés might be?' she prompted.

Justine's eyes were heavy, as if dragged from the dream of a long-gone time. She shrugged. 'It's hopeless.'

Rose was determined to get all the available facts before giving up.

'Do you have any photographs?'

Justine stood and went to the dresser. From a bottom shelf she took an old-fashioned photo album. The sort with a plastic covering for each page to protect the glossy photographs, each held in place by tiny plastic corners. She handed it to Rose.

'I'm not sure if this will help. All the photos were taken in Spain before I was pregnant. They're just snapshots really, a record of my time there. And I don't have a photo of Federico. I saw him every day so there didn't seem any urgency to take one. I never imagined.' Her words tailed off.

The album contained exactly the same sort of pictures Rose had of her own student days. Poorly framed pictures of groups of people, grinning, holding glasses of beer, tops of heads cut off, whitewashed by bright sunlight or cast by shadow, red eyes and bright shining teeth. She spotted a young April in one photo sitting alongside a dark-eyed beauty with long hair past her shoulder blades. They were wearing incredibly brief bikinis, lying on towels on a beach.

'That's Catalina, our third in the flat.'

But I don't want pictures of the girls.

'So Andrés could be the father?'

'Yes.'

'Weren't you on the Pill?'

'Yes, but it was the kind you had to take at exactly the same time of day and I was hopeless at remembering. You remember being that age; how could *I* ever get pregnant? That happened to other girls, not me.'

'So you and April and your third.' She hesitated, unable to remember the other name.

'Catalina.'

'You all shared a flat. Did you share boyfriends too?'

'No, we didn't. Catalina had her college sweetheart, Juan Antonio, and April kept herself to herself.'

'That's not what I heard. I heard the two of you fell out over a man.'

'Who on earth told you that?'

'Jeremy Bottle'.

'God, not him, he's a worm. Why were you talking to him about me?'

Rose explained about Kate. 'He'd read the interview in *Gallery*** and told me you'd been at college with April.'

'You don't want to believe a word he says.'

'So you didn't shag your tutor then?'

Justine's face blanched.

'He said that? He doesn't know, how could he know? No, I didn't. It didn't happen like that.'

She stood up, went to the sink and turned the cold tap on full. She stood, a glass tumbler in her hand, but made no move to fill it, watching the running water, oblivious to the aura of splashes on the worktop, tiled splashback and the front of her jumper. Eventually Rose stood, prised the tumbler from Justine's fingers, filled it and then turned to Justine and ushered her back to her chair. She stood while Justine gulped the water down as if she hadn't had a drink all day.

Rose didn't know what to think. She'd obviously pushed a trigger but to press Justine further about it now could be counter-productive. She explored the contents of the cupboards until she found a pack of expensive-looking biscuits topped with Belgian chocolate. They each chose one. Rose felt the welcome buzz of sugar and hoped Justine felt it too.

'Jeremy doesn't know what happened. No one does. I never reported it.'

'Can you tell me?'

A fleck of chocolate was lodged at the corner of Justine's mouth and Rose wanted to reach out a finger and wipe it away, but she made herself stay still.

'I've never told anyone.'

'Who was he?'

'Paul Willow, my tutor. I will never forget his name. He was brilliant, the best teacher we had. But none of the girls liked him. He was – smarmy.'

'He was English? How come he was teaching in Spain?'

'Do you know, I have no idea. It never occurred to me to ask, we were just grateful that he spoke English. He was my tutor so he took an interest in how I was settling into Spanish life, coping with the language, the workload, that sort of thing. He even lent me some money to get me through until my grant cheque arrived. But when I was late paying him back, he – well.'

'I can guess what happened.'

'No, you can't and I need to say it.'

Rose stretched her hand across the table. 'He hit you.'

'No, he raped me.'

Justine's face was wet with tears as she told how this man, this tutor, this teacher responsible for the well-being of his students, had abused a young woman in his care.

Rose felt so angry. She remembered her own university tutors, how supportive they'd been, encouraging when she wrote her first journalistic assignments, firm when she failed to hand in work on time. That Justine, who had had such a hard time in Málaga, should then have a tutor who was an abuser was so unjust. She walked round the wooden table, sat next to Justine and hugged her.

That evening, Rose sat on the balcony. Taking frequent, rather large gulps of cold white wine, she re-ran the conversation in her head. London was quieter now as it settled for the night; a solitary car drove across Battersea Bridge, the last helicopter of the day had departed the heliport. She was home alone. Nick had left earlier dressed in black tie, bound for some association dinner in the City. The flat was empty but the space felt good. Free air. On the table at her elbow was the now empty bottle.

She wrote a list of possible fathers. Federico, Andrés, Paul Willow.

She sighed. She wasn't convinced that knowing the birth father would help find Jenni. The men were in Málaga. Jenni was born in the UK.

Accepting she couldn't stop searching, she swallowed the last of the wine and turned her back on the dark river.

Just as she was drifting off to sleep, Rose realised she hadn't asked Jeremy Bottle about Kate.

47
LONDON AND SPAIN,
MAY 2010

After confessing her rape to Rose, Justine felt physically
battered and bruised. As if it had happened all over again.
Working hard at keeping her behaviour normal, she settled
Darya into bed for the night, clicked the toddler gate at the top
of the stairs and then ran a bath filled with calming pine bath
oil. She sunk up to her chin, breathing deeply of the scent. It
helped, but was not soporific and the hour was still early. So
she pottered for a while round the house, straightening things,
putting newspapers into the recycling bin, deleting a few
unwatched, never-to-be-watched things off the Sky digital box,
laying out breakfast things for tomorrow. Something drew her
to her studio. Not paint or leaves; instead she logged on to her
email. In her inbox was a message from Maud titled: 'Urgent:
Exciting Invitation'.

Justine had never returned to Málaga. She had been to
Madrid three times for temporary events at small galleries. But
Madrid was three hundred and fifty miles further north and felt
safe. The Exciting Invitation forwarded by Maud was a show
at the CAC, the Centro de Arte Contemporáneo. In Málaga.
When Justine lived there the building which now houses the
CAC beside the dry Guadalmedina river was boarded up. It
had been the city's wholesale market.

In her email, Maud practically begged Justine to say yes.
'This is a Huge Opportunity, Justine. We can break into a new
market.' That was Maud's vocabulary: route to market, positioning, merchandise offer, presentational merit, cost/benefit
analysis, margin, bottom line, cash cow. Justine wasn't sure
who the cow was supposed to be but had a horrible feeling

it was her. She didn't speak business jargon, and something in her rebelled at the commercialisation of what it sometimes felt was dragged from her body against its will. Galleries were opening everywhere now that the world had been reduced to the size of a long-haul flight. She wanted her work to be bought by the big three museums and put on permanent display. She'd made it into one, Tate Modern. Nothing so far in the Centre Pompidou in Paris or MoMA in New York.

Twice in the last three years, Maud had suggested putting on a show in Málaga. Twice, Justine said no. But saying no was getting more difficult and Maud was both irritated with and baffled by her continued refusals. Málaga was firmly on the global art map. When Justine had studied at the Escuela de Bellas Artes, General Franco had been dead only eight years. It was a kiss-me-quick-hat destination for tourists venturing abroad for the first time. Now people went to Málaga for art weekends to visit the Museo Picasso, Centro de Arte Contemporáneo and Museo Carmen Thyssen. The city had spent millions of euros on the arts, with more planned. Málaga branches of the Centre Pompidou and the St Petersburg State Russian Museum were being discussed.

She wished the Museo Picasso had existed when she'd lived in the city. It was because of Picasso that she chose Málaga, not Paris or Amsterdam. The thought of being able to see his mixed media, paintings, ceramics and collages, in the flesh, every day, made her heart burst. The Casa Natal was new since her time too; the ruined building of his birthplace with which she was so familiar had been reconstructed and opened to the public. A new airport terminal had just opened with more flights from European destinations, while traffic was diverted away from the coast by an outer ring road. The Escuela de Bellas Artes was not in a grey concrete block on the shabby *polígono* any more; instead it occupied one of the new modern glass and steel buildings forming the Campus Universitario Teatinos.

Justine knew all of this because, as well as the Málaga Turismo website being top of her favourites list, she had also developed the habit of googling 'Málaga photos' and followed no fewer than fourteen bloggers writing about life in the city. No matter the pain associated with the city, something pulled her back. On hot days in London, she compared temperatures on the BBC Weather page. She did the same on cold days. When she ate tapas-style food at a new trendy restaurant – *tapas* and *pinchos* were Instagram hits, Justine had eaten them everywhere from Shanghai to Cape Town, Milan to Santiago, Chile – she would remember Federico's olives, the slippery slices of *mohama* and *jamón*. No matter how expensive the restaurant, no matter how many titbits and pre-desserts served, none of it tasted as good as those meals she had shared with Federico on the bench beside El Jazminero. Perhaps Spanish food tasted best in Spain, as tea outside England was insipid.

Maud's email ended with a killer statement. The theme of the exhibition was to be Picasso and his sphere of influence. The CAC's permanent collection specialised in Spanish artists after 1980 – Victoria Civera, Juan Muñoz, José María Sicilia, Miquel Barceló, Santiago Sierra and Juan Uslé – but the curator also wished to include current non-Spanish art. Hence Justine's invitation. 'Man with Guitar' was to be loaned by the Musée Picasso in Paris, drawings for 'Guernica' were to come from the Reina Sofia in Madrid. The Museum Ludwig in Germany had promised to send Picasso's head of Dora Maar, plus two paintings, 'Harlequin' and 'Woman with Artichoke'. Best of all, the National Gallery of Art in Washington DC was to loan his lithograph 'La Colombe'; the dove.

The picture that had started Justine's lifelong obsession with art. Her dream, to be hung on the same museum wall as Picasso, seemed within reach.

That is how Justine and Maud came to be wedged into narrow airline seats, surrounded by a cheerful group of women all wearing pink t-shirts and headbands with silver pom-poms that danced in the blast of the plane's aircon. They drank champagne and ate chocolates ordered from the breakfast cart, while Justine nervously cradled a large cardboard cup of what the airline thought was English Breakfast Tea. Maud put on an eye mask and went to sleep.

Justine was struggling to deal with the contrasts with the last time she was in Málaga. Flights to foreign cities had to be reserved at a travel agent. The internet did not exist. Mobiles did not exist. She used cash, very occasionally she wrote a cheque. The Falklands War began and ended. The *Mary Rose* rose from Portsmouth Harbour. Mark Thatcher disappeared in the Sahara during the Paris–Dakar rally, and Michael Fagan broke into Buckingham Palace and sat on the Queen's bed.

The hens were singing, 'My Heart Will Go On', so Justine selected Joan Jett on her iPod and settled her noise-cancelling headphones comfortably on to her ears. With her eyes closed she could see nothing, but her mind was in full-on anticipation mode.

What will it look like? How will I feel?
And, most frightening of all.
Who will I see?

As guests of the CAC, which hadn't existed in 1982, they were staying at an expensively cool boutique hotel, which hadn't existed either. Málaga's Old Town, the only part of the city not flattened during Nationalist bombing raids in the Spanish Civil War, where the hotel was located, was achingly familiar to Justine. When she had left the city twenty-seven years earlier, she had put a sticking plaster of fictions and obfuscations over the truth of what happened. She wasn't sure if she was ready yet to rip it off.

Their rooms were on the top floor, quiet and all white. Justine unpacked, poured herself a glass of Lanjarón fizzy water and looked out of the window. She could just see the roof of her old building on the Plaza de la Merced where she had lived for seven months. She downed the water in one and, after rummaging in the mini-bar, re-filled her glass with vodka. That went down in one too.

And now, she was free for the afternoon and evening. Maud had drinks with a friend and dinner with another agent tonight. Tomorrow was crammed with meetings with museum officials and curators at the CAC plus chats with the directors of existing and proposed Málaga museums. Lunch was to be a formal affair with the British Council's director and various local tourism and culture people. Tomorrow evening, it was the *Noche Blanco* when Málaga threw open its doors for everyone to celebrate culture. Events included music on the streets, free museum entry, dancing on the beach, food, wine, beer and all kinds of free entertainment that would last all night. Justine had checked out it out online before she left London, watching video highlights of last year's event on the official website. The Spanish did one thing really well; they could party all night long.

She pulled on a hat and sunglasses and walked towards the Plaza de la Merced, amazed how the narrow *pasajes* near the *catedrál* were unchanged: cobbles underfoot, the walls leaning inward from vertical, balconies with black railings. To left and right she dodged round revolving postcard stands outside tiny shops packed inside from floor to ceiling with racks of flamenco dresses for children, fruit bowls made of olive wood, blue and white ceramic ashtrays and posters of bullfighting. The intervening years melted away in the afternoon May heat. She turned the corner into the *plaza* where she had lived. Where there had been boarded-up empty buildings were now tourist shops selling expensive sculpture and paintings. A line of red double-decker tourist buses queued at the kerbside. The biggest change was Picasso's birthplace, the Casa Natal, now a stylish cream building with tourists waiting patiently for admission. Justine joined the queue, shuffling along, experiencing a patience so unfamiliar; her impatience stilled by the magnetism of at last walking in the footsteps of the boy Picasso. This was where he finished his father's drawing of a dove.

And that's where it started for me, with Davy Jones.

Her memory was clear and unadulterated by the intervening forty-something years.

The woodie was getting restless in his box in front of the Rayburn. He could move his wing and her mother was making noises about him being shifted from the kitchen to the shed. Justine wanted him to get well and fly again, but she wanted to keep him too. So far she had thirty-three sketches of him. On Saturday the touring library van arrived, and she quickly found a book about Pablo Picasso. She flicked through the illustrations and found one of a dove, but it was not what she expected. It was a black line drawing on a white background. Pigeons weren't white. Davy Jones was mostly grey with a pink breast and two white patches where his collarbones would be, if birds had collarbones. Justine made a mental note to ask her father.

She closed the book with a bang.

'Are you all right, dear?' The lady who drove the library van was sitting at the tiny desk where she kept the wooden box in which were stored everyone's library cards. They were little envelopes, really – blue for children, red for adults – into which the library lady slipped the ticket for each book borrowed. When you returned the book, the ticket was put back into the book, which was returned to the shelf.

'Are you searching for something in particular?'

Justine was standing beside the adult section of the book-shelf, out of bounds to children.

'I'm trying to find out about Picasso because my dad said he drew a pigeon and I've got a pigeon. Davy Jones.' She waited for a reaction.

'Davy Jones,' she said again, 'like the Monkee. The English one.'

There was no sign of recognition on the library lady's face.

She started to sing 'Hey Hey We're the Monkees', including some dance moves popular in the playground. The library lady did not smile. Justine stopped dancing.

'He's not a pet, he's wild. But he's injured and I'm trying to make him better. But,' she held up the Picasso book, 'this isn't a drawing of a pigeon. It's white.'

Maybe Picasso didn't draw a pigeon after all, or maybe it wasn't Picasso who drew it but another artist altogether. But her father was always right. He knew everything about birds: where swallows went in the winter; why owls sicked-up their poo; why a woodpecker's beak didn't break with all that hammering.

'Well now, let's have a look.'

They both leant over the page, studying the illustration.

'Yes, I see what you mean. This is actually a print, a lithograph. The title is French for dove; it's called 'La Colombe'. Picasso made it in 1949 when he drew another very famous dove picture, 'La Paloma', which is also sometimes called 'The Dove of Peace'. I know it's confusing; two pictures of doves, made in the same year, one title in French and one in Spanish. But, you see, although he was born in Spain Picasso has lived in France for many years.'

Justine nodded, not wanting to admit she was a little muddled up.

'And are you learning Spanish at school?'

'No, French.' She hated French. She turned a page, wanting to talk about Picasso again.

The library lady bent to the bottom shelf and pulled out a small thick book with a robin on the front cover. 'Dove, dove,' she said, running her finger down a page at the back. 'Here we are. "Pigeons and doves".'

Justine watched as she turned the pages. Rock dove. Stock dove. Woodpigeon. Collared dove. Turtle dove.

Davy Jones was a woodpigeon. Picasso's *paloma,* or *colombe,* was not there.

She shut the book with a bang, feeling cheated.

'Perhaps Picasso,' the library lady hesitated, 'perhaps he improved the bird.'

'What?' Her mother said saying 'what' was rude. 'Sorry, I mean, how did he improve it?'

'Well, artists don't just paint what they see. They change things; they use their imagination to improve what they see and to invent totally different things. If they paint a portrait of a person, they might make a big nose slightly smaller, or sticky-out teeth a little straighter.'

'You mean Picasso lied?'

'Perhaps.' And the library lady smiled at her.

It was the smile that confused Justine the most; for an adult to smile when talking about lying contradicted everything she had ever been told. She considered the fact that painters lied. It had never occurred to her that they didn't just paint what they could see. She considered the art book again. There was a strange picture on the front cover, painted in grey, black and white, no colours, showing people and animals screaming. They reminded her of demons.

'Do you like drawing?'

Justine looked up. She nodded.

'Well, in that case I think we can break the rule this once and let you withdraw an adult title. Do you want to take that one home with you? You'll have to promise to take care of it and bring it back next Saturday morning.'

'Really? Thank you, thank you very much.' Justine handed over her junior blue library ticket. The library lady slipped a yellow ticket from the front of the art book, wrote a date on it, slipped it into the pocket of Justine's blue card and filed that in the wooden box. Justine couldn't wait to show her father the picture of Picasso's white dove and compare it with Davy Jones.

The library lady watched as Justine tucked the book carefully under her arm. 'Next week, I want to hear what you think about Picasso. He is a brilliant artist. Thankfully people have realised exactly how brilliant he is while he is still alive, although he is quite elderly now. Many artists, you know, are very poor all their lives. Van Gogh for example had to borrow money from his brother. His pictures only become recognised and worth a lot of money after he died.'

Justine thought this sounded most unfair.

As she jumped off the bottom step from the van to the pavement, the library lady called after her.

'Did you know, Picasso called his daughter Paloma.'

As she stepped out of the Casa Natal into the evening sun, Justine dwelled upon a photograph of the boy Picasso. He looked four or five years old, hair neatly parted, white bowtie at his neck, buttoned jacket and a pleated knee-length skirt. She found it difficult to reconcile this boy with the effortless artist who oozed art from every pore. She turned towards the cathedral, her feet knowing the way, and in a few hundred yards there it was. The Museo Picasso. With excitement bubbling in her chest, she stepped into the lobby and felt the coolness of the white marble chill her flesh. Her goosebumps were induced by excitement. The Palacio de Buenavista, the building which housed the museum, was a national monument, built in the sixteenth century by Diego de Cazalla. She wondered fleetingly what Federico would think of the architectural restoration if he were here, and suddenly it struck her that the team of local architects who worked on the project may, just may, include someone Federico had studied with. She had walked along the Calle San Agustin many times, it was the main route between the apartment on the Plaza de la Merced and her bus stop to college, but she had no memory of this building. In all probability it had been one of many anonymous places boarded up and covered with posters and graffiti.

She bought her ticket and was admiring the proportions of the internal courtyard with its heady mixture of Renaissance, Mudejar and contemporary architecture, when there was a small cough and click of heels on the marbled floor behind her.

'Señora Tree? It is Señora Tree?'

Wishing she had worn a bigger hat, she turned. In front of her stood a small, bespectacled man wearing a very expensive lightweight linen suit. He was beaming at her.

'What an honour it is to entertain you here. *Encantada, encantada.*'

So in that way Justine's impulse became an official visit with the director of the museum, various curators and the PR. In the way of the modern art world, business cards were exchanged. Everyone spoke English, though she was surprised to find at least half of them were fluent in Russian, Chinese and Arabic too. Perhaps Maud was right about business opportunities here.

By the time she left, Justine had agreed to ask her agent to confirm details of a contract for a Justine Tree exhibit in a side gallery currently full of Giacometti figures. She thanked them politely in Spanish, to their surprised nods of appreciation, and excused herself by inventing a dinner engagement in Marbella.

Never in her wildest dreams did she expect to exhibit at the Museo Picasso. She'd expected it to be full one hundred per cent of his works. She wanted to shout out loud. But as she walked towards the cathedral, the walls of the narrow passages seemed to brush her shoulders and she saw, as she knew she would, the café where she met Federico. Where she learned about coffee and fried fish.

The last time I was here, I was looking for him but he was already dead.

She turned, feeling tears blur her vision, walking, pushing past bodies, almost running towards the light where the narrow passage widened. It was early evening now, tourists were eating at outdoor tables and the smell of food wafted through the air. *Patatas a lo pobre*, a peasant dish of fried potatoes, tomatoes and peppers. *Albondigas*, spicy meatballs. *Berenjenas con miel*, deep fried slices of aubergine dripping with honey.

A hundred yards further on, she found the pitch where she had tried to sell her paintings to tourists. Now another group of students stood beside their easels. On display were kitsch scenes of Málaga but also black-and-white photographs of beaches, distorted line drawings of architecture and faces, a mosaic of Picasso's face made up of bits from different Picasso paintings. There was a lot of Picasso-style on sale. Justine watched as a student talked to a customer for an instant portrait, settled the elderly lady in a canvas chair and with a finger beneath her chin, moved the lady's face left and right before settling on a position.

Justine walked on. Across the road was her old bus stop; she had run here so many times to catch the college bus. Not wanting to miss a class, desperate to see Federico. Sometimes in the intervening years it felt as if he had not existed, that her mind had invented a love that was not there. Conjured it from need. Filled a vacuum. Or turned a student friendship into something else. She had nothing tangible to remember him by, not even a photo, and longed to hold something which had belonged to him, which he had touched, so she could place her fingers where his had been. It would be a sort of connection. The most real thing of Federico's that she'd had, was lost.

Perhaps.

She turned another corner and walked into another memory; they were coming now with each step.

The last time I was here, Federico held my hand for the first time.

She stood on the edge of the Paseo del Parque. The ground beneath her feet was the same but this was not the city she remembered, of grey concrete blocks and dereliction. It had been a city without confidence in itself. This Málaga had machismo. It was a bullfighter, strutting in his sparkling suit ready for the performance to begin, serving its delights to tourists who had money to spend. And she liked it. The sun was sinking and, as if a bell had chimed calling everyone outside, local people were emerging from stuffy houses out into the cooler air. Just as she remembered, couples walked arm in arm along the paths, teenage girls linked up in a line sometimes six and seven abreast, small boys kicked footballs and small girls skipped while the old men sat on benches in the shade of palm trees and plane trees, talking quietly and puffing on cigarette after cigarette. It was cleaner than she remembered, the gardens more manicured. There was a rose garden she couldn't recall. She was searching for a familiar bench beside an old friend. El Jazminero.

The statue wasn't there. Feeling dislocated, she wandered in circles, doubting her memory but knowing she was correct. She stood in the centre of the small shaded square, surrounded by trees and bushes, where they had so often sat. But the circular garden did not enclose the flower-seller; instead there was a tree with a label. A Chinese gingko.

She walked to the next enclosed garden, hoping to see El Cenachero, the fish-seller, but he had been replaced by a tree too. There were tears in her eyes as she set out to walk the entire Paseo, back and forth, each footpath. She found a couple of old friends: the nymph with the water jar, and Bernardo, the bust of a solemn man with a Shakespearean-style manicured pointy beard. She finally found El Cenachero sidelined beside the main road, near the entrance to the vast underground car park. Weary but determined not to leave until she found El Jazminero, she asked at Tourist Information. Her request was greeted with bemusement. She spoke in halting Spanish, frustrated that she could not make herself understood. Then another assistant arrived wearing a small metal Union Jack badge on his lapel. She repeated her question in English.

'*Sí*. Now he is named El Biznagero, but is not in Park of Málaga. He is in the Rosaleda.' He saw the blank expression on Justine's face, and unfolded a city map. With his pen he drew a circle.

'Here.'

It was the rose garden she had passed earlier. Her feet were tired now, and as she retraced her steps along the Paseo it seemed twice as long as it had earlier. When she finally reached El Biznagero, the magic had gone. It was the statue she remembered, but he stood in the open, no sheltering trees to give privacy. He was set on a plinth and reached high to the sky. He was unreachable, untouchable. And there was no bench to sit on.

It was as if El Jazminero had never existed.

She walked along a side street, threading her way between parked cars. Mourning the loss of their special place, angry with the town council for changing things, she stopped dead as another memory bludgeoned her.

The last time I was here, it was after Andrés.

The assault of the past started to overwhelm her. This was why she fought against returning. Her pace quickened, not stopping until she reached the Plaza de la Merced again. She circled the monument to what she thought of as Picasso's bench facing the Casa Natal, where she had often sat, asking him for advice. But someone was sitting on it. She was disappointed. She wanted to be alone. Turning half away, the moonlight caught the arm of the person. A dull bronze. A statue. Picasso sat on her bench in this nineteenth century square where he must have sat as a child, watching life unfold in front of him while doves flew overhead. She sat beside him. The bench seemed the same, the rough concrete providing no comfort to her bottom. She twisted to look at the opposite side of the square to her old apartment and picked out the window which had been her bedroom. So many times she had stood there, staring across at the ruin of Picasso's home, its plaster peeling like a cheap clay face mask, its windows boarded up and covered with peeling posters.

I was a ruin too, when I ran.

Hard to believe this elegant cream mansion was the same place. Everything was changed, time had passed.

The last time I was here, I despaired of being a real artist.

She had felt such a fraud, as if someone would eventually work out that she was a makeweight, a lightweight, a no-weight, a girl from the dead-end of East Yorkshire who'd drawn pictures on the back of old bits of wallpaper and her father's carpet brochures.

Now I am a different sort of fraud.

She was exhausted after so many years of squashing her memories, beating them flat like a piece of tough meat being tenderised. At this precise moment she was terrified of seeing Andrés or Willow walking towards her. As the sun set and the lights came on in the smart tapas bars around the *plaza*, she walked slowly back to her hotel. Ready for a bath and bed.

Then someone was calling her name.

'*Guapa. Justina. Soy yo.*'

And there was Catalina. A huge smile on her face. Beside her stood two children. Boys, both with her dark chocolate eyes. About twelve and eight, Justine guessed.

From nowhere, envy flooded every inch of her body so she ached as if beaten.

They talked until the early hours, perched on high stools at a dark bar down an alley, busy with locals not tourists. Juan Antonio came to collect the boys and Justine greeted him with affection.

So some things do last. I was so consumed by my love, I didn't see anyone else's.

She tried not to stare. Maria Catalina Alba Roman was beautiful. She had always been pretty but now she had matured into a gracious elegant Spanish lady. A mother. Beside her, Justine felt vacant. She struggled to put a word to it.

They talked easily about art school, art today, Justine's art, April, Juan Antonio who was now a successful architect and local politician, and Catalina's work teaching sculpture at the Escuela de Bellas Artes.

Justine laughed when she heard this. It felt right, it completed the circle.

'It has changed. *Todo*. Everyone we knew is gone.'

'Gone?'

'*Sí.*'

'How gone?'

Catalina ran through a list of professors who had taught them. Retired. Moved. Dead. Promoted. Living abroad.

She had to hear it said out loud.

'Willow?' Justine forced the word from her mouth.

'*Muerto.*'

Justine breathed out, deep from the furthest corners of her lungs where the dirty mucky air lingered.

48
LONDON, MAY 2010

Rose found Paul Willow listed on an art industry website. Next to the dates of birth and death was a list of his employment including 'Professor of Art, Escuela de Bellas Artes, Málaga, Spain.' She didn't waste time trying to trace the escort agency on the assumption that the clients would use false names and that Justine had never known the surname of Bernadita. Rose did google the address given to her by Justine but it was now listed as a shoe shop. The image was clear on Google Street View. She found an online listing of Spanish genealogists, selected one based in Málaga, and sent off an email requesting information about Federico Gala.

Curious at the growing discrepancies between Justine Tree the Artist and the real woman who in her head Rose referred to as Justine King, she explored the official Justine Tree website. She was seriously impressed. The depth of content was way beyond what she expected and she made a mental note to mention this to Justine. There was the usual biography, works, press cuttings and reviews but also a section aimed at primary school teachers with suggestions for art projects, and a blog. Justine seemed to update this weekly with entries ranging from what she was working on that day, to her thoughts on the latest big London exhibition, to her feelings of loss at the recent death of an American artist.

Rose spent fifteen minutes watching a video about Justine making art in Yorkshire, on a remote clifftop where she grew up. It showed her walking along a path, gathering bits and pieces as she went; pieces of grass, leaves, pebbles – things that Rose could have walked past without considering them as art materials. Then Justine had knelt on the ground, folded out a wooden board and secured a canvas to it with bulldog clips, and proceeded to combine all her foraged things together with glue and paint to create, what? A work of art? A painting? A collage? Outdoors? Rose didn't know how to define it, but the finished effect was beautiful. Wild, like the scenery, wind-swept, bleached by sea salt. 'Cliff/Wind/Sea 53' was later sold at auction, according to a linked news article, for a six-figure sum.

I haven't considered the Yorkshire connection.

She searched online for 'Justine Tree' and 'Yorkshire' and got thousands of entries, articles in local newspapers, talks at libraries, charitable fundraising by Justine for her local RNLI at Flamborough Head and a photograph of her planting a tree at a bird reserve.

She checked her UK atlas. Flamborough was a village and Flamborough Head was a large promontory of land sticking out into the North Sea roughly halfway between Hull and Middles-brough. The local paper was the *Bridlington Free Press*, so Rose logged on to the website and searched for 'Justine Tree'. Up popped some of the stories she'd already found via Google. Then, on a whim, Rose searched again for 'adoption' and set the date limits at 1982-1985. In the way of selective seeing, when you fancy buying a red car and suddenly notice all the red cars on the road that had previously been invisible to you, one headline leapt from the page in flashing lights.

'Happy ending for baby left on doorstep'.

She gasped. All the elements were right. A baby girl was left on a doorstep in Bridlington in 1983.

It's her. It has to be. How many babies were abandoned in Bridlington that year?

In her enthusiasm she jumped up and knocked her chair backwards, sending it skittering across the wooden floor-boards. She reached for her mobile. Each ring seemed to take a minute.

Pick up, pick up.

'Justine, it's me. Rose. Where was the doorstep where left your baby?'

'Hackney.' Her voice sounded faint against a noisy back-drop. Wherever she was, it was windy.

Aaagh.

'You're sure?'

'It's not something I will forget.'

'I'm sorry, that was crass of me. Did you leave anything else with Jenni that might help connect the two of you?'

'Like what?'

'I don't know, a letter?'

'I wrote a letter to her afterwards, the one I gave to you. You do still have it, don't you?'

'Yes, it's safe.'

Rose put the phone down, feeling unsatisfied. If finding Jenni was as simple as making a few searches on Google, Justine or Lily would have found her easily.

So why does Justine need me? What can I do that she can't? What am I missing?

And that's when she realised she had allowed herself to be sidetracked by her belief that Justine was wilfully misleading her. She had resented Justine for telling lies, for wasting her time. But what if Justine was telling her the truth, at least as much of the truth as she was able, and that she simply didn't know?

I have to think of the places that either Justine can't access, or she doesn't know exist.

She knew just the person to ask.

'What is it exactly that you need to find out?'

Was there a hint of weariness in Bella's voice, or was she being over-sensitive? Rose believed facts were black and white, set in stone, not imaginary. To her, *Star Wars* meant Ronald Reagan's space defence system, not a movie. Facts had finally let her down, and so had her training. Her lack of social work accreditation was hindering her access to official records. Only so much could be achieved by journalistic schmoozing and it was clear now that being a journalist wasn't enough. Not all records were digitised or in the public domain. Rose was embarrassed at having to ask Bella for help and vowed to do something about it, vaguely wondering how one qualified as a social worker. It was top of her to-do list once Justine's commission was finished.

'Only two things.'

Confirmation of whether Jenni had lodged a letter of contact with the Adoption Contact Register saying that, if her birth parents wished it, she would consider meeting them. And whether a paper trail existed to prove Justine's story that she left Jenni on a doorstep in Hackney.

Rose was new to the subject of abandoned babies. Had never considered how anyone could do that – put a baby down, and walk away – though she'd seen occasional stories on the television news about an unwanted infant being named after the person who discovered it or the nurse who cared for it. Now she tried to imagine how it must feel to give birth, alone, probably somewhere grim – a public toilet, an abandoned building, a lonely bedsit. Being cold and coping with the pain, the fear, the uncertainty. In these imaginary situations, it was always cold and raining. Rose couldn't imagine being so stupid as to get into such trouble, not to be in total control. She remembered how Lily, when she was pregnant, had described her body as acting with a mind of its own. She likened it to being driven by someone who had never had a driving lesson. Rose hadn't fancied that and, from what she knew of Justine, she didn't think she would either.

So how do you abandon a baby?

The thought process must be agony: to keep your baby knowing you would do a bad job, or sacrifice your own motherhood and hand your baby to someone else who could be a better mother than you? It must feel like the utmost failure.

No wonder I didn't get those 'Green' paintings.

For the first time she felt protective of Justine and wanted to shield her from the worst of Jenni's anger. Because there would be anger.

This is why Nick and Bella told me to disengage.

49
LONDON, MAY 2010

It turned out that the reason Justine's voice sounded so faint on the phone was because she was in Spain. Málaga. Where, Rose understood, she could not bear to revisit. But she was bubbling, that was the only word for it. She'd been offered an exhibition at the Museo Picasso and had met Catalina, the third girl in their apartment. Justine was flying home tonight, and they agreed to meet at Tate Britain tomorrow afternoon.

Rose arrived early and took the opportunity to stroll the halls. She hadn't been here for, oh, at least three years. Admiring the Turners, she vowed not to leave it so long next time.

Perhaps working with Justine has given me a taste for art.

She found Justine standing in front of David Hockney's huge 'Bigger Trees near Warter'. It filled one whole wall. The two women sat side by side on a narrow stone bench. The room was empty.

As Rose was working out how to start, Justine spoke first. She gestured towards the canvas. 'I grew up only a few miles from there.'

'Where is it exactly?' Rose was fed up of playing games.

'A few miles south of Brid.'

'Brid?'

'Bridlington.'

Rose swivelled to look her straight in the face. 'I'm facing a dead end. There's one long shot which a social worker friend is checking out, but I have to tell you I don't know what else I can do. If there's something you haven't told me yet, now would be a good time.'

She raised her hand because Justine had jumped as if pricked by a needle.

'Yes, I know there are secrets. If you really want to find Jenni, you have to tell me everything. Everything. The smallest detail, all the irrelevant things of daily life, the embarrassing things you are still hiding.'

Justine put her head in her hands. 'I don't want to go back there. I am so ashamed.'

'Well then, I'll never find her.'

Justine closed her eyes. She didn't want to remember, had spent a lot of hours in the middle of the night and a lot of paint trying to erase the memories, had constructed a professional persona of 'single woman fulfilled by her art'. She could feel the heat of Rose's gaze upon her, knew she was trying to help, but wished she would go away.

'Please, Justine. Try.'

Justine opened her eyes and found Rose was watching her with excitement, as if she suspected everything Justine had fought so hard for so long to hide was about to be told.

'Okay, okay. Just give me a moment.' She closed her eyes and let her mind drift back to 1983.

'A friend from secondary school helped me. Susie. I bumped into her in the supermarket queue in Brid. One glance and she seemed to know everything without me having to speak. She was the first person who actually understood why I couldn't stay at home to have the baby. She'd grown up where I did, she knew my parents, her upbringing was pretty much the same as mine. She was very kind. So when I said I thought London was best because there I could be anonymous, she told me about her cousin.'

'In Hackney?'

'Yes. Bridget lived in a bedsit in a house in Hackney and was advertising for a room-mate. She couldn't afford the rent on her own.'

'She had a baby too?'

'She miscarried.'

Rose didn't know what to say.

'Bridget was amazing. She helped me find a job as art assistant at a primary school and I worked there until just before the birth. The rent was low so I was able to buy baby things at bring and buy sales, church halls, Women's Institute, you know. I was proud that I managed, and I know Mum and Dad would have been proud too.'

Oh, if only you'd had the courage to tell them.

Rose felt sorry for Mr and Mrs King.

'I crocheted a beautiful lemon cot blanket.'

So she did want to keep the baby.

She opened her mouth to speak, then shut it again.

'I gave birth on August second. Between us, Bridget and I, we managed. I still worked part-time and she did shift work at a printing company. She was amazing, I could never have done it without her. Most of the time we took it in turns to care for Jenni, and our downstairs neighbour Mrs Gledhill was always happy to help out for the odd hours in between.'

Rose didn't think it was a secure, long-term arrangement.

Justine looked at Rose and glared with such intensity that Rose wondered if she had spoken aloud.

'It wasn't a proper solution, I knew that, but it felt secure compared with how life had been. And after all that's what women always used to do. They supported each other and managed while the men disappeared. That summer was wonderful. We went out every day, some days we'd walk for miles. I took her into central London to the National Gallery and showed her all the paintings, and we visited all the monuments and sculptures in Whitehall and along the river. Her favourite was the Neon Tower on top of the Hayward Gallery, which was new and quite edgy for London then. One hundred and eight fluorescent tubes, flashing colours. It seemed magical. I even entertained the idea of becoming a light sculptor. I could see a life ahead of me with art and Jenni. Then one teatime we got home and there was a policewoman waiting.'

She took a long swallow of tea.

'There'd been an accident at the print works. Bridget was in hospital, being operated on. Her arm had somehow got caught in between rollers and she was dragged into the machine. They were trying to save her arm, there was talk of amputation. Well I left Jenni with Mrs Gledhill and went straight to the hospital, but I was too late.'

The tears were hovering at her jawline again but she didn't seem to notice. Rose leant across the table and gently brushed the wetness away.

'She died?'

Justine nodded. 'I struggled to pay the rent after that. It was too much for me on my own and no one wanted to share a cramped room with a woman and a baby. My hours were cut at school because they had to teach less art. They let me go. And then Mrs Gledhill had a stroke.'

'You couldn't cope.'

'I tried.'

'Of course you did.'

'I know I should have asked for help, gone to Social Services, gone back to Yorkshire, but I was afraid of the questions and I wasn't thinking straight. I can see that now. It's exhausting, being a single mum surviving in one room, living from minute to minute. There's no escape, no rest, no privacy, no respite. I set the alarm for 4am one morning and dressed Jenni in as many pieces of clothing as I could get her into. I wrapped her up in the blanket I'd made for her, so tightly she was swaddled like a terracotta baby from Ancient Greece.'

Rose stared at her.

'I saw a figure, in the British Museum, years afterwards. As soon as I saw it, it reminded me of Jenni that night.'

'Where did you take her?'

'I thought if I left her early in the morning she would be found soon. I didn't want to leave her at night, it would be freezing cold and I worried she'd catch pneumonia. I wanted to do it right.'

Rose didn't doubt her.

'So where?'

'I left her at Clare Scott's house. She was the headmistress at my school. She was a good woman, I knew she would do the right thing. I was sure she wouldn't connect it with me, after all I was just another ex-employee at Hightrees Primary and our paths hadn't crossed much.'

'In Hackney?'

'10 Rusham Close.'

'And then what did you do?'

'I ran away.'

50
LONDON, SEPTEMBER 1983

She felt thin, stretched, like a cheap rubber band pulled too tight to the brink of snapping. Clouds, heavy with the grey of night, began to thin and lighten as morning arrived. A triangle of blue sky appeared. Justine walked, unaware of direction; just away from that house with its neat front garden and painted gate. Cars were passing her now, buses, hurrying pedestrians, groups of schoolchildren in uniforms. Every footstep was another step further away from Jenni.

Don't think about it, don't think about it.

But that was all she could think of. The swaddled bundle. The doorstep. At a zebra crossing she waited for a pause in the traffic, then turned and looked back in the direction of Hackney.

Is she still there? Has Mrs Scott found her yet? Is she cold? I could just pop back and check.

But she knew she couldn't, shouldn't. But it was so hard.

Someone will find her, take her home and put her in a warm bedroom. Be there with her every minute of the day. A mummy and a daddy to introduce her to crisp apples and roses and the seashore. To draw stick men and teach her the piano. I can't do any of those things. I don't deserve her.

She walked for hours without direction, stopping once to drink water from a public drinking fountain, and again to use a public lavatory. The cold was seeping through the thin soles of her shoes now. There had been a heavy shower at midday but she had continued walking. She didn't pause until she saw, set back from the pavement, a wide archway and then double doors, wooden, studded with iron nails. A porch. She hesitated. Just a short sit down, then she would go on.

It was a church unlike any she had been in before. It made the Methodist Chapel at Flamborough seem a temporary affair with its corrugated-iron roof and two tubs of weedy daffodils flanking the plain front door. This place was cavernous. It seemed empty, dark; a heavy scent hung in the air. Warm. Quiet. Just what she needed. She took a deep searching breath and fatigue hit her like a bus, pressing her feet into the cool marble floor. She should think of a plan but first she would sit, rest. She glanced round for a pew and realised why the place seemed so huge. There were no pews, no pulpit. She turned on the spot. Lined up along a back wall were a dozen wooden chairs. She sat down and leant her head back against the wall, closing her eyes. When she opened her eyes again she had no idea how much time had passed. Her surroundings came into focus, lit by sunlight from an ornate glass panel in the ceiling. The rain must have passed because sun was streaming through the window on to dark wooden walls covered with lavish gold and richly coloured panels. Gold reflected everywhere. Jesus everywhere. To Justine, raised on a meagre religion of hard seats and plain walls, this was food for her creative soul. Drawing energy from the art, she sat up straight. That's when she noticed she was not alone. A figure stood in the shadow alongside the opposite wall. A thin figure, head draped in a shawl.

Justine stepped into the pool of light. The woman, for now Justine saw the handbag hanging over her forearm and heard the jingling of bangles at her wrists, raised her head and smiled. Her high cheekbones, upright posture and simple, elegant clothes made Justine feel like a rag doll.

Years later, Justine would wonder what would have happened if she had not met Darya Kushkupola.

51
LONDON, MAY 2010

They were thrown out of the Tate at six o'clock just as the red light on Rose's digital recorder started to blink. They parted at the kerbside. Justine called a black cab. Rose crossed the road to the bus stop; she was heading straight home to Battersea. As soon as she got in, she went straight to her desk and rang Bella.

'I have the name and address of where she left Jenni.'

'And?' Bella's voice was calm, as if she knew what Rose was going to say.

'10 Rusham Close, Hackney.'

'Yes.'

'Mrs Clare Scott?'

'Yes.'

'Have you any other information?' Rose was surprised, her heart filling her chest.

'She was healthy, released quickly from hospital into short-term foster care, and listed for adoption. Because she ticked all the popular boxes – girl, white, less than a year old, healthy – there were a lot of enquiries.'

'And?'

'She was adopted by a Mr and Mrs Weatherington from Islington.'

'Islington?'

'Yep.'

'Are they still in Islington?'

'No. I've done some preliminary checks but haven't found them yet.'

Is nothing in this case straightforward?

Rose stifled a sigh.

'You will find them, Rose. They are called Naomi Grace and Sebastian Albert. That should be a sufficiently unusual combination, together with the surname Weatherington, for you to track them down. I'm sure they're still in London. Statistically, people don't move far from home throughout their lifetimes. I think the average is thirty miles.'

Rose tried to feel a big sense of satisfaction at what they had achieved today.

'Okay, I'll go online and search for Jenni Weatherington.'

'Think a moment. The name Jenni does not exist in connection with this baby. Justine is the only person who knows that name.'

'Right. So I still can't find her.'

'Better to try the parents.'

'Thanks, I will. You're brilliant, Bella.'

'That's my middle name.'

'Seriously, without your help I couldn't access the records.'

'But without your digging in the first place, we wouldn't know which records to look for.'

'So we're a double act.'

'We are.'

The smile in Bella's voice as she said goodnight made Rose smile too.

With a guesstimate of the Weatheringtons' ages, Rose searched first of all for their marriage record. She found it in 1981. They were married at Islington Town Hall. There they were in the index: Weatherington, Sebastian Albert to Naomi Grace née North. Not for the first time, Rose wished the census records weren't frozen for a hundred years. What she wouldn't give to get a glimpse into the Weatherington household in Islington in 1983. But the current generation's secrets were put away for a century, supposedly to save everyone's blushes. So Rose searched the local electoral roll instead and there they were again. Mr and Mrs Weatherington of 115 Copley Avenue, Islington were registered to vote. Every year until 1984. Then nothing. With frustration she logged off and slammed down the lid of her laptop with a crack. Swearing, she examined the case. There was a splinter-thin line along the lid.

With half a glass of wine inside her and dinner prepared ready for Nick's return – a tomato sauce bubbling on the hob, parmesan grated, basil washed and ready to be torn, and a bag of fresh tagliatelli waiting to be tipped into the saucepan – Rose felt a little more in control.

She taped up the crack in her laptop lid, then logged online again. 'Jenni Weatherington' produced nil results. She hated it when Bella was right. So she tried 'Sebastian Albert Weatherington' and up popped twenty-three pages of entries. Son returns to family dairy business. Quoted in a farming magazine about milk production processes. Local farmer's son wins agri-feed grant for university. In a conference speech, professor challenges traditional diet of dairy herds for optimum animal performance. Annual results for Bempton Valley Foods. A taste test on the Waitrose website for Woldtopper, a 'deliciously flaky and salty cheese, ideal with a tart apple'. Local businessman Seb Weatherington to stand for Bempton Village Council. Directorship listing for Bempton Valley Foods. Bridlington Beer Festival, sponsored by Bempton Valley's Woldtopper.

Bridlington?

She checked her UK road atlas. Bempton was the next village to Flamborough. Rose's head was spinning at the irony of it.

Please tell me that Jenni didn't grow up a couple of miles from her mother's childhood home. So much for Bella's thirty miles theory.

She read the search results again, sorting, making notes, looking for a timeline, for knots and twists. Checking she'd got the correct Sebastian Albert Weatherington. Born in Bempton, son of a dairy farmer. Won bursary in YorkFeeds 'new talent' competition. Attended university in London, BSc Zoology. Worked for various agri-foods businesses including a period in America. Returned to the UK to his old university, various positions, finally professor. Inherited the family dairy farm. Returned to Yorkshire, transformed an almost bankrupt farm into an award-winning cheese producer using milk from its own Guernsey pedigree herd.

Rising excitement made her fingertips fly across the keyboard. With a lump in her throat, she started a fresh search for 'Naomi Grace Weatherington'. Top of the search list was a newspaper listing under Deaths.

'Naomi Grace Weatherington, née North. Died after a long illness, sadly missed by husband, daughter and two brothers. Funeral at St Michael's Church, Bridlington. No flowers please, donations to Marie Curie Cancer Care.'

A daughter? Rose logged on to online records of gravestone inscriptions, crossing her fingers that the gravestones at St Michael's had been digitised.

They had. The text of Naomi's headstone read:

Naomi Grace Weatherington
Now at peace
Born October 22, 1957
Died January 2, 2010
Sadly missed by husband Seb and their beloved three children Elsie, Tom and Joe.

Elsie?

Rose's heart fluttered as it hadn't fluttered since she read the name of her own birth mother. Her fingers fumbled on the keyboard now as she searched the birth records for Elsie Weatherington, putting the year of birth at 1983. Nothing. 1982, nothing. 1984, nothing.

Ha!

She searched every year. Elsie Weatherington had not been born.

Where did you come from, Elsie?

She so wanted to share this with someone. Bella didn't answer, so Rose left an excited message on her mobile, curious if Bella was out with her father. Bella and John had been dating for two years now and Lily recently predicted an imminent announcement. Both girls loved Bella and saw how much she loved their father. A demonstrable love, evident in the way their fingers sought each other, a hand resting on a shoulder, a cup of tea proffered without request, the sort of gestures Rose realised she had rarely observed between her father and her mother Diana. She was just about to call Justine's mobile when a key rattled in the front door.

'Hello-oo.'

It was Nick. A brief kiss and a quick hug, and then she poured out the story of her monumentally successful day.

'It has to be her. I was just about to call Justine with the news.' She gave him another kiss to which he responded enthusiastically.

'I'm always happy to interrupt you.'

More kissing, until Rose tried to extricate herself. 'I have to ring her now.'

'Why? To tell her what? That you might have found her daughter? Might.' Nick pinned both her hands together with one of his and stroked her cheek with his spare hand. 'I know you're excited, love, but are you one hundred per cent sure?'

'Ninety-nine per cent.'

'Not enough. I thought you believed in facts?'

'It's just that I want to be honest with her. I swore to myself when I started this that I wouldn't hide anything. I won't lie to her.'

I'm lying about too many other things at the moment.

She flushed as she thought of her stash of contraceptive pills.

'I'm not suggesting you do, honey, just that you confirm it before you get her hopes up. This is such a huge thing.'

He's right, damn him.

'Won't you find more documents in Yorkshire and be on the spot to set up a meeting straight away?'

Drive to Yorkshire? Ugh.

Rose felt Nick staring at her, as if he could hear her thoughts.

'You don't want to go to Yorkshire because you're afraid of being car sick. So take a sickness tablet and get the train. Trains go everywhere you know, Rose. Go first class, it's a smoother ride. You can keep the receipts, I'm sure Justine won't mind paying.'

Rose grimaced.

'I thought you were brave.'

I am, I'm Strong Rose.

So she went online and booked two train tickets for the next day. Bella was coming with her.

52
YORKSHIRE, JUNE 2010

Next morning, the platforms of Stevenage station were flashing past their train window when the call came. Rose sat opposite Bella, her hands clutching the edge of the table to stop them drumming the chipped Formica as she struggled to contain her excitement. It was difficult, listening to half a telephone conversation as Bella talked.

'What? What?' Rose mouthed the words silently at Bella, who responded with a thumbs-up.

'We've got it.'

Rose sighed with relief. Bella had insisted that they have the documentary proof before they contacted Elsie.

It's really going to happen. We've found her.

She wrote notes as Bella outlined the document trail. The foundling discovered at 10 Rusham Close, London E8 on 12 September 1983 was named Clare Rusham and put into temporary foster care in Ilford. She was subsequently adopted by Mr and Mrs Weatherington and re-named Elsie Clare.

They agreed to stay the night in a hotel in Hull. Both felt strongly it was important not to invade Elsie's territory. They would travel on to Bridlington once Elsie said yes to a meeting.

Bella made the initial call. As an intermediary, she explained to Rose, she was in a position completely impartial and unthreatening to the person who had been found. Unlike Rose, who could be assumed to be on Justine's side. Sometimes in adoption reunion, the person being sought did not want to be found. In these circumstances, contact with the researcher, who represented the searcher, could be fraught and counterproductive. Although with her head Rose understood this, had always known the protocol, with her heart she couldn't help feeling pushed aside. For the moment, she listened. There was a brief explanation and a long period of silence as Elsie talked, Bella listened and Rose got increasingly fidgety. The outcome was that yes, Elsie would meet them. Yes, she knew she was adopted but knew nothing about her birth parents.

After one long, interminable night in the Hull hotel, the final leg was via another train. It crawled as a snail, leaving a trail of iron tracks behind reaching all the way to London where Justine had awoken, eaten breakfast, and was probably now painting, still in ignorance. Rose's head was full of Justine and Elsie, yes, but also of the future and her identity detective agency. She would reunite people lost through adoption.

The fields and hedges flew by in a blur as Bella read a novel and Rose made notes in her notebook. They passed level crossings across narrow empty roads, old abandoned signal boxes. She noticed a lot of tractors. The train meandered through the flat countryside, straining and rattling round long curves, so many curves that Rose wondered if they were going in circles. They passed through station after station. Cottingham. Beverley. Hutton Cranswick. Driffield. Nafferton. Country names. Weatherington was a country name too, it could easily be a village along the railway route.

The meeting was held in the café of a country house called Burton Agnes Hall, a few miles south of Bridlington. Rose and Bella arrived half an hour early, anxious to find the right place. Standing outside the café's half-open stable door was a younger version of Justine. Taller, Rose thought, with black hair and glowing skin. She didn't need to check a photograph to be sure this woman was Justine's daughter. Her eyes filled with tears. It was a reaction she hadn't expected and she blinked them away.

They were the only customers. They sat at a table in the corner, with mugs of tea and a plate of chocolate brownies in front of them. There was a pause, the sort of pause you get in a blockbuster film just before the volcano erupts. Rose took a sip of tea and stole a look at Elsie who was answering a question Bella had asked about Burton Agnes Hall. If this was an interview for an article, she would have described Elsie's emotional state as 'bubbling with supressed excitement'.

Rose waited for silence, and then put her mug down. Its tap on the table was like a full stop to Elsie and Bella's polite exchange.

'So, Elsie, on the telephone yesterday Bella explained how your birth mother has been trying to find you and wants to meet you. Now you've had a day to think about it, how does that sound to you?'

Elsie nodded. 'Yes, definitely. I want to know everything.'

'Good. We're here today, Bella and I, to talk about what happened before we introduce the two of you.'

'Is she here?'

Elsie stood up suddenly, her knee banging the table so the crockery clattered together. Tea spilled. Bella caught a wobbling milk jug. Rose stood too and put a hand on Elsie's arm.

'No, Elsie, she's not here now. Just us. We'll arrange another meeting, when everyone is ready.'

They both sat and Bella offered round the plate of brownies. They each took one and for a few minutes the air was full of the sound of chewing.

Elsie broke the silence, her voice higher than before, sounding younger than her twenty-seven years.

'I don't really understand why you are here, and not her? Why couldn't she find me herself?'

'She tried. Many times, over many years.' Rose paused, searching for words.

Bella picked up her thread. 'The process is not easy. The document trail for adoptions is practically non-existent, done on purpose to protect the people involved from being found if they want to remain anonymous. Some people never know they were adopted and some birth mothers deny they ever had a baby. There are protocols in place to protect families today from past secrets being revealed without care and due process.'

Elsie shook her head, not side to side but with a little upward twist to the right which made her long, beaded earring swing like a quivering aspen leaf. Rose smiled; Justine shook her head in the same way.

'I have always known, since I was small, that I was adopted. I can't imagine not knowing. How it must feel, to sit here now and not know I was adopted?'

I didn't know.

Rose remembered the smell of dust in her social worker's office, the cheap light bulb casting yellow light on the paper Mrs Greenaway was trying to read. The sound of her heart thudding so hard against her chest wall she thought it must be moving her blouse.

She heard a quiet cough, and another. Bella spoke.

'This can be an emotional process for everyone, Elsie, and that's why we will take it one step at a time and not rush.'

Rose was grateful that Bella took charge. She felt incapable of pronouncing her own name.

How arrogant of me, to assume I could do this when I have no training. To assume I can do it better than a professional. I am so lucky to have Bella with me. Without her, I wouldn't be here now.

With that thought came a realisation about the future.

I need her, if I'm to make Kindred work.

She gave her head a tiny shake to re-order her thoughts away from her business plans and bring herself back into the room. She focussed again on Bella and Elsie.

'I've always wondered why.' Elsie's voice was small and quiet, asking the question but not as if she wanted to hear the answer. 'Why she didn't keep me.'

Ah, the whys.

'Your mother was a student when she became pregnant. It was unplanned, a big shock. She was young, abroad on her own. She had little money and no support. She tried to keep you, but couldn't manage. It was very hard for her to give you up.'

Elsie nodded slowly. 'I thought it must be something like

313

that, I hoped it was.' Her fingers twisted and untwisted through the handle of the mug.

Rose noticed her fingernails were edged with a dark line, as if her hands had been insufficiently scrubbed. Dirt, or old nail polish? And then she remembered Justine's nails marked with a similar stain.

Oil paint.

'You say she was abroad when she got pregnant, so does that mean my parents are foreign?'

Oh, why does she have to ask that?

'Your mother is English. We're still in the process of identifying your birth father, and,' she glanced quickly at Bella who nodded, 'I think it's best to warn you we may never know who he is.'

Elsie nodded slowly, as if the nodding were helping her to absorb the information. Her eyes were focussed on the plate in front of her, chocolate crumbs dotting the plate's design of strawberries entwined with a gold line.

Bella caught Rose's eye and made a minute movement with a white envelope in her hand. Rose nodded back.

'Would you like to see a photograph of your mother?'

Elsie drew her hand across her eyes and Rose noted the sharp arrow of her brows, shaped as a wrong-way-up V.

'Yes please.'

She took the envelope from Rose and opened it. There was one photograph inside of a middle-aged woman with short dark hair, dark eyes, and brows like upside-down V's.

'Oh.' Elsie's hand flew to her mouth. 'She's familiar, as if I've always known her.'

She studied the photograph carefully, her eyes lingering on the woman's features one by one.

'I've seen her somewhere.'

'She lives in London but she grew up in Flamborough.'

That was a shock.

'Flamborough? But that's the next village.' She studied the photograph again. 'What's her name, are you allowed to tell me?'

Rose looked at Bella again, who nodded.

'She's called Justine.'

Another gasp. 'I know who she is. She's an artist. I'm taking art and photography classes at college in the evening. We did a project on her last year.'

Rose smiled. 'She's written a letter to you.' From her bag, Rose withdrew the blue envelope Justine had given her on the day she commissioned her to find Jenni. 'Just in case you find her,' she had said, 'this is what I wrote on the day I gave her away.' The envelope was sealed.

Elsie breathed deeply then ran her finger beneath the flap.

My dearest Jenni,

Today I did something I am ashamed of. I gave you away and know I will never see you again. I did it to give you a better life. I am alone and have no money, I can't pay the rent on our room or buy food, I've been trying to manage but the nights are getting cold and I fear the winter will make you ill. I want to protect you from pain, from unhappiness, from unkindness. You are such a cheerful baby, you blow spit bubbles when you giggle and it is such an infectious irresistible sound. I love you so much that it hurts me to leave you. I don't want to let you go, but I know I must. For your sake. You deserve a Mummy and Daddy who can give you everything you deserve. Please don't hate me because I couldn't cope.

I love you and you are forever in my heart.

Your mother, Justine

Tears were on the brink of spilling down Elsie's cheeks.

'I was called Jenni?'

Rose nodded.

After the signature was a second paragraph written by the same hand, in black ink, not blue. It was dated this year.

Darling Jenni,

Not a day has passed since I wrote the note above that I have not thought of you, loved you, and wished you every happiness in your life. I did what I did in the hope your life would be better than the one I could give you. I was so poor and in a rough place in my life, I was doing a bad job of being a mother and you deserved the best start in life. Now I wish I had tried to cope, but I am stronger now than I was then.

Not a day has passed when I haven't wished we could meet so I could tell you I love you, and that I did what I did through love. I know you have your own family and I do not want to upset anyone or cause any distress to your adoptive parents to whom I am so grateful. They have done what I could not. So if you cannot meet me, I do understand. But be sure that I will always love you, as long as I live.

Wishing you a happy life, your mother, Justine.

Elsie breathed out. It was a long, slow sigh, Rose thought, as if she were expelling a breath held deep within her since her birth. Her eyes did not leave the blue sheet of paper. And then she drew the letter to her lips, and kissed it. She held on to it tightly, her fingertips bleached of blood by the pressure.

Rose didn't know what to say. The intensity of the moment was nothing she had experienced, to be sitting alongside someone at the moment of such a personal revelation, of being the vehicle of that revelation.

Without me, Elsie wouldn't be sitting here now.

Finally, what she had achieved sunk in.

Not yet, an internal voice of caution warned. *It's not finished yet.*

Elsie passed the letter to Rose and gestured for her to read it. It moved her to tears. She realised the main emotion she was feeling was jealousy; she was jealous of this tearful young woman, jealous because she was going to meet her birth mother.

And I never will.

Bella's words broke the emotional spell. 'Justine wants to meet you, Elsie. You can say yes today, or no, or think about it for a while. This process goes at your speed, no one else's.'

Slowly, Elsie lowered her gaze to her hands, folded neatly on the table before her.

'She's in London.' Rose spoke quietly. 'She doesn't know about our meeting today, so it'll take a while to arrange.'

'That's okay then, because I have to talk to Dad first.' Elsie stared at Rose then. 'You won't know, there's no reason why you should know.' She paused as if trying to extrude something alien. 'Mum died at the beginning of this year, so I'm back home helping Dad with my two younger brothers. I have to tell him about this the right way.'

'Of course you must. Take as much time as you need,' Rose said. 'You're very fortunate, Elsie, being able to meet your birth mother. For many people, this chance comes too late.'

Elsie looked closely at Rose's face, as if seeing her for the first time. 'You're adopted too?'

Rose felt the burn of Elsie's stare and wanted to turn away, but with an effort she maintained eye contact. She summarised her own story. 'So you see I know a bit about what you're feeling, the questions you must have.'

'And now you know everything.'

'No, not everything. I'm not sure that's possible for an adopted person.'

Elsie was waiting. Rose knew she wanted more but didn't know what to say. Avoiding her eyes, she looked out of the window at the formal garden surrounded by towering trees. She waved her hands about in what she thought was the shape of a large oak tree but then recognised was heart-shaped.

'I think of myself as a tree, many hundreds of years old, which has been cared for by many different people who pruned me and watered me and gave me fertiliser. I can't say which part of me is the result of a particular person's efforts. I am the whole tree, they made me *me*, and I'm grateful they did.'

Elsie was nodding.

'Mum and Dad told me I was always colouring and painting from when I could first pick up a chunky crayon. They encouraged me even though neither can draw for toffee. Dad's attempt at drawing my pony looked more like a mouse than a horse. Then at school I was good at computing and realised I could apply it to art, so that's what I do. I design brochures for Dad's business. He makes cheese.'

She smiled and shrugged then turned to Bella. 'Are you adopted too? Is it a qualification for your job?'

Bella shook her head. 'No, I'm a social worker. My mum was a teacher, my father a probation officer. All pretty standard boring stuff.'

'Absolutely not boring,' said Elsie. 'What you do, reuniting people like me and my – my mother. Justine. That's an amazing job.'

Oh how Rose recognised that pause.

Mum, Mummy, Mother, Ma, Mam.

She was trying it on for size and Rose knew the feeling.

Elsie reached her hands across the table and the three women linked fingers, connected, sharing the moment.

'Thank you so much, for what you've done.'

The atmosphere was heady with good vibrations and it came as a shock to Rose when she realised she hadn't said the difficult thing. In the strategy she had agreed with Bella beforehand, the subject of the abandonment would be covered today. But Rose hesitated about breaking the mood.

How to bring things back down to earth?

She decided to change the mood, do something. Food. She jumped up suddenly, so abruptly that she knocked her chair backwards. In the flurry to right things, she was aware that Elsie and Bella were staring at her.

'More tea, I think.'

She strode over to the counter and ordered tea, rapidly changing her order when she saw the clock on the wall. It was lunchtime. Three other tables were now occupied and Rose realised she was hungry. When she returned to the table with a tray laden with sandwiches, flapjacks and assorted soft drinks, Bella was sitting there alone.

'I don't know what to do about the abandonment,' Rose hissed, as she transferred the food from tray to table. 'I should have said it earlier, and now I'm afraid it'll put her off meeting Justine.'

'Just say it.'

'I can't. Not without leading up to it. It'll be a shock. We don't know how she'll react.'

'How I'll react to what?'

Neither Bella nor Rose had sensed Elsie's return. She was standing behind them and for the first time Rose recognised how tall she was. Nudging six foot. Surely Justine wasn't that tall?

'If there's something bad, I'd rather know.'

Elsie sat in the seat opposite Rose. She reached for a ham and salad sandwich. Rose watched her crumple the plastic wrapping into a ball, which immediately un-crumpled itself back into its original sandwich shape.

Elsie took a bite of thick sourdough bread, and set the sandwich on her plate. Her teeth were white and straight, orderly and neat. She chewed and swallowed.

'Please tell me.'

'Okay.' Rose's mind had gone blank. Why hadn't she rehearsed how to say this bit?

'This isn't going to be easy to hear, Elsie. Your mother didn't give you up for adoption in the usual way, I mean she didn't formally hand you over to a social worker.'

Elsie waited, her fingers folding the sandwich wrapper into neat squares again and again as each time it unfolded. Finally she gave up and smoothed the wrapping flat and pushed it beneath her plate. Her abandoned sandwich had a single mouth-shaped bite missing from it. Pieces of lettuce and York ham overlapped the slices; rough bread edged by a pink and green frill.

'Did a neighbour report her or something?'

'No.' Rose looked at Bella for help, but Bella was staring at her tuna sandwich.

'She gave you to a work colleague, someone she trusted to do the right thing. The headmistress of the school where she worked as a part-time art assistant.'

'Right. And?'

'In Hackney, she left you in Hackney. At Mrs Scott's house.'

'What, left me as if I was an Amazon package?'

It was coming out all wrong so Rose told Elsie the whole story from the beginning, keeping as close to Justine's own words as she could. Then she waited. For Elsie to cry, to shout, to get up and walk away.

For a moment she said nothing, then reached again for the blue letter and read aloud.

'Today I did something I am ashamed of, I gave you away and know I will never see you again.'

Her voice wavered slightly, but there were no tears in her eyes.

'That's it, isn't it? That's what she means. That's what she was ashamed of. But she did it because she loved me.'

Rose knew she should stay quiet but instinct told her to speak.

'And she still does.'

'When you said something bad, I thought you were going to tell me she left me in a wheelie bin. But she didn't, she left me with someone she trusted.'

'The teacher's name was Clare Scott.' Rose smiled as understanding flooded Elsie's face.

'Clare? Mum and Dad called me Elsie Clare. Oh.' She was smiling through her tears now. 'Justine must have been so strong to do that, mustn't she? To walk away from her baby, to walk away from me. Oh my.'

She held on to the blue letter as if she would never be parted from it, while her right hand was thrust deep into her coat pocket as if searching for her mother's grasp.

'Do you want to meet her?' Rose held her breath.

53
YORKSHIRE, JUNE 2010

One day later, Justine's train travelled on the same rails as the train that had carried Rose and Bella. She felt more scared than she had since she ran from the Astraea Clinic twenty-seven years ago. It was a different sort of fear; her heart was pounding like a turbine and her eyes were prickling. She rubbed them and felt the smear of mascara which she knew would make her eye bags seem double the size. She pulled a used tissue from her jeans pocket and spat on it, dabbing at the soft skin beneath her eyes, knowing it was absolutely the last area you should rub ferociously, but rubbing ferociously all the same. She rubbed her sleeve over the back of her mobile and squinted at her reflection.

Great.

Now her eyebags were red and puffy.

What will she think of me?

Her fear was both logical and illogical. She couldn't wait to see Jenni but wanted to run in the opposite direction. She wanted to see her baby blue eyes, wondering what colour they were now. Wanting to know, but not. Wanting to run, but not. To steady herself, she let herself sink into the memory of Federico's eyes, knowing there was danger in doing so in case Elsie's eyes were not deep velvet brown, but unable to deny herself this glimpse of what was still a vacuum in her life. Strangely, the memory gave her strength, as Federico himself had given her strength. She could see now that her pregnancy and what followed had made her a stronger woman. Not at the time, of course; at the time she had been a mess. But afterwards, once she'd come through the shock and grief and shame and out the other side, she had attacked the world. Would she be an artist today if she hadn't met Federico, hadn't struggled in Málaga, hadn't borne Jenni and lost her? She certainly wouldn't have met Darya, wouldn't have painted 'Green', sales of which had surged beyond even Maud's expectations. Not that it was all profit; huge expenses had to be deducted plus Maud's commission and salaries for her staff, but enough would be left for her to help Elsie, in whatever way she needed help. Because Justine was determined to be there for her, even if Elsie at first didn't want her. And she was prepared for that, expected it. She had tried to imagine herself in Elsie's place, a woman turning up out of the blue, claiming to be the mother who had not wanted her years ago, but now did.

She is brave enough to meet me. The least I can do is be as strong as she is.

54
YORKSHIRE, JUNE 2010

Justine spent the night at Seaview Cottage in her childhood bedroom, but hardly slept. She'd been up for hours when, the next morning, the village taxi pulled up outside ten minutes early. It wouldn't take long to get there, but Justine would not risk being late on this, of all days. As the taxi approached Burton Agnes Hall, she was taken with the beauty of the place and wondered how she had never visited it before. She'd checked the website on her iPad while on the train yesterday and knew it had been owned by the same family since the original manor house was built in the twelfth century. Family connections going back that far were beyond her comprehension. The house now combined the original Norman house and its later Elizabethan addition.

Old and older, living side by side.

It made her wish her parents were here to meet the granddaughter who grew up within walking distance of Seaview Cottage.

She was an hour early for her meeting. The café was empty, except for a young girl serving behind the counter. Justine shifted in her chair, her eyes darting to the doorway then back to her watch, like a lizard watching a fly just out of reach. She wanted to be seated at a table when Elsie walked through the door. Why? A power thing? A control thing? She didn't want to think what that said about her.

Fear. Insecurity. Shyness. Yes to all of them.

She ordered a coffee. She'd never been a great coffee drinker, but it was comforting to hold the hot mug and somehow tea didn't seem strong enough. Coffee was part of putting on a uniform, getting ready, preparing for the unexpected. In her head, she ran through what she wanted to say.

'I'm sorry.'

Two words said it all.

Most of all she was desperate to see what Elsie looked like. *I hope she hasn't inherited my non-existent earlobes.*

Another glance at the door.

I can't assume Elsie will be like me, Mum and Dad, Grandma and Granddad. After all, I resemble Dad but behave worryingly like Mum.

Only now was Justine beginning to realise how their parenting had been influenced by their own childhood when they had lacked so much that, nowadays, people took for granted. Central heating, university for everyone, workers' rights, equal pay for women, maternity and paternity leave, satellite television, the internet and mobile phones. She was sorry that Elsie would never meet her King grandparents, never know how similar they all were. Any dissimilarities didn't matter because they were family.

There is a primary genetic connection that can only be severed by death. Jenni and I connected so briefly. I broke it knowingly, cruelly and Jenni was so young she couldn't know something was missing.

And with that recognition came the worst memory, still so clear it could have happened that morning.

55
LONDON, SEPTEMBER 1983

She found the cardboard box beneath Bridget's bed. It was full of clothes, washed and folded. There was a faint smell of must, as if the clothes had been put away slightly damp. The box was strong, stapled, just the right length and depth. She emptied it. Inside, the base was patterned with orderly rows of rings, the indentations of cans. Peach slices. Into the bottom she placed a cushion covered by a clean, brushed nylon blanket, folding and re-folding it so it fitted snugly in the bottom and up the sides without uncomfortable ridges. She was creating a nest, warm and padded, so Jenni would be safe inside, protected from the elements and shielded from the curiosity of passers-by. Over the top she would tuck the lemon blanket.

She tried to think of every eventuality. The one which most concerned her was the possibility that someone should pass by in the early hours of the morning and stop to investigate a brown cardboard box on the front doorstep of a perfectly ordinary house. She prayed for a lack of nosiness. She also worried about air and considered piercing holes in the cardboard but decided to simply leave the top open and unsealed. She re-arranged the folded blanket in the shape of an envelope so Jenni could be slipped between the folds, her face free of covering. She worried about the limited space because she did love to kick out on waking up; stretching, limbering up for a new day of exploration. The box would have to do.

It was their last night together. Jenni fell asleep in the cradle Justine had bought for £1 at a bring and buy sale. It listed slightly to the left and the paint was chipped, but it did the job. She made sure to stick to their normal bedtime routine, a feed, a lukewarm bath, tickling tiny fingers and toes. Justine didn't know the words to any children's songs so she hummed 'Eye of the Tiger' and another whose title she didn't know but it was about how hard it was to say sorry. Neither seemed particularly suitable for a baby, so she switched to 'Twinkle Twinkle Little Star' for which she could remember both tune and words. Jenni went to sleep and woke as usual for a feed. Justine treasured these last few hours. She sat beside the cradle, hearing every breath, seeing each twitch and snuffle, amazed that she had given life to this independent being so similar and yet unique.

Too soon, the hour hand of the clock approached three in the morning. Then four. Time for one last feed. Justine had done her homework, consulted an A-Z of London in the library to check the route and written step-by-step instructions so she wouldn't get lost. She calculated it would take thirty minutes, which was a long way to carry a baby in an awkward cardboard box but instinct told her not to use the pram. She knew she would be an odd sight. There was a risk she may be seen by someone walking to the industrial estate in the next road on their way to the early shift in a warehouse. She was banking on the fact that a woman carrying a box at five in the morning would seem less strange than one pushing a baby in a pram.

Now. It's time to go.

She tried not to think things such as 'this is the last time we will both be in this room' and 'she won't come here again', but thought them anyway. Her plan worked, she didn't take one wrong turning, saw no one as she passed from commercial buildings and storage units to terraced streets, then lines of bungalows with front gardens. She arrived in Rusham Close five minutes ahead of her estimate. She would kiss her gently, one last brush of the soft hair on her head, and then she would go.

Then something happened she had not planned. She put the box carefully on a crumbly brick wall round the corner from her destination, taking the chance for a breather. She pulled the cardboard flaps apart and, as she bent forwards, two large eyes stared solemnly back at her. Wide awake eyes. It was an unwavering look, as if Jenni knew something out of the normal was happening. Justine stifled a yelp but her daughter did not murmur. Justine gently stroked her face with the tip of a finger, and hummed 'Twinkle Twinkle' again. So softly that someone walking on the other side of the road would not have heard. But there was no one there. This was a quiet suburban road; bedroom and kitchen lights were still off. Justine watched her daughter's eyes close again, her lids heavy with sleep and the security that comes with the sight and scent of her mother.

I am a traitor. I am a despicable being. I don't deserve to be a mother. I don't deserve to be alive.

She almost picked up the box and walked home. The only thing that stopped her was her empty purse. No coins for the electricity meter, no money for food.

She deserves better than that. She deserves a proper mother who can care for her. I can't give her the things she needs.

With her heart breaking as if split by the heft of an axe, Justine folded the cardboard flaps shut, picked up the box and walked to the house of the headmistress Clare Scott. She was glad afterwards for the interlude on the crumbly brick wall as there was no chance to say farewell. The front gate was open and she tiptoed up the path. The house had the sort of porch with a little roof but no door or walls, designed simply as shelter from the rain, somewhere to stand for a moment while groping for your house keys. On either side of the path, two ranks of large white daisies bobbed their heads in the soft night breeze. Justine placed the cardboard box on the front door mat, next to the white plastic milk-bottle holder, its arrow pointing to '1', then heard a front door slam nearby. She crouched, not moving, trusting to the shadow cast by a large shrub in the front garden to hide her. A man walked past along the pavement, swinging a rucksack, whistling 'Let's Dance'. It was a jaunty tune for the early hours and the man walked with a swagger of the shoulders as if he thought he was Bowie.

She waited for his footsteps to fade, knowing every second of delay meant potential discovery.

'Farewell my Jenni, my little bird. Live a good life. Please, please don't hate me.'

Each word was more a breath than a whisper, her lips so close to the cardboard she could almost taste it. She slipped something from her pocket and tucked it beneath the blanket.

After a quick check she tiptoed down the front path and out of the gate. Once she had turned the corner, she started to run.

56
YORKSHIRE, JUNE 2010

Justine heard the creak of the café door open and knew it was her. A certain shimmer in the air. A breath of wind from outside carried with it a scent of something flowery; roses, and another tone of skin and warm soft hair. It was this scent Justine had worked so hard over the years not to forget. She looked up and her eyes met the eyes of a young woman standing framed in the open door, the daylight spilling in from outside making a silhouette of her.

She's here.

If she had been standing she would have fallen, like a conscious faint. Justine didn't want to faint, didn't want to miss a single moment. She took a deep breath and watched as Elsie walked towards her, each step slowed with the same effect as using the pause button. She saw a tall girl with dark hair brushed away from her face, white shirt, long elegant legs in narrow jeans. She was holding a large black bag which dragged her right shoulder low. There was a nervous lilt at the edge of her mouth, a crinkle, a wrinkle of the lips, a smile to charm everyone.

She looks like Mum except her hair is Spanish.

Elsie was three tables away now and the slow-forward effect speeded up.

I met Federico sitting at a café table and after a few cups of coffee I believed he was the one. I have never loved anyone except him. Jenni is older than I was then.

She stood and held out her hand. 'Hello Jenni.'

The hand which met hers was cool, its palm was wide, the nails untidy and rimed with a dark stain Justine recognised as Prussian Blue ink.

'Hello. I'm sorry, I don't know what to call you.' Her voice was surprisingly low.

Then she smiled and with horror Justine knew she had seen that crinkly smile before. Her breath caught in her throat. The room began to spin and she was the maypole again. But she did not fall. A strong hand supported her elbow, her daughter's hand, guiding her down into the chair. She stared into her face. She could see none of Willow in her.

But would it be visible? And can I love her, if he is her father?

It was mathematically possible. Paul Willow could be Jenni's father. With that thought came a memory of that night. She pushed it away. She had tried, after Málaga, for years after she became successful and financially secure, she had tried to make a relationship work. One boyfriend said she was cold, another that she was seriously messed up. A third called her a control freak.

None of that mattered. Willow didn't matter.

She is my Jenni.

'Please, call me Justine.'

'I – I don't know what to say.'

Her East Yorkshire accent took Justine straight home to Seaview Cottage, to primary and secondary school, to growing up, only ten miles from where they now sat. She realised she was staring, dropped her eyes then looked up again. She wanted to drink her in.

Her legs were wobbly, her stomach full of lead. Clichés, but true nonetheless. Here she was, sitting before her daughter. Justine King, daughter of Lorna and Peter King, obsessive collector of leaves, chocolate-eater and teenage fan of Joan Jett and The Runaways. She felt split. Self-promoting, successful Justine Tree. Lying Justine Tree, sad and full of regret. Neither persona was fully her. If she didn't know which of the two was the real her, how could she face this confident girl who was waiting patiently, expectantly and, Justine saw now with wonder, with love.

It was that which gave her courage to look at Elsie again,

really look. She was no girl. She was a woman, sitting straight, eyes clear. Justine couldn't make sense of the fact that this flesh and blood and bone woman was the same baby who blew the most enormous spit bubbles. Whose tiny feet were rectangular-shaped with toes almost all the same length.

She became aware that Elsie too was assessing, studying Justine so intently that a crinkle appeared between her brows.

Like Granddad Bill, Justine thought with glee, *frowning when the Saturday teatime football results didn't match the predictions on his Pools form.*

She tried for a smile, and in finding one it squashed her fear of Jenni's anger. Elsie's anger.

'I don't know what to say either, but that's okay. We'll work something out.'

Jenni, Elsie. Elsie, Jenni. The two names swirled in her head and she regretted drinking all that coffee.

A hand rested on her arm, patting gently.

She is helping me, supporting me. I should have done that for her, all her life. Not for seven weeks. Seven measly weeks. I have failed her and I don't know how to say sorry.

She heard mumbled words, and a carafe of water and two glasses were placed on the table, followed by a pot of tea, a plate of sandwiches. Egg and cress. Ham and tomato. Salmon and cucumber. The sort of sandwiches her mother would have made, would have felt appropriate for the situation, cut in triangles and arranged symmetrically on a large plate patterned with blue forget-me-nots.

Not that Mum could ever have imagined this occasion.

It was the thought of her mother that did it, guilt that Lorna never knew her granddaughter, didn't know she existed. Justine drunk a glass of water down in one go, took a deep breath, and said what she had prepared, sitting up in her bed last night at Seaview Cottage, writing notes using the short pencil and the thin notepad she found in the bedside drawer.

'Elsie.'

'Yes.'

'There are some things I want you to know, I need to

explain, about what happened and why I gave you away.' That wasn't right; she had vowed last night to tell the truth. She forced out the words between her teeth. 'Why I abandoned you.'

It felt good, saying the A word, getting it out there. Her hands rested on the table in front of her, clenched so tight her skin had blanched white.

A hand held hers. Justine looked up into her daughter's eyes.

'I want to understand, but before you start I need to say something to you. I don't blame you, I don't hate you. It all happened a long time ago. I had a brilliant childhood, I've been very happy, my parents loved me and I loved them.' She paused and patted Justine's hand, rhythmically. 'Take your time, Justine. I'll wait, I'll listen to everything you have to say.'

She called me Justine.

So Justine told her everything that happened after her birth. Well, almost everything. She kept it simple. Everything she said was true. Anything she did not say was omitted for reasons of sensitivity or lack of proof, not purposely to obfuscate, just saved for another time. She talked for fifteen minutes, their hands clasped together. She hung on to Elsie's warmth, the strength of her grasp which promised so much. She hardly dared hope, even now.

'What was I like?'

Justine sucked in a deep breath.

'Your hand would wave like a pink sea creature, stretching toward my mouth, your fingertip pressing between my lips as if you wanted to catch my words. You were surprisingly heavy, asleep in my arms. And every day since I've wondered if you missed me. If somewhere deep in your sub-conscious there was a longing for a smell that was me.'

Elsie's eyes brimmed with tears. She reached to the floor and pulled her large black bag up on to her lap. From it she took a grey pebble.

'Oh.' Justine's gasp sounded loud in her own head, as loud as a shout. She received the stone from Elsie's outstretched hand, cradling it in the flat of her left palm, rubbing it gently with her fingers, feeling the bumps and troughs, smoothed by the Mediterranean Sea.

'This is my Málaga pebble. I left it with you, in your cardboard box.' And the tears exploded from her.

Elsie pulled her chair alongside Justine's and hugged her, rocking her side to side, until the sobbing quieted.

'I confess I thought my birth name must have been Freda or Flora or Florence. Or that my birth mother's name was.' She pointed to the stone.

Justine turned it in her hand so the flattest side was uppermost, the large 'F' scratched in the surface worn by the years.

'Federico.' She knew what Elsie would ask and tried to forestall her questioning. 'He was someone I loved very much.'

'Is he my father?'

Years of anticipation, thinking about this most obvious question, did not prevent Justine's brain from freezing. There were a number of stories she could tell, occasions she could remember, which would offer Elsie some sort of answer, something that might satisfy her to be going on with. But they would not be the whole truth and Justine only wanted to tell her the whole truth.

'I can't, I don't. I'm sorry, I don't actually know.'

'It's okay. We can talk about something else, if you'd rather.'

And Justine was so grateful to Mr and Mrs Weatherington for raising this beautiful young woman.

'I will tell you more about it, just not today. I'm feeling rather overwhelmed.'

An hour drifted by, then two. They talked, drank tea, then wine then more tea, and spent passages companionably together in silence. Justine felt out of it at one point, as if she was observing a distant tableau. Not planning to do it, she reached for her sketch pad and started to draw. Elsie was talking about growing up on the farm, her pony, the jobs she did before school, helping milk the cows, the cakes her mother used to bake. They ate a lot of cakes. Justine captured a line drawing of Elsie's face, her nose which was so like Federico's, her hands.

Her hands.

She stopped as cold overwhelmed her body as if she had been doused with ice cubes. Elsie's hands had long elegant fingers and flat oval nails she recognised. Andrés. Justine pushed away her pencil. She felt sick. Málaga came rushing into that calm café on the quiet eastern coast of England where they sat with a cold teapot between them.

Andrés had played the piano before the sex, that night at his house. Probably a well-meant attempt to set her at her ease; it had the opposite effect. It was a piece Justine now recognised as Debussy. She listened to a lot of classical music, but avoided solo piano.

He was a kind and considerate man.

But her anger with him, at his presumption that it was acceptable to pay women for sex, still burnt deep. A part of that anger, she knew, was directed at herself, for finding no alternative.

Her pocket diaries were stored safely in a black box file at the back of a tall shelf in her studio. She had done the maths, counted the pages of her 1982/1983 diaries obsessively, deciphering her monthly notations. The sum was the same each time. It was mathematically possible. Andrés could be Jenni's father.

57
LONDON, JUNE 2010

It was the peace after the storm when the trees and shrubs drip, the earth steams, the sky clears and the sun emerges. Five days had passed since the meeting at Burton Agnes. Justine was back in London. Today was her fiftieth birthday. A landmark day, but not because of that number. Everything was different. It wasn't that she felt like a mother, just that now she had someone to cherish. For the first time she fully understood what she had denied her parents, the chance to meet their granddaughter, to really know her, and Justine was so sorry for denying them that experience.

It's true, I am a fake. That woman at Jupiter Tower was right.

But now, from somewhere beneath the hard outside bark and inner rings marking each year without her daughter, Justine King was re-emerging. Each conversation with Elsie stripped away another layer. There were a lot remaining, but her fear was beginning to lift.

Supported by Bella and Rose, and with the encouragement of her daughter – how she loved to use the phrase, 'my daughter' – Justine had told Elsie the full story. Her unexpected love for Federico, the grinding poverty, her pride and determination to manage on her own, Bernadita and the escort agency, Andrés, Willow, the rape, the clinic, the abandonment. Nine monumental things to admit to, and she had ticked them off on her fingers as she went. Everything was on the table. She knew the truth was essential if they were to move forwards, Elsie and she. Rose was right. 'Ninety-nine per cent of the truth is not enough.'

The trouble was, there was no way of knowing that final one per cent. Federico? Andrés? Willow?

58
SPAIN, JULY 2010

The woman was alone on the beach. She walked, hands in her pockets. The wind roared off the ocean waves, dark grey and tipped by a frenzy of white froth. When she did look up, her eyes hardly focussed on what was in front of her. She wandered slowly north where a thin spit of rock acted as a natural break-water. She climbed without hesitation from flat rock to flat rock until she stood on the top, facing the windward side. Her long dark hair escaped from her purple cotton hat, whipping round her face. She reached up with her hand to control it. She turned, hopped back the way she came, and stood for a moment on the leeward side in the shelter of the tallest rocks. She felt closest to him here where they had played so often as children.

Finally she turned and walked back the way she came, her right hand thrust deep into her coat pocket, the bulge of the fabric moving as her fingers kneaded something special held there. Tomorrow she would finally find the answer.

The incoming tide brushed her plimsolls. She stopped, took a moment to choose a pebble, threw it into the sea. Again and again, she threw stones in the direction of a particularly jagged black rock. They all fell short. He had always been better than her.

With a rumble of thunder, the sky changed. Where there had been blue, there was grey cloud tinged with black. A storm.

Bueno.

She pulled a camera from round her neck.

59
LONDON, JULY 2010

A month passed during which a number of things happened. Justine asked Rose to find the truth of what happened to Federico and to order DNA tests. She simply wanted to know. She met James Watercliff for lunch, then dinner a week later, and was at once terrified and excited by what it meant. Elsie said just to enjoy it and not worry about any meaning. Justine had filmed her part in a new television series called *Art/Collage/Imagination* and was developing the basis of her next series. She was playing with the title 'Connectedness'. The inspiration had come from Elsie who, one night on the telephone, had said, 'Do you know what I love most about this? I feel connected to you.' It had made Justine cry. So she was exploring the idea of things that belonged together, which could be separated in space but never detached, because they were attached invisibly, forged together, welded, melded, stitched and linked. Flesh, stone, metal, biological matter, timber, people, family. Memories, knowledge, thoughts, experience, history. She was grappling with the scope of the concept; the subject was vast. Huge. Organic. Alive.

But how do I do it?

She was tempted to go big.

Rose was late and Justine was irritated. Her email had been concise. 'Wednesday afternoon at three. Your studio.' Elsie had arrived last night having received the same message. It had been their first night together under the same roof, and Justine set aside the memory of it to be enjoyed later. Mother and daughter together again. While they were waiting for Rose to arrive, Justine went to a shelf, selected a book and gave it to Elsie who received it as if handling a delicate object.

'It won't break,' said Justine. 'It was a present from Federico. There's a marker in the page of a poem he read to me.'

Elsie removed a postcard which marked the page. The picture was the Millais painting of *Ophelia* in the river. She studied the poem.

'It's in Spanish.'

'Yes, but he told me what it means. Let's see if I can remember it right. "You justify my life, if I had not known you I would never have lived. And if I should die without knowing you, I would not die because I would never have lived." She paused. 'I think that's it.'

The two women gazed at each other in silence. With tears in her eyes, Elsie handed the tattered paperback to Justine who shook her head.

'No, I want you to have it. You see that's how I feel about you. I haven't been in your life nearly enough, and I want to change that. If you will allow it. Now I've found you, I have started to live again. All the years without you were not a real life, I was unconnected from you. From everything, really.' She had only just realised that last bit.

'Okay, we can swap because I brought something for you.' From a bag Elsie withdrew a lemon-coloured crocheted blanket.

More tears ensued.

'I've realised something, now you're here with me, something I'm so ashamed about. But I've vowed to myself I won't lie to you or hide anything from you. So,' she drew in a deep breath, 'it's my fault that you never knew your grandparents. My parents, Lorna and Peter King. When I found out I was pregnant, I didn't ask them for help. I told myself I was protecting them from the shame of having an unmarried mother for a daughter, but I can see now that I was protecting myself. And I am so, so sorry. How different it would've been if I'd allowed them to help me, and I'm sure now that they would have done without censure. I would not have lost you. And they would have known they had a beautiful granddaughter.'

'What matters now is that you found me again. No one can change the past, it's what we do now that matters.'

Then the doorbell rang and Rose was there, with a blue folder of information and photos. She stayed long enough only to wish them well and say she would leave them to read. She would return in an hour.

Irritation with Rose displaced by anxiety, hunger and fear, Justine tipped open the folder and out fell a selection of newspaper clippings, school reports, and school and family photos. Most of it was in Spanish; some pages had an English translation attached. One headline was the loudest, most brutal, the blackest.

'Local student killed in head-on collision'.

It was as if it was happening again. She was in the apartment at the Plaza de la Merced with Catalina's hand on her arm, her lilting voice, her broken English.

'There is accident.'

Every fear she had fought to repel was proven true.

She had never read a report of Federico's death. She had been the girlfriend no one knew about. It never occurred to her to trespass on his family's grief, to introduce herself, to ask about the funeral. So she had written that letter which now made her cringe; so crude, worded so awkwardly. Hopefully they had understood the grief and sympathy expressed. And she had run away, left the country, never gone back.

Now, as the tears fell, the supporting arm belonged to her daughter and not to April or Catalina.

The doorbell rang again and Rose came into the room, followed by a woman whose skin was the colour of Caramac. It was a long time since Justine had seen skin like this. Federico's skin.

The woman held out her hand to meet Justine's. '*Soy* Leona Gala'.

Gala?

Justine's brain could not process the name but her eyes recognised that face.

'*Encantada.*'

The Spanish reached her lips without any conscious reaching for the correct phrase.

I wonder how much Spanish I could remember if I tried.

The thought that she and Elsie could study Spanish together appealed.

It turned out that Leona spoke English, learned, she explained, because her job as a landscape photographer took her round the world. First of all, she apologised for not being able to tell them much about the day Federico died.

'I was young, I had only eight years. Of course my father explain to me *Mamá* and Federico died in a car accident. It was long time before I know about *Abuelito.* But you want know about Federico.' She smiled at Justine and Elsie.

Justine's head was spinning. It was like being with Federico, but not. She turned to Rose. 'How, how did you find her?'

Rose explained how a local genealogist in Málaga had searched the Spanish birth and death records and discovered Federico Gala was survived by a sister, Leona. Rose traced Leona by her marriage and divorce certificates but then the trail went cold.

'Until I googled her and found this website with the most amazing photographs.' She smiled at Leona. 'Really beautiful.'

'You take photos?' Elsie leant forward, her eyebrows raised, a mirror image of her aunt's.

Leona smiled and nodded. 'I live always near Cádiz. It is a beautiful place and so I am photographer of nature.'

Justine listened to Leona's speech pattern. Federico's voice was as clear as the Málaga sunshine.

'It is difficult to say about Federico. I know is not good to believe all my memory of him because I had little years but my father tell me stories. Most of all I remember the smiles of Federico. *Actualmente* I hate him because when I am little because he call me Lioness. For my name. And he make this.' And she growled like a lion, her fingers clenched as a big cat's paws. The noise was remarkably loud and she laughed.

Justine's heart skipped a beat. Federico felt so close. Leona was saying a lot of what she had felt. Feeling unsure whether to trust memories which were only positive, and worrying that the memories become distorted by time. The meeting with Elsie had been such a cleansing experience that she dared to wonder if it would be healthier to release her memories, to let Federico go and allow him rest, to leave him dozing in the shade on that hillside at Istán, as if he would walk towards her, laughing, tossing an apple core at her head. And at the same moment, she knew it was impossible to let go. She focussed on Málaga 1982, drinking coffee in the sunshine, walking on the beach, doing nothing amazing except being together.

When she came to again her cheeks were wet. The others were drinking tea, looking at photographs, allowing her space. After she dried her eyes, Leona gave her a package wrapped in colourful birthday paper. Inside was a diary.

'No one know he write diary,' she explained. 'It was found beside his bed in the bedroom which is his for all his life. In it, he wrote about loving a girl called J. There are lots of words and one *poema*.'

Justine could hardly breathe.

Leona held the diary in her hands as if it were a Bible. Before opening it, she spoke quietly, looking directly at Justine. 'We never know who is this girl J. Spanish girls are not many called J, only Jimena and Juliana. It is not a name *muy común*. We think we never find J. But here you are; my sister.'

She reached forwards and kissed Justine's cheek, and then began to read. Justine's heart afterwards felt so full of love and longing and loss that she was dumb.

Elsie moved to sit next to her. 'If it will help, I'll type this into Google Translate and print it off, so you can have your own English version of his poem.'

Justine nodded. She was bursting with love for Federico, for Elsie, for Rose for bringing them together, and for Elsie's parents who had tended her as she grew into this fine young woman.

Leona reached into her pocket and pulled out a pebble.

Justine and Elsie gasped. As Justine reached hungrily towards Leona and took the stone, Elsie's hand delved into her own pocket. Side by side were the two pebbles that had last been together in 1982.

F and J.

Justine was crying now, and Elsie was stroking her hair. It was an intimate gesture and Rose felt like an intruder. Wondering whether to get up and walk away, she didn't want to make a noise that shattered the spell and settled for shifting her chair so she faced away from the mother and daughter, looking out of the window. She searched for something to think about that was unconnected with adoption. Work. Adrian's television documentary was in production for broadcast. He was pleased with her research and promised to put more work her way. Rose had not asked Justine to be a witness. April had come through with another commission, a profile of paper sculptor Bogdan J Brownhill. Now the Justine case was finished, the research work for Lily had also stopped, which Rose regretted. She enjoyed working with her sister who had proved herself thorough and reliable. Perhaps Kindred could encompass Lily as well as Bella. She had proposed a partnership to Bella, who had accepted. Her plans were coming together.

Except Nick. She'd been trying not to think about him all day, had managed to be out of bed and in the shower before his alarm went off this morning, breakfast skipped and an early meeting invented so she could leave with a perfunctory peck on the cheek. She had to do something, but didn't know what, about the received text she had read on his mobile yesterday. No, she shouldn't read his texts. Yes, she should respect his privacy as she expected him to respect hers. Yes, she had been tempted to check his emails, as Lily had checked William's.

But do I want to know the full story, or is it better not to know?

Should she maintain the status quo and hope the wobble would stabilise? She hadn't been checking up on him, there had been no suspicious behaviour that had caused her to spy, just his phone beeping with an incoming text while he was in the shower. Seemingly innocuous. But not. It had opened a pit of vipers.

For a while now it had felt they were taking parallel paths, running side by side, separate railway tracks made of steel. Not diverging, not converging. Confident this was a phase, part of their growing maturity as a couple, she had not paid attention, trusting their mutual love had space for space. But this text message had separated the train track, sundered and re-directed so they were now separately heading north and south. Unless she changed things.

Do I want to?

Truth was, she didn't know. She knew she loved him; she just wasn't sure how much. She liked some of what she had with Nick, was less keen on other bits. And though she knew this was the deal you signed up to when you entered a long-term relationship, she had wanted, expected, more. What if he wanted more too? That's what that text was about, after all. A feeling of indigestion pressed against the inside of her ribs, between her breasts, regret for that which had once seemed so bright.

If we are so easily broken, we are not meant to be.

The words of the text were burnt on her brain.

'I want to come home. I miss you. I HATE this place. I'm sorry, I was wrong.'

From his ex-wife.

Time seemed stationary but Rose's watch worked at double time and the three women would not be separated. She transferred Leona's booking to the last flight of the day to Seville and then, sitting at Justine's desk, checked her inbox. There was an email from *The Sunday Times* requesting Rose interview Scottish sculptor Geraldine Bronze whose retrospective at the Royal Academy had just been announced.

The real world was calling and the voices of Justine, Elsie and Leona faded into white noise. With the cold slap of inevitability, she knew she could not, should not, postpone her talk with Nick. Just the thought of it made her close her eyes to stop the prickle of tears.

The sound of unfamiliar laughter drifted in from the garden. Justine, Leona and Elsie were giggling over something, a photograph perhaps, and Rose wondered that she had never heard Justine laugh before. Her face seemed whole, complete, as if it had been unfinished before. Not unfinished, so much, rather as if something had once been extracted which only today was replaced.

Rose's phone beeped with an incoming email. There were no words. Just a photograph of a packet of contraceptive pills.

60
YORKSHIRE, AUGUST 2011

She lay flat on the ground, and the sun burnt her cheeks. Her eyes were closed. If it was a test, if someone had blindfolded her, befuddled her and asked her to identify her location, Justine would know. The cliff top. Her cliff top. Home. The early morning August heat bore a tinge of autumn chill. She wriggled her toes. Her bare feet tickled with dew from the grass; another sign autumn was on its way. The ozone smell of air so fresh she wanted to breathe in and in and in. The waves breaking on the chalk rocks below were splashing, crashing, weathering. Herring gulls were screeching above. She smelt the golden stubble in the nearby fields, newly cut, the dusty remains of wheat. A hoot in the distance, the mid-morning train to Hull, the driver approaching the unmanned level crossing near the village. She could fall asleep here and be happy never to wake up. Time seemed to both march quickly by and be still, but today she was waiting.

The delivery had been promised 'early' but the morning crept on. She was itching to get started. Space had been set aside, lifting machinery installed, cutting equipment acquired. Maud had so far fielded four requests from museums to show the premiere of 'Connectedness'. This would be the key piece. Lying on the cliff top this morning, she decided to dedicate the new series to her mother.

To keep her hands busy, she rolled up the sleeves of her blouse and turned out the understairs cupboard. It contained the last of her mother's possessions. A year and a half had passed since her mother's funeral. It had taken six months to buy the adjoining terrace cottage and knock the two houses into one, to negotiate with the neighbouring farmer to buy the paddock that adjoined the cottage's garden, to build a large barn/studio. Her last link to London disappeared when Darya died a few days after Christmas. London suddenly seemed irrelevant. The Kensington house was sold to a Chinese investor who Justine never met. Finally she was able to return home. She felt less stressed, older, flesh-aged but not worried by this transformation. The process of changing her surname back to King had begun. Maud argued strenuously against the change, citing PR backlash and a slashing in value of Justine's art. Justine told her just to do it.

And so her first public appearance as Justine King was at Burlington House. In a short ceremony a month ago, the terms of obligation were read out, and she was asked to sign the Roll of Obligation then receive her medal. Silver, with a burgundy ribbon. Now she was Justine King RA. She remembered her conversation with Catalina and April all those years ago in Málaga; of the seven things they agreed were required in order to call themselves 'artist', only two were now unachieved.

There was of course another reason for this new mood. The thought made Justine smile. Elsie would call by later, as she did most days. Just to say hello and to be.

This isn't getting the cupboard emptied.

She dragged out boxes, an old vacuum cleaner, her father's toolbox and pots of paint, until one thing remained. Her mother had hated the tall chest of drawers, hence its banishment to the glory hole. It had belonged to Justine's grandparents, an oak tallboy, utility furniture dating from the war. How like her mother not to throw out something she hated, but to find a use for it where it was out of sight. There were two drawers at the top, two tall cupboard doors beneath. She pulled out the left-hand drawer, took it into the kitchen and tipped the contents out on to the table. The detritus was the kind which mysteriously accumulates in at least one kitchen drawer of every house in the country: three bulldog clips, a jam jar full of screws, blunt secateurs, a single gardening glove, a torch without batteries, a dog-eared manual for a twin-tub washing machine long since discarded, freezer ties and labels, and assorted batteries. The second drawer contained a shoebox full of torn packets of plant seeds. Inside the cupboard was a pile of scrapbooks, the tall kind with rough grey paper that Justine remembered using as a child for school projects, bought from the local shop. Each was labelled on the front in her mother's handwriting with 'Justine'; one for each year of her career as a professional artist. She carried them to the kitchen table, her heart pounding.

The years 1984 to 1988 were thin, few press clippings. This had been her leanest time. The first fat edition was 1989, the year of her first solo exhibition. A box labelled 'Justine's things' yielded more treasure. As she searched carefully through the papers, the clock ceased to tick. In a large envelope were old school certificates – Neatest Handwriting, and Most Imaginative Drawing – a rosette for winning Best Miniature Garden at the village fete when she was eight, old school essays, a leaf picture made at primary school, a newspaper clipping of sports day with Justine kneeling in the front row in a pair of shorts that, although the photograph was black and white, she remembered were lemon yellow towelling.

She was taken aback at the volume of stuff her mother had saved. Tears started, although she had been crying less of late.

Is this what being a mother is? Following, supporting, being an invisible cheerleader?

How she wished she had boxes full of Elsie's early life.

However it had to be said that if Justine had known at the time that her mother was stockpiling press cuttings and photographs, she would have hated it, mocked it. Her mother's pride would have made her wrinkle her nose in embarrassment. Now, she knew that if you weren't embarrassed by something in your past, you weren't really living.

I'm glad you kept it, Mum. Oh, I wish I could talk to you now about Elsie. You would be so proud of her, I promise.

She would learn from her mother and try not to embarrass her daughter. Instead she would watch quietly from afar, saving a scrapbook of reviews and souvenirs of her promising photography career.

The last box to emerge from the tallboy was full of piano sheet music, her mother's maiden name written at the top of each in pencil. She had an elegant hand; Justine had never noticed before how even and composed her mother's handwriting had been. She collected a handful of papers and knocked the edges together to line them up neatly. Bigger and fatter than the others was a brown envelope. From it she withdrew a tiny matinee jacket in fluffy blue wool, folded neatly between tissue paper. It smelled new and unworn. And a birth certificate.

Alan Peter King.
Mother: Lorna King.
Father: Peter Brian King.
Born stillborn.
Date: February 26, 1957.

I had a big brother?
She had longed for someone to look up to, to pave the way for her.
Why didn't they tell me?
Because they wanted to forget. Because they wanted to protect her from grief. Because it had happened and could not be changed. A cocktail of anger and sorrow and pity for her parents swirled in Justine so she could not stand. She held the thin paper tightly, and sat down heavily on a box.
Alan.
And in a moment, so many things about her mother started to fall into place.
The hullaballoo of an engine startled her.
Is it here?
With Alan's birth certificate clutched in her hand, she hurried outside. It was Elsie's boyfriend Jed on his old Kettle Suzuki motorbike, restored from a heap of rust found abandoned in a patch of nettles.
He waved and grinned as he pulled his helmet off. 'Is it here?' Then his eyes refocussed and, smiling over Justine's shoulder, he shouted again and waved.

'Heh!'

Justine turned. Walking along the cliff path was Elsie with a dog at her heels. Jacko was a yappy dog with a big heart. Elsie released him from his lead and he bounded towards Jed, jumping at his heels, his tail wagging like windscreen wipers in a storm. There was a touch of Labrador to the shape of his floppy ears, and his long narrow muzzle was whippet, but the rest of him was Jack Russell. Justine watched Elsie and Jed hug. It made her feel, if not old, then finally grown up. For years she thought of her life as being before Federico, and after. His death had taken a slice out of her life, removed a brick from the wall. Now the wall was being rebuilt a brick at a time with the additions of Jed and Leona. Justine watched as the young couple looked into each other's eyes and for the first time knew the definition of lonely; it was what she had been and was no longer.

A thunderous clatter approached along the track from the village as a flat-bed lorry came into sight, swaying over the ruts. Jed ran to open the gate to the barn as, with a welcoming beep of the horn, the driver negotiated the bend and pulled to a halt beside Justine's beat-up Land Rover. On the back of the truck, secured with cables, was a tree. English oak.

THE END

AUTHOR'S NOTE

The Flamborough lifeboat in the story, the *Dorothy and Gordon Hardcastle*, is a fictional version of the lifeboat I knew in my childhood in North Yorkshire. The real lifeboat at Filey was the *Robert and Dorothy Hardcastle*. The *Lady Mary Fountwell*, Dorothy's predecessor in the book, is my invention. I also re-arranged the displays of art at Tate Modern, London and Ferens Gallery, Hull.

All authors love to read reviews by readers, so if you enjoyed reading *Connectedness* please leave a review at Amazon and Goodreads. Thank you!

ACKNOWLEDGEMENTS

My name is on the cover but I have a team of brilliant people working with me who have helped bring *Connectedness* to life.

To Dea Parkin at Fiction Feedback for the copy edit and proofread.

Thanks to Jessica Bell for the brilliant cover.

To Nicky Stephen Marketing for website and marketing support.

To my writing group, who have each read this manuscript in so many forms: to Alison Chandler, Lev D Lewis and Lisa Tiger. Thank you for your input and patience.

ABOUT THE AUTHOR

Sandra Danby is a proud Yorkshire woman, tennis nut, tea drinker. She believes a walk on the beach will cure most ills.

ALSO BY SANDRA DANBY:

NOVELS
Ignoring Gravity

HER SHORT STORIES ARE INCLUDED IN
Diaspora City: The London New Writing Anthology
The Milk of Female Kindness: An Anthology of Honest Motherhood

ABOUT THE 'IDENTITY DETECTIVE' SERIES...

Rose Haldane, journalist and identity detective, reunites the people lost through adoption. The stories you don't see on television shows. The difficult cases. The brick walls. The people who cannot be found, who are thought lost forever. And each new challenge makes Rose re-live her own adoption reunion, each birth mother and father, adopted child and adoptive parent she speaks with reminds her of the tragic story of her own birth mother Kate. Each book in the 'Identity Detective' series considers the viewpoint of one person faced with the dilemma of adoption reunion. The first book of the series, *Ignoring Gravity*, follows Rose's experience as an adult discovering she was adopted as a baby, realizing her parents had lied to her all her life. *Connectedness* is the story of a birth mother, her hopes and anxieties, her guilt, fear and longing to see her baby again. Coming soon… *Sweet Joy*, the third novel, will tell the story of a foundling, a baby abandoned in The Blitz and how the now elderly woman is desperate to know her story before it is too late.

To be one of the first to hear when *Sweet Joy*, third in the 'Identity Detective' series, will be published, sign-up for Sandra Danby's e-newsletter at her website.

To find out what makes Rose Haldane tick, see photographs of where she lives, read true life adoption stories and discover how *Connectedness* was researched, visit…

Author website: www.sandradanby.com
Twitter: @SandraDanby
Facebook: www.facebook.com/sandradanbyauthor
Pinterest: www.pinterest.com/sandradan1

NEXT IN THE SERIES . . .

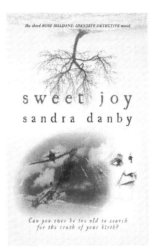

It is 1940 in Twickenham, west London, after one of the worst nights of The Blitz. A baby is found alive in the wreckage of a bombed house. The house is shut-up and unoccupied, its owners moved to the countryside for the duration of the war. So why was a baby left there, alone, and what happened to her parents? Decades later when identity detective Rose Haldane moves to Twickenham, she notices an elderly woman watching her from across the road. Except the woman is not interested in Rose.

IF YOU MISSED *IGNORING GRAVITY*, READ THE FIRST CHAPTER HERE...

1 PROLOGUE 1968

There was a sharp slap followed by a cry. The sound of an animal echoed in my ears and my soul and my empty womb and didn't fade.

'4lb 3oz. Girl. Write it in the Statement Book, then take it away.'

2 THIRTY-FIVE YEARS LATER: ROSE

Someone took her by the arm, forcing her to sit down. Breath warmed her cheek. She was icy all over. She could see nothing, nothing except one word written in the diary.

Adopt.

Suddenly pain, starting at her cheek and spreading through her head. Again, and again. Each slap beat that word deeper into her unconscious.

Adopt.

Rose Haldane fell off the edge of the world.

Three days earlier, it was 10 a.m. on Thursday morning and Rose was sitting on a sofa the size of a generous double bed. Black, low, leather, polished steel feet, it was positioned on one side of a glass coffee table bigger than her kitchen. Opposite was a black-leather swivel chair that screamed 'executive.' She sat on the sofa gingerly, lowering her bottom until, just as she expected to hit the floor, she sank into the sumptuous cushions.

'He'll be at least ten or fifteen minutes,' his PA Amanda had said when she showed Rose into the room, using the tone that meant, 'he's very important and you're not.'

The room was silent, the air still, no movement except for her chest, which she realised was heaving up and down as if she'd run up the thirty flights of stairs instead of taking the glass-and-steel bullet lift. This had happened only once before, at a big interview. Nerves. She touched her cheeks. Burning.

Do something, she told herself. *Yoga.*

She lay backwards on the sofa as if it were a bed, her head touching the wall behind her, her legs stretched out in front. Ignoring her pulse, she breathed deeply.

In, out. In, out.

She focussed on the questions she was going to ask, her eyes closing as she concentrated…

3 NICK

Nick Maddox, managing director of Biocare Beauty, was sitting at his desk, thinking about face cream. In particular, the failure of the bottling machinery at the Scottish factory that manufactured his best-selling Natura-Refresha Night Flower serum. Should he shift production to Devon? Or cross his fingers that the machines would be fixed in time to fulfil his export order to France next week?

At that thought, he leant back in his chair and allowed himself a small smile of achievement. *Me, exporting face creams to France. It's like selling an English striker to a Brazilian football club.*

Having decided to trust the Scots, his mind shifted to the press interview with a financial journalist that was due to start

– he glanced at his watch – five minutes ago. He sighed. It was the last in a schedule of PR interviews about his management buyout of the company. This was his least favourite part of the job, talking City talk with business journalists wearing expensive suits and carrying all the latest techie gadgets while examining his desk for similar gadgets, and who were sure they knew more about face creams than he did.

4 ROSE

'Miss Haldane?'

Rose sat bolt upright and stopped breathing. Her notepad and pens scattered across the smooth grey slate floor, coming to a stop beside a pair of well-polished black shoes.

She looked up. A neat man with cropped pale-blonde hair stood in the open doorway. His lips twitched, Rose was unsure whether with disdain or amusement. Neither was the response she wanted to provoke.

'Sorry to keep you waiting. I'm Nick Maddox.' He bent down to retrieve her stationery, placed it on the coffee table in front of her, then sat down in the Mastermind-style chair and looked at her.

She sat up straighter and tugged at what she now realised, given the depth of the sofa, was an unsuitably short skirt. Her mother would have disapproved.

'I'm Rose Haldane, from the *Herald*, but of course you know that. Thanks for the opportunity to interview you, it's…' she couldn't think of the right adjective, '…good of you.'

He looked at her, one eyebrow slightly raised.

She tried to shuffle her bottom into a more comfortable position without seeming to fidget or nudging the hem of her skirt even higher.

'So, so… shall we start? Tell me… what's it like being your own boss?' *Rubbish, Rose. What a predictable opening question to ask an MD who liked the company so much he bought it.* To gain a little time, and to avoid looking at him, she opened her shorthand notepad.

When he didn't answer, she looked up. He was staring at

her like a university professor waiting for her to provide an answer he knew she didn't know.

'You know, being in control of your own destiny? Making your own history?' *Shut up, Rose.* Journalism rule number one: don't put words into his mouth.

'Destiny?' He leant back in the swivel chair. 'That's an interesting word.'

Boy, is he confident. Arrogant. She hated arrogant men.

'I wouldn't say I'm in charge, the bank is. I just have a new boss.' His voice was strong, as if he were answering questions he expected to be asked. Every now and then he glanced down at a paper in the folder he'd laid open on the coffee table. A briefing paper supplied by his PR, she guessed, a list of predictable questions and answers. His smile just about reached the edges of his mouth but fell short of his eyes.

Politeness guarantees boring copy. Journalism rule number two: if in danger of boredom, use shock tactics. 'You're very modest for a man who's just completed a £50 million MBO. You've upped your salary and bonus to seven figures. What will you do with the cash? Buy a yacht?'

Too much. She waited, wondering if she'd blown it.

When he spoke, he was so quiet she had to lean forward to catch his words.

'You shouldn't believe all you read in the papers.' His smile tightened.

Ooh, he's hiding something. 'I don't, that was in the disclosure documents provided by your merchant bank.' This was one of the things she'd read online before leaving the office. She was subbing for a sick reporter so there'd been no time for proper preparation, no time to buy a pot of Biocare Beauty's top-selling face cream and try it at home.

'Right.'

Rose watched the displeasure tighten across his cheeks. *Perhaps now he'll stop treating me like some unqualified reporter on* Back-of-Beyond-Gazette. True, her first job was for the *Littlethorpe Mercury*, but she'd worked her way up to the *London Herald* and had interviewed people far more intimidating than Mr Nick Maddox. So she held eye contact as he studied her, determined not to flinch. Most people she interviewed wouldn't look her in the eye.

Journalism rule number three: think, say, feel, do. Was Maddox saying one thing and thinking another? Many people did, the trick was to unlock the puzzle.

His eyes narrowed slightly, then he smiled without warning. It lit up his face, and she forgot to wonder what he was thinking. 'You have done your homework. That's refreshing. I'm tired of journalists who research online and think they're instant experts on my company. It's insulting.'

Why is he being nice?

He turned in his chair. 'Look at them.' He pointed to the people sitting at desks in the open-plan area on the other side of the tinted glass partition. 'They made it happen, not me...'

While he talked, Rose noticed his hands. Light golden skin with long fingers suited to playing piano octaves. She found herself wondering how it would feel to be touched by those hands, and was horrified to realise she hadn't heard a word of what he'd just said. She nodded and stared down at her pad, her face hot. Carefully, she wrote the shorthand symbol for 'Maddox'.

'...banks are only interested in cash flow, covenants and the bottom line, they want their repayments. The bank doesn't care if I make face creams or screwdrivers.'

'So, now you can enjoy running your company.' Her eyes were still fixed on her notes. *Wrong again, Rose.* Journalism rule number four: statements are not questions.

'I've always enjoyed it, and it's not strictly speaking *my* company. The MBO is the beginning, not the end. You wouldn't believe...' His sentence ground to a halt and he slowly took a sip of water. 'No, I shouldn't tell you that. You're a journalist,' he spoke softly, as if to himself.

Hell yes, I am a journalist. Irritating man. Why did he start a sentence that sounded juicy, only to stop halfway through? She'd expected him to be media-savvy but things weren't going well. First, his PA refused to admit her because she wasn't Alan Smart, the slick, sick journo she was subbing for. Anyone less than Alan Smart, who regularly featured on *BBC Business News*, would be a waste of her boss's time, the PA implied with a glance down her aquiline nose. Then, there was the lying down on the sofa thing. Her cheeks had only just cooled from that blush when she caught Maddox trying to read her shorthand notes upside down. She offered the notepad to him, but he refused without a flush of shame. The chemistry hadn't recovered.

She put down her pen. 'Look, if you want to tell me something that's off the record, that's fine.' She adjusted her face into a no-compromise look. 'It's fine as long as you say so now, before you start talking. I won't quote you until you say it's okay. We can go back on the record later. But you can't decide after the interview that some bits are on the record and other bits are off. I don't work like that.'

She held her breath.

He swivelled in his chair, his eyes fixed on her. 'Sounds fair.'

She exhaled and smoothed her hands over her skirt to hide their trembling.

He called for more coffee. Rose watched Amanda's procedure with cups, milk, sugar, and chocolate digestives without a word. *She loves him, maybe not romantically, but she'd throw me out of the window if she had to. What is it about him that inspires such loyalty? Perhaps Amanda likes his golden hands too.*

He talked for half an hour without pause, at the end of which she could see glimmers of the real man sitting in the black leather chair.

Ask him something personal now. The barriers are down, ask him...

But his mobile rang and he excused himself to answer it. Rose glanced at her watch. Jim, the photographer, was due in five minutes.

'I'm sorry, that was a call I had to take. Shall we continue?' Maddox was playing with a black fountain pen and studying her legs.

She sat up straight with her knees pressed together. She wished her mother could have seen her ladylike posture.

Maddox didn't hurry his appraisal of her legs, and when his eyes rose to meet hers, they showed no embarrassment at being caught out. *Damn him.* To her dismay, Rose felt her cheeks grow hot again. She wasn't ashamed or embarrassed or angry. *It's just a bodily reaction beyond my conscious control.* That was how her father had explained it to her when she was five and blushed every five minutes. 'The blood vessels in your skin get bigger to let the hot blood reach the surface so your body temperature is balanced,' he'd said.

Where is Jim, for God's sake?

Maddox poured water into two glasses, watching her discomfort with obvious amusement. Rose clenched her teeth and stuck her tongue in her cheek to prevent it forming the words that her mouth wanted to unleash.

Arrogant, pompous, self-important... *I didn't say that aloud, did I?*

'Are we finished here?'

'Almost. We just need to take the photograph.'

'Right.' He was looking at her knees again.

What a creep. When would she stop being attracted to the same type: gift-of-the-gab salesmen who sold themselves as energetically as they flogged advertising space and houses and... face creams? *Does he give all his female employees this treatment? Shut up before you say something you'll regret.* She stuck her tongue back in her cheek again. *Come on, Jim.*

'Did you know that the phrase 'cheeky' means tongue-in-cheek?'

What? Can he see inside my mouth now?

'Er, no.' Her face grew hotter.

'The Victorians thought it was rude to show your cheek in this way. They were the first people to tell children off for being cheeky.'

'Really?' *How does he know stuff like that? He must be making it up.*

She tweaked her blouse, which was clinging to her breasts,

then sensed him watching her. Instantly, her nipples hardened. *Oh shit!* She took a deep breath and folded her arms over her breasts. *Take control. Say something, quickly. Before he does.*

'So, how long have you been at the *Herald*? Do you enjoy it?'

Too late. Now he's making polite conversation.

'I love it.' *Liar, that sounds so insincere. It is insincere.*

He raised his left eyebrow. 'Really?'

He said 'really' as if she'd said she'd always wanted to be an exotic dancer. Feeling the flush building again, her eyes dropped to her hands and she babbled about university, work experience, and the farming magazine she'd worked on before breaking into local newspapers. The school nativities, council meetings, obituaries, police briefings. Then the job at the *Herald* and her flat in Wimbledon and–

At last... Jim shuffled into the office, laden with camera gear.

Rose stifled a sigh of relief and ran a hand over her brow. Her face was burning.

Thirty minutes later, Maddox shook her hand. His grasp was firm, his palm cool and dry, his fingernails neatly clipped and filed.

'Anything you need to ask, facts you need to check, just email me or give me a call. Amanda will put you straight through.'

You bet she will. 'Thanks.' Rose's eyes were magnetically attracted to the philtrum connecting his nose and upper lip in a line like a dot-to-dot picture. It was deep and dark, with a hint of afternoon stubble, and she wanted to run her finger along it.

'Here's my mobile number.'

She took his business card without touching his fingers, and shoved it in her pocket. *Did he see me staring?*

He held the door open for her. 'I'll be glad to help, anytime.' His voice dropped low on the last word. Then he turned into his office and the door closed.

Amanda didn't get up from her desk but simply pointed towards the lift in the lobby. Rose smiled at her graciously. It was always worth keeping the secretaries on-side, but she'd need a blow torch to thaw this one.

Outside, she lingered on the pavement and looked up at the top floor of the glass-and-steel building, trying to work out which was Maddox's office. A shadow flitted across one panoramic window. She ducked behind the bus shelter. After waiting for what seemed like ages, she sneaked another look.

The shadow was still there, an arm lifted in a wave.

Oh. My. God.

Rose tucked her chin to her chest and walked away very fast.

5 NICK

He stood with his nose pressed to the window, his breath misting the glass, watching her disappear. Knowing he would never see her again, knowing he shouldn't want to see her again.

'Can you sign these?'

Amanda's words made him jump. She had entered his office silently and was standing close behind him. Too close. Sometimes he suspected her of creeping. He took the folder and signed the documents without reading them, like he had a million times before.

He waited until the door closed, then went to the window again. She'd gone. What was it about her that drew him to her? She was a journalist, a type he avoided on principle, but… there was a vulnerability beneath the efficiency which attracted him. And her eyes, blue… almost aquamarine.

A knock at the door and he jumped again, startled from his reverie by a line of people filing into his office. The finance team. Within moments, he was absorbed in packaging costs, and forgot all about Rose Haldane.

Enjoying this preview? To keep reading
***Ignoring Gravity*, buy the paperback at Amazon.**

.

Made in the USA
Lexington, KY
14 May 2018